THE
OCTOBER
MEN

DAVID IMPEY

BIGBEAR

For
Judith

PROLOGUE

MATT JENNINGS

Oxford. Sunday October 11th, 1900hrs.

Have you noticed how many documentaries on World War Two nowadays seem to be in colour?

When I was younger, World War Two was always in black and white. Grainy, foggy images of slaughter and destruction rendered somehow distant and surreal by the monochrome film of the day. Reality has more focus, surely?

Even the movies were monochrome: stark black and stark white. No mistaking the fight between good and evil. Maybe that's why the SS wore black uniforms: so you could tell the angels were not on their side.

I suppose the first time World War Two was ever fought in colour was when *The Great Escape* was released in 1963. Before that, John Mills led the fight against the Nazis in his homespun monochrome; quite a contrast with Steve McQueen coursing around the lush alpine meadows of Bavaria (it was supposed to be Poland) under a swooning sky.

And now this. I dislike TVs in pubs, even when they have the sound off, as in this case. I go to the pub for a conversation; the alcohol is incidental. That's why sitting in a pub drinking by yourself is one of the loneliest things in the world. But today, the TV has something that is holding my attention like never before: World War Two in colour. Sure, there have been countless documentaries featuring colour footage, but this is different, even if it has been repeated from a month ago.

It looks like it was shot yesterday.

Here is Pearl Harbor. Apparently, some Hollywood film crew were scouting locations for a new movie and happened to have a camera loaded with widescreen colour stock when the Japanese Zeros tore across the Hawaiian sky like swifts.

7

They must have had more than one camera, because the action is presented from a couple of vantage points, with the terrible majesty of the USS Arizona's demise captured with breathtaking silent clarity: the plume of black smoke belching heavenward as the magazine blows; the bloom of oily red as the munitions and oil detonate; the strange sense of awkwardness in knowing that, however many times you view it, nearly twelve hundred men died right there and then, and here I am, watching it within the walls of a nice, warm pub. And it doesn't even make a sound.

With their backs to a declaration of a war that would end with a bright light and a mushroom cloud, the pub customers sit and chat and drink and live in the moment. The din of war is drowned by the clinks of glasses, the strained voices as each tries to be heard above the others. The laughter, the mock seriousness, the what-the-Government-should-*really*-do of it all.

And where is Otto?

Otto is always late. Typical Oxonian: more doctorates than any sane person would know what to do with. He could solve some obscure mathematical theorem before getting up in the morning, but you'd be risking your life if you asked him to wire a plug for you. And as for telling the time…

As with any academic, if something happened to grab Otto's attention then time would lose all meaning for the man. Day and night would merge into an infinite grey light and he would only emerge when he had either satisfied his curiosity or dropped to the floor unconscious.

And as with others of his level of sublime brilliance, his social skills were… well, let's say that he could be well described as being a little flaky. I have often watched him when surrounded by a group of others: students, friends, fellow travellers. They would be wrapped in their conversation and Otto would sit there, having fixed one or other of the group in apparent rapt attention. But Otto would actually be working out some abstruse physics problem, using the camouflage of talk and laughter to hide himself in his own calculations.

If you can't get there directly, work it out from first principles.
If the mountain won't yield itself to you by one route, try another.
You can see the top from where you stand.
You know what the answer is. Now find the proof.

Otto isn't antisocial or a recluse. Otto isn't even his name. I think it's Oliver or something. There's somebody else with the same name in college and he doesn't want to be confused with them. So he chooses to be called Otto instead. And anyway, it is kind of a cool name. No one could object to someone called Otto joining them down the pub.

To be fair, he doesn't even look like your typical academic. Otto has a mane of tight, curly hair that falls down his collar and onto his hooped polo shirt, like an avalanche of Slinkies. The look is complemented by a pair of jeans and trainers. It's all rather reminiscent of the 1970s, I always think. I suppose that look must be coming back again.

By contrast, the stereotypical academic would wear trousers of some man-made fibre that would be slightly too short: the bottom of the legs would be suspended in lofty grace above the wearer's ankle, revealing a pair of grey or wheatmeal socks. His shirt would protrude from the triangle of space left by a maroon V-necked jumper: a colour calculated to drain what life remained from an otherwise pallid complexion. Open-toed sandals are more for your Death's Head Academic, but not out of the question.

And the glasses! Walk into any high street optician where you can select from a thousand different frames from numerous glitzy designers. None of them would stock Otto's glasses, and wouldn't have done for over thirty-five years.

So Otto has managed to preserve his academic credentials without turning into—what did he call it?—a 'dweeb'. He mixes it socially with the best of the university set and, crucially from a professional perspective, certain institutions fund his research.

As a representative of one of those institutions, this means he can translate his flashes of theoretical insight into worldly propositions for which I can calculate net present values.

But I can only do that when the bugger actually turns up at the time agreed.

I sigh as I hitch back the cuff of my shirt to look at my watch. To be fair, he's only fifteen minutes late. For Otto, that's practically punctual. I have always had what practitioners of psychometrics call a 'Type A Personality'. So for me, bang on time is actually five minutes late.

Also, being a Type A, I find it hard to accommodate the peculiarities of other people's personalities, especially when they jar with my own value sets. So, I have to take a deep breath and soothe myself with some platitude about how it takes all sorts.

I could order another pint. This one is getting low and I still haven't done half of today's crossword, so I could be justified in having another. I brought the crossword in the expectation of Otto's behaviour. I'm stuck on 8 down: 'Try to shuffle over a dune'. Nine letters, first letter 'E'. Buggered if I know. This might take more than alcohol alone.

It's a pleasant enough evening; the light is hanging on in the October sky even though the sun has long since set. I take a table outside and divide my restless attention between the crossword and the movement of bikes, tourists and the occasional furtive car, moving up and down Broad Street.

The Carolian sandstone buildings take on a natural quality at this time of the evening. They start to resemble the sandy bluff of some lethargic river, pock-marked with the nests of martins and bats. The cyclists weave past them, as they have done for over a hundred years.

The bike is the best way of getting around Oxford, despite the growing problem of bicycle theft. There's nowhere to park, few places to drive, and the city fathers have conspired to discourage the car as much as possible. I wish they could do the same for the teeming multitude of smoky buses.

If it wasn't for the fact that I should be having a conversation with one of the scientific officers of one of my former vested companies, this would be a pleasant enough way to kill time. A crossword, a beer, a cigarette.

Of course! The answer is so fittingly Oxford. I fill in the empty squares and award myself a celebratory slurp of beer.

Thirty minutes late. Let's give him a call. I tap in the first letters of his name, select it (nobody else in my contacts list has a name that begins 'OT') and press the green button. Silence for a while, as the phone searches for a signal and transmitters around the area throw glances at each other for the best line of sight.

The ringing. It has an empty, hopeless quality. The network has found Otto's phone, unlike Otto. And then the inevitable voicemail message: 'Hi. Otto here. I've obviously got my head somewhere else just now so leave a message and I'll call you once I'm back on the planet.' *Beep.*

God, I hate talking to these things; it's like trying to communicate with your fridge! 'Hi, Otto. Just checking you're still able to communicate with those plebs among us who are constrained to a Newtonian universe. I'm at the King's Head and... erm...' How can one be articulate and talk to these bloody things? 'Anyway, just to politely remind you, we were supposed to meet a half-hour ago. Give us a call if you're held up or something.'

My voice trails off, unconvincingly. Although I'm not sure why it's supposed to sound convincing at all. I'm here, he's not. *He's* late. How much more convincing do you have to be?

Sod it!

I stub the remains of my third cigarette out in the volcanic ashtray, drain my glass and stride across the street into Broad Street and past the stately Sheldonian and the nuclear-bunker Bodleian, stuffing my newspaper into a street bin as I go. The crossword remains unfinished, dammit.

I'll try Otto's place; he's bound to be there. It's only a ten minute walk from the pub. He hates working late in the office and the lab has to close at 7pm because the Health & Safety wonks say so. And life is far too short to argue the toss with them. So, if he's anywhere, he'll be at home.

Otto's place is a small terraced house in Jericho, a quiet but gently bohemian area of Oxford. The area feels slightly detached; it seems to back onto the City of Oxford, rather than being an integral part of it. As such, it is a retreat from the city and the haunt of dons and intellectuals.

I've always liked Jericho. It's not pretending to be anything other than that what it became; a rather slow-geared shelter whose engine chugged along to a more relaxed rhythm, on a lower flame. It's rumoured that the community grew out of the congregation of travellers who, arriving too late to enter the city gates, had to rest outside the walls. Joshua and trumpets notwithstanding.

A bit like Otto, Jericho seems to be comfortable in its own skin. The cafés are nice places to enjoy coffee, apple cake and read the newspaper for a morning. It's not flash and it's not outwardly wealthy. (Although the colleges and the university have bought up most of the properties around the area, so to get one now would require a king's ransom.)

But it takes a gentle pride in itself. Which is not what I find when I push open Otto's front door. Splinters in the frame where the lock had been and a sinking feeling that what happens next is unlikely to be good. The door bumps halfway open, obscuring the hall within. There's a book on the tiled floor. The house is dark.

The thought flickers that Otto has forgotten his key or some such. But why the darkness? He'd have put a light on somewhere, if only to find the phone book to call a locksmith. His phone! I call the number again from the front doorstep. Again, the wait for the connection and then the metallic tone in my earpiece.

For the second time, and this time for definite, I feel a sense of dread. I call his name. But if he didn't answer the phone, why would he answer me in person? I use the light from my phone to find a switch and the hall is bathed in a slanted, blue light. A lamp at the end of the hall lies on the floor; the ghostly glow of my phone throws shadows from the coatrack and the bookshelves along the walls.

From what I can see, there has been a terrible disturbance. Books, ornaments and glass litter the tiled floor. If there's been a struggle, there doesn't appear to have been any blood spilled.

On TV, I would have gingerly pushed the front door and stepped into the house, peeling back a layer of the mystery with every room explored. Until, in one room…

But I'm not on TV and I am not brave enough. There is nothing in my former life that would equip me if I met any assailant.

So I call the police and wait on the doorstep for them to arrive. 'Help!' I say, rather pathetically. 'I am at my friend's house and his front door has been broken down and his stuff is all over the floor and I think there's been some sort of—'

'We'll send a car round straight away, sir. What is your name?' And is this my phone I'm calling from? And they ask me lots of other questions and they promise they will send someone around as soon as possible. And would I mind staying put until the officers arrive? And that's the end of that and I'm left alone outside a darkened house and gradually the air begins to curl with a distant, echoing keening. And the noise grows and grows until my head starts to swim in the ululating, swirling noise and the blue bursts and the black wells and high visibility jackets and the peaked hats with the mouths under them moving and asking questions and they are just routine sir and am I the person who called 999 just now and would I mind waiting while the officers have a look around inside and you haven't disturbed anything have you or touched anything have you and how well do I know the occupant of the house and am I able to answer some questions down the station as they need to know as much as they can about whoever it was who lived here and the brilliant blue and the blinding darkness pulses in my head and on the walls of Jericho.

Perhaps now these walls will fall. Not to trumpets, but to sirens.

PART ONE

RIPPLES

CAPTAIN HENRY PARFITT

Le Cateau, France. August 1914.
(Excerpt from Captain Parfitt's memoirs,
published privately in 1932.)

The Field Ambulance has been positioned about three miles to the south-east of Le Cateau, some distance from the artillery who have started to pull back to the south. It was a bit nerve-wracking having them so close as we knew this would render us fit targets for the enemy. Indeed it so proved, as we came under shellfire for a brief but disturbing period. I shouldn't like to be subjected to that sort of an onslaught too often.

We have received our orders to pull back to St Quentin in the morning which is going to be something of a labour given that we have all but finished unloading the FA with all three sections operational a few hours ago. The Sergeant Major in Section A is trying to put a brave face on things but he is no poker player and has taken to venting his fury on the junior warrant officers and other ranks in the administration section. These poor chaps are going to have to gather up all their paperwork and file it neatly and in an orderly fashion on the general service wagon. The concern shared silently by all is that the retreat will not rest at St Quentin and that we have much farther yet to go.

Our quandary is that, unlike most of the infantry, we know we are both coming and going; we are charged with preparing to decamp whilst still taking in wounded from the field. It has been all hands to the pumps, what with the enemy having mounted a new and even more savage offensive. I hear that our generals have contrived a rather effective means of extricating our troops by having a rear line bring down covering fire enabling the forward line to retreat to their rear and so on.

Rather like a backward game of leapfrog, only with bullets and men's lives at stake.

What has made everything substantially more difficult has been the dust. I suppose one must be grateful for small mercies; I can only assume that the ground would be transformed into a quagmire at the first drop of rain. Heat is something one should expect in August here in northern France, but I didn't anticipate how dry it would be. I suppose the air has had all summer to desiccate and, while we have basked in its glory back home, we were little suspecting what discomforts it would bring to bear later on.

The dust pervades everything. All the instruments and the bedding, all the field dressings, the liniments, the syringes and needle housings, the operating tables, our clothes, our food, our eyes and our ears and our nostrils. Everywhere imaginable and a few places one had thought unimaginable. One is never trained for this. Years spent studying and then practising medicine at St Thomas' were as nothing to this. They never trained us for this; in every emergency one simply falls back on one's training and it is as though all the procedures undertake themselves. My hands are the vehicles by which care is dispensed, but they seem not to be in my charge. Without the rigorous discipline, one's practice teeters on a writhing bed of barely concealed panic.

We first encountered this almost as soon as we landed in northern France nearly a week ago. Our FA had initially been loaded onto trains and, after having crossed the Channel, we had regrouped at Rouen before being dispatched on yet another train which disgorged us about a mile from our present position. We unloaded the horses and wagons from the train and set off on the road. It was there that we met our first column of artillery, so we filed in as best we could; each of our wagons had to wait for a suitable gap between the horse-drawn guns as it was considered bad form to force them to slow down. The poor beasts were having a hard enough time drawing these mighty weapons without us impeding their forward travel, but we were keen neither to attract the opprobrium of the gunners nor risk being trampled underfoot.

We made it to our present position, about two miles to the north-east of the town in the early hours of Saturday night and, by the time the FA was operational, it was starting to get light again. We were all of us tired as there had been precious little in the way of sleep on the boat crossing or the trains, but we managed well enough and our spirits were lifted marvellously by the smell and then the sight of breakfast.

As ever, the dust seasoned our repast and sweetened our tea. The battle, only a few dozen miles away, was throwing up warm, ochre clouds that were borne on a lazy summer wind. We had stationed ourselves near the edge of a small wood of delicate poplar and beech trees and I fancifully imagined myself in summer regalia contemplating a picnic with friends. The reverie was shattered by the report of a shell exploding somewhere in the wood and the unnatural applause of soil, leaves and branches falling to earth.

That was probably the last opportunity I had for any respite. That day had seen the first engagements with the enemy which, if field reports were anything to go by, had been successful with our cavalry having repulsed the Germans. I wrote in my diary that evening of the fervent hope that this would be a portent of things to come and that this meeting of two great armies would be settled with a mere skirmish. However, I was aware of the vast numbers of men deployed and the vast reputations of nations and empires and even then I feared that these first actions would not be the last. A sentiment that turned out to be prescient.

Our first casualties arrived soon after breakfast, probably about 0800hrs. I have never counted how many we ever saw in any one day or in any one battle. There seemed little point, and there were more pressing matters to attend. I know that the FA Sergeant Major had kept thorough accounts of our operations and I am sure that the RAMC has archived the numbers diligently. All I know is that after the first sporadic arrivals, the pace became relentless.

By the evening of the Saturday we had come to appreciate that the sleep of the surgeons was going to be of paramount importance as without it we were likely to be more dangerous to our patients than the enemy.

I was tasked with setting up duty rosters for surgical cover. We had twelve medically qualified staff, all accorded officer status by a grateful monarch, of whom half (myself included) were territorials and the remainder regulars. I arranged that, at any time, there would be eight surgeons able to operate. This was contrived by having three groups of four surgeons all doing eight-hour shifts in every twelve hours, with each group starting their shifts at four-hourly intervals.

It sadly meant that no one ever got more than four hours' sleep in one stretch. But we were rested well enough to perform our duties with professional efficiency. The nurses, administrative staff and other ranks had their rosters organised by others, usually the warrant officers.

While the battle intensified throughout the Sunday, I slept close to the FA even though the local mayor had arranged lodgings for the officers in the town's houses. *Delogement*, it was called. We had had no time off other than that I had contrived in the roster. The padre was leading a service of sorts—Church Parade would have been too grandiose a title for it—and I could hear the rather unconvincing strains of various hymns and prayers through the canvas of the FA while I fished a number of unpleasant-looking pieces of shrapnel from a young fusilier's leg. It occurred to me that one could conceive of an amusing game in which one suggested inappropriate hymns to be sung in the field. With Harvest approaching, 'We Plough the Fields and Scatter' would have a certain ironic ring.

I finished my shift and settled down at 0300hrs.

I was roused by a sergeant at six-thirty in the morning of the Monday who presented me with new orders from the Surgeon General in which four of our medical staff were to be driven to another FA about fifteen miles from our present position to a small town called Avesnes-sur-Helpe where a large contingent of wounded had been taken. Transport was waiting for us, so myself, another captain and a lieutenant traipsed toward the vehicle with a sister scurrying after us, all carrying monkey boxes: the name given to a small case of dressings and instruments carried using a shoulder strap. Before long, the car was lurching across the countryside. I remember thinking at the time that there was a strange quality to the morning; it was like a surreal tableau with the sky brightened by an unrisen sun and the earth still clinging to the night.

What with shell-holes and other obstacles, it was a good hour and a half before we arrived at our destination: again, another FA on the edge of another wood which afforded everyone the mistaken sense of concealment and sanctuary. This FA was somewhat smaller than our own, having only two sections compared to our three. The urgency of the request for additional medical staff was apparent.

The wounded were laid out in serried ranks of stretchers either side of the path leading to the admissions tent. Inside were warrant officers and orderlies frantically recording the names and serial numbers of the men outside in readiness for their short journey to the operating table. The sight was less upsetting than the noise. As a surgeon, one becomes inured to the sight of blood, even organs. What one cannot get used to is the involuntary, unstoppable and bone-chilling sound of more than a hundred moans and cries of pain. The threnody of a host of angels, dark and unseen.

We were soon directed to our stations and our work began in earnest. The story we heard suggested that the early successes were short-lived and that the enemy's strength far exceeded that of our own. We were being attacked on two fronts and the assault had been relentless.

First, the enemy had marched in parade-ground fashion into the sights of our machine guns and were mown down where they stood. Then they changed tactics and began to attack our men in a less regimented manner that turned out to be much more effective. Their artillery was also starting to take effect and this had begun to take its toll. The evidence of that toll was laid before me on the operating table and it was a terrible thing to behold.

It was also dawning on us here in this forward position that our time here was measured in hours, not days. We should soon be heading south lest the Germans overrun us. Reports had already come in of Medical Officers being taken as POWs by the Germans with scant regard for the precepts of the Geneva Convention.

I cannot say how many wounded we treated that day nor indeed how many we saved, let alone patched up sufficiently for their return to the front, but the numbers must have well exceeded a hundred and fifty. I had not appreciated the passage of time but when I finally saw any sort of timepiece (it was a stretcher bearer's watch), I learned that I had been operating for twelve solid hours.

Not every man beyond the canvas made it inside. Probably a quarter yielded their last on the French ground and lay under khaki blankets in the fading light. Khaki, I learned, is a Hindu word meaning 'dust'. And so to dust they return. I inspected their ranks, ambling silently and exhausted until I happened upon one stretcher where something caught my eye. This casualty was different.

At first glance I thought it might have been the body of a civilian; certainly the shoe which jutted out from under the blanket was no army boot and there was no evidence of puttees. It was too dark to see the body in any detail and, for a moment, I considered illuminating the scene to get a better view. I quickly thought again; shining a light would give away our position and direct a barrage of artillery on our heads. I buttonholed a couple of bearers and had them move the corpse into the tent where my investigations would go unnoticed by the Germans.

Once the stretcher was inside and it was safe to remove the shroud, an unexpected sight greeted me. This was no soldier. Indeed, I was not sure it was a civilian, either. I looked up from the table to a nearby corporal and asked how the body got here. The NCO was obviously on some sort of urgent mission (all missions in the army are urgent, I soon learned) and proffered some non-committal answer before dashing off.

A sergeant wandered over, intrigued by my question. He peered at the body, gave a low whistle and rubbed the back of his neck in bewilderment. 'Where did *he* come from?' he eventually gasped. I said that I had no idea and asked if he had heard anything from any of the bearer parties or the horse ambulance drivers. He agreed to see what he could find, muttering something about this being a 'right puzzler and no mistake'. I never saw him again; he was quickly detailed to the task of dismantling the FA for movement, but his sergeant major did show up about two minutes later.

He asked what the problem was and I replied that I was rather perplexed by one of the bodies which I had found outside. He (for the corpse was male) had obviously been dead for anywhere between twelve and fifteen hours as rigor mortis had fully set in. The conundrum was his presentation, which was like nothing I had ever seen. The sergeant major agreed that the corpse was most peculiarly dressed.

The first thing we did was to search for some identification. Item number one in the army book is the 'dog' tags, with name, rank, serial number and religious affiliation. Not unexpectedly, there were no tags, nor any sign that any had ever been worn; there were no tell-tale marks around the neck. We rolled the body over and went through his pockets, all of which were empty. The mystery deepened.

It wasn't the fact that there was no identification in the usual places, but that there appeared to be *too much* identification everywhere else. This is where I must describe his attire and his general appearance.

He was about six foot two in height and weighed about twelve-and-a-half to thirteen stone. He was athletic in build and, judging by his soft hands, did not have a job that involved much manual or physical labour. He had a shock of wild curly brown hair that would have picked him out in any crowd and which had grown to more than shoulder-length. It seemed to roll some considerable distance down his back.

A shell exploded in the wood close by and startled everyone in the FA. Preparations to move gathered pace. The tent at the other end of the FA fell and the canvas and poles were swiftly packed onto a GS wagon by a team of orderlies and bearers. No sooner was this done than a volley of shells landed close by, tearing off branches and splintering the tops of the trees. Jagged shards of wood flew over and past us, with one or two piercing the canvas of the tent I was in. The canvas reeled and convulsed and the noise of that alone was truly awful. The breathtaking percussion of the shells enhanced the sensation of hell approaching.

The sergeant major looked up from the table; he was as dazed as I was and he had temporarily lost his concentration. He bawled out orders, threats and encouragement in equal measure and the men hurriedly began dismantling the second and last tent. 'Please look lively, sir', he pleaded. 'We can't loiter here too long. We're in the range of their guns now. We've got to move, sir. Sorry.'

'Give me one more minute.' I ran the light up one side of the corpse and down the other, trying as best I could under the distraction of the barrage to memorise what I was seeing. He was wearing a sporting shirt, open-collared with long sleeves, blue and white hoops, possibly the sort of thing worn on either the football or the rugger field. His trousers were blue also. I wondered if he was in some way connected with the French army, but these trousers were cut differently and had pockets in all the wrong places. This was no French uniform. The trousers were cut from some sort of hard-wearing serge and were slightly faded. The hems on the legs were worn, probably because they were too long for him. His footwear also had a sporting feel in that he appeared to be wearing plimsolls or shoes for the gymnasium. But whereas plimsolls were normally either white or black, these were blue again and had three stripes down either side.

But the biggest conundrum was that every piece of clothing carried a name. I couldn't be sure if these names were his or those of his tailor. His trousers were apparently styled by 'Strauss and Company' (there were more details but it was too dark to see clearly and the name was partially obscured by earth) and, emblazoned on his left breast just above the stab wound that had caused his demise, was yet another name: Hacker or Hackett or something. It seemed most likely that this last name was that of the mystery corpse and, while I was absorbing this, a volley of shells screamed into the wood and detonated with a heart-stopping report. This was too close and I knew I had to leave right then.

I dropped everything including my monkey bag and ran for the wagons. The tent was all but down and there were a few men struggling to pack it away. They all fled, dropping what they were holding. It was a short distance to the waiting wagons—fifty, maybe sixty yards over uneven ground and long grass—but I could sense the creeping barrage behind me and the pulses in the ground beneath my feet growing ever stronger with every shock.

The wagon nearest me was starting to move off and I became terrified that my attempts to catch it would prove fruitless. The gap between the tailgate and my outstretched hand was widening and I could hear the shouts and encouragement of the men. One or two reached out to me but it became obvious that their efforts were too late. A couple of the other men who had been the last to drop their tents had managed to lunge at the tailgate and scramble to the comparative safety of the vehicle. I was obviously not as fit or as fleet of foot as they, and I came to realise that I would be left behind to face whatever maelstrom would follow.

The shells were unending and their growing ferocity seemed without limit. Looking back, I realise now that they must have still been some distance from me as I was unharmed by any shrapnel. But the thought of remaining in this place was unthinkable and somehow I kept running.

My lungs were burning. It could have been the cordite or just the sheer exhaustion, but I was now struggling to draw sufficient air to fuel my headlong rush for the receding wagon. The grass whipped at my legs and my ankles crunched and twisted with every pothole. The men continued their exhortations; I was all that was left of this company to be saved. A couple of men yelled at the driver to slow down but he had his orders to retreat with all due haste. The needs of the many outweighed my predicament.

I was on the point of giving up when the wagon hit an unseen pothole and the rear of the vehicle pitched upward as the front wheels dug into the dusty ground. It decelerated sharply and the driver was forced to drop the engine down a gear or two, enabling me, for the first time, to gain some lost ground. The shells landed closer still and the ground trembled, threatening to unbalance me. I was beginning to feel faint, my lungs only able to capture dwindling amounts of oxygen. I was aware that I had started to stagger and that my running was becoming more of a meander. I might have been drunk; I wished I'd been drunk. My first chance at salvation and my wretched body could not grasp it.

There was another explosion. This time it was not a shell but the engine of the wagon backfiring in protest at the driver's inexpert attempts to engage the correct gear. I could hear oaths issuing from the driver's cab and renewed shouting from the men on the wagon.

I was three steps from the waiting arms.

Two steps.

One.

My hand was wrenched away. I tripped and my legs collapsed beneath me, but I was safe. Hands clawed at my uniform and I was hauled rudely but gloriously into the back of the wagon. My heaving, gasping, retching carcass was hurled onto the floor where I lay with a rictus of both pain and elation etched on my face. I knew that, momentarily, I was free.

The ordeal was far from over, however. The wagon had yet to pick up sufficient speed to carry us all from this increasingly dangerous place and it was too dark to see and too risky to ignite the headlamps. More potholes lay in our way and there was the very real fear that one would cripple the wagon. And still the barrage crept towards us from behind. Towering blooms of earth, giant polyps of soil throwing high their arms and scattering the scenery to the winds.

With one more belch of smoke, the wagon regained its momentum and accelerated away from the position and we watched in awe and silence and tempered relief as the Field Ambulance succumbed to the onslaught and disappeared beneath an irresistible cliff of fire and earth. Within seconds, all of it—the canvas, the tables, the equipment and the bodies— was gone.

VINCENT VAN GOGH

Arles. April 1888.

Dear Theo,

I am overcome with excitement. I have had such a happy few days lately and I cannot believe my good fortune.

Firstly, I am in good health. You are always agitated, dear brother, about my cough and it seems to have abated at least for the present. I don't feel the same tiredness as I had suffered the last time I wrote to you and the tonics I was able to acquire with the money you sent me seemed most efficacious.

I admit that I felt so exhausted after the weekend. However, after the respite of the last two days, I am ready to pick up my brushes and return to work again.

I am much encouraged by the kind words of Eugène since he visited me from Fontvieille last month. Indeed, he was so complimentary and has offered to purchase one of my paintings. I am not sure which he would like to buy but I feel moved to work on something new for him especially. I am much inspired by his wife's exhilarating pointillist technique and I might see if I can do something along the same lines.

The days here are so hot. The light is so strong and everything under it is bleached and brittle. The only colours in the middle of the day are white and pale ochre and deep blue. But, in the morning it is so lovely, so gentle. The light is like a cool white wine.

The vineyards hereabout are sunk in a pale green glow. As the sun rises, the golden aura of the grapes and the vine leaves fills the day. Between the vines are deepening blue and brown shadows that throw that golden light into ever sharper relief.

It is then that the peasants come to tend the vines. They are bent over each leaf, every twig.

They arrange parasols of greenery for the bunches of sweet fruit and snip off the dead or dried foliage. It is slow, deliberate and graceful work. It is a painting in waiting.

Secondly, I have heard from my dear friend Paul who has finally consented to come and stay with me in Arles. I have a spare room for him here at Place Lamartine and I am sure that he will be most comfortable. It is not opulent, as I have described in fine detail to you before, but I am sure he will find it agreeable.

I know he and I will fill the days painting and laughing. I have so many ideas on how we might amuse ourselves and each other. I have exciting plans on how we might test our skills and ingenuity beyond the current humdrum routines we have set for ourselves. It will be a time we will both remember for the rest of our lives.

And lastly, dear Theo, I have left the best, the most exciting news till last.

I have sold my first painting! It is of the café in Place Lamartine and I have called it *Veuve Venissac's Café*.

It shows the front of the widow's restaurant with a number of diners eating and drinking. The shade of the lime trees contrasts wonderfully with the livid pink walls of her establishment.

I was going to paint it for her in payment for a few meals but, the day after I had finished it, a gentleman visited my atelier and asked about my work.

The gentleman was strangely dressed. I find it hard to put my finger on what it was about him and his manner that seemed odd but he had the air of someone who belonged neither in Provence nor, for that matter, in France or even the Netherlands.

His accent suggested he was from England but I couldn't be sure, even having lived among the English for all those years.

His clothing seemed so thin and lightweight and yet he had an otherwise ordinary black suit. Perhaps it was because his shirt was open at the neck rather than complimented by a tie. Who knows?

Anyway, am I going to deny a man one of my works of art because he is improperly dressed? First Eugène Boch and now this man.

He spent about thirty minutes peering at the work in the studio before alighting upon *Veuve Venissac's Café* whereupon he offered me twenty francs for the canvas. I bid him up to twenty-five.

You would be so pleased with me, Theo.

All those exhibitions in Paris and now I start to sell work in Arles. Who would have thought it?

Your ills still give me cause for concern and I hope that Doctor Gruby is being as attentive to your case as his professional skill will allow. I hope that the pains will subside before too long and that the medicines you are prescribed will be taken as Gruby has set out for you.

Perhaps, like myself, you are enervated by the city's foul air and should repair to a more rural area. I am certain that it has done my health no end of good as I have said already in this letter.

Perhaps you should leave Paris and come to Arles as well. Together we may thrive both in our health and our artistry. You should be careful to get better as it seems both our health will benefit. I shake your hand firmly.

Ever yours,

Vincent.

THE ASSASSIN

Rastenburg. July 1944.

It's the dogs that worry me the most.

Dogs have an almost preternatural sense of smell that transcends anything we can comprehend. It's as though it's linked to some psychic ability to convert mere scent into an understanding that something malevolent is lurking. Not just nearby, but *over there*. Over there in that bush. Behind that mossy jumble of rocks. Under the shade of that pine tree. Not that one over there, but *that* one. *Over there.*

First the ears. Up they go like some naval signal. Then the draw of the first breath before the cannonade of barking and the convulsive straining on the chain. The handler's arm jerks and twists as the dog bids for freedom. And then, two possible outcomes; neither of which are good. The handler can choose to let the dog lead him to me— jerking, barking, writhing with outrage—or he can let the dog go.

If the handler chooses the first option, then he will die before his dog. A puff of air like a pea-shooter and a small rose will appear on his forehead. He will heave a sigh of disappointment and he will fall to the ground without ceremony. The dog will not look round; he will be fixed on my scent and my hideout and I have at most two seconds before the dog realises that he is no longer restrained and begins his lunge forward.

If the dog is let slip, then it will die before the handler's unbelieving eyes. The handler will hesitate: not long, but long enough. He will be drawing breath to shout an alarm when the bullet hits and the cry will never come. Instead, a thin keening noise as the lungs deflate through his already tensed vocal cords. No one will hear him but, in both cases, they will hear his dog. And that will be all they need.

Two thousand people work here and all but three hundred have one job to do. They have to stop me. It won't take seventeen hundred to catch me. Probably a dozen, maybe half. More than that number will hear the dog and they will know what that means. And only what that means.

And every hour I have to run the same gauntlet. Through the undergrowth, I see the gleaming black and brown coat and the training takes over and I can hear its breath and the rhythmic beat of the handler's boots on the sandy earth.

The principles of marksmanship. First, keep a steady eye on your target. The target, the front and back sights and your eye must form a straight line and must be fixed. Breathing must be controlled. Take a slow, deep breath and hold it. The position and hold must be firm enough (firm, that is, not tense) to support the weapon. The trigger should be squeezed gently, almost with affection. And the shot should be followed through: continue to squeeze the trigger to avoid disturbance to the position.

With every passing dog, the position, the breathing, the fixed eye, the firmness. All must be there. You become the terrain into which you merge. Camouflage is more than blending in; it is *becoming* where you are. You can never smell like the terrain: not entirely. Rubbing the dust over your face and hands, rubbing it into your clothing, webbing and scrim, will all cover most of the scent. But not all of it. There is always the gnawing anxiety that your luck will run out and that gentle zephyr will telegraph your position to a nose several times more expert than your own. To make matters worse, it's hot and humid. I'm lying in a shallow depression I dug for myself nine hours ago, trying to keep dead still, and it's nearing the middle of a July day under a canopy of pine trees all exuding a resinous, sappy odour; all this sucks the oxygen out of the air and the sweat through my pores. In a while, I am going to be detected by one of these dogs. I am not sure how much longer I can go undetected.

The handler mutters encouragement to his dog: *good dog, well done, what can you smell?* All the time they come nearer to my position; their path is not likely to pass directly over me but there's always the dreadful chance that this time they might veer a bit too close: close enough to catch that stray scent. God knows, this happens every hour, give or take, and every hour my heart starts to pound. The deep, slow breathing, the relaxation techniques I use as a sniper: it makes no difference. The adrenalin in my bloodstream has a will of its own and my heart is its faithful servant. If it pounds any harder, they will surely be able to hear me. My chest and my arms twitch imperceptibly with the beat; I am not still, not as still as I'd like. Can the dog hear the rustle of my clothes or am I just imagining it?

I can certainly hear the pounding. It's like a piledriver going off inside my ears and it makes it hard to hear the approach of the handler and his dog. And I want to be able to hear them; I want to be able to know everything I can about them. I want all the advance notice I can get to enable me to make that decision: do I kill them or do I let them go?

The dog—head down, scanning the ground—comes level with my position. He and his handler are now in my killing zone. The SS flashes on the handler's tunic make him a tempting target and my finger involuntarily tenses on the trigger of the rifle. He is looking straight ahead, to the left of my field of vision, and appears to be distracted by some movement elsewhere. The dog, though, has looked up from the earth and his ears have pricked up. His bright eyes switch in my direction and he raises his head, nostrils flaring and twitching. His mouth opens and his tongue lolls out from behind rows of teeth glistening with saliva. He is about to turn to face me directly and the game is about to change completely.

Another dog barks somewhere and his head snaps around in the direction of the noise. The game is still on. Nothing has changed yet. The handler moves off, the dog leading the way.

Even though this only seems to happen about once every hour it takes a good ten minutes before the pounding in my chest and ears subsides and I can return to the job in hand.

The patrol comes by every ten to fifteen minutes. There will be about a dozen black-clad sentries pacing the same course. They look neither to the left nor the right so it seems as though their manoeuvres are for show rather than security. But their rifles are loaded and they are well trained. Very well trained.

The *Reichssicherheitdienst* are a different proposition compared to their opposite numbers in the *Fuhrerbegleitbrigade*. Behind me are the massed ranks of the FBB, their minefields, watchtowers, checkpoints, artillery, tanks and heavy weaponry. But they are mere conscripts compared to this elite, motivated troop of fanatics. I have one job to do and RSD also have one job to do. They are there to stop me.

Every ten to fifteen minutes the patrols go by and their passing is a helpful break in the tedium. I've been squinting down this telescopic sight for the past three hours. The rifle has been trained on one spot only. My target will move, dazed and confused, into the crosshairs in about twenty minutes from now and when that happens, no one at all will be looking in my direction. For about five minutes, I won't have to worry about dogs, handlers, patrols of crack soldiery, nothing. Except the shot I'm about to take.

I will probably get the chance to loose off three, maybe four, rounds of silenced ammo. I want to do it with the first. In all the confusion and smoke and shouting, no one will have noticed where the first shot came from. Nor will they have had the chance to notice any flash or—God forbid—smoke (I cleaned that rifle bore till I was in danger of enlarging it; smoke shouldn't be an issue). But all eyes will be on my target and one wound will tell them that they are under fire, two wounds will give them a good idea where from.

So, one shot it is. For my professional sake.

All's set. The rifle is cocked and ready. It was properly zeroed just before the operation, well away from the notice of the guards hereabouts. I'm getting regular sips of water through the straw from the bottle in my webbing so I am sufficiently hydrated though not enough so I need to pee; that would attract the attention of the German Shepherds in a heartbeat. I'm breathing slowly, regularly and I'm calm. Calm like a stone.

The exfiltration is all arranged; by the time they realise what has happened, I will be well away from here and they will never, ever, ever find me.

Here we go. The one-eyed man with the gold German Cross is leaving the hut and is getting into a waiting staff car with another man. They issue some curt orders to the driver. We've got two, maybe three minutes to go.

The staff car drives off, leaving the right side of my field of vision heading for the first of the three checkpoints. The car will make it out and the occupants will be safe for the next few hours at least. As the noise of the car's engine fades into the distance, the forest seems to hold its breath. Nothing seems to move: no birdsong, no patrols, and the few men I can see are functionaries with nothing to do other than smoke desultory cigarettes and count down the time to when their superiors emerge from the hut. Which they are about to do.

Now.

The hut swells and lurches and the windows all burst as the roof peels back. The splintered roof trusses arc upwards, stripping the adjacent trees of branches. Glass and smoke spews across the compound. And then the blast hits my ears. I'd expected it to be muffled by the wooden walls; instead it's sharp, piercing, staccato.

Then it all kicks off for real. First the shouting, then the running, then the sirens. Vehicles appear from nowhere. Troop carriers, ambulances and fire tenders are accompanied by squadrons of men sprinting toward the explosion. Most are in full uniform, but some who had obviously been off-duty after a night watch, are in vest and braces. An officer in a black uniform takes charge of the situation and starts detailing men to either fight the fire or to gain entry to the hut and begin to remove the wounded; the dead can wait their turn.

The vehicles position themselves to best acquit themselves of their duties: the fire tenders are close to the seat of the explosion, coursing water through the contorted opening in the roof or up the sides of the trees which are alight. They are obliging me by generating yet more smoke to obscure the scene. The mounting sense of confusion is providing greater cover for my work than I had anticipated. The officer directing the fire and rescue details is good—I can't help thinking he's done this before somewhere—but even he can't blow the smoke away by himself. Still, he's already established a clear line of command; he has warrant officers each assign men and duties and it is they who are screaming and yelling at other men. The RSD have set up a defensive ring around the hut with men lying prone, their rifles pointing away from the scene in the direction of any potential attack.

The first casualties emerge, helped out of the wrecked building by their rescuers. They are dazed and helpless, their uniforms are scorched and torn and their heads and hands are spattered with blood. As more stagger out clutching at their wounds or rubbing their smoke-salted eyes, I hear their moans for the first time, even above the shrill siren. Order is being rapidly established, and the shouting has subsided. Everyone knows what has to be done now; no one needs to talk any more. Control has been regained: a tense, uneasy control. First, the casualties will be determined, the damage assessed and the perpetrators found and dealt with. But there is still one key matter that must be addressed by the rescuers: is he alive?

The minutes tumble by slowly as, one by one, survivors of the blast are helped or carried out or stumble out of their own accord. They all look ragged and pathetic; a company of the once all-powerful reduced to vagrants in a fraction of a second. But it's what they do on leaving the smouldering wreck that is so revealing. They all turn round and face back toward the site of the explosion. There is a sense of expectation, of hope.

These men gain certainty and purpose from the adoration of one man. And he is not in their midst yet. Will he ever be? Their future depends on it, or so they think.

I know he will be coming soon; I know he will lift their spirits. And I know much more besides.

The time arrives, marked by the sound of heels clicking as half a dozen black RSD guards snap to attention. It seems so ridiculous that even amidst this smoke-ridden tumult, everything should stop for the paying of military tributes. But this is what happens as a shambling, broken figure limps out of the smoke and into my view. His hair is chaotic like a rocky shore and streaked with blood coursing down the side of his head; his light brown tunic is blackened with soot and torn by shards of wood and metal and his trousers are completely ripped from hem to hip. He looks like a circus clown after having performed an unsuccessful trick with a cannon. But nobody is laughing.

He is in my crosshairs. I am aiming for his heart as head shots can be unreliable and there are enough vital organs near the heart to increase the chances of a kill; the dum-dum bullets I have loaded in my magazine will take care of business very nicely, thank you. My finger begins to squeeze the trigger. Gently, gently. My breathing has stopped. I am calm and the rifle is firm in my grasp. He has walked into the line of sight.

And so has an RSD officer. I ease the tension in my finger and exhale. The officer is obviously fussing to check the man's condition and, for his cares, he is waved away. My target wants room, he wants space. He doesn't want to be crowded by underlings who don't deserve to stand on the same soil as him. My target is recovering his composure and has started to shout obscenities at people around him, particularly the other survivors of the explosion.

The officer, shocked by the reaction, recoils a couple of steps and then, chastened, stiffens to attention, surely hoping that his misdemeanour will not lead to further action.

And my target is once again in my sights.

This time there will be no obstruction. Everyone else has seen the tongue-lashing meted out to the hapless RSD officer and none are willing to incur the same. They are all keeping a respectful and convenient distance and leaving him at my mercy.

The finger tenses, the trigger draws back millimetre by millimetre and I await the gentle recoil of the rifle as the round squirts past the silencer at the end of the barrel. After that, events would be unstoppable, irreversible and utterly final.

The rifle lurches and there is an ugly clunk.

A dud, for Christ's sake! I've waited nine hours in this fucking place and the first round I load into the chamber is a dud. So much for all my training; my ears are filled with the squelching of blood pumping at high pressure through my arteries. I withdraw the magazine and cock the mechanism, hoping to eject the 7.62mm round from the chamber. Nothing. I try again and still nothing.

I don't want to move if I can help it. The only time I want to move is when I crawl away from this position and make for the exfiltration point. But I've got to shift forward to peer into the chamber and find out what the hell is going on. I hope the excitement and chaos around the hut is occupying the guards sufficiently to allow me to creep the foot or so I need. I look like a small bush and it's a windless day, so I shouldn't be moving. Still. Needs must.

What I see spoils my day. The round has jammed well and truly and it looks at first glance as though the dum-dum bullet has somehow disintegrated when it was stripped from the casing. In short, the rifle is utterly fucked and my job here is has been an embarrassing and ignominious failure. A sitting target, a state-of-the-art sniper's rifle and my only option now is to crawl back to base with my tail between my legs. It's only ever happened once before and I *really* hate it. Alternatively, I could come over all heroic and try to kill the target by chucking stones at him. The first option is distasteful in the extreme but it affords me the opportunity of having another go; the second option either ends with my brains all over northern Poland or my being strung up with piano wire for the amusement of the SS.

I glance at my watch. I've got ten minutes to get to the exfiltration point round of the back of one of the other huts used as a senior official's secretariat. They will be running around like headless chickens so won't be on the lookout for a pile of undergrowth.

I am truly pissed off and I am going to spend some quality time beating myself up when I get back. When all is said and done, the target may have got lucky this time, but I only need to get lucky once. And I try my damnedest not to leave things to luck.

MICHEL DUPUY

St Aubin de Lévéjac, Provence. June 1957.

'...Deinde, ego te absolvo a peccatis tuis in nomine Patris et Filii et Spiritus Sancti. Amen.'

Amen.

Absolution reverberates around the nave, mingling with the dust and the cool damp of the ancient stones. This church has offered sanctuary from the sun for all these centuries yet still it tries to force its way into the sacred gloom, barging through the leaded windows, searing into the limestone flags.

The blasphemous sun. Now there's a thought. Sitting at the back of the long, cool church, Michel shrugs his shoulders. He wonders if the must of the old stones carries the smell of the plants that once sprang from its hillsides. Michel often finds himself thinking of fanciful matters in church. Maybe it's the hypnotic drone of the litany, the vacuum of silence which nature fills so obligingly with thought.

Michel squirms at the notion that, so often during the most sacred and transcending moments of the mass—the liturgy of the Eucharist, the homily—he finds himself thinking about sex. It transports him to when he was an altar boy at this very church, just old enough to admire, if only from afar at first, the girls in the choir and the congregation. Mass is supposed to be an act of faith and purity and yet his mind is led far away. Then again, there is something of the sacred about that, too. Here is a place where a growing boy and a fully grown man can harbour less than worthy thoughts. Storm in a harbour, perhaps.

It could at least give him something to confess; one of the abiding burdens of Catholicism is the guilt that one might not have done anything worthy of atonement. But, somehow, telling the priest that his service was a source and inspiration of carnal pleasure, no matter how furtive, was going to make for an uncomfortable exchange.

It was, and still is, a small community. The people are of the land and make their living from it. Such as it is. The soil is rocky and barren with few, if any, fields large enough to entertain the growth of any real crops. A few meagre vineyards, some maize, the odd animal. Meeting girls was limited to those within the parish and, particularly, those who presented themselves chaperoned by their family to the weekly service. It was either that or the village café and bar when they were old enough or brazen enough.

Michel thought about his wife and how she had first materialised during one mass many years ago. She had been coming to church with her family long enough before, but it was that day when Michel *noticed* her for the first time. He can't have been more than sixteen; she was not much less. Epiphany!

The congregation shuffles out into the sudden day, its gentle murmur fading with the echoes of the Mass into the countryside. Michel stays, allowing himself one last prayer: the same one he always intones silently to himself, if not to God. Whether God listens or is at all bothered Michel cannot say, despite the protestations of the priest that the love of God, which passes all understanding, is his.

At last, serenity. All have gone and the empty church gradually fills again, but this time with the sound of the breeze outside, the birdsong and the puttering of vehicles departing for home. There is the usual sound of the priest's footsteps on the flags, scuffing over the sill of the west door, regaining composure and steadily but resolutely pacing the length of aisle back to the vestry. There he will no longer be God's messenger on Earth. Once again, he will be just the priest. The priest does not look back at Michel. His work is done for the day.

Once the church is swathed in silence again, Michel rises to his feet, picks up a small bunch of flowers that's been by his side throughout the service and saunters out into the daylight. The late morning sun has caught its heat and now it presses down on those immodest enough to challenge it. Michel still has a short journey to make across the bone-white ground. Across the road and through the gate. There he will rendezvous with his wife who has been waiting for him.

Marie does not come to church anymore. She does not have to. God Himself had excused her these past five years and so she waits for Michel in a cool plot shaded by the spires of a row of shimmering poplar trees, bathed in soothing winds.

Michel stands by her and whispers about the previous week.

The chickens were laying well despite the heat, and the milk from the goats had been sold to the local *laiterie* to be turned into *chèvre*.

The crops were starting to fill out nicely so there was likely to be food on the table for most of the year, provided there wasn't a heatwave again.

The van was playing up; Gaston reckoned it was the carburettor, or the timing, or the points. Why does he commend his only vehicle to a mechanic who doesn't seem to know the first damn thing about cars?

The commune had agreed to relieve him of his crop of grapes once they were harvested. As every other year. But one still has to go through the annual ritual of applying to them for their patronage. So many people expect genuflection it's a wonder that his knees don't seize up.

Ah well, Michel supposes, knees don't seize up. At least not in your late thirties.

'All things considered, Marie, things are hanging together okay. There's food to eat, enough money to enjoy life, even if the horizon is not that far off. And this is one of the loveliest places on earth. Even if you are only there to share it with me once a week.'

Michel kneels to lay his flowers upon her, stands back up and stares vacantly at her stone, thinking all the time of her face as it laughed, scolded and smiled at him. *Dorme bien ma cherie.* Until next Sunday.

The village bar is a short walk down the hill from the church. Like a thousand other villages in France, it's situated in the village square. And, also like a thousand other villages in France, the bar is surrounded by the usual companions: the *mairie*; the *patisserie*; the *boulangerie*; the general store; a few houses and flaky lime trees, and a memorial to the Glorious Dead of the Great War, now with a new plaque added to commemorate the fallen of the more recent one.

Jean-Pascale has just opened. It has gone midday but there is little point in opening when the customers are all at Mass. Michel muses on why everyone is required to attend Mass when the word itself was derived from the Latin for 'dismissal'. If you thought for an instant you were dismissed from the duty of attending Mass, the priest here would promptly disabuse you of that.

Michel chooses a table in the shade of a faded red awning and orders himself a *pastis*, a bottle of Vichy water and a coffee. He contorts himself to retrieve his lighter and cigarettes from one or other of his jacket pockets.

At last, the drinks arrive and Michel feels vindicated to light his cigarette, savouring the spicy taste of the tobacco smoke in his mouth and the glorious euphoria once he's drawn it into his lungs. A *pastis*, a Gitanes, a shot of coffee. On a beautiful day what could possibly be better?

The week was a routine and Sunday was a routine within itself. Michel would get up, attend to the livestock, prepare breakfast, stroll to church, stroll to the bar, stroll home to lunch and spend the afternoon in a daze drawn from the bottom of a bottle of wine. Tomorrow is another week like the one before. And so on.

Routines become automatic: the conveyor upon which life will progress. There are few if any turnings off this path so Michel accepts and enjoys, relishing the pleasures no matter how simple. Things that happen do so of their own accord and seldom impinge on his routine. Which is why Michel has not noticed the gentleman who shares the awning's shade with him.

Michel nods a guarded greeting at the man who returns the nod with a cautious smile and a tentative, '*Excusez-moi*'.

Excusez-moi is the prelude to a conversation, so Michel shifts in his seat to regard the man more formally and to put aside the view of the village square and its occasional flurries of movement: villagers, a child on a bicycle, two blackbirds eyeing each other combatively and a gang of hooligan sparrows rattling around one of the lime trees.

'Can I help you?' he asks.

'What a lovely place.' An uninspiring start to a conversation! Of course it's a lovely place, even if it's not actually *my* lovely place. It's just where I come for a drink and to meet my friends. And to get away from them, too, sometimes.

'Yes. Yes, it is.'

That was supposed to have been the exchange's rejoinder, but the gentleman persists. He leans forward. 'Is that your farm at the bottom of the lane? I thought I saw you leaving it when I was out walking earlier this morning.'

Michel decides to pay the man greater attention. This is not some *paysan*. He is dressed in a summer suit, cream or beige, with an open-necked shirt, brown suede shoes and a Panama hat. Apart from his grey beard, he looks effortlessly cool in the heat of the day. It's the little touches: silver buttonhole holder with iridescent blue cornflower; ring on his finger bearing some sort of crest; elegant Swiss watch. He is drinking a tisane and has a bottle of sugary, gassy orange juice on the side.

'I do live round here.' Non-committal; it's a good policy to open proceedings.

'Forgive me, monsieur. I don't mean to pry into your private life.' A brief pause for response from Michel, but there is none. The man opens his hands slightly to indicate that he is no threat. 'I didn't want to cause you any alarm, either. I am sure you would rather have been given time to yourself on a Sunday and for that I apologise.'

'No alarm taken, monsieur.' Michel relaxes his position to show that he is willing to be congenial. 'This is a nice bar and it would seem rather bad mannered of me not to give a visitor the time of day. Especially when we are the only two people here.' Michel points into the dark interior. 'Jean-Pascale doesn't count!'

'Thank you for that.' And there the conversation ends. Perhaps.

Michel is, at heart, fairly outgoing, although it is too hot to be so right now. But his nature means that he has little stomach for a pause, pregnant or otherwise, when given the proximity of a newcomer, and, other than drinking, smoking and staring at the scenery, there is little else to do, so what harm could a pleasant chat pose?

'You don't seem to be from round here,'

'Originally, no. I was born in Switzerland. The Valais.' *That explains the accent and the watch.* 'But I'm now living in Avignon.'

'Avignon.' Michel repeats with an effort to sound impressed.

'Yes. I've been there with my family for a few years now, I suppose. We love Provence. Almost as much as… Well, it's very different to Lac Leman.' He laughs.

Michel opens up. 'To be honest, I've never ventured too far from St Aubin. I have been to Avignon a couple of times but there's not much there that draws me to the place. It's a bit noisy for my taste.'

'Oh, some parts are less frantic. The old city, round by the cathedral and the university, are a bit more relaxed but, I grant you, the roads beyond the wall are like some enormous chariot race. And you French do make driving more exciting than other countries!'

Both men laughed.

'So what brings you here on a Sunday?' says Michel. 'And, if you don't mind my being inquisitive, alone?'

The visitor moves forward. He tries to hide the fact that this is the moment he has been waiting for; a signal for the real issue to be given an airing. He composes himself. 'I think I will have a glass of wine. This tea is too hot for the weather. Stupid choice, really. Can I get you anything?'

Michel thanks the visitor and asks for another *pastis*. Jean-Pascale sweeps across to the tables and the visitor joins Michel. He offers his card, a sudden formal gesture. Michel takes the card and reads it.

Professor Bernard Croce
Chair of Anthropology
Université d'Avignon et des Pays de Vaucluse
74 Rue Louis Pasteur

Michel looks up. 'Anthropology?'

'Yes.' The professor takes a sip of his chilled wine. Michel chooses the moment to light another cigarette. 'You might have noticed some young guys walking across your land up to the rocky outcrops the last week or so?'

They didn't seem that young to Michel but he nods all the same.

'They are students of mine and they have been doing fieldwork into cave dwellings, looking for evidence of inhabitation by early man.'

'How early?' Michel isn't particularly interested but the professor seems to be getting excited at the prospect of finding someone to talk to about his pet subject and, anyway, after this morning's endless homily, he was more interesting.

'Have you heard of the Lascaux caves in Dordogne?' Michel nods; they are the pride of France. 'They were discovered back in 1940 and, ever since the end of the war, teams of academics, including anthropologists like myself, have been scouting likely locations in search of similar sites.'

'Are there many others?'

'No, not really. The conditions in Lascaux were very particular. They were dry, well ventilated, but not prone to flooding or seepage. This is despite the fact that they're limestone caves, like the ones in the outcrop near your house.'

Near my house, Michel thinks. The professor can see the penny beginning to drop. He continues. 'Those paintings had been there for over seventeen thousand years, since the Palaeolithic era. So they had to have special conditions if they were to withstand the changes in climate, let alone the general passage of time. We've had a couple of mini ice ages since then.'

'So, these… *students* of yours…' Michel's voice trails off. The next question seems rather superfluous.

'Yes, well…' The professor begins as though he is addressing an academic congress with the conclusions of ground-breaking work, 'We think we may have hit on something.' He leans forward conspiratorially and lowers his voice. 'There is definitely evidence of Palaeolithic man having inhabited the caves above your property. I'm not saying it's conclusive yet, but it's highly… suggestive. (One has to be rather careful what one says at junctures like this.)'

'In what way is it "suggestive"?' By now, Michel is becoming wrapped up in the professor's excitement. On reflection it was obvious the man was brimming over with something he had to tell someone.

'How well do you know the caves up there?'

'I went in there a couple of times when I was a kid. I've always lived here, you see. It's my father's place which I inherited about three years back. I never went in there much. There were always too many other things to do on the farm. I was an only child so my parents had no one else to help around the place. I didn't get much free time at all, thinking about it.' Michel flashes back to his childhood: its brevity, its predictability, and the predestination of his future. He snaps back to the present. 'But I don't remember finding anything in there.'

'How far did you venture into the caves?'

'Honestly, not far. They were dark and I suppose I was a bit scared of them. A part of me was worried about getting stuck in there for some reason. What if the roof fell in?' Michel rubs his chin, a gesture of small embarrassment. 'I've never really liked confined spaces.'

The professor relaxes back into his chair and sips some more of his wine. 'Quite. You would have been perfectly safe, but I am grateful for your insecurity in the caves. The paintings in Lascaux have been badly damaged in just the last few years. Their increasing popularity has meant that too many people have been looking at them, breathing on them, rotting the paint. They lay undisturbed for seventeen thousand years and in barely five they are already threatened by annihilation. That's why the authorities are having to consider closing the caves to the public completely. In my opinion, they should do it immediately.'

Michel nods. He has his cigarette in one hand, *pastis* in the other. 'You were saying something about evidence of these paley... What were they again?'

'Palaeolithic. It means in effect "Old Stone Age".' Michel nods again, even though he is still not quite sure what he is nodding for. This isn't a normal conversation for him, and his companion isn't the usual, either. 'We've found a couple of trinkets. Palaeolithic Man seemed to have a bit of time on his hands so he spent it making rock art and jewellery and such.'

'You have to make your own entertainment, don't you?' Michel laughs, seizing an opportunity to leaven the academic dough.

The professor chuckles. 'Very much so. The next step for us is to work our way through the cave system more thoroughly to see if we can find any more art or artefacts from that time. Um...'

Time holds its breath. Michel is unaware that he is perched on the edge of his chair. An invisible string joining him to the professor has pulled him forward, reflecting the academic's transit from the table's edge to his now more reclined position. The professor exhales abruptly:

'I've got to come clean. I'm not here by chance. I know the house where you live. I saw you leave it this morning. But it's not the first time I have laid eyes on you. Myself and my students have been here a few times before. I didn't want to disturb you until I absolutely had to, but we are all… Well, let's say that matters have crossed a threshold and I need to engage your help.'

'*My* help?'

'Yes. You live next to the caves. Your house is by the only track that leads to them. Anybody who ventures up there must, to some extent, disturb you. Therefore you are ideally placed to be the guardian, the *custodian* of the site. We need someone who is willing to keep people away from the caves and who is willing to keep their existence quiet. At least for the time being. Until we've had the chance to survey the caves completely.'

The professor lets the words hang under the awning, safe from the afternoon breeze. Michel doesn't move; he knows that a proposition is about to present itself but he doesn't want to pre-empt anything. One thing he learned from his father: when striking a deal, let silence be your ally and let the other guy do all the talking until he's named his price. Then ask for double.

The professor interprets Michel's silence as encouragement to go on. 'So, the university would like to pay you a stipend.' Michel gives a quizzical look, 'An annual fee for standing watch over the caves. And for keeping other people away.'

'How much "annual fee"?'

'The university would like to offer ten thousand francs a year.'

'I would prefer twenty thousand.'

'Oh, come on now! How much does your farm make you at the moment?'

'Firstly…' Michel has the upper hand at last; horse trading is his meat and drink. And livelihood. 'We are not discussing my farm. My farm is my farm and, as such, is a separate matter entirely. And secondly, with respect, I'm not sure that it's your concern.'

The professor puts up his hands in surrender. 'I'm so frightfully sorry. I didn't mean to be intrusive. I was merely trying to put twenty thousand francs into context against the revenue your farm generates.' He lets his head fall a little. 'And you are quite right. It was improper of me to have asked. The heat of the day and the occasion has got the better of my manners. I apologise.' The professor nods and Michel accepts his apology with a nod of his own.

Again, silence falls between the two men and they sip their drinks once more. The professor carefully, thoughtfully places his wine glass on the table before him, looks at Michel and smiles.

PROFESSOR DAN SIBLEY

Oxford, May 2005.

His rooms are empty now; the tutorial is over. The students are departed, yet their presence lingers as though the ghosts have not yet decided to follow on behind. The aura slowly fades. The chatter and scuffing of soles on the ancient steps recedes and a silence gradually filling with air, birdsong and the distant thrum of the city washes into the rooms.

Sibley exhales and leans back in his chair, tilting it away from his cluttered desk.

Professor Crispin Daniforth-Sibley likes to project the image of a louche, aged hippy despite not being old enough to have partaken in the bacchanalia of the 1960s. (He was only nine years old in the Summer of Love.) He has developed his own uniform: jeans, garish suede waistcoats, floral shirts, bead necklaces, earrings and fawn leather shoes. He has long, greying hair which he pointedly never ties in a ponytail.

His rooms at college are festooned with ornaments, rugs and throws collected over the years from various souks and bazaars in out-of-the-way towns in North Africa or the Indian subcontinent. There is the vague smell of patchouli masking the scent of other herbal materials. He experiences a faint disorientation, glancing out of this bohemian room, redolent of a Marrakesh *riad* and into the august, splendid and sublimely English vista of an Oxford college quadrant.

He has strived for many years to cultivate his outwardly laid-back demeanour; this has had the effect of setting him apart from both his academic peers and his students. As such, it lends him a pleasant but forbidding air and sets his charges on edge. He likes to project an image of the brilliant but temperamental *wunderkind* and surrounds himself in the paraphernalia of his own mystique.

But it is all artifice. And well he knows it.

The *wunderkind*—for once he was that star child—has long since slipped into the past. His early flashes of inspiration which launched his ascendance to the select company of quantum physicists are all spent. He has built up quite a bibliography of published papers and monographs, but every new one adds less to the sum of human knowledge than the one before. He is in danger of repeating himself.

And was that *wunderkind* a younger, hippy version of what teeters on an Oxford chair today? No. In those days, Sibley was a Nice Young Man who dressed conservatively and had a haircut that met with his mother's approval. The affectations followed The Breakthrough. But few either remember or know and so the myth of the groovy professor has prevailed.

It was about the time of The Breakthrough that his name became 'Dan': short for Daniforth, but few were aware of that, either. He has loathed that his parents chose to name him after a distant and long-dead ancestor. *Crispin*, for God's sake; that's what you call a vicar of a parish church in some lost Devonian valley, or some gaudy-jumpered presenter on children's television. Who has ever heard of a physicist called bloody Crispin? And woe betide anyone who ever called him 'Cris'!

So here he sits, alone in his fusty splendour, trading on a reputation that had been all too fleeting and yet was sustained, if not camouflaged, by his swagger and exotic accoutrements. He had led a life of discovery that had been so vibrant and new, but was now becoming predictable. Before him stretches fifteen more years in academe, teaching students ever more repetitive courses freshened occasionally with the advances of other people's work.

Sibley leans forward and the front two legs of his chair return to the floor with a satisfying clunk. A book on a nearby shelf topples onto its side. He walks to the shelf at the opposite end of the room and reaches for a bottle of scotch; it's still only five o'clock but what the hell. It might relax his ossifying brain and help him absorb the contents of the buff folder on his desk.

There is still one chance that he might repulse the inexorable, creeping tide of mediocrity. King Canute knew that he had no power over the elemental forces of nature and went to extreme lengths to demonstrate it to his fawning courtiers. But many of the secrets of quantum physics remain undiscovered and a new insight might yet lift the beach from the sea and turn the sinister tide.

Otto is onto something. Sibley can sense it. The boy is still an undergraduate but he was born to describe the universe. Equations, proofs, conjectures and arguments flow from him effortlessly. He is hard to keep up with, even for an Oxford professor approaching his half-century. But the basic principles are always in line with the very bedrock of marvellous science: simplicity. No one ever says, 'That's genius. It's so complicated!'

It isn't a thesis; it's a discussion paper. A pitch. The document is only about fifteen or so pages, hardly comprehensive, but the mathematical concepts and accompanying narrative are compelling. If Otto could persuade his professor-cum-tutor that his concept could be demonstrated in the laboratory, then his theory had to be intellectually and scientifically watertight.

Dan scribbles some notes on a separate block of paper. Stab points, scoring out, quick sips of whisky. The sun starts to dim, lowering the quad below into a soft spring gloom. An angry blackbird remonstrates with an intruder.

The first hypothesis is that all dimensions are grouped in threes, all at mutual right angles: the scalar dimensions (up, forward, sideways); the electromagnetic dimensions (electric field, magnetic field, motive force); the thermal dimensions (kinetic energy, light, dark energy); and the gravito-spatial dimensions (gravity, light, time). So far, so-so. Otto has taken the established concept of a universe with eleven dimensions and categorised them. Others have worked on this before and emerged with broadly similar findings. Otto's inspiration is the grouping together.

The second hypothesis: at a quantum level, there is no mass, there is only gravity and mass *per se* (indeed, all matter) is a manifestation of gravity, not the other way around. Revolutionary stuff, Dan thinks; an interesting way of describing the nature of matter. But has he missed something? He has made the leap that, by altering one dimension's value, it will automatically express a different value for the other two.

Dan pours himself another scotch and returns to his block of paper. He bends over the paper and surveys the marks and scribbles. His gaze switches from his jottings to Otto's notes, back and forth. He can feel his younger self, a faint distant voice encouraging, insistent. The tide of dullness may yet be resisted; a new future may yet present itself. He knows his fate is to be no more the star child, but he can be the midwife. There is much he can add to this proposition; quite apart from his experience, there are his contacts.

If this hypothesis is true, then it will require substantial university resources to demonstrate it experimentally. For one thing, they are going to need some time on the new-generation synchrotron that is nearing completion. Dan has heard that his old colleague Hugo will be installed as director of the establishment so maybe he can get some time on the initial runs while they calibrate the massively powerful beam. Then there's the funding. The tech transfer people at Illumina are going to get a call for sure.

But there's nagging doubt.

The role of the specialist, the *expert*, is that of historian: the custodian of the sure and certain knowledge of everything that has happened in the past. The expert is the jealous guardian of that bank of knowledge and the esteem of the expert is challenged whenever someone comes forward with ideas that extrapolate that knowledge and propose new theories. These will be beyond the expert's ken and will constitute a threat to his esteem, his reputation, his legitimacy.

The expert can respond in one of two ways: repudiate or embrace. In the first instance, if the experiment fails then his reputation will remain unstained, but it won't win him any popularity prizes. In the second, if the expert adopts an open-minded position and the experiment is a success, then he will transcend into the new age of knowledge and he will re-establish his supremacy as a leading light in the field.

The risk: guess wrong and you look a fool. Dan strokes his beard; to be resistant to new ideas would confirm his fossilisation and blow away all trace of his cool, hippy fabrication. His clothes have made the choice for him; Dan will do what he can to make this happen.

THE OXFORD MAIL

Oxford. September 2014.

[Headline] *HUNT ON FOR OXFORD DOUBLE JACKPOT WINNER*

[Copy] *A mystery Oxford man has apparently won an unprecedented TWO lottery jackpots worth nearly an amazing £146 million within twenty-four hours.*

*The winning tickets for the National Lotto and the EuroMillions draws were both purchased last Thursday evening from a shop on Walton Road, Jericho. The Lotto jackpot is estimated to be worth £7.3 **million** thanks to a double roll-over, whilst the EuroMillions jackpot was worth over £138.4 **million**! According to the organisers of the lotteries, neither prize has been shared with anyone else.*

Shop owner Amandeep Rai will not be drawn on the identity of the lucky man. 'I have to be very careful to protect people's privacy,' he tells the Mail, 'especially when considering the very large amount of money at stake here'. Mr Rai says that he can confirm both of the tickets were jackpot winners and that the man in question is 'due a very pleasant surprise.'

The Mail has learned through other sources that the man is likely in his late twenties and is believed to be a student or a postgraduate at the university.

Latest reports from the lottery organisers suggest that the lucky winner has yet to come forward. He has six months before his ticket becomes void and the winnings automatically go to charity.

With nearly £146 million in the bank, our mystery winner will join the ranks of the UK super-rich, beating such superstars as Daniel Radcliffe (reputed to be worth over £50 million) and even Oxford's own Thom Yorke (£35 million). But he is not quite in the same league as the Beckhams (about £200 million).

This combined win means that he will be the UK's third largest lottery winner ever, just behind Adrian and Gillian Bayford who won over £148 million in 2012 and Colin and Chris Weir who scooped over £161 million on the EuroMillions in July 2011.

Mr Rai says he is 'absolutely over the moon' about having sold the winning tickets and wishes the winner the very best for the future. Asked what he would do with so much cash, Mr Rai modestly says, 'I would probably give most of it to my family and leave enough for me and my wife to have a few nice holidays.'
[Copy ends]

THE ASSASSIN

Vienna. February 1911.

This is the last time, as far as I am concerned. I have chased this bloody man all over the place and he continues to elude me. No one has managed to do this before, at least not for this long. This time I'm going to make a proper job of it and finish this once and for all.

I've been staying at the dormitory on Meldemannstraße for three weeks and they have been the coldest bloody three weeks of my life. The building is a forbidding edifice and what passes for heating amounts to a pathetic fire in a single grate of the grandiosely named 'Reading Room'. Even the term 'fire' is an exaggeration. It's nothing but a couple of bits of wet wood that sit in the grate and send smoke up the chimney (some of the time; I don't know when it was last cleaned). There are gas lamps and steam heating, but the fucking things are never turned on unless some board member from the charity is expected to drop by.

The building is cold, but the staff are colder. Everything is too much trouble, with the feeling that you're here because you're too worthless to be anywhere else (a bit rich given that I'm here because, like everyone else, I've paid). Not much, granted. Only two and a half crowns. But it's still money after all. It's just that ingrained snobbery of the Viennese. If you're not twirling around some glittery ballroom whilst some screechy little palm court orchestra murders Strauss or Lehar, then you're just a random piece of shit. As if *they* ever get invited to swanky military balls. Arseholes!

We're just the *bettgeher*—the bed lodgers—and we are a threat to their cosy, petty-bourgeois notions of society. We are airbrushed out of their postcards, their picture books and their minds.

The residents here seem largely unbothered by the attitude of their supposed servants, which makes me hate the staff even more. They all spend the time engaged in various empty pursuits. Most are in Vienna to pull themselves out of the rut their lives have fallen into. There's work to be had here, but overcoming the innate suspicion of the business proprietors is an uphill struggle. You want to work as a waiter in Vienna? How polished are your shoes? What is your accent like? How would the esteemed clientele react if they encountered you? You're not from round here. I'm not sure about you. It's nothing personal. Goodbye.

Yeah, whatever. Goodbye, and fuck you!

Once you've got your foot on that first greasy rung, then things start to become a bit more straightforward. They don't become easy, though. Work well and keep your nose clean for a good nine to eighteen months and you acquire a record of note; you become a 'good character'. You're still treated like shit, though, because that is your place. And if you know what's good for you, you rejoice in your new-found status as a piece of shit and blow plenty of smoke up the arse of everyone in an Astrakhan coat. Because then you advertise the fact that you are inferior and that is good for their self-image (especially if they are out parading some high-class whore before their peers, presenting her as their 'niece'.) And then you get tips and your boss is happy because the man in the Astrakhan coat will come back, probably with another 'niece'.

And that would be your ticket out of here. Hard graft and an inability to find anything distasteful, at least not overtly.

What *wouldn't* be your ticket out of here would be to adopt my target's routine.

At 9am they shut the cubicles where each man sleeps. So, he crawls out of bed at 8.59am, probably still wearing the same shirt and trousers he wore yesterday. He then takes up a position in the non-smoking part of the Reading Room and quickly annexe the supply of newspapers which he reads through at length. After a quick lunch in the canteen—

tafelspitz or *rindsuppe*—he takes up his easel and brushes in the same corner where he has spent the morning, producing works of unimaginable mediocrity. At some point in the afternoon he has Löffner run along and get something tasty from the local delicatessen, after which he resumes his artistic pursuits.

(It must be lovely on this lunatic's planet, living the life of the effete country gentleman in a boater and blazer, painting scenes of riparian bliss as punts patrol up and down the river.)

After dinner, he resumes his life of splendour, expounding on the political issues of the day with a collection of his intellectual Jewish friends and a couple of other obliging lickspittles. And, after a bracing evening of discourse and debate, he traipses off to bed and a lovely night's sleep.

Annoyingly, he spends almost no time at all on his own.

That rules out taking up some distant vantage point and waiting for him to embark on his regular morning constitutional down to the banks of the Danube at 10.30 precisely. Because he doesn't make one. It also rules out the casual walk-past silenced shot from under a rolled up jacket. Manual extermination— stabbing, garrotting, cervical fracture—is not feasible as there are too many people around him and it would take too long for him to die. There is also the practical problem of getting close enough. It could be made more possible if I developed a personal relationship with the target, but this is something I never do; I prefer professional detachment as it helps me sleep at night. And anyway, in this guy's case, I really don't want to get to know him. I suppose I could always poison him, but that's not my style and there's always the risk that the poison would end up being ingested by someone other than the target.

That brings me back to shooting. I need to find some reason to get him away from this place and on his own. The key may have presented itself to me in a small *bierkeller* and *brauerei* on Muthgasse round the back of the Heiligenstadt *bahnhof*. The man had been drunk and from the right social stratum: if it's wearing black tie, is shitfaced and feeling sorry for itself, it can be persuaded to do things it wouldn't otherwise countenance.

He was perfect: from a well-to-do family with the right connections and a reputation to uphold at all cost. He had found himself in a spot of difficulty with a gentleman who was planning to take him to the cleaners—both socially and financially—for an indiscretion with his fourteen-year-old daughter. Leaving out the sob story that this was not the fourteen-year-old's first dalliance, it meant that my prospect was highly suggestible. So I suggested something that he agreed to so readily he knocked his own beer over in order to grasp my hand and shake it. He was weeping with gratitude and I was concerned he was going to draw attention. But then again, in a Viennese boozery late at night, no one is going to be in much of a fit state to notice anything.

My part of the bargain was to be fulfilled the next evening in the Praterpark. I felt a little bad about the prospect of what I had to do to the fourteen-year-old but consoled myself that she had been a complicit party in the family business of extorting money from high society. It would be a fairly simple stroll-by affair performed with the aid of a silenced Beretta hidden under a coat.

I had to impress on him that I would do my part after he had done his; besides, doing my part first would weaken my position and might give him the nerve to welch on the deal. He had one job to do and it wasn't going to be complicated. He, or his representative, would come to Meldemannstraße and ask to see Löffner about commissioning his friend to paint a house in a well-heeled part of the city.

It was going to be a surprise for his father whose birthday was next Thursday. Owing to my target's busy diary, the only day that would be practical for the exterior work to be done would be next Monday (in three days time). That, at least, would give the artist a couple of days to finish the artwork and deliver it to him at the same address at the end of the day on Wednesday.

Löffner readily agreed and informed the well-dressed man that the fee for the *meisterwerk* would be fifty crowns. After some pleasantries masking mutual enmity, the price was settled at thirty-five crowns and it was agreed that the artist would show up at the address at eight o'clock on the Monday.

This gave me the best part of three days to locate and establish a suitable position and scope out exactly how long it would take for me to get from there to the exfiltration point in one of the more densely wooded corners of the Praterpark at noon.

So here I am atop a block of swanky apartments in the old heart of Vienna near the Domkirche St Stephan freezing my balls off waiting for some haphazard little painter to turn up and start doing his thing. I derive some pleasure— why was it only the Germans who coined a single word for *schadenfreude*?—from the fact that he has had to get his sorry arse out of bed three hours sooner than usual, that there is a marrow-chilling easterly wind bearing with it occasional flecks of hateful wet snow, and that I get to finally shut the fucker up. As I already said, I don't like developing a relationship with any of my targets, but by God, this one was going to be an absolute pleasure.

To his credit, at five minutes to eight, he shuffles into view. He knocks at the tradesman's entrance and is met by one of the servants who peers at him disparagingly, then shows him the exterior of the house (as if it couldn't be seen already). The street is busy with horses and pedestrians on their way to their places of business for the day; it will be a while before things settle down and the street empties. Which is fine by me; I can get nicely settled on my roof nestling against the chimney stack and the parapet and adjust the telescopic sight on the rifle until the target is fixed in the crosshairs, marking a point just to the left of his spine. He won't feel a thing; at this point, that's justice enough, since he hasn't yet done anything that warrants him suffering.

And I wait.

And I rehearse in my mind the route from this point to the exfiltration: forty-five minutes on foot, allow an hour if I choose to saunter and behave like a visitor to the city rather than someone escaping from the scene of a crime. I could do it in under twenty-five minutes if I take a tram and walk only part of the way. In an emergency, I could always hail a cab but that would be a last resort. The fewer people who know I even exist today, the better.

It is now 10am. The painter is absorbed in his work; he has taken to sitting under an umbrella which he has managed to sweet-talk out of the valet in the client's house. This at least is keeping the sleet off his canvas. I'm no painter, but I imagine it's not easy to work when the surface you are using is getting wet. The street is all but deserted, with every honest citizen of Vienna at work or indoors. The artist is sitting on the corner of the house where two roads meet, just across the road from it. This affords him a reasonable aspect from where he can give some depth and perspective to his frightful composition. It means that the rifle has to be angled down fairly sharply, but I've had worse shots to take and not missed before. My location is such that only someone flying directly overhead in a silent dirigible is going to see me, and flying machines of that sort are going to be pretty rare on a day like this.

A quick check all around, a glance at the rifle itself.

All looks good. Time to do this thing and get out of here.

I squint into the sight, steady myself, slow my breathing, force myself to calm down.

I gently squeeze the trigger. It is just me and him; there is nothing else. It is an intimate moment, almost sacred. The trigger retracts and the rifle recoils, just as something blurs on the telescopic sight.

At first I think it's me: an eyelid, a hair, I don't know what. Then I hear the crump of a body collapsing on the cobbles, skidding wheels and a cab driver's cry of alarm. The cab lurches down and over as it tries to avoid the body of the horse. Instead, the shafts dig into the horse's body and pushes it over to the side of the road, into the gutter. I peep out from my position.

The painter, obviously alarmed, staring at the dead horse.

The weeping cabbie and the screaming passengers inside and the rolling tide of blood that spreads along the ground from the horse's head.

I don't bother to look any more.

I don't bother to swear.

I don't have time to sink my head into my hands. I have to go.

Nothing it seems will kill this bloody man. Not my best efforts. Nothing. It is going to be a long couple of hours between here and the Praterpark and it will be even longer trying to explain why it's all been fucked up yet again.

He won't be happy.

GERALD MURPHY

Cap d'Antibes. August 1925.

His eyes are closed, whether in ecstasy or concentration it is hard to know. People watch him and sense a beatific aura envelope him in this, his moment of creation. The rattle of the ice in the shaker; it is the rattle of Buddhist prayer wheels or the toll of Shinto bells. He stands, shoulders back, hands clasped about the chrome shaker. The incense of the air fills his senses: juniper, black pine, sage and the flowers in the herbaceous border mingling with the hot, red scent of the earth itself. He has no need for sight; that would be a lesser sense. Superfluous.

The glasses wait ready, cloaked in condensation, their rims coated in sugar. The rattling ceases and he strains a clouded, garish potion into each vessel. Orange, grapefruit, lime, lemon and, of course, gin: the Juice of a Few Flowers. The juice of the Cote d'Azur sun which is reddening and sinking behind dull, blue mountains framing a milky sea.

Gerald hands a glass to Sara and to his new guest, both of whom are seated at the table on the terrace of Villa America with the others—Fernand and his wife Jeanne-Augustine and the saturnine Dottie—all bedecked in evening finery. They have been spellbound by the rites performed for them by the high priest of the cocktail, a spectacle lent an even more sublime quality side-lit by the setting sun. Small candles in lanterns flicker on the table and they raise their glasses in friendship and appreciation before taking their first sip.

'God, I love this!' Gerald lifts the glass before his eyes, admiring his handiwork.

'Thank you for this. For this marvellous drink.' The guest recoils from the tartness of the cocktail which the sugared rim is unable to counter. If anything, the sugar accentuates the acidic mix. But it is a glorious concoction: the equivalent in taste of a firework display, with the fruit giving colour, the gin detonation.

'Mikhail, it is my supreme pleasure.' Gerald slumps as far back into his chair as the structure will permit and awards himself another sip. He laughs and regards his glass yet again. He shakes his head with disbelief. 'It's a frightening thought, my friend. I'm sitting here in these beautiful surroundings, in the company of fine people doing nobody that I can see any harm and yet I'm violating the Eighteenth Amendment.' He permits himself a wide grin. 'I'm a traitor to the United States of America.'

The group all laugh heartily. Fernand, who is sitting next to the new guest Mikhail, claps loudly and shouts, 'Vive la revolution!' while Sara passes a small dish of olives to Dottie and Jeanne-Augustine. Dottie turns her nose up at the olives at first, then blithely picks one between forefinger and thumb and drops it into her dry martini. There, it coils down the sides of the conical glass like a ball in a roulette wheel and joins its incumbent cousin.

She looks up at Gerald. 'There's a certain irony, I suppose. You could be shot at dawn for a shot at sunset.' More laughter. It seems so ludicrous that they should try and ban something that makes people so happy.

Gerald leans across to Mikhail. 'So, I trust that my friends at the Hotel du Cap are looking after you well enough?'

'Royally. Thank you, Gerald. And thank you once again for your invitation to join you here this evening in your wonderful villa.' He nods his head. 'I feel most honoured.' Dottie tuts and rolls her eyes.

'And how are things back in *Gaye Paris*?'

'I am not really in much of a position to tell you, I'm afraid.'

Gerald raises an eyebrow. 'Oh? How come?'

'I have been travelling rather a lot since I last saw you at Étienne de Beaumont's splendid parties. As you know, I have been trying to finalise arrangements for the rest of my family.'

Gerald addresses the rest of the group. 'I should explain. Mikhail had to flee Russia after the Bolsheviks took over. Something about your mother's—'

'My aunt.'

'Ah, yes. Something about Mikhail's aunt's close relationship to the Tsar. Second cousin or something. Am I right?' Mikhail nods. 'Naturally, the Bolsheviks won't hand out travel permits without the necessary paperwork.' Gerald rubs his thumb and forefinger together in the universal gesture for *baksheesh*. 'Otherwise, the only travel they encourage is in the direction of Siberia, am I right?' Mikhail shudders. Sara takes a sharp intake of breath.

'It is not the money,' says Mikhail. 'The biggest problem I have is finding who I can give it to, such that it will make any difference. There are legions of apparatchiks who will accept my gracious donation to the revolutionary proletariat cause without doing anything specific in return.'

'Who are you trying to get out?' says Fernand.

'My wife, my mother, and my brother and his family. He has two children who are still quite young. They all live in Petrograd.'

'How come you managed to get away?' Dottie is nestled behind her dry martini like a cobra.

'I was out of the country on business when the revolution happened. By the time I knew what was going on, it was too late to get transport home. The war in Flanders made travel arrangements harder still.'

'So what did you do?' Fernand is obviously distressed by the tale and is trying to be sympathetic.

'Nothing, really. I gravitated toward Paris and found myself caught up in society there. In many ways it has turned out to be useful. There are many other Russian émigrés there. With this and the many American contacts we have made in Paris, it has enabled us to build a campaign. We want exit visas for those the Bolsheviks consider 'undesirable'. That will be my family.'

Gerald looks across at the Russian. Despite the surroundings, the glamorous evening wear, the cocktails and handmade cigarettes and the effete company, this man seems small and pinched. His bird-like features are accentuated by his black, back-combed hair. He has the brooding countenance of a small bird of prey. A kestrel, perhaps. Waiting, calculating. A distant gong chimes and the reverie is broken. The group all stand and file in to the villa, greeted by the first aromas of the evening's meal.

Mikhail is the last guest to step through the terrace windows, followed closely by Gerald. The room is brightly lit, contrasting with the muted evening outside. At the far end, near a cabal of armchairs, sofas and coffee tables, stands an easel and a large, square painting.

'I like that,' says Mikhail.

Gerald smiles. 'Thank you.'

'Did you do that?' Mikhail is incredulous.

'Well, yes.' Gerald tries to sound modest.

'It's very good.' The Russian tiptoes up to the canvas and squints. 'Very good, indeed. It must have taken you quite a while to paint this. The detail is very fine.'

'Thank you again. I suppose it's taken about a month or six weeks to get it right. But I was only working on it off and on.'

Mikhail returns to scrutinising the canvas. 'Do you ever sell any of your work?'

'Heavens, no.' Gerald is truly amused by this notion. 'I've exhibited a few of my pieces before now, back in Paris. But I'm not intending to make this any kind of profession.' He stands in the middle of the room on the path between the terrace and the dining room, hoping that the Russian's stomach will overrule his artistic hunger. He clears his throat.

Mikhail gives a start and whips round to face Gerald with wide eyes. 'Oh my goodness. I'm so sorry. I was completely swept away by this. It is just marvellous.' He sounds to Gerald like an adolescent who has just spied the love of his life for the first time. An infatuation has begun.

The two men walk to dinner with the Russian continuing to extol the artistic merits of the painting. Gerald hopes that this does not become the predominant topic of conversation all night. Dottie would never forgive him and would probably kill Mikhail by immortalising him in some of her caustic verse. Although that could be rather fun.

After dinner, Gerald and his guests play cards and listen to music. They drink more of Gerald's cocktails and talk of art and love and the joy of being in France, on the Cote d'Azur, and they drink some more and gamble like children for childish sums over their cards, and gradually the evening fades to slumber and the company yields of the inevitable, of every wonderful occasion, and gracefully dissolves.

In the morning the painting and the Russian are missing.

Gerald sees neither of them again.

PART TWO

THE OXFORD
HISTORY UNIT

JACK BRADEN

Corona, New Mexico. June 1947.

Jack is checking fencing. He likes to check fencing. It gets him out of the homestead and into the deep country. It gets him away from the men, away from the human race altogether. The boys have been tasked with making good the fences so the sheep don't stray too far and it looks as though they've done a fine job. Nothing to complain about here.

He climbs back onto his horse and rides further south along the line. The country here is fairly undemanding; it rolls a bit but nothing major. No high mountains round here, other than the land itself which is already near enough seven thousand feet up. In the winter it gets pretty darn cold, but here in the middle of June it is fine and dry and warm. In fact, it's going to be a real nice day, especially if he can keep it to himself.

The horse lopes and rolls its shoulders across the jumbled terrain; the dirt is hard-packed enough to cause the animal no problems. He takes it steady, though; no need to do anything stupid. It's a long, hard walk back to the homestead and it's probably two or three days waiting to die otherwise. Slim chance of being found out here if something goes wrong.

It's getting on for eleven now and Jack's been riding and inspecting for nearly five hours with the sun in his eyes most of the way. He kicks the horse on up to the top of the next ridge where he can get a good all-round view of where he has to go next and take the opportunity to make some coffee and have a cigarette. The view from the ridge is big and glorious. It's not so much the view of the land that is so fine—the land itself is pretty featureless with the trees all but given way to scrub—but the huge sky is like a cathedral roof. The angel-white clouds drift and curl overhead, drawing Jack's gaze ever upward. It puts him in mind of something he learned in Sunday School.

I will lift up mine eyes to the hills from whence cometh my help. My help cometh from the Lord which made heaven and earth. He will not suffer thy foot to be moved. He that keepeth thee will not slumber.

Braden had best not slumber. There's still a way to go yet and the day isn't eternal, but nothing's going to get done until that coffee and that smoke. So he sits on a nearby rock and savours the moment. It's not his land, but he loves it like his own, and it feels good being back here. It's the strong sense of place, after having been wrenched from home for so many years.

The kids'll be coming up to stay at the ranch in a day or two, so this kind of work needs to be done now. After that, Jack will try to focus his time on doing chores around the ranch and pulling together all the management stuff: accounts, paying the men, getting some stores in from Corona on Dubois and Main, or Albuquerque if it's anything larger.

He raises the coffee mug to his mouth and takes a long, slow sip of that rich, rough, brown taste and complements it with a rewarding draw on his cigarette. He knows they are probably no good for him, despite the doctors advising on which brand to favour, but it does make a good day a whole lot better.

As he lowers the cigarette from his mouth, something catches his eye. He sits stock still and tilts his head slowly from side to side like a big cat or dog. He doesn't know if it makes any difference, but he thinks he can see more that way.

Nothing.

Maybe it's just some trick of the eye…

There it is again. A flash. He didn't imagine it.

Jack gets his field glasses out and has another look. He can't be sure, but… *People*? What in the hell are they doing out here? There isn't a road for miles in these parts and they don't have a horse or a Jeep. Nothing. They got tents, but that's about it. And what the..?

He discards the coffee dregs and gets back on the horse, riding off in the direction of the people. They are a good couple of miles off so it's going to take him about ten minutes, but they don't seem to be going anywhere; they're just sitting there by the stock tank watching him approach. It looks as though one them has got an eyepiece of some description. A telescope?

As he gets nearer, Jack can see that there's three of them, and two tents. They are all men, dressed in outdoor gear. The thing that's really out of place is the large piece of silver material hooked onto a rock, blowing around. As the wind is from the south, the material is being billowed in the direction of the tank and that's going to scare the sheep. If they don't drink water when they should, then they could get dehydrated and have accidents. Thirsty sheep don't think too good and act even worse.

Sure enough, the sheep had wandered some way off. Dammit!

The horse slows its pace as it nears the men and, before he gets too close, Jack gives a cursory, 'Howdy!' The men all respond by waving. 'Can I help you? This is private property.'

'We're sorry to trespass,' says the man nearest him. Strange accent, maybe east coast. He has one of those strange beards: goatees. Jack thinks they look kinda stupid. The other two also seem a bit weird; one guy has long hair, real curly. The guys back at the ranch would soon sort that out; they'd probably call him a girl.

'Can I ask what you're doing here?'

'Of course. We were just passing through when we—'

Jack cut him off. 'No one "just passes though" here. And especially not on foot. It must be ten miles to the nearest track from here.'

'We're not on foot,' says the first man with the odd accent (Boston?). Jack studies the second man behind him. He can now see what he's holding to his eye: a small home movie camera; he's seen photos of them in magazine ads. 'We left our truck back on the track over there.' He points in the vague direction of a low rise. Jack knows there *is* a track out there, but it hasn't been used since Adam was a boy.

'Okay.' Jack begins slowly and patiently. 'Mind if I ask the nature of your business?'

'We were following that,' says the Bostonian, pointing at the flapping fabric. The sun flashes off its silver skin. Jack draws a breath and is on the verge of asking the next, obvious, question when the Bostonian shows he has the manners to answer it first. 'It's the remains of a weather balloon. It's nothing special but we like to get them back as a rule.'

'Where you guys from exactly?'

'National Oceanic and Atmospheric Administration,' he says. 'NOAH for short. I'm Bob Crowmarsh, one of the directors of the south-west climate project. We're trying to map the different wind patterns over the south-western states at different altitudes.'

'Where you based?'

'Maryland. Where you from?'

'I work at the ranch up north from here. I'm the foreman and I gotta check on the stock from time to time.' Jack waves at the thrashing balloon. 'This thing is gonna scare the stock and I'm going to have to ask you to help me get it packed up.'

'Of course,' says the Bostonian. 'That'll be our pleasure.'

Over the next twenty minutes, the four men gather up the flapping material and bundle it all up in a roll, then weigh it down with rocks.

Once all the material has been safely stowed, one of the other men lights a fire and they brew up a coffee. Jack joins them, hoping to learn more, but no one says very much; the only one doing any talking at all is the Bostonian. One of the other men is taking long, slow panning shots with the movie camera, including a few shots of Jack himself.

'I appreciate the attention,' say Jack, 'but do you mind if you point your camera somewhere else?' The man does as he is asked, raising his hands in a wordless apology.

He notices that one of the men is sitting next to a small piece of equipment that has been salvaged from the debris. 'Do you mind me asking what that is?'

The Bostonian takes a noisy slurp of his coffee. 'That's the data recorder from the balloon.' Jack shrugs his shoulders; what does he know? Still, everything else they've picked up seems wrecked, but the "recorder" is pristine. It's about the size of a child's toy blackboard slate, but white and smooth and shiny with rounded edges. He couldn't be sure, but it looked like the outline of an apple on the back of it.

'So what's next with all this…?' Jack tries to find a word for trash that isn't likely to offend his visitors but gives up and just waves his hand in the direction of the heaped wreckage.

The Bostonian nods his head. 'Well, we'd need to report it to the County Sheriff first and then arrange for some guys on horseback to come and get it all. We can't carry it back to the truck from here. There's too much of it for the three of us to carry. Along with all our other gear, I guess.' His voice trails off as he sits and stares at the pile of bits under the silver balloon.

A silence settles on the group. Jack speaks up. 'Look. I'll tell you what. My kids are coming over to join me for the summer in a couple of weeks. There can't be more than four or five sacks here. We can come back, pick it up and hand it over to the Lincoln County Sheriff. I know the guy, he's a friend of mine. He'll know what to do with it.'

'That would be very accommodating of you, sir,' says the Bostonian. 'Thank you very much. Can we give you anything for your kids' trouble?'

Jack thinks for a second 'Yeah, I guess they'd appreciate that. Though God knows what they can spend it on out here. I'll put it to their college education. Or something.'

The Bostonian reaches into a back pocket and pulls out a wallet. He removes a twenty-dollar bill and gives it to Jack, who whistles in surprise. 'Uncle Sam is paying,' says the Bostonian. 'Don't worry.'

'Where you guys heading now?'

'Well, now we've tracked this balloon down and we've got the data recorder, we'll just head for the truck and go back to Albuquerque. If you like, we can stop off at the Sheriff's office and let him know that you'll be coming by in a week or two with the equipment. It's useful that you know him already. That'll save us a job.'

'After that? I mean, don't you guys want all this stuff back again?'

The Bostonian clears his throat. 'Technically, this all belongs to NOAA although actually it's a heap of garbage now. So I guess we'll ask him to contact NOAA and they'll send someone official out to pick it up from him, otherwise it's going to make his office look a mess. Then they'll fly it back to Maryland.'

Jack nods. 'They should be able to make that happen real quick round here. There's an Army Air Force base not twenty miles away.'

'Oh? Which one's that?'

'Roswell.'

MATT JENNINGS

Oxford. Monday October 12th, 0900hrs.

Now what?

I've been left waiting here for bloody ages. They asked me to come in at the appointed hour and I did my civic duty and presented myself accordingly to the... whatever he is. Certainly not a real police officer, let alone a desk sergeant. The DI is obviously running late as she should have been here over thirty minutes ago. While I am always happy to help our local constabulary (except when I want to get up the A34 a bit faster than the speed limit allows) I also have a job and it won't wait for me. And they've left me to fester in the bit next to the front door and facing the reception desk with a very closed door next to it. I suppose you'd call it a corridor, except it doesn't exactly allow for free passage, since it's little more than a space between two closed doors with a bench along one wall. It sure as hell isn't a waiting room, either. There isn't a single magazine to read; just lots of patronising posters reminding me to 'Lock It Or Lose It' (my bike, that is) and a number of notices featuring blurry CCTV stills or fanciful identikit pictures of felons the police would like to eliminate from their enquiries. After a bloody good hiding, most likely.

I seem to spend most of my time waiting for someone or other. Yesterday it was Otto. Today it is Detective Inspector Pauline Campbell. At least that is what the Police Support Officer said when he rang me this morning. The police seem to have lots of hangers-on working for them, but very few actual policemen.

Someone is coming to the door. The latch turns. False alarm?

No! This time, we're on. Finally!

DI Campbell, I presume: business-like, in some form of trouser suit. Fairly tall and blonde with scary black-rimmed specs; she certainly doesn't want to project a girly-girl image. I can imagine that wouldn't do you any favours in the police; whatever their PR might say, they still have an unofficial reputation for being stuck in the nineteen fifties. And they still don't let women in the masons. So, if you wear a dress you're probably scuppered.

How do you do and all that. Thank you for taking the time out of your busy blah, blah, blah. Would I come this way? Hopefully this won't take too long.

Through the very closed door with the combination panel, follow meekly past various desks and milling people. All rather chaotic but I'm sure they know what they're about.

Up a set of stairs laid with a kind of plastic fabric that passes for carpet but looks indestructible and on to the first floor.

Along a window-lined passageway flanked with more offices and rooms, then through yet another door with a metal sign 'Meeting Room C' and a slidy thing to let you know if Meeting Room C is Occupied or not.

Today it is going to be Occupied by myself and two women who introduce themselves formally as DI Pauline Campbell and DS Amanda Hayes.

Would I like coffee or tea? I would like a bloody large scotch but I politely request a glass of water. I'm not a great coffee drinker and I wouldn't trust the police to make a cup of tea. It's probably the same sweet, soupy brew they offer to road accident victims to take their minds off the fact that their entire family has just been wiped out in a pile-up.

I'm shown to my seat and, whilst we're waiting for the beverages to appear, I'm taken through all the formalities again: name, address, telephone number, work address, work number, mobile number, blood group, shoe size, etc. To be honest, what with the shock of discovering Otto's place last night and the raging cacophony of police sirens, blue lights and the rest, it was amazing I could remember any of it.

I'm gagging for a fag, but the blue-remembered, homespun days of the 1970s and *The Sweeney*, when one could light up in a public building, are well behind us. I'd probably get manhandled to the ground by a SWAT team if I tried. Okay, here we go.

Tell me about Dr Parsons. What is your relationship with him?

My first inclination is to utter some witty retort about our not being in a 'relationship', but I catch the eyes of DI Campbell and her colleague: a younger, more demure woman who seems less concerned with trying to look masculine. I have their full and undivided attention; they have a well-practiced patient look that tells me that they're in no hurry. Just as well, since I would be setting the pace of things around here for a while. It also told me that I wasn't going to be leaving until everything I knew, or thought was relevant, had been imparted faithfully, and that right now was not the time for buggering about. Otto's disappearance was Real Life writ large.

I begin. 'Otto is someone I know through work. He and I have been doing business together for nearly ten years.'

'What kind of work is that, Mr Jennings?' DI Campbell draws a sip of her milky coffee and swallows it noiselessly; nothing to disturb the concentration of the interviewee. A quick adjustment of the specs and all attention is back on me.

'I work as a Technology Transfer Partner for Illumina Innovations. It's an organisation that was set up by the university back in the 1970s to help raise seed capital for spin-out companies from university R&D projects.' I look at their faces again; the patient gaze is still there and I must obviously say more. 'Otto was working as the Technical Director for an SME. That's a small-to-medium-sized enterprise. Sorry for the jargon.' My bread and butter is a language comprised almost entirely of acronyms; I can go hours without uttering a sentence consisting of whole words. 'The company and the project as a whole was almost his own idea. Originally it was something he and his then tutor Professor Dan Sibley came up with in one of their endless tutorial sessions. Dan lectures in Quantum Mechanics. He felt that Otto's idea had mileage and ran a few experiments down at the Exatron to see if it had proof-of-concept feasibility. Apparently, it did.'

'What's the Exatron?' asks the sergeant. 'I've heard about it, but I don't know too many details.'

'It's basically a very big, very powerful particle accelerator. The Exatron is a next-generation version of the Diamond synchrotron that used to be down near Abingdon. It's all part and parcel of the Penrose Science Park.' That patient look must be a gift; you couldn't just train that into someone. 'It's a big doughnut-shaped building and they blast either really intense beams of light or intense beams of sub-atomic particles round and round in a circle, to explore the nature of matter. Physicists get off on this stuff. It's also bloody expensive to fire up, which is why Dan and Otto eventually ended up approaching Illumina for funds.'

'Where did they get the initial funds for the proof of concept?' says Campbell. She has been scribbling notes in a small block pad, despite the fact that a cassette machine has been recording the interview.

'The Penrose Science Park is funded by the university. In essence, the physics faculty gets a few "free turns" in order to keep the academics happy. After that, you have to pay. The Exatron is a cost centre as far as the university is concerned and so it has to pay its way. They rent out their facilities to all sorts of commercial and research institutions around the world and, from what I hear, it does pretty well for itself, thank you.'

'Why was Otto using the Exatron at all?' Campbell has put her block pad down for the moment and is giving me that look of undivided attention again. I'm glad I'm not being suspected of any foul play; I feel sure that this technique of hers could be intimidating.

'He thought he had worked out a theoretical way of creating weightlessness here on Earth.' The two policewomen look suitably impressed. 'If it could be shown in the lab, then this would have all sorts of benefits to various commercial concerns. Pharmaceuticals, chemicals, agrichemicals, etc. Because it would obviate the need for sending expensive equipment into space. Otto and Dan had already spoken to a number of dons at the university and they were getting rather excited about the project.'

Campbell looks up from her pad. 'So why did Illumina Innovations get involved?'

'Dan and Otto did their homework and came to us with a draft business plan. It was a bit ropey, which is what you'd expect from academics. But Dan has had practice at this before so it wasn't too much of a pig's ear. They proposed setting up a company called Oxford Gravity and I helped with pulling the initial finances together and setting them up with a structure and some offices. If you can call a bench in the Penrose Science Park an office. Otto was styled as Technical Director-cum-CEO and Dan was given the rather honorary title of Chairman. Board Meetings and AGMs consisted of the three of us plus a couple of non-executive hangers-on from other parts of Illumina. Legal, corporate governance, that sort of thing.'

'How was the business going?'

'Cash-negative, basically. Things were still at the R&D stage. For what was in essence a fairly simple proposition, the technicalities have turned out to be predictably complex.'

The sergeant's brow furrows. 'In what way?' Before I can formulate a response using words with one syllable, she volunteers that she did a science-based degree before choosing to join Oxford's finest. That said, it wasn't in theoretical physics (biology, as it turns out) and it wasn't at Oxford (Keele) but nobody's perfect. I can't claim to have the best academic chops myself, having only read Chemistry at one of the London colleges, followed by an MBA from the Open University part-time. I was lucky to get the job at Illumina, being something of a low-caste in Oxford terms. But my experience working for a small venture capital outfit stood me in good stead and Illumina welcomed me with arms nailed open.

The level of theoretical physics Otto and Dan had immersed themselves in was way beyond my ken and I have to think back to Otto's explanation, illustrated with a matchbox over a couple of pints on the terrace of the Victoria Inn, overlooking the serene prospect of the languid, willow-fringed Cherwell river.

'Well, there are two aspects to the apparatus.' Otto is sitting with the matchbox poised above the table, a cumulus of curly hair trembling as he talks animatedly. As ever, he is wearing his trademark rugby shirt with blue and white hoops. With one hand he cradles the matchbox, while the fingers of his other hand twist and screw the air caressing its surface. 'Firstly, we need to build a pod. It's a big egg-shaped box basically made of aluminium and welded together. Rather Heath Robinson, actually. Then we fit it with rediffusers.' His fingers dance over the box, furiously indicating a myriad of locations for these rediffusers. 'They are like lenses that will deflect the beam over and around the pod's surface. Except the lenses aren't optical. They're magnetic.' As he says 'magnetic' his fingers form a cage in the air and tighten, the muscles in each digit standing proud and reddening. 'The rediffusers then have to be able to alter the path of the beam very subtlely in all three dimensions. But, and this is the tricky part, the beams must all be entangled. That's the quantum equivalent of coherent, like a laser, so that when they are recombined on the trailing edge of the pod, there is no net disruption to the beam. Got it?'

Of course I haven't fucking got it. I'm just nodding in what I suppose to be the right places because I don't want to look like a brain donor. Otto is always heartened by my apparent comprehension; he treats me like some sort of soulmate from the other side of the tracks: a non-believer who is slowly turning to the faith. In truth, I'm a fraud; I'm the dope dealer who feeds his addiction. I give him money and he does physics and pretends he is doing it as some fledgling enterprise that will ultimately gratify me. (He'd read the bit about 'fiduciary duty' when boning up on what a CEO does.)

But what is the second bit of the apparatus? Otto plonks the matchbox down on the pub table and bends his head hard over his chest as though he is summoning up some huge effort.

'Making the controls for the rediffusers. They all have to be computer-controlled and the tolerances for the software are ball-achingly slim. The bizarre thing is that it was harder to get this right with the lab model than it was with the full-scale thing.'

'Excuse me, but have you built the full-scale apparatus?' Otto suddenly has my full attention. Firstly, because it is good manners to tell your Board what you are up to and, because I sit on that Board, I would have known if he had. Secondly, because he hasn't told me specifically. Thirdly, it would be rather important—momentous, even—and wasn't on the timescale of events that the Board had agreed at the previous AGM about three months ago. Lastly, where did he get the money?

Otto doesn't look remotely sheepish. Being an academic must be a benign form of Asperger's, because the concerns of other people are as dust. 'Well, the rediffusers were full-size, so it made sense to stick them on a full-size pod. We just spent the money allocated to Quarter Three this year. Dan and I didn't think you'd mind.'

'And?'

'And we ran the experiment the day before yesterday.' I obviously have an expression on my face that Otto can't interpret. For the record, I am stunned. This is an example of loose-cannonry that is one of the few things that I go off at the deep end about. I have very few rules with my vested companies; one of them is to not do things behind my back. Ever.

'Otto, we've talked about this before and I—'

'Calm yourself, dear Matt!' He only ever calls me that when he knows he's upset me. He takes a large slurp of beer. 'It's all in the budget. The cost of the full-size pod is miniscule in the grand scheme of things. We're spending the money on the diffusers, the controls and the Exatron. And anyway, it didn't work. One of the diffusers was mis-aligned and the beam suffered a net disruption.' He sees my downcast expression. 'But the sparks were amazing!'

'I hope that I explained that reasonably clearly,' I say to the two policewomen. Campbell makes a few corrections to some of her notes on the block pad, while the sergeant just sits there, trying to absorb my amateurish retelling of Otto's explanation. I wasn't as good; I didn't have Otto's boyish enthusiasm, or a matchbox.

'How far did the experiments get with the full-size apparatus?' says the sergeant, finally. I shuffle in my seat a little before replying.

'I don't actually know.' They both look at me, the patient expression bit more blank, a bit less warm. 'I haven't seen anything of Otto or Dan for the last eighteen months to two years. Dan invited me to a meeting at his college rooms one afternoon. He poured me a large Calvados and told me he'd secured third-party funding and was dissolving Oxford Gravity and thanks for my help.'

The sergeant sits up. 'Didn't he have to repay the initial funding to Illumina or do you just offer funds in the form of grants?'

'We take the money, thank you very much. Dan and I did some horse-trading, agreed a buy-out, subject to a few pending calculations, and a couple of days later, that was that. The funds were transferred to Illumina, the documents were drawn up to strike off Oxford Gravity from Companies House, and all parties went their separate ways. Illumina were happy enough. They'd got the expected return on the investment, and I had plenty of other fledglings to nurture. Never been busier, as it happens.'

'Then why were you at Otto's house last night?' says Campbell.

'Because he called me. Out of the blue, yesterday morning. I hadn't heard from him in over nine months and then he calls to say that he needs to talk urgently, that it's all gone pear-shaped and he needs advice. It wasn't like him at all, so I took it seriously.'

'Was he often overwrought?' says Campbell, pen poised over the block pad. I take a swig of water.

'Never. That's what was so unusual, and why I took it seriously. Otto lives on his little private planet where the weather is always lovely. For him to get agitated like that… I was concerned. So I agreed to meet him.'

'Where?'

'At the King's Head on Broad Street. I got there at seven and waited. It wasn't unusual for him to be late. If anything, it was routine. But I then tried his mobile and got no response. And that wasn't routine. He had that thing grafted to his hip. At this stage, I was curious rather than concerned. And I decided to walk over to his place in Jericho. It's only a ten minute walk or thereabouts.'

'What did you find when you got to his house?' says the sergeant. It's a routine question and we both know it; I've watched enough police procedurals on TV.

'The same as you. The door was open. Jericho is a reasonably safe place but you don't leave your door open. So I knew right then that something was wrong. I pushed the door wider and looked down the front hall. '

'Go on…'

'I didn't get a detailed look but the hall was a mess. There were books everywhere and smashed ornaments and coffee all over the hall carpet. There must have been some kind of fight or disagreement.' I take another gulp of water; I am not enjoying recounting this bit. 'It was enough of a scene for me to know I shouldn't disturb it, so I called you, I mean 999, right there and then. You were over pretty quick, I must say.'

'Thank you.' Campbell didn't look up from her notes.

'Had you had any other communications with Dr Parsons earlier that day? Since the original phone call?' The sergeant rests her head on one hand and looks at me intently.

'No.'

'Or any communications with anyone else from Oxford Gravity? Or members of staff at the company? Colleagues of Otto's?'

'No.' I see where she's going. Oxford Gravity hadn't existed for a while, but those responsible for setting up—particularly Dan and Otto—were still a unit.

DI Campbell's eyes narrow. 'What about Professor Sibley?'

'Do you think he's mixed up in this?'

'We're not speculating on anything at the moment as we don't have any facts to go on just yet.' There's something Campbell is keeping from me.

'Have you found Otto?' I ask, with a hint of desperation cracking my voice at the edges.

'No,' replies the sergeant. 'We are still looking for him.'

'He wasn't in the house, then?'

'No. At present we are treating him as a Missing Person.' I'm surprised by this. I thought a certain amount of time had to elapse before anyone could be declared missing. 'There are still certain circumstances that we need to clarify. The most telling thing is that he had arranged to meet with you and didn't turn up. That is cause for concern, which is why we've put him on the Missing Persons list.'

'So why the question about Dan Sibley?'

'Mr Jennings…' DI Campbell has adopted a mellifluous, civil-service tone that is clearly meant to sound a touch overbearing and therefore put me in my place. 'We are examining all possible avenues with regard to Dr Parsons' disappearance. Professor Sibley is just one of many lines of enquiry we are pursuing. And that includes you.'

'Me?'

'You are not a suspect. But you *are* a material witness. Therefore we need to know who you have interacted with in regards to this matter. I don't mean to raise any concerns on your part or flag anything as being significant. Right now, we have a Missing Person and no idea as to how we might find him.'

DI PAULINE CAMPBELL

Oxford. Monday October 12th, 1030hrs.

'Coffee!' Campbell watches out of the station window as Matt Jennings strides off into an Oxford city centre afternoon. 'Coffee!'

She blows an exasperated sigh. DS Hayes sits at the table and watches her boss as she stands at the window.

'Well,' says Campbell at last, 'what have we learned from that?'

Sergeant Hayes wrinkles her nose. 'We know he didn't get a close look at the interior of the property and, in all likelihood, he didn't interfere with the crime scene.'

'That much is clear,' says her boss. 'Coffee!' Campbell pauses for a moment to think. 'I suppose from outside... it is starting to get dark after all... there is no light inside the house...' She trails off.

'Has Forensics come back with any estimates of how much blood there was?'

Campbell tots up the size of the pool on the hall carpet and tries her best to think positively about it. Maybe the carpet has some kind of special stain repellent treatment.

'Not yet, no. But I don't see our Missing Person popping by in the flesh any time soon, do you?' Campbell continues to stare out of the window across the barnacled college roofs and the more distant spire of Christ Church Cathedral. She muses briefly on how business people don't seem to wear ties anymore; Jennings had a nice enough suit with a white shirt, but it was open-necked with no tie. Strange.

She takes a deep breath and turns to Hayes. 'Okay.' She claps her hands together. 'I will go back to Jericho and comb over the crime scene. Amanda, I want you to get White and Reynolds to start poring over the CCTV footage for last night.'

'I'll get them to start looking from about six-thirty. The blood was still wet when we got there so they couldn't have left more than half an hour before.'

'That should be okay. Keep an eye open for any vehicle with two men. Three would be a clincher, especially if two of the three are on the back seat.' She rolls her eyes. 'And pray to God almighty that they didn't use a van. On second thoughts, also get White and Reynolds to make a note of any vans they see coming up on the cameras before about nine, I guess.' She rubs her forehead and sighs. 'It's just a hunch, but I don't think they used a van. I don't know why. It all seems a bit... ad hoc. If it had been planned, they wouldn't have left the mess.'

Hayes angles her head. 'It's as though they were expecting Parsons to go with them willingly.'

'Only he didn't. I wonder why not?'

NICK YOUNG

Oxford. September 2011.

Nick is feeling pleased with himself. Barney had been a great help and would probably be a linchpin in the whole project. The two had first met as undergraduates, both in the same college and both keen members of the university Gilbert and Sullivan society. He couldn't have asked for a better partner in such an enterprise.

Nick walks past the Holywell Music Rooms: an unassuming building which resembles a small Methodist chapel rather than a venue for choral and chamber music. The building is set back from Holywell Road which is usually quiet and crowded on both sides by old terraces of rooms and apartments all owned by the university and inhabited by post-grads. The occasional car dares to creep by, but most of the time, the greatest risk to life and limb is posed by cyclists who will only let you know of an impending collision at the last possible moment.

Barney had been most accommodating. He had met Nick in his college rooms; he is a Senior Lecturer now in the history faculty and gets his own grace-and-favour rooms in his old college. The quadrangle below is as serene and timeless as it had been when the two studied there together ten years earlier. For Barney, little had changed, bar the passing of the years and the gentle ebbing of his hairline. He had stayed put, pretty much; Oxford agreed with him, as did the academic life and he needed little in the way of distraction other than his teaching and research.

Nick, on the other hand, had kicked the Oxford dust from his heels as soon as he could and had celebrated his first in physics by taking a year out to travel the world, including a three-month gambol across the face of the globe, racing a beaten-up car from Southern England to Ulaan Bator in

Mongolia. He had taken a camcorder and produced a ninety-minute documentary of the trip which won the admiration of a friend of his father who worked at a TV production company in central London. After that, physics took a back seat.

The two men begin the session by ruthlessly ribbing each other's attire. The only thing they can agree upon was that they have each conformed to stereotype: Nick with his goatee beard, dark blue denim shirt, black jacket and black jeans, rounded off with a dashing pair of winkle-pointed black boots; Barney with his moon-face, tortoiseshell-effect glasses, fusty checked shirt and corduroy trousers of estuarine grey, Nick called Barney a fogey and Barney called Nick a media luvvie. They pour some more scotch and laugh like the children they had been when they first met.

'Are you still gainfully employed?' Barney enquires.

'Asks the permanent student from the comfort of his grace-and-favour armchair!' Barney snorts; he has a mouthful of scotch to contend with. 'As it happens, my patronising friend, I do.'

'Pray, tell.' Barney likes to use medieval language as mild seasoning.

'It is because of my current employ that I have come to see you.'

'I'm not sure how your occupation could possibly… Oh, you want me to be an 'Historical Advisor' on one of your entertainments.' Barney flicks air-quotes with his fingers.

'In a word, yes.' Barney can always be relied upon to get to the heart of the matter in a short time; a rare quality for an academic, especially one in the humanities. 'We need an Historical Advisor, with or without quotation marks.'

'What are you working on?' Barney sat back in his armchair and waited for some sort of briefing.

'I can't tell you.'

'Then one is going to be hard-pressed to give you any really meaningful advice, then, isn't one?'

Nick leans forward in his chair and rocks the liquid in his glass back and forth, watching the legs of the liquor hanging there before being swept up once again. 'Of course. There will need to be all sorts of confidentiality agreements and things you will need to sign before I can say anything concrete.'

'As long as it doesn't interfere with my research, I doubt I will have a problem signing anything like that.'

'Excellent.' Nick is always hesitant about approaching friends in a work context, so it is a relief that Barney is willing to comply with the legal constraints, if only in principal at this point. Nick pauses, thinking of how to move on to the next item on his agenda.

'Come on, Nick! Out with it.' Barney shouts a bit louder than intended. But this coyness is starting to become tedious. 'It's going to be a long evening if you're going to try and communicate using only the power of the pregnant pause.'

Nick nods; the scotch is starting to exert some effect and he remembers he's not had anything to eat. 'You're quite right. I'm sorry. I shall be more candid. After another scotch. What is that by the way?'

'Talisker.' Barney tops up Nick's glass with another two or three fingers of the copper liquid.

'Very nice it is, too. Thank you.' Nick admires the replenished glass. 'Right. Where was I?'

'You were blathering fecklessly!'

'Right-oh! I have a question for you. What do you consider to be some of the most beguiling historical mysteries of, say, the last one hundred and fifty years?'

Barney whistles and rolls his eyes. 'Jesus! I don't know… let me think… Couldn't you have given me advance notice of this question? It's like being asked which birthday cake was your favourite.' Barney's brow furrows and Nick fancies that his glasses may have fogged over, but it could have been his imagination. Barney shrugs his eyebrows. 'A perennial favourite is the identity of Jack the Ripper, I suppose.'

Nick leaps in his seat. 'Absolutely fucking brilliant! I knew you'd be perfect for this. Anything else?'

'Erm… who was the Man in the Iron Mask?'

'Was that in the last hundred and fifty years?'

'It has to be during that timescale, does it?' Nick nods and Barney rubs his cheek with the heel of his hand. 'Pity. Pre-Norman Britain is really my area of expertise…' He trails off and muses for a bit before snapping his fingers and jumping up in his chair.

'I know a good one.' Barney looks triumphant. 'This would be a crowd-pleaser on an unprecedented scale.' Nick's expression urges Barney to continue but Barney is relishing the moment and the mischievous joy of tantalising his old friend. 'This is something that a zillion potty theses have been written about and a million bolt-necked Americans have obsessed over for fifty-odd years.' Nick is starting to look exasperated; Barney has him hooked.

'Fucking *what*, Barney?' Nick enunciates each word as if it were a sentence all its own.

'Who killed John F Kennedy? I mean who *really* killed him? Could Oswald shoot straight? Was anybody actually there on the grassy knoll? What role did the police play in the assassination?'

'Inspired! Totally inspired.'

'I'd love to know the answer to that one. Everybody wants to know the answer to that one. Except, of course, those pinheads who have created an industry peddling all that conspiracy theory bollocks.' Barney slumps all the way back in his armchair and beams. He sits up straight again. 'So, why are you asking?'

Nick leans toward him. 'I can't tell you. Sorry. I can tell you that you've passed the interview. Or audition. Or whatever you want to call it.'

'You can't just stop there, you annoying git! What happens next?'

Nick rises to his feet, a little unsteady. 'Next, I go and see my colleagues back at the production office and I tell them that you'd be a perfect Historical Advisor. After that, we get the paperwork drawn up, I bring it to you, you sign it in blood and then you get to meet the team.'

'"The team"?'

'Yes. Back at the office.'

'And where is that nowadays? Some dusty, rubbish-strewn back alley in Soho frequented by creatures of indeterminate gender and easy virtue, perchance?'

'No. Just up the road in Summertown. I'm back in Oxford, so we'll be seeing a lot more of each other.'

And with that he walks off, feeling pleased with himself, a slow sea swell rolling beneath his feet.

MIPCOM NEWS

Cannes. April 2012.

[Headline] *HISTORIC AGREEMENTS FOR HISTORIC NEW SERIES*
[By-line] *James Corcoran*

[Body copy] *Atlas Media Rights has announced today that it has signed 21 distribution agreements with channels for its four-part history series* Witness: History.

The series has been produced by new outfit The Oxford History Unit and boasts rare footage and stills of key historic events as they happened. Atlas Media have been tight-lipped about the content of the series other than to say that it is 'unique and ground-breaking'.

Atlas say that they and the channels to whom the series has been sold are bound by confidentiality agreements not to disclose any content.

So far the show has been sold to 14 different countries including the US, China and India, and the sums paid for each episode have apparently broken records for a debut offering from a small independent production company.

We approached Nick Young, Producer of Witness: History *for further information but he would only say that he was proud of the work his team have done in preparing the footage for each episode and that the show will more than live up to the hype he expects the channels to generate in advance of the programme's broadcast.*

Dirk Postema of Atlas Media was also evasive about the show itself. 'I am truly thrilled to have been asked to help sell this show around the world. It is a real once-in-a-lifetime event. It is going to be hard to top this, I can tell you!'

Atlas say that, with only a day left of MIPCOM to go, they have had approaches from many more channels who are keen to learn more about Witness: History *and are prepared to broadcast it despite, or possibly because of, the much-rumoured high price tag.*

[End.]

DAILY TELEGRAPH

[Headline] *WITNESS: HISTORY*
THE IGNOMINY BROUGHT HOME
[By-line] *Susie Hopwood*

[Body copy] *Readers of this column will know that I am not one for hyperbole. Nor, I like to think, am I prone to hysteria. I have been, as they say, round the block a few times; I have seen it all. Or, until last night, I thought I had.*

After last night's opening episode of Witness: History *I admit to being so stunned that I nearly missed the copy deadline for this edition simply because I was rooted to my sofa with my mouth agape and my mind trying to make sense of what I'd seen. Or perhaps 'witnessed' is a better word.*

The surprise—shock, even—was all the greater because this programme has been shrouded in secrecy and no preview screenings have been available. This usually gets alarm bells ringing in any reviewer; a late reveal minimises the chances of a potential audience being scared off by a mauling review before it is aired.

Last night's episode retold the bombing of Pearl Harbor in December 1941. Heaven knows there have been enough documentaries rehashing the same old stock footage of the attack (of which there's about 30 seconds' worth that's usable) fleshed out with old interviews of survivors and some cutaway shots of 'Pearl Harbor as it is today'.

What was astonishing about Witness: History *was that the Oxford History Unit—this is their first output—had somehow uncovered a wealth of footage of the actual attack seen from about three different angles and all shot in fabulously sharp and vibrant Technicolor. For the first time we see the Arizona's forward magazine exploding, catapulting the souls of nearly twelve hundred men heavenward on a terrifying column of oily red flame and black smoke.*

The programme begins with a long, slow panning shot of the island of Oahu, the Harbor, and the opening to the ocean beyond. The only sound is the morning breeze. There is a low thrumming and, shortly after, the first specks of movement are seen over the glittering sea. Just then, the soundtrack crackles into life with an ominous soundbite of an anonymous serviceman stating that Pearl Harbor is a great place to be stationed because there's no fear of any attack. Quickly, the specks become Japanese Zero fighters and they fly past the camera like arrows.

Soon after, the devastation begins. The three different camera positions each have a terrible vantage of the destruction wrought on the Harbor and the nearby airfield. I remember having to sit through Tora! Tora! Tora! *as a child while my parents and older brother sat there feasting on the horror. But we all knew that it was a Hollywood confection, even though it was based on real events. But* Witness: History *does not afford you that comfortable luxury. That's because, this time, it is very real indeed.*

Isn't it? That is what is probably going to keep me awake all night after writing this piece. Was this real or was this some work, some incredible work, of artifice? I cannot say and maybe this is the true art of this documentary. So much of it seemed to be about the moment itself and not, as has been the usual constraint of history documentaries, its recollection. How did the filmmakers of the day have the prescience to interview sailors and airmen the day before the attack? Their responses were so bone-chilling. When asked about the security of the base, they all dismissed any chance of an action.

It is a testament to this production that the documentary carried itself without the need for intrusive voice-over. This meant that, to some extent, we saw the attack through the eyes of the servicemen. We felt their anguish and pain. And outrage.

The footage of the attack and the contemporaneous interviews were intercut with sections on how the film was discovered by the Oxford History Unit. Their access to the Bodleian Library enabled them to trace rare footage and then track it down to a small farmhouse in Wyoming of all places. The Oxford History Unit film crew interviewed the owner of the farm who, as it turned out, was the grandson of the senior cameraman responsible for the unseen reels of film.

It transpired that he had been commissioned by the US Navy of the day to shoot a propaganda film on 'A Day in Pearl Harbor' and he had chosen to centre activities about service life on a peaceful, God-fearing Sunday morning. Like all film crews, they cheated and started to film a couple of days early, hence the interviews.

So, after ninety minutes, I found myself rooted to my sofa, mouth agape, my mind boggling with conflicting emotions: the sheer awe of what I had just seen scrambled with my professional questions, starting with the straightforward, How Did They Do That? After the electric fog had cleared I found myself asking what Witness: History had just shown us that we didn't know already.

The answer of course is nothing. The attack on Pearl Harbor is probably one of the most extensively documented military actions. There is very little of any consequence about it that we didn't already know. But now, thanks to Witness: History, we have an emotional dimension; we have a sense of what it felt like to be there.

There are three more episodes of Witness: History to go, and we know that the next two will tackle Jack the Ripper and the Roswell incident. The broadcasters are being cagey about the fourth episode, but they promise it will be astonishing. If it is only half as astonishing as tonight's instalment then it will still be nothing short of ground-breaking.

I am certain that this programme will be repeated before too long and, if you missed it last night, I urge you—I oblige you—to watch it. Witness: History is history being made before our eyes.

[End.]

DI PAULINE CAMPBELL

Oxford. Monday October 12th, 1730hrs.

Forensics have been and gone. The small terraced house in Jericho is quiet now. save for the sounds of Walton Street some distance away: cars, students, residents and visitors to the bars and restaurants. Some sounds are nearer to hand: the ticking of the central heating pipes, the shivering thrum of the fridge and the listless flapping of the police cordon tape in the evening breeze. *Police Line: Keep Out!*

The house is darkening. It's just how Campbell likes to start; clear the site of human presence, including other police officers, and let the evidence be your guide. Every person writes their biography in the stuff with which they surround themselves: books, letters, bank statements, phone records, address lists, computers, pictures, photographs, postcards on the kitchen corkboard, the choice of furniture, curtains, lampshades, the colours of the walls, the textures on the floor. It all speaks; it announces you; it defines and describes you.

Campbell lifts the cordon tape and approaches the front door. It is locked now; the Scene of Crime Officer had found the house keys on the bookshelf in the hallway. The latch had been kicked halfway down the hall, but the deadlock hadn't been thrown at the time of the intrusion, so the premises are secure. Campbell has uplifted the keys from the police station with a simple signature; she has the life of Otto Parsons in her hand. Hayes follows close behind as Campbell unlocks the door and enters.

First, the hallway.

Campbell turns the light on and the two detectives survey the scene. A long passage. To the right, about halfway down, is the door to the main living room. Running up the left side of the hall, commencing just beyond the living room door, is the foot of the stairs. Also to the right is the low bookcase with some ornaments on top: a mixture of tribal art obviously purchased as tourist souvenirs from some African adventure, and pieces of garish pottery (Poole, perhaps). Other ornaments litter the floor: old, polished pieces of former Soviet-era ordnance (again, tourist knick-knacks, albeit with attitude), and another piece of tribal art, this time broken in whatever struggle there might have been.

There are a number of books on the floor: an eclectic mixture of high science (textbooks on quantum mechanics and transformational mathematics) and literature (Dostoevsky, Wittgenstein, Orwell, Ma Jian, Kundera). So, Dr Parsons was an armchair freedom-fighter; he liked to rage against the iron grip of totalitarianism from between the pages of a good book. Then there were the travel books: Vietnam, Namibia, India, Morocco, Chile, Mexico. No photographs anywhere. Interesting. You'd think he'd have a framed memento somewhere of these places. Then again, maybe he only read about them and never actually visited.

In front of the living room door, the bloodstain. Forensics had given a rough estimate: it was not enough to kill him but he would be in a bad way and would probably need carrying from the scene. He certainly wouldn't have walked anywhere. The trauma alone would have incapacitated him. They probably shot him or stabbed him, because he was trying to cling to the side of the bookcase as they were dragging him from the house. It would seem his assailants didn't have a patient nature. It would also seem that, wherever they were planning on taking Otto, he wasn't expected to return. Not alive, anyway.

'No reports of gunfire last night?' It is a question rather than a remark. Hayes confirms it. So, whoever paid a visit had a silent, or silenced, weapon. So our felons are more than likely professional and they are obviously dispassionate about their work.

A couple of pictures on the wall; nothing momentous. A few largely abstract pieces in oil, probably painted by a friend or acquaintance. Campbell lifts one of the frames and peers behind. There is an inscription on the back: 'To Otto. Beyond space and time. Love, Amy'.

'Any idea who Amy might have been?'

'Amy Duncan, ex-girlfriend,' says Hayes. 'As far as we know, Otto hasn't been in any kind of relationship for at least a year now.'

The hallway dog-legs past the foot of the stairs and carries on past an under-stairs cupboard terminating in another door, presumably to the kitchen. Nothing of any apparent interest down there, but they'll have a good look in due course.

The living room. That's where people's lives really open up.

The room runs the length of the house and has been opened to the kitchen which takes up the width of the premises along the back wall. The general theme of the room is 'boho'. Campbell chides herself for being so *female* in her assessment, but then she nods to herself. It comes with the gender.

Bare floorboards, random placement of oriental rugs: cheap ones, either bought in second-hand markets or ersatz versions purchased in some furniture chain. Indian-style coffee table and bookcase (Thakur?) made from dark wood and ironwork. Large sofa smothered in throws and cushions and probably a lot less comfortable than it looks. Battered armchair on the window side of the sofa, also smothered in soft furnishings to hide its modesty. Both items of furniture are faced toward the corner of the room in the general direction of the flat-screen TV above the hi-fi system. The hi-fi is fairly high-range equipment: Campbell was always amused by the notion that the quality of a hi-fi system was usually in inverse proportion to the number of buttons; this amplifier has an on-off and a volume control, and is connected to a turntable and a CD player. The speaker cabinets are stationed either side of the front window like sentries. The whole lot was likely to have been expensive.

Otto seemed to like classical, jazz and world music. Very little rock. Quite a lot of choral: Tavener, Pärt, Gregorian chant. She opens the CD tray and finds a recording of Brahms'

Clarinet Quintet. Music to watch paint dry, she thinks. Come on now! This isn't about you; we're here to listen to Otto, find out what he has to say.

So, Otto, you like music of the spheres. You want refuge, from all your science and your fervent beliefs. Interesting that there's nothing overtly religious here other than the music, but that's a diversion rather than a pursuit, isn't it? You have gods enough already, don't you?

Low table by the side of the sofa with a small vase part-filled with essential oil and sticks. (Campbell sniffs: ylang ylang.) Mere affectation, Campbell imagines; this is all just to create some kind of blissed-out ambience in the event of there being company. In which case, ylang ylang is the wrong stuff to use: you might get them into bed, young man, but all they'll soon be snoring like an old train.

Opposite the sofa and to the left of the TV is the fireplace: small and blocked off with a pine mantelpiece which has been stained to give it a patina of age. There are a few ornaments on the mantelpiece: a pottery vase (probably crafted by a university colleague), some dried flowers imposed by a female friend to de-bloke things a bit, a small brass Buddha, two brass candlesticks with a couple of half-spent candles, and a folded piece of paper.

Coffee table. The usual assortment of large books: the ubiquitous *Earth From The Air*, some massive tome of photos of the Himalayas, *The 1,000 Best Films Of All Time*, a large Iberian-looking ashtray with the remains of a few roll-ups.

'Has Forensics had a look at these, Amanda?'

'The dog-ends? I believe they took some away for DNA but, given that we found only three of them, it looks as though he liked the occasional solitary spliff. We're not expecting to find anyone else's DNA.'

The living room and kitchen area all look reasonably orderly: no blood, and no more chaos than you'd expect to find in a small house occupied by a single male. The assailants were probably let in by Otto and they only got as far as halfway down the hall before things turned unexpectedly ugly for him. It doesn't look as though they made it this far into the house, which means they didn't linger to look for anything or pick anything up.

To the right of the doorway is a fold-away table with the accoutrements of Otto's home office: an in-tray piled to its rim with paper (letters, bank statements, brochures from scientific institutions, yesterday's *Guardian*), a laptop, mouse, mouse mat, cordless telephone, stapler and a Japanese Daruma doll with only its right eye painted in. The printer is under the table; no paper in the out tray. Above the table are two shelves laden with box files and ring binders stuffed with more papers. The spines declare their purpose: Oxford Gravity, OGL Board, Lectures, Bank, Holidays.

'Amanda, will you go through his in tray? I'll see if his laptop is easy enough to get into.'

Hayes picks up the tray and wordlessly carries it off to the sofa. She's a wee slip of a thing and she practically vanishes into the upholstery as soon as she sits on it. Campbell allows herself a private smile. The lid on the laptop opens and the machine comes to life; thankfully, Otto must have had the thing on sleep mode and… yes! No need to worry about passwords. We're in. First things first: the emails.

Otto is tidy and has filed all his emails in different folders. The inbox has a few notes in it, most of which seem to be undeleted spam: the local cinema and theatre, what's on at the Holywell Music Rooms, local supermarket, a dubious offer to deposit a huge sum of money into his account purporting to come from some lawyer in Dubai. The folders consist of 'Oxford Gravity', 'Exatron', 'Illumina', 'University Stuff', 'Family', 'Friends', and a number of miscellaneous subjects.

She stares at the list of folders and opts for 'Oxford Gravity' first, on the grounds that it was Otto's big project.

Over five hundred emails.

The last two weeks have seen a tedious exchange concerning settings for rediffusers and electron-volt readings for the particle beam. Something about 'acceleration of split beam from the pod and temporal displacement'.

More emails about calculating coordinates for different displacements. Helpful remark from one of the programmers: 'It's like trying to land a jet on an aircraft carrier travelling at over 900,000 kilometres per hour.'

A whole load from Professor Sibley, with at least thirty in the last week. Wouldn't it be easier by phone? Campbell supposes that, with subject titles like 'OGL winding up', Sibley would need a paper trail. Corporate governance is one thing, but covering your own arse is something entirely different.

Behind schedule... Illumina baying for their investment... Still cash-zero... Initial seed funding exhausted... Exatron use now at full rate... (She assumes this means that they are not going to get any more academic rates.)

One of the Sibley emails jumps out at Campbell, for its tone and urgency.

Otto,

Forgive the brusque tone of this communication, but I need to be plain with you about OGL and its future, or lack of it.

The initial objectives of the project have failed. We have proven this time and again and, as Einstein said, the definition of insanity is repeating one's mistakes in the expectation of a different outcome.

The attempt to neutralise gravity is not feasible and, thus far, we have not been able to achieve it. The fact that we have stumbled on something of far more interest to science is an obvious serendipity and one that we can capitalise upon with appropriate levels of funding.

This is well beyond the scope of Illumina and, as you know, I shall be seeking the Board's agreement to dissolve the company at the next meeting, pending the return of Illumina's initial investment once the next stage of funding has been raised for the daughter company we have discussed forming.

As you know, I am very keen for you to be involved in the new venture. Your talent as a quantum physicist is unparalleled, in my opinion. However, getting this off the ground is something that will require greater financial expertise than either of us possess and I urge you strongly to go along with what is being proposed. I am confident that it will benefit all of us far more greatly in the long run, if not indeed in the short.

Your offer to put up some of the funding is much appreciated, but I doubt that you have access to the kinds of continued funding that we will initially require and, I might suggest, your offer is probably too little, too late.

Please leave this matter with me for the time being. I only have our continued best interests at heart.

With best regards,
Dan

The email originated from Sibley's faculty and was hallmarked with his imprimatur, the university crest, faculty address and direct phone number. It's dated May 2012. About two and a half years earlier; about the time that Sibley bade a rather abrupt farewell to Matt Jennings, if Campbell's memory served. Campbell wonders what Parsons' response might have been. She clicks on the 'Sent Mail' folder, selects all the emails addressed to Sibley and scans again.

The response is a surprisingly meek note agreeing with Sibley and saying that he concurs with the approach for the time being, although he has some concerns about the funding sources and wants to be involved in the selection.

Back to the inbox. Sibley didn't reply to Parsons' response.
'Fuck!'
A long, low gasp from the sofa.

Campbell wheels round to see Hayes hunched over two pieces of paper she has lifted from the in-tray.

She is shaking, her mouth open and eyes wide in astonishment. Campbell leans across, takes the papers and scans down the pages. They are bank statements: a dry list of transactions. When Campbell reaches the bottom of the page, her eyes widen. She's never seen a statement like it.

'So we've found the mystery lottery winner. Bloody hell. To win one Lotto…' She is about to make a reference to Lady Bracknell but can't make it work in the circumstances. Instead, she opts for the bald facts. 'Seven million on the UK Lotto and one hundred and forty-six million on the EuroMillions.'

'There's more.'

'More? What more? What more can there possibly be?'

'El Gordo,' says Hayes, staring at a gold-coloured certificate she has just dug from the in-tray pile.

'The Spanish lottery? The one that pays out a billion Euros? Don't say he scooped that as well.'

'Only fifty-odd million quid's worth of it.'

'So, all in all, he's totalled wins on the major lotteries of over two hundred million quid.'

'It would seem that way.'

'So, quite apart from being the brainiest physicist in Britain, our Dr Parsons is also the luckiest person alive.'

No, he isn't. No one is that lucky. The odds against it are so astronomically small. It must be fraud. But how do you swindle the largest, most secure lotteries in the world? Once would be hard enough. But three times? Campbell checks the statements again; the seven and hundred and forty-six million wins were credited to the account less than a year ago, but there's no sign of the jackpot from El Gordo. There has to be another account somewhere.

'Amanda, we will have to get on to his bank first thing tomorrow and find out what other accounts he has stashed away. I'm sure the Gordo cash will be in one of them. After all, the draw was ten months ago. Maybe he's got a string of accounts with lots of jackpots in them. What do you *do* with all those lottery wins, Amanda?'

Hayes gives Campbell an old-fashioned look and continues to rifle through the pile of papers. She looks up, holding a colourful brochure in one hand. 'Guv, have you got anything on the laptop about the Oxford History Unit?'

'Let's have a look.' Campbell strains her eyes at the screen and, finding nothing related in the emails, types a search into the computer's 'C' drive. After a while, the files and references line up on the screen. Ten, thirty, then fifty files and documents all referring to the unit. Campbell waits for the hard drive to stop searching, then scans the list. Quite a few references are double-counts but the term occurs in at least one hundred different files. And there are files of all different types: documents, presentations, emails, one video and even a spreadsheet.

The connection might not be obvious, but Otto appears to be linked to the Oxford History Unit in some way. Mostly, it's all stuff related to one of his former students, Nick Young. A couple of times, Professor Sibley gets a name-check, but it looks like a passing interest compared to Otto's close acquaintance with Young.

Emails from Young congratulate him on *Witness: History*. Great achievement, turned out even better than he was expecting... Can't wait to see the one on JFK...

The email referencing *Witness: History* was written two weeks ago. What does Otto know about this? The content has been a closely guarded secret and only the Pearl Harbor episode has been seen so far.

'Amanda...' Hayes hums her acknowledgement. 'We need to go and see Nick Young at the Oxford History Unit tomorrow.'

Hayes looks up, her brow furrowed. 'What have they got to do with all this? I mean, what has a TV programme got to do with... anything?'

Campbell shrugs. We surround ourselves with our own biography, but by God, this is turning out to be some life story. They will need to take the laptop away tonight, together with anything else they find. This house is turning out to be a treasure trove; the victim seems to have more to answer for than the perpetrators.

She lets out a long sigh, rises from the laptop and directs Hayes to call in uniformed back-up. They can't go ferreting around in here by themselves for any longer. For one thing, there is a lot of evidence that will need to be bagged and tagged. For another, whoever abducted Parsons may want to return and retrieve something. And she'd rather there were enough bodies in the way of the front door to make that notion unattractive.

There's still the rest of the house to go through and, above all, Campbell's favourite hiding place for clues, the kitchen. This is where the obscure and seemingly random bits of information are housed: the postcards from friends with first names only; the bit of paper on the corkboard with a couple of initials and a phone number; the reference number for something scribbled down for reference sometime in the near future; times, dates, assignations. The kitchen is where we keep our minutiae; usually not for long, but it is a snapshot of our lives in the very moment of action.

The kitchen build is fairly recent: a tasteful cream colour in a Quaker style with a wooden work surface. It's the type that looks as though it's been made up from different off-cuts of wood pressed together. It's reasonably tidy (for a man, Campbell supposes) with a few plates and pans awaiting transit to the dishwasher. Few crumbs around the toaster. Nothing Otto's mother would find much fault in.

The corkboard is present and correct and festooned with memorabilia: ticket stubs from Sugarloaf Mountain cable car; the local tandoori takeaway menu; a calendar featuring paintings by Gustav Klimt; a Post-it note with a phone number for a local plumber; IT support. And, loitering in the corner, partially obscured by the menu from a Thai restaurant around the corner, there's a scrap of paper torn from a pad of lined foolscap, with a number, or part of one. It's only four digits long, and two initials: 'LP'.

Campbell calls Hayes over for a closer look. Hayes takes the scrap and squints at it before handing it back to her boss. 'Initials and a number. It could be a fragment of a phone number but that leaves at least six digits we need to guess at.'

'Maybe. Maybe not. Otto didn't need to write down the first digits because he knows them off by heart. That means the number is either an Oxford number, in which case the first digits are going to be 01865, or it's a mobile number that's similar to one he knows well. His own, perhaps?'

'I'll get the team to start trawling through his phone book and see if we can see any commonly used examples.'

'Also, can you get on to the service provider for a breakdown of who he has called most recently, both from the landline and the mobile. Who has called him the most? See if you can find any matches to our four-digit friend here.'

Campbell's radio cracks into life. She responds. The voice from Control informs her that uniformed back-up are about to arrive at their location. The night outside strobes blue and black and there is a loud and insistent knock at the front door.

DR JANET HOOPER

No, she had not seen it. No, she had been out for an evening engagement. No, she hadn't heard anything about it. What is he talking about?... A *what*?

'My conference room. Fifteen minutes. I want my section present. No excuses.'

Dr Hooper squints as the lights are turned back on and the blinds raised. She swivels her capacious chair away from the screen and back to the ten people sitting round the table. They all look at her for a reaction. A nervous quiet occupies the room.

'Well, that answers that!' There is a muted shuffling and chuckling and clumsy attempts to convert the chuckles to throat-clearing. Janet Hooper is not smiling; this is not funny. Not at any level. 'I imagine the DNI will want to see me in the next five minutes, so any theories you guys can come up with between now and then would be cordially appreciated.' Janet surveys the faces around the table. Their fear reflects her own feeling at having to explain herself to the Director of National Intelligence when she has nothing to say.

Zwerling, the specky kid from Yale, raises his hand. 'It goes some way to explaining who those two guys were near the triple underpass. That must be where the film was shot.'

Janet looks at him coolly. 'What two men exactly?'

All eyes are on Zwerling now. 'There was a railroad guy who gave evidence at the Warren Commission. He claimed that there were a number of men in the yard behind the stockade and the pergola on the grassy knoll. Two of them were standing over by the underpass, seemingly doing nothing much.'

'Go on…'

'Jed's a conspiracy geek, Director.' Coates, the Football Major, as Janet disparagingly calls him. Originally from Idaho, of all places. Majored in economics from some big-league university—Duke, she thinks—but wasted his intellectual talent on playing football. Doubtless he used that as a means to chase up a fine score in the bedroom. Usually has most to say when he's not talking.

Zwerling retorts. 'Well, the Conspiracy Geek has read up on the subject.' Coates rolls his eyes. 'The railroad guy's testimony seemed to change between his first interview and the Commission. At first there were all these guys peppered around the yard. And then there was no one behind the stockade.'

'So it appears that his first testimony may have been the most accurate,' says Janet. 'Colin, you're the analyst. Give me your assessment. And make it brief.'

Colin Sandberg cranes his head over his notes and, without looking up, darts over the scrawled ballpoint trails. 'The basic thesis is that President Kennedy is shot to death in Dallas because of his stance on civil rights and not, as we've been led to believe, over Cuba. The evidence for this, as proposed by this documentary, is that the humiliation of Governor George Wallace by JFK and the submission a week later of the Civil Rights bill to Congress precipitated a conspiracy led by prominent members of the Ku Klux Klan and executed by affiliated members who were in the employ of the Secret Service.

'The footage, taken presumably by the two unidentified men by the triple underpass, of the shooter behind the stockade first crawling and then walking to a car belonging to a family member by marriage of one of the Secret Service agents stationed in Dallas strongly suggests the assassination was indeed an inside job.

'The irrefutable link made by the film between the car owner and the Klan in Alabama and, again, with the Secret Service agent, ties the whole thesis together. And Lee Harvey

Oswald *was* a patsy who probably got one lucky shot off which hit Connally.'

Sandberg looks up, not so much for applause, but to see where the missiles might come from.

Before anyone can say anything, the silence is shattered by the trilling of the phone. Janet picks up the receiver. She nods and frowns and says, 'In ten minutes'. She replaces the handset.

'Questions, ladies and gentlemen? We have a lot of answers now, but we don't have the questions.'

Kimberley Mader speaks up, stammering a little. 'Question One, I might suggest… How come none of this footage has seen the light of day for fifty years? Why wasn't it submitted at the same time as the Zapruder film?'

'That's good, Kimberley. Any others?'

'Who produced this?' says Coates. He isn't going to be upstaged by Mader who is still on his list of potential conquests. 'The Oxford History Unit are… Well, who the hell *are* they?'

'What's the FBI response going to be?' says Gruber, the latest addition to the team who is shaping up to be a sharp analyst and will give Sandberg some competition.

Janet shrugs. 'I imagine that the Director is going to tell me that himself. The only reason why I haven't been hauled across his carpet already is that he has been getting his ducks in a row and talking to the other agencies. This is probably going to end in the White House before the close of day and I can only imagine how crowded that room is going to be. For one thing, Fitts at the Secret Service is a bit of a good ol' boy himself.' She affects a Southern corn-pone drawl. 'So he's not just going to be angry. He's going to be pulling the floorboards up with his teeth!'

Janet looks at her watch. A couple of minutes left. 'Right. This is what I want to know. I don't care if we are treading on other agencies' toes. Get me the information first and then we can start to share resources. I don't want this agency to turn up to a White House conference with us being the only ones to say, "I didn't know that."'

She stands up and points at individuals around the table. 'Jarmin. Find out how they traced the licence plate of the assassin's car. *I* don't know how to find a fifty-year-old plate, so I wanna know how they did it. Sandberg. You and Gruber follow the trail. I want to know everything about that Secret Service agent. Who he worked for, his work record, his family connections, his bank records, his health, his family's health, anything and everything. For three generations, at least. Kimberley. You and your team, get me everything on the Oxford History Unit. Who are they? What are their backgrounds? What are there political affiliations, if any? Bank records, anything else they've worked on. Yada, yada, yada. It's eleven twenty-five now. I'll probably back out of the Director's office in an hour and, if I know anything about how Washington works, we'll be summiting around 4pm.' She raises her voice. 'I want the answers to all these questions on my desk by two-thirty. That's in three hours, ladies and gentlemen. Lunch is cancelled. Get all the help you need. Those of you I have not mentioned by name, find yourself a job helping out.'

Janet sweeps out of the conference room. The other attendees follow in her wake.

Later that evening, Janet is seated Business Class on a United flight to London Heathrow. She has packed for a long stay in the UK.

DS AMANDA HAYES

Constables White and Reynolds have been cooped up in a darkened room for the last two days, poring over endless CCTV footage. They must be boss-eyed by now or, at the very least, have stinking migraines. I think I'm getting one myself.

I've tried every Oxford combination I can find to complete Otto's partial number. Once you assume that the dialling code is Oxford and the four numbers we found are the last four numbers, then there are, theoretically, one hundred possible numbers. The phone company has helped to narrow it down a bit by eliminating sixty numbers. So that leaves us with forty to try.

Good, old-fashioned police work is what it's called. Me and another constable I saw checking up on holiday destinations during her lunch break are ringing them all. So far, no good. Half are not picking up; it's likely they're domestic premises and the occupier is at work or shopping or just out. We've had a few chats with a number of plumbers, insurance brokers, one undertaker, a vets' surgery and a doctors' practice on the Cowley Road. There have been a number of householders who have picked up the phone but they've all tended to be elderly subscribers or children who are off school because they're sick (or playing truant).

I've got about half a dozen more to go before calling it a day with this list. I look at the other constable enquiringly; she holds up five fingers. So we're nearly there. At least until this evening when we have to go over the numbers who didn't pick up during the day. Joy!

There have been four LPs so far: the plumber, a Mrs Lilian Plowright, one of the GPs in the Cowley Road practice and a

Mr Leonard Pritchard; both he and Mrs Plowright were rather elderly and, unless they were good mimics, unlikely suspects.

With the help of the IT geek, I managed to get a printout of Otto's phone directory from his mobile. We also got his service provider to send us a full log of incoming and outgoing calls over the last three months. They were extremely helpful and even sent it to us in electronic form so we can sort the number any which way. We started by searching for any number with our four digits in the right order. Nothing.

It begs the question: why would you write down the phone number of someone who doesn't seem to have rung you and who you haven't rung either?

Maybe the landline? Jen has obtained the phone company's log, again for the last three months, on a huge printout. She's been going through it by hand whilst ringing the Oxford numbers. That's why they say that women can multi-task.

Paul White comes by my desk, out from his hole.

'What is it, Paul?' I start to dial Oxford 95….

'I need some air. And daylight.' He rubs his eyes, picks up Otto's mobile. 'Can I have a look at this?'

'Don't you have other things to do?' I say, as the ringing tone trills in my ear.

'I guess.'

'Well, I guess you'd better… Hello! This is Detective Sergeant Amanda Hayes calling from Thames Valley Police in Oxford. I wonder if you could help me?' I wave at White to go away, or leave me alone at the very least. I concentrate on the call, but I'm still aware of him lurking beside me. I persevere with what turns out to be another dead end—a student called Emily Wilkinson—and then politely hang up. White is still hanging around, engrossed in the mobile.

I start with, 'Are you still here?' and then wish I hadn't. I'm not a sarcastic person but sometimes it's easy to lapse into hierarchical cliché. I apologise and make some remark about having a headache which is supposed to be a balm between us, but still comes out sounding self-absorbed.

Paul continues to scrutinise the mobile. He has me intrigued now.

'What is it?'

'I'm not sure, Sarge. But, if this was my phone…' He trails off.

'Yes?' Sometimes it's harder to get information out of colleagues than it is from suspects under caution in the interview room.

He wrinkles his nose and rubs his eyes again. He's tired. I'd be tired too if I'd sat through hours and hours of CCTV. I'm tired enough as it is, and flat-eared from being on the phone all day.

'It's all mates stuff.'

I look at him uncomprehending.

'Everybody and everything on it seems to be his social life.' He holds the phone out to me and shows me the screen. 'You've got his Facebook page, his Spotify account. All the contacts are friends and family, or the local hospital, cinema, restaurants, that sort of thing. I can't find a single person on here who *works* with him.'

'So, you don't think this is his only phone?'

'How many mobiles have you got, Sarge?'

Two. I take a deep breath and nod at him. The Police give me one as part and parcel of the equipment. Otto must have a work mobile, too; one that we haven't found yet. He's probably still got it with him and we don't even know the number for it yet.

'Paul, give yourself twenty minutes off the CCTV. In fact, get Chris in here. I want both of you to go through this like a dose of salts. Ring Otto's company and find out if they have an agreement with a mobile provider and if so, which one. If not, you'll have to ring round all the mobile operators in the book and ask them if they have any accounts listed with Dr Otto Parsons in or near Oxford.' I call up the local mobile operators' from the internet. 'I'd start off with this lot.'

An hour later I am standing in front of DI Campbell in her office. We have some results; just when we thought we were never going to find anything, it all seemed to come at once.

'The car is a light coloured Ford Mondeo, registration HX14 TWS, driven by a male with one male passenger in the back. There appears to be some sort of large package on the back seat next to him. We've traced the reg and the car belongs to a hire company. The company has branches in Oxford and I have sent White and Milton over to interview the manager there. White and Reynolds did a good job of tracking the car's movements. They picked it up proceeding south down Walton Street about the time that Mr Jennings said he was walking to Parsons' house. From there, we've picked it up outside Oxford Station, the Botley Interchange and again at the Milton Interchange on the A34 which is where it comes off. Finally, we see it enter the Penrose Science Park where it stays for about four hours before leaving, this time with only one person inside, at around 12.35 in the morning.'

'Have you tracked it back after that?' says Campbell.

'Not yet. That's the next job. The other thing we don't know is where it went on the Science Park. We'll need to get hold of the security tapes. I've sent Reynolds down there to dig them out.'

'Are you sure that's the car? You couldn't be mistaken?'

'We're fairly certain this is the one. There were a few other contenders, but they eliminated themselves pretty quickly. One turned out to be a couple of bakers delivering a cake to the Randolph Hotel, another was a couple with a sick daughter heading for the John Radcliffe. This one seems to be acting in the right way, driving at the right sort of speeds. If nothing else, we can do the driver for doing at least ninety on the A34. The timings match the witness statements.'

'Nice work. We'll see what Reynolds has to say when he gets back. What about the phone number?'

'"LP". Well, the first thing is that the phone we lifted from Parsons' house isn't his work phone. White called Otto's place of work, when we tracked it down. It's basically an office in the South Oxford Science Park Building. They have an office manager who tells us that Oxford Gravity didn't have a phone policy of their own, but they piggy-backed on the Science Park's arrangement with their provider.

'We spoke to the provider who told us that they have an account for a Dr Otto Parsons and they can provide us with all the incomings and outgoings. Jen had a spark of inspiration and asked them if they had any accounts listed for the Science Park with the same four digits as our friend "LP". And they did.' It's hard not to sound triumphant.

'Go on.' Campbell is looking impressed, but I can tell she's getting impatient.

'"LP" is Ludis Pahars. I think that's how you pronounce it. That's all we can say at the moment. He's got a couple of addresses. Obviously the one at the Science Park, but his domicile is given as an address in Blackbird Leys.' I hand over the piece of paper with the name and address of the college.

Campbell stares at the piece of paper for a moment, then looks up at me. 'Find out what you can about this character. He's obviously not local. Have you any idea what nationality that name might be? Check with the college. Is he a student? What information do they have on him? I'd like that all on my desk by close of play today.'

'Should we try and bring him in?'

'Yes. If possible. I'd like to find out who his friend is in the car. And I'd like to find out what he's done with Dr Parsons. And I would like to find out why you take someone who is badly injured to a science park in the evening in the middle of the Oxfordshire countryside.'

LANDLORD OF THE KING'S HEAD

Oxford. Saturday October 10th, 2145hrs.

'Hello. I wish to report a disturbance. I'm the manager here at the King's Head on Holywell Street...

'There are two gentlemen creating a noise...

'No, they're not fighting...

'Yes, I've asked them to leave after having warned...

'No, we gave them three verbal warnings to pipe down or we'd call the...

'One is a youngish man, late twenties I'd say, with dark curly hair, wearing a blue and white rugby shirt...

'The other, yes...

'Sorry, the other one is older. He's wearing a large white woollen sweater and has long grey hair, so....

'Yes, they're still here now...

'No, I can't be sure what the commotion is about. Money has come up, mostly...

'Yes, money. The young guy says he wants to pay and the older...

'No, he says he wants to pay. I don't know what it means...

'The older one says it's too late for that now...

'Look, I just want them to go away. My staff aren't bouncers and the language is upsetting some of them. Especially the...

'Yes, it is offensive and I want them...

'Before it gets violent! I don't know, maybe it could...

'I'm not sure about pressing charges. They haven't broken anything but a few customers have left. Just get here as quick as you can. They're upsetting some of the girls here. It's not right.'

121

HUGO PATTERSON

Oxford. March 2013.

It's been a long day and it's time to set off home. It is the time of day that Hugo likes best; that moment of anticipation as he climbs into the car, clicks the seatbelt into place and turns the engine over. Not that he doesn't like his job at the Exatron. It's truly fascinating. The variety of uses for a large high-powered beam of electromagnetic radiation is truly mind-boggling. And every day some wild-haired academic will pop up with another outlandish application for it.

It was the Management Team meeting today and that is usually a bit of a dogfight as the different heads of department try to put their interests ahead of everyone else's. As ever, the Technical head and the HR Director were ganging up on Hugo to get more cover as the facility grows busier. But the budget is the budget and, at the end of the day, the Exatron is expected to turn a small profit, and that means keeping a lid on expenditure, irrespective of how much additional revenue is coming in thanks to increased usage.

The Technical head was moaning about how one of his staff had apparently walked out two days earlier. It was lucky he had managed to employ the new chap a fortnight or so ago; in effect, he's back where he was at the start of the month when it comes to human resources. And everyone was coping then. Hugo knows they were busy, but *everyone's* busy. If anything, this new chap is something of a star and has already made a few improvements to the system by himself. Although he does seem to be exclusively focussed on whatever it is Sibley and Parsons are doing. And that seems to be causing headaches when it comes to scheduling some of the other projects, especially the academic ones.

Hugo turns the key in the ignition and the engine of the saloon car splutters into life. He engages reverse gear and checks the rear view mirror before pulling back from his parking space. Just as well he did; there is someone immediately behind his car. What are the chances? The car park is practically deserted save for this lost soul and, for some reason, he is blocking Hugo's route home. Hugo cranes his neck round and sees Ludis Pahars' face grinning back at him. To Hugo, Ludis has the bright-eyed countenance of a school prefect about to bid farewell before taking up his university scholarship. Irritatingly, he appears to be endowed both with brilliance and a portrait in the attic. Hugo winds the window down and leans out.

'Ludo, what can I do for you?'

'Actually, doctor, I have something I think I might be able to do for you. Can you give me a lift, by the way?'

Hugo opens the passenger door and the technician climbs in. 'Where do you want to go?'

'I was wondering if you could head in the direction of Wantage for me.'

'Can this wait another day, Ludo? I live in the opposite direction and I am rather keen on the idea of getting home right now. How far in the direction of Wantage do you want to go?'

Ludis wriggles uncomfortably. 'Well, just the other side of it. Couple of miles only, I assure you. Please.'

'Ludo, it's getting dark.'

This is intolerable, really, Hugo thinks. He's the director of a major scientific facility, not a bloody taxi service for Baltic immigrants.

'I assure you, doctor. This will be worth your while. I promise.'

Hugo rings his wife and lets her know he's going to be at work for another hour hour. And they drive.

At the other side of Wantage, at the entrance to the Oxfordshire Downs, the anonymous loops of modern housing estates peter out and the countryside begins in all its dark majesty. Ludis directs Hugo off the main road and the car winds its way along ever narrower lanes. Eventually, he points to an opening to a field and asks Hugo if he wouldn't mind driving in there while he gets out.

'What on earth for, Ludo? What is this place?'

'Please, doctor. It will be worth it. I promise.' The plangent tone is back in Ludis' voice. With a sigh of exasperation, Hugo manoeuvres the car through the gate and into the field. Once in, he turns off the engine and nearly jumps out of his skin when a back door opens and another man dressed in a black leather jacket sits down uninvited. Hugo stammers with outrage.

'Excuse me! But who the hell—'

He is cut off by the muzzle of an automatic pistol jabbed into the back of his neck. A voice from behind growls and tells him to shut up.

'I'm sorry about this, doctor,' says Ludis.

'What is going on here, Ludo? Who is this man?' Hugo is frozen in place.

'Relax, doctor. My friend and I have a proposition we would like to put to you.'

NICK YOUNG

Somewhere in England. Monday October 12th, 1030hrs.

White noise.

It fills my head. It sounds like some large boiler is in the room but I can't be sure if I'm hot or cold.

My neck feels stiff. I've been asleep and I'm sitting up. Why can't I see? Why is it so dark? And what can I feel on my face? I can't move my arms; they seem to be behind my back. I want to scratch my face but there's something covering it. My arms. My wrists. *Ouch! They hurt.* I can't move them. They're tied together.

'What's going on?' My words are swallowed by the white noise. I'm alone. Or maybe not. How can I know when I can't move from this chair, I can't see anything and all I can hear is this noise. My God, it fills my head like cement. This endless rushing noise like a stream of metal shards. Or glass. I listen: for footsteps, breathing. Nothing.

Am I cold? I still can't decide. What am I wearing? I rub my cheek against my shoulder. I think I'm still in my shirt. I rub my knees together. I'm definitely wearing trousers. I don't think I'm cold. I'm not sure if I'm hot. Why does this noise make it so hard to be sure? Does the use of your ears block other senses? What is this machine here with me?

'Hello?' Still nothing. How did I get here? What happened before I ended up like this? Whatever 'this' might be.

I trace it back to where I started the day: in Summertown, at the office. At the office, yes. It all started just like every other day, I suppose. Or did it? *How did I get here?*

Think, damn it! Think! What's the last thing I remember? The office? Home? The street? The street! Yes. No! I can't be sure. I can't be sure of anything. Except my name: Nick Young. Okay, we've got that established. One, two, three. Four. Five.

Where is this leading? I am a TV producer. I produce TV programmes. I am tied to a chair, fully clothed, in a room with some sort of machine. And I can't see anything because I have a bag over my head.

'Hello?' Still nothing. More noise, more rushing noise.

Something lands on my shoulder. Oh, Jesus! What's that? A hand. There's someone in here with me.

'Hello!' The hand lifts off but no response. *'Hello!'* I need contact, some form of contact. What's going on? How did I get here? *What's going on?*

Nothing but the noise. I sniff the air. Anything? Sniff again. Nothing. I can't smell anything or anyone, but I know I'm not alone. There's definitely someone with me. I can feel their presence now. They're standing somewhere nearby, watching me. I'm not alone. I'm not alone.

Whoever it is, they put me here. That hand: it was no friend. That's why they're not talking to me. Just watching. And that noise covers them. I can't hear them move or breathe or swallow or anything. But I know they're there. I can feel it. I can feel them.

'Who are you?'

Are they smiling when I cry out? Are they making fun of me? Or do they just sit there, or stand there, and look at me impassively, dispassionately? Like people looking at a vase? That's all I am right now: an empty vessel. I'm a TV producer for a successful TV programme. I'm not an empty vessel. Talk to me, you fuckers! I know you're there.

I turn my head from side to side; maybe I can dislodge the hood slightly, see something under it. Maybe...

A chink of light! So I'm not in darkness after all.

Bang! My head lights up. I can see shafts of white behind my eyes. First the burst of light and then the pain. It feels like some huge scaffolding pole has swung across the left side of my face: unyielding, unstoppable, solid. Jesus Christ, that really hurt.

Bang! And again, but from the other side. The light is not so bright this time; maybe you get used to this. But not the awful pain. My cheeks feel like they have been shattered. Do I still have all my teeth? What's going on? How did I get here? What's going on?

'What's going on? Please don't hurt me. What do you want?'
Another blast of force and pain to the left cheek.

'Please! Stop!' A salty tang. Is that blood in my mouth? And still, that relentless noise.

Then, no more force, no impacts. Just noise and darkness. I try to move the chair, but it's probably fixed in place. I can't move it. Whoever is with me, they are just standing there, watching me. Is this amusing them?

'Please. Just talk to me.' What can I say? What can I say that will change anything? What do they want me for? They haven't captured me like this just so they can stand there and watch me writhe in my chair with a fucking bag over my fucking head.

'You bastards!' *Bang!* Face struck again by the boom. Or fist. Or baseball bat. How should I know? I'm just some kind of toy to them. I can't move. I can't see. I can't reach out. Nothing. All I can do is speak and then get hit. I'm bleeding quite a lot now. Am I going to bleed to death? Are these bastards going to let me bleed to death? Is this how it ends?

I'm sweating; perhaps I'm hot after all. All that I know and trust, everything I've ever taken for normal and safe and ordinary... That's all gone now. What's Jane going to think? Jane...

'Please!' Nothing. I'm alone. It doesn't matter who else is in the room. I am truly alone now. I am standing on the shore as the ferry approaches through a veil of mist. This is the last thing I shall know.

I start to cry. Childhood tears. The tears of loss and forgiveness missed. The tears of not knowing how this can end. I haven't cried like this for a long, long time. I cry now because it's nearly over; I cry because there's so much left unsaid to so many people; I cry because all that I hold dear—my hopes for the future, my ambitions, my desires—will be unfulfilled. Above all, I cry because I don't understand.

'Please. I'll tell you whatever you what you want to hear. Please!'

A sharp stab of pain in my upper arm. A needle. And then a voice. A woman's, American.

'I was hoping you'd say that. We have so much to talk about.'

PROFESSOR DAN SIBLEY

Heathrow Airport, London. August 2011.

'Good morning, sir. Welcome. Can I have your passport, please?'

Dan Sibley pulls his passport and booking confirmation slip from his inside jacket pocket and hands them over. The girl behind the counter checks the name on the passport, the details on the booking slip and lifts her carefully made-up face in order to lock eye contact.

'Thank you, Professor.' She hands back the passport. 'Will you be checking in any baggage?'

'Yes. Just the one piece, please'. Sibley lifts the suitcase onto the conveyor belt at the side of the desk. He tries to do it effortlessly. Even though it probably won't impress her, it might make him feel a bit better.

'Would you prefer a window or an aisle seat, Professor?'

'Window, please.' The route is mostly overland and through daylight, so there may be something worth looking at. 'I've got an empty seat right at the front. Is 1A acceptable?'

'Certainly.'

She prints off a boarding pass and spends a few moments getting the luggage tag sorted out: one long strip for the suitcase, one stub to be stuck to the boarding pass.

'Do you know where our First Class Lounge is, sir?' Sibley shakes his head. 'Just go through Security and follow the 'Airport Lounges' signs. Ours is up one level from there. They will announce the flight to Dubai about forty-five minutes before it's due to depart. Have a nice flight and I hope we will welcome you back again soon.'

'Thank you very much.' Sibley gathers up the Boarding Pass, his carry-on bag and his lounge invitation and strolls off in the direction of the Departures gate.

PART THREE

THE OCTOBER
FOUNDATION

JOSEPH BOYLE

New York. October 1929.
(Excerpt from Boyle's memoirs, published in 1958).

And then came that day in October 1929; that day which has been my making and which has been my greatest perplexity. I have kept this to myself for all these years for, oh, how such a story will grow and reform itself into the image of those who tell it and how it will reflect so ill on myself. So I have chosen this moment to recount the episode in my own words and to cast them in print such that there is only one version of the event, and one alone.

It is still hard for me to be sure if the day was some kind of divine gift or just dumb luck. I had worked in my position as Senior Partner in the bank and secured it such that my tenure was unassailable. Ten years' work had established me on Wall Street as a Name and one that sat amongst the most august company in Lower Manhattan. I had built up profits upon profits for the bank and all of it on the single, compelling premise that one could make money from the Stock Exchange without having any—or, to be more accurate, very little—of your own to start with.

I doubt very much that I was the bright spark who dreamt up the concept of Buying On The Margin, but I certainly prosecuted it within the bank and, latterly, with the bank's clients.

It was an arresting proposition for anyone with a modicum of financial ambition: you select the shares you wish to invest in; the bank then puts up on average 85% of the face value of the shares and you put in the remaining 15% plus the bank's commission; the very act of purchasing the stock will increase demand for that stock and, consequently, the value of that stock will rise. The next time you put in an order for more shares, the price will be higher. On top of that, the bank would allow you to borrow against the value of your share portfolio in order to acquire yet more stock. And so it went.

And our clients became very wealthy, very quickly. At least on paper. The bank, by contrast, became very wealthy, very quickly, and paper had nothing to do with it. We amassed a fortune in just the commission alone. Our exposure to the large client base who had bought on the margin was, to a great extent, offset by our physical deposits and, of course, the bank's own shareholding. So we had insurance and the market was rising and rising and the sun shone and times were so very good.

I can remember the long summer months spent out in our house on the road to Montauk. The sea glittered and danced on the sands at the end of the garden and the sea grass swayed in the exhilarating ocean air. I would take long walks with Anne and the kids over the heathland, and Anne would point out the different trees and fruits and the kids would cry out their names: blueberry, beach plum, bayberry, rose and rosehip, black cherry, black huckleberry. Anne was always good at naming the plants; something, alas, I never had the talent for. Despite our good fortune and the luxury in which we could afford to live, she never lost touch with what lay beyond the front door, and instilled in our children that sense of enquiry and respect.

We would spend the weekends in Montauk as a family and socialise with our friends in the Hamptons, including the Jamesons and the Murphys and their artistic retinue. Then I would travel back to the city in time for the start of work on the Monday. I had an apartment in Midtown which afforded me ready access to Wall Street should I need to return at short notice. Thankfully, I was rarely expected to drop everything and return to work at all hours; that time was receding, if not completely behind me. I enjoyed the ministrations of a sizeable staff who were able to react as and when circumstances dictated. In Wall Street, those circumstances would dictate frequently and volubly and insistently. In fact Wall Street was a creature with a life and a rhythm all of its own. Those who fed and watered the beast learned on the first day that the beast never slept and that it was always demanding. But in those days, the rewards for keeping the beast well were almost without limit.

Success, it is said, breeds success. I have never subscribed to this view. For me, original thinking and a pioneering spirit breeds success; maybe not the first time, but certainly in the end, as long as the road to success doesn't break you first. Thereafter, success spawns latecomers: those without the imagination or creativity to devise new ideas for themselves. They will clamber with tooth and claw upon the coat tails of the innovators and bask in the reflected glory. At first, the latecomers will be successful and they will flaunt their good fortune and exaggerate their financial prowess before those who have not yet clambered aboard. And thus, the hangers-on will join the latecomers and they too will enjoy their own brilliance for a short summer. But with every summer, there must come a fall.

It is to my eternal shame that I was not bold enough take a step back and wonder if our unstoppable upward trajectory was truly unstoppable. I pride myself on my objectivity; I try to be detached from what I observe. What I saw—or thought I saw—was the impossible: the defiance of gravity writ large; men of commerce proving that the laws of physics and nature could be broken or ignored. I too was swept up in the great exuberance of the financial miracle. But I never found the time or the will to sit back and consider whether this miracle would be eternal. I like to write it off as youthful inexperience; it helps to moderate the degree with which I chide myself. The myopia of arrogance.

No, indeed, it fell to a stranger to open my eyes; someone whom I had never met before and who, to this day, I have encountered but once more. His was a most startling proposition and he opened it with a gold brick.

My secretary led him into my office and, as the door opened, he entered on a pillow of open outcry from the floor below. He told me his name was Bernhard Croce and that he was from France. He was, as I would have expected for a Frenchman, well dressed and had something of a military air about him, although he sported a full silver beard. I took him for a naval gentleman as I could only think of his bearing and his beard being acceptable to that service; but what did I know? He walked across the room and waited for me to proffer a chair, then sat himself down.

I offered him a drink and he politely asked for a small Armagnac which I was not able to supply; he settled for a Cognac instead. The secretary returned a few moments later bearing a tray of coffee for us both. Monsieur Croce was carrying a small leather portmanteau which he placed on the floor by his seat and, after sipping the Cognac (of which he approved, I am happy to report) I asked him how I might be of service. He replied that it was he who would be of service to myself and for a moment I was concerned that he was merely a representative of yet another investment fund seeking to use our bank to endorse or promote his products. He saw me bridle and raised his hands in a reassuring gesture.

'I am here as a sole agent. Please do not be alarmed.'

I relaxed and he began again.

'I… er… I am not sure how to, or even *where* to start. Forgive me, but I need your help. And, perhaps more importantly, you need my help.'

'Monsieur, you will forgive me if I respectfully ask you…' I trailed off; I was never adept at asking people to get to the point and have them still like me afterwards.

'Of course. *Alors!* Tomorrow is Thursday.' I nodded. 'That is when a large number of companies are going to be posting their quarterly results. Is that not so?' He looked at me for confirmation and I nodded yet again. So far Monsieur Croce had not said anything that I didn't know or was of special interest. 'They are going to be bad.'

The abruptness of this statement brought me up short and I was temporarily at a loss for what to say or do next. 'How do you know?'

'How I know is unimportant. What is important is that I *do* know and that I am not surmising this, at best, or making it up, at worst.' I thought I detected an air of mild triumph as he broke to sip his Cognac once more before he continued. 'Take Ford, for example.'

'What about Ford?' I enquired nervously; I had some considerable exposure to the stock.

'They have pioneered the use of assembly line construction and they have been phenomenally successful.' I started to relax at this point, perhaps misguidedly. 'They have made it possible for the average man in the street to afford his very own automobile. Beforehand, a motor car was an unthinkable luxury, a plaything of the very wealthy which was hand-built by craftsmen bespoke. The price of a Ford Model T is a small fraction of the cost of one of its competitors before the introduction of the assembly line.'

'Okay. But where is this all going?'

'How much do you know about the company's inventory, Mr Boyle?' he looked me square in the eye and waited for a response. He had to wait for me to think first, though. I wasn't sure of what he was driving at, or perhaps I was in denial of it. I shrugged my shoulders and waited for him to continue. 'The company has a huge number of unsold automobiles, Mr Boyle. American industry's technological capability has improved and grown and developed over the last ten years to the point where production now outstrips demand. Real demand!'

'But Ford's growth has been meteoric,' I countered. 'We have been living off the company's dividends for years and there have been no signs that the company is in trouble.'

'Who said they were in trouble? I simply said that production is now outstripping demand. By itself, that's not "trouble".' He leaned forward in his chair and spoke in a low voice laden with menace. 'But when you take it together with all the other disappointing results from all the other companies...'

'I ask you again. How do you know? If the results aren't published, you either have a lot of privileged information or you are surmising.'

'Privileged information is what Wall Street runs on, Mr Boyle. Everybody knows everything, especially the inside track. That's why people go to stockbrokers and use bankers and investment funds. Because all those expensive dinners and weekends in the Hamptons buy you access to that information. Isn't that the case?'

'As you said, Monsieur, that's why people go to stockbrokers and the like,' I retorted.

'I doubt it will always be like that,' he added darkly. 'So,' he began again, 'let us recap. The stock market is racing skywards. The Dow Jones is at an all-time high and looks like it's never going to stop. All the share prices are buoyed up with a strategy of buying on the margin which means that they don't really own very much at all. It's all just debt, Mr Boyle. You're all skating on thin ice and it's already started to crack. Look at what happened back in March.' He had a point; there had been a minor market correction but the momentum of blind greed had rapidly overcome the fall in values.

'That rebounded quickly.' I tried to sound confident but I was starting to doubt myself now, and I think my words came out sounding cocksure instead: the classic sign of someone who is trying to defend an indefensible position.

'Yes, it did. And the Dow Jones has grown steadily ever since. But it is the first crack in the ice. You can call me a doom-monger if you like, but, as I said at the outset, I am here to make us both a lot of money.'

At this, he reached into his portmanteau and, with a small effort, hoisted a large gold brick onto my desk. It thudded down with an awesome resonance. I regarded it for a few moments, then looked back at him, expecting him to continue.

'Tomorrow is Thursday,' he announced. 'And, as I said, that is when the company reports will be published. The Dow Jones will fall. The banks will try to staunch any loss of confidence by buying shares to prop the market up. Friday will be the last day the sun shines for twenty-five years.'

'How do you know this? How can you be so sure?'

'*How* is not something I am prepared to discuss with anybody. The important thing is *what* can be done about it. And that "what" is sitting on your desk right now, Mr Boyle.' He sipped some of the cognac and followed it up with a draught of coffee. He again reached into his portmanteau and produced two sheets of paper bearing close typescript. 'These are my instructions. I have here a list of three hundred or so companies. On Monday morning you will instruct your traders to sell these shares short. I have indicated the amount for each stock.'

He handed the first piece across to me and it took a couple of seconds for the full horror of what he was proposing to present itself. I admit I am no poker player, but I could feel my face declaring my shock as I read through the list. And the amounts! His instructions would probably bankrupt some of these companies. I looked up at him; he was sitting in his chair quite impassive. 'What if you're wrong?'

'I am not wrong. I am well-informed, Mr Boyle. This is Wall Street. It runs on information. I have information. And it is information that no one else has. Yet. The reconciliation period is, what, five days?' I nodded. 'Good. Then I wish to instruct you to command your traders to reconcile the position before close of business on the following Friday. Immediately upon completion of the position's reconciliation, I wish you to purchase the following.' He handed me another sheet of paper. The list was much shorter and consisted of a few mining stocks. The remainder was gold itself. As with the first list, the sheer volume of stock he expected to acquire was staggering.

'How do you plan to raise the capital to purchase these?'

'With the proceeds of that week's transactions. I am confident that the profit I make from the short-selling will cover the costs for the second list.'

'Yes. But if you are wrong—'

'I'm not wrong. I told you that.'

'But if you are, the level of debt you are racking up in this second set of transactions will constitute an unjustifiable exposure for this bank. In my position within it, I cannot countenance such a proposal.'

'I thought you'd say that,' he replied coolly. 'That's why I thought it prudent to visit you today. As I mentioned earlier, tomorrow is going to see some unpalatable activity on the Stock Exchange. I have written down what the extent of the losses is to be and the desperate measures some financial houses will take to redress the situation.' He fixed me with his pale blue eyes. 'If I am in any detail wrong, any detail at all, then I expect you to disregard these instructions and we shall have no further dealings. If I am not, then will you execute these instructions, Mr Boyle?'

They say that love is blind and euphoria can blind a man, too. I had been wrapped in the euphoria of the last seven years and taken a significant role in feeding the frenzy. I could have had a pang of conscience about it, but at no time had I ever pretended to be some sort of social worker. My job was to make money for my employer, my clients and myself. Period. I looked back at his pieces of paper. '*Any* detail?' He nodded.

'I will ask my secretary to book you an appointment. For tomorrow, at four o'clock in this office. If your predictions are in any way inaccurate, Monsieur, then I can predict that our meeting tomorrow will be brief.' He sat there, his gaze fixed on mine. After a time, his expression softened and he nodded, smiling. He stood to go, picked up the gold brick from my desk and replaced it in his portmanteau and moved toward me to shake my hand. As soon as he grasped it, he held it firm.

'Tomorrow it is, Mr Boyle.' I expected him to let go of my hand but he just stood his ground. 'You might want to consider what you have just heard. I did say that this meeting would help you as well as myself. It will only help you if you are prepared.' With that, he left.

He returned the next day as per the appointment. We spent over two hours together with two of my associates as we planned the investment strategy for the coming days and years. We set him up with an account and, after that, I never saw him again.

JULIA KITAGAWA

New York, March 2013

The auction room is still; it's as if all present are holding their breath. The previous lot, a sublime landscape by Sisley of a river softened by a summer haze, is being carried off the rostrum to its new home. As the last echoes of the gavel fade, a few throats harrumph. Seats are adjusted. A deep well of expectation has opened up.

Julia is standing at the back; she is not going to miss this moment. She had assisted David, the Director of Fine Arts, in the preparation of the auction: cataloguing the lots; inviting guests; notifying collectors on the Armstrong's database; confirming provenance; and, in some cases, establishing the authenticity of the work by consulting experts.

This last issue was essential for the next lot: thirty-eight. As expected, *Veuve Venissac's Café* has caused a sensation. Van Goghs do not come up for auction every day. Once an art institution has acquired a work of global significance, it is loath to let it go; even the large corporations which like to have prestigious pieces of art in their boardrooms will do their utmost to protect these assets, since they represent the honour and the importance of the owner. To relinquish such a gem would constitute irredeemable loss of face, especially in the Far East. It's practically unprecedented for a Van Gogh that no one has ever seen since the day it was painted to come up for sale.

Julia knew the eyes of the world would be focussed on this sale room tonight. Her role in helping organise the event was one thing, but her role in authenticating the artwork was quite another. Should the painting turn out to be a forgery, it would result in the most appalling loss of trust in the auction house. Armstrong's would become a laughing stock overnight. The company didn't charge 20% commission plus taxes to the purchaser for nothing. Julia is part of the core structure of maintaining the reputation of the company and the integrity of its clients and their lots.

It took over six months of travelling back and forth to different institutions to have the painting X-rayed, photometrically analysed, and examined by experts in Van Gogh's use of brushwork, pigments, composition and correction. They pored and cogitated and deliberated and squinted at print-outs and graphs and X-rays and even specks of pigment. Lastly, they matched the description of the painting with the letters to Theo, the artist's brother. And they tried and they struggled as best they could to prove the artwork a fake, but the artwork stood its ground.

The painting is truly *Veuve Venissac's Café* painted by Vincent van Gogh in Arles in 1889. All doubt removed. Lot 38.

David is taking the sale, and he has not had too long to wait for the painting to have been carefully borne onto an easel at the back of the rostrum. Julia imagines she can hear a faint gasp from the gathering, but she could be mistaken; maybe it is just wishful thinking on her part. The Great and the Good of New York society are here together with a smattering of faded rock stars and supermodel royalty, and art critics and art correspondents from the world's high-end media. These people are far too cool to gasp in the presence of unimaginable wealth; they bathe in it as standard. To the side of the sale room are the telephones; Julia counts them with her finger. Ten. Or is that eleven? She's rarely seen so many. And there are those faceless bidders on the Internet, poised at whatever time of the day this might be for them. Julia still finds it extraordinary that someone might be waiting for their grapefruit and muesli to be served to them for breakfast while they are hanging on a phone to make a multi-million dollar purchase like this.

David clears his throat and describes the lot as seen. As he does so, he scans the room; he has a good notion of who will be bidding and is using this brief interlude to seek them out. They will give the most delicate of movements; they will not want to attract attention. They have rivals in the room and they will want to convince them that they have given up bidding. Behind him is the vast electronic board looking for all the world like the departure screen at some major international airport. It quotes the latest bid in ten different currencies. David, however, will be calling the bids in US dollars. And it begins.

David opens with a commission bid of one hundred million: already higher than the most ever paid for a Van Gogh. His strategy is to raise the price in twos and threes (one hundred and two, and five and eight, and ten) until one hundred and forty, when he will up the bids in fives. It seems to take no time at all before the price has passed one hundred and fifty million dollars.

David signals he will increase the price in increments of ten million dollars. The bidding, as far as Julia can see, is as intense as it was at the start. Perhaps he should have started much higher. But then his purpose is to snare as many bidders as possible early on and let the excitement of the moment carry them onwards and upwards. Those in the room using subtle gestures will have been spotted by now, and so to pull out at this point would be acknowledged as showing a lack of backbone by his peers. The bidders are riding an enraged tiger; to dismount now would be fatal, if only to reputation. But that can still count for so much.

One hundred and eighty million dollars. Julia can see that at least half of the dozen or so bidders have dropped out, but most of the phones are still live, their handlers whispering urgently and listening intently. The internet bidders—there seem to be about five from Russia, China, India, the US and the UAE—are still in play and the rise of the price seems inexorable.

Two hundred million dollars. Only one other painting has ever achieved this level before. Three men are left in the room: two of them obviously Middle Eastern and one Julia cannot say. Eastern European? They are seated in different parts of the room and David is having to work hard to keep an eye on all three and their tiny movements. The Middle Eastern gentleman nearest Julia is ever so slightly raising his head whenever David looks in his direction; she cannot say what signals the other two are giving. Four telephone bidders remain; the handlers are keen to ensure that David will see their bids. The internet seems to have dropped out altogether, with no activity for quite a while. (Julia muses that time in an auction is measured in money and not seconds; the internet last bid thirty-five million dollars ago.)

David now raises the price in twenties. Two-forty, two-sixty, two-eighty. The numbers drop like the beats of a metronome. Two remain in the room, with two on the phones. The Middle Eastern man has fallen by the wayside. The assembled are trying not to gawp at the two bidders in the room; it would not be seemly, after all. Instead, they opt to focus on the two phone handlers. Julia's colleagues, Jeanette and Colin, are doing their best to wipe out any acknowledgement of their surroundings; it is just them and the metallic voice at the end of the line.

Three hundred and eighty million dollars. There is a pause. The amount quoted is not a statement, it is a question. It hangs in the air and in the ether. Colin, the phone handler, signals by nodding his head emphatically. David confirms the price, immediately countering with a flick of a programme. Four hundred. All eyes revert to the phones. Jeanette shakes her head and quietly thanks her client. She replaces the receiver and sits down. Colin stares hard at the floor; his client will be considering his options. He obviously wants this painting. To have it would be the culmination of his ambition and his existence. He is anonymous to all but himself and now all that he desires is to be able to regard himself with quiet admiration. He will want to impress himself. But can he justify this?

Colin nods again. Everyone takes a collective breath and all focus returns to the bidder in the room. Four-twenty?

Four hundred and twenty million. No artwork has ever sold for so high a price. In the aftermath of a global financial crisis, this is the first indication that there are those for whom the storm has abated.

A flick of a programme and all necks switch back to the phone. Four-fifty? There is a buzz in the room. One of the internet bidders— Chinese—has put forward a bid of four hundred and twenty-five million dollars. David calls the amount. The man with the programme shakes his head dolefully; this is not his night but he has fought valiantly and his honour remains unimpeached. He can dine out on this.

So. Colin. And the phone. He murmurs something to the client; it looks like an invocation, a gentle encouragement but in truth all he is doing is reminding the client of the current bid and asking if he wishes to raise the price yet further. The instinct of everyone is not to hurry the man, but David can smell that the end is near. From the rostrum he quietly says, 'I'm afraid I must ask for a bid. The offer stands at four twenty-five. I can take four-thirty.'

More murmuring. Colin listens and nods silently as he receives his instructions from the other end. Colin then looks up at the rostrum.

No.

The room erupts into applause and the hammer falls. *Veuve Venissac's Café* has been knocked down for four hundred and twenty-five million dollars, not including the twenty percent commission with federal and local taxes. The anonymous purchaser will have to part with in excess of five hundred million dollars before he can take delivery of the painting.

Julia allows herself a smile and her colleague Kimberley congratulates her; this has been Julia's first big authentication and her first big sale to organise and she knows that this will have been noticed within Armstrong's if not across the auction world generally. David's place at the rostrum is taken by another auctioneer and, with an apparent lack of ceremony, Lot 39 replaces its illustrious predecessor. And the auction continues.

DS AMANDA HAYES

Oxford. Tuesday October 13th, 0930hrs.

The Exatron is a large circular building clad in what appears to be corrugated aluminium and sits in a gentle curve of countryside beneath some chalk downs. DS Hayes, accompanied by DC Jen Carlisle, parks her unmarked car in the visitors' spaces and the two gather their bags and coats from the back seat before walking towards the main entrance.

Inside, the reception area is large and high-vaulted but utilitarian and uninspiring; no effort has been made to give the visitor the impression that they are setting foot in the future of science. The receptionist invites the two officers to take a seat, and they retire to a small circle of blue fabric-covered sofas and armchairs gathered around a glass coffee table covered by a selection of unreadable journals. They sit and stare at the stark architecture: exposed metal beams and lattices, more corrugated aluminium, a few bas-relief artworks. There's a background hum of distant machinery, punctuated by the receptionist answering the occasional phone call and the remote swish of a car passing by.

The two women sit playing with their mobile phones, answering emails and text messages (or pretending to, anyway; DC Carlisle is actually playing a game she had downloaded over the weekend but Hayes is none the wiser). Every so often they check their watches, look up at each other and tut. The receptionist had said he was on his way and that was quite a while ago. Hayes shifts in her seat and twists round to look accusingly at the receptionist. We're not here for an interview, she thinks. We're the police, for Heaven's sake. The receptionist carries on, unaware of the psychic assault.

A door opens with a click which reverberates around the reception area. Shoes click-clack across the concrete floor in their direction. The owner of the shoes—a middle-aged man, slightly balding with a belly that hangs over his belted trousers like a geological feature—holds out his hand to Hayes. 'Good morning. I'm Gerry Ridder, Facilities Manager here at the Exatron. Sorry I couldn't get here sooner. It's quite a large site and I was at the other end when I got the call that you were on your way.'

'Delighted you could see us,' says Hayes. Ridder doesn't have a choice, but it's always good policy to be gracious to the public. She produces her warrant card. 'I'm DS Hayes and this is DC Carlisle.'

'I gather you wanted to see the CCTV footage for Sunday night. I met with your DC Reynolds who asked if he could take it away but I'm afraid that's not going to be possible. My apologies for that. It's just the system limitations. I'm more than happy to take you through the security files if you have the time.'

Hayes nods. 'As long as it's no bother.'

'Of course not. Please follow me.'

The receptionist takes Hayes and Carlisle's photos and produces visitors' badges. As ever, the photos are moon-faced and fish-eyed distortions of how they actually appear and Hayes wonders what purpose these pictures ever serve.

The office complex adjoins the reception area, so it is not too far to go to Ridder's office on the second floor. The three pause by a coffee machine and help themselves before entering his office and sitting round his desk.

Ridder swivels round a large computer monitor so that the two women can see it. He presses a number of keys and the screen lights up with a mosaic of eight TV images.

'This is the live feed from the CCTV cameras we have around the site. You can monitor up to eight at a time, though you'd need the eyes of a fly if you were going to do it properly.' The attempt at humour elicits no response.

Carlisle leans forward. 'How many cameras do you have throughout the site, Mr Ridder?'

'In total, thirty. Nine of them monitor the outside of the building, the rest are all watching the operations internally. To be honest, the main purpose of the CCTV is to record what happens with the scientific equipment. More data-gathering than security. But they can serve both functions.'

'And how far back do tapes go for each camera?'

'Well, we don't have tapes. It's all done on hard drive, of course. But they hold back images for eight days. So, for Sunday evening, you shouldn't have a problem. What would you like to see first?' Ridder's fingers are poised over his keyboard.

'Let's start with the external cameras first,' says Carlisle.

'In that case, I suggest focussing on those that cover the three entrances to the building.' Ridder taps away at the keyboard. He arranges the images so that the three cameras facing the doors are enlarged, compared with the other five. 'What time would you like to view them from?'

'Can we start it off from 7pm?' says Hayes. Ridder taps a few more keys and the eight images all play. The cameras take a still every five or ten seconds and Ridder speeds them up so a new still is loaded every second. It doesn't take long before they get to the time when the car from Jericho is due to turn up. At 7.43pm, a light-coloured Ford Mondeo pulls into the parking bays and stops. A man is in the driver's seat, but it's hard to make out any distinguishing features other than the fact that he's wearing some sort of dark top. A sweatshirt, perhaps?

Carlisle squints at the screen. 'Can you zoom in on the driver?'

'Yes, I can, but I doubt it will be very much help. The resolution on these cameras is not brilliant. If I zoom in too much, all you will see are some large, grey pixels.'

'So there's nothing you can do to sharpen up the image?'

'Look, this isn't the movies where they have some magic button where the pixels all turn into pin-sharp images. You, of all people, should know that. I'm afraid that what you see is what you're going to get.'

'Let's spool the tapes on, then' says Hayes, defusing.

They watch for a while but nothing happens. The car sits in the parking bay and no one moves in or near it. The entrances to the building remain silent and untroubled by traffic. The three of them scan the images for any clues, any signs of life, but still nothing.

Then, Hayes notices something.

'Where's the driver?' she asks pointing at the image of the parked car. 'Where did he go?'

'He must still be there,' says Carlisle, leaning in closer.

But he isn't.

'Can we run the tapes backwards?' says Hayes. Ridder taps the commands into his keyboard. After a while, Hayes shouts. 'There!'

Ridder and Carlisle study the screen, trying to work out what it is she has spotted. 'Look at the time code. It's jumped back twenty minutes.'

Ridder runs the tape forwards slowly and, sure enough, there is a jump in the time code of about twenty minutes and the driver in the image just vanishes. Ridder runs the tape backwards and the driver instantly reappears and sits motionless with a frozen time code for a period of twenty minutes. When the time code unfreezes, the car reverses out of the parking bay and disappears off-frame.

'So there you have it,' he says. 'They arrive and then, whatever they did for the next twenty minutes, they've wiped it from the system.'

'Can you do that?' Hayes asks in exasperation.

Ridder motions to the screen: 'So it would seem.'

'How?'

'I don't know. I've not done it myself, you understand.' Ridder tries not to sound too sarcastic, but it is a stupid question.

'I notice that they haven't tampered with the other camera feeds,' says Carlisle.

'Well we'll need to check the other tapes as well, I suppose,' says Ridder, irritated. 'We now know when they left the car, because they froze the feed at this time here.' He points at the screen. 'So, we can assume that they used one or other of the entrances to the building a couple of minutes afterwards.' His gaze returns to the screen. 'A-ha!' he declares. 'The camera to the main entrance.'

Two minutes after the car park camera is frozen, the feed to the main entrance also freezes. They scan forward until the time code starts up again. But this time the freeze is only two minutes long. A couple of minutes later, the camera watching the southeast entrance freezes: again, for two minutes.

'I imagine,' says Hayes, 'that the driver entered the building via the main entrance and then walked through the building to open up the entrance at the rear. If our assumptions are correct, they wanted access to that door so that they would minimise the chances of their bumping into anyone else. Do you have a log of all those who came and went that evening?'

Ridder punches some more keys and reports that there were a couple of cleaners, one maintenance man and the security guard who was probably doing his rounds at the time the suspects were entering the building.

'Would our driver have had a security pass?' says Hayes.

'He wouldn't have got past the reception area without one.'

'So he could have wiped the record of his entry from the system along with the camera feeds?'

'If he's wiped the feeds, then he probably did that too, yes.' Ridder concedes.

Carlisle frowns. 'Where would he have had to go in this building to do that?'

'Unless he hacked into the system, which I might suggest would be entirely plausible given what he's done to the CCTV log, he would have had to break into this office.'

'And any sign of a disturbance when you arrived for work yesterday?' Hayes weaves her head from side to side as if trying to physically jog his memory.

'Not that I can recall, no.' Ridder is emphatic.

'Then hacking seems the most likely answer. Could it be done remotely, or would they have to use an access point to the system?'

'I'm not an expert on hacking, so I couldn't tell you for sure. But if you access the system using one of the PCs here, you would bypass quite a few firewalls that might otherwise cause you a headache.' Ridder rubs his forehead and grimaces. This is going to require a complete security upgrade.

Carlisle checks her notes. 'We know the car was spotted heading away from this facility at around 12.35. So, we need to check all the camera feeds between the time of the first freeze and then. So that's thirty feeds over about five hours.'

'What are you thinking?' says Hayes.

'Well, they've interfered with the external feeds presumably to cover their tracks when they were outside the building. I reckon they did the same with those cameras that might have monitored their activities when they were inside the building as well.'

'I have a suggestion,' says Ridder. 'Let's go through each of the cameras in turn and note which ones freeze, when they freeze and when they free up again. We could plot that out on a graph or something and that will give you a schematic of what their progress was through the facility on the night they broke in.'

The two women nod and, over the course of an hour, they sit glued to the screen watching the time codes counting down the hours. When a time code freezes, they note the time and plot it on a rough chart that Carlisle sketches out on a piece of paper with the aid of a book's edge, drawing the axes. As soon as the time code jerks into life again, the new time is recorded and plotted.

At the end of the session, Hayes takes Carlisle's graph and hands it to Ridder. 'Talk us through this.' It's a challenge as well as a request. Ridder regards the untidy chart and rubs his chin. He steps outside and fetches another strong black coffee.

'Okay. Camera Eight and Camera Eleven. This is the car park and this is the main entrance. The car park is frozen for twenty minutes, but the main entrance is frozen for only three. That means that they only used the reception area briefly, presumably to walk through it. But whatever they were up to in the car park took longer to sort out.

'Camera Twelve. That's looking down the east perimeter corridor which would get you from the front of the building to the south-east entrance. This one freezes two minutes after our friend enters via the main entrance and restarts again three minutes later. So, Chummy used that corridor only once.' Ridder checks the chart again. 'Yes. Just the once. So this and the main entrance was used just to access the south-east door and not used again. If we look at Camera Seventeen which looks over the south-east door…' He runs his finger across the chart. 'We can see it was used twice. Once about two or three minutes after Camera Twelve freezes, which would tally with the amount of time it would take to get there from Camera Twelve. Like I said, it's a big building. And they've frozen it for…' He counts, muttering under his breath. 'Twelve, thirteen… fifteen minutes. Which adds up to the length of time Camera Eight, the car park, is offline.'

'This is piecing together really nicely,' says Hayes, using her best encouraging tone. 'Keep going.'

'Then Camera Twenty-Three… Let me look that one up.' He pulls a crib sheet on a clipboard from on the top of the return unit of his desk. 'The Beam Hall. Bloody hell. They went into the Beam Hall.'

'What happens in there?' says Carlisle.

'Well, nothing at the moment, but it's where the main beam is housed, together with some other equipment from whoever is using the beam to run experiments. But no one was running anything on Sunday night.'

'Are you sure?' says Hayes. 'Could there be any records of unauthorised usage of the equipment?'

153

'I'd need to check the power logs for that. Every time we power this stuff up, it would heat your house for about eighteen months.' Hayes rolls her eyes in astonishment. 'But that would take a bit of time. So I suggest we persevere with our camera hunt for the time being.' Ridder quickly drafts an email to one of his colleagues, enquiring whether the beam had been used that evening. He returns to the chart.

'Camera Seventeen was the next to go AWOL. Both that and Camera Twenty-Three were offline for over four hours.' Hayes looks quizzically at Ridder. 'Camera Seventeen is the one in the Control Room. So they entered the facility via the back door, crossed straight into the Beam Hall and did something in there whilst, one assumes, operating the equipment from the Control Room.'

Carlisle gazes at the screen, pondering. 'Is it possible to set up the equipment and run, I don't know, some sort of experiment in four hours?' She has been totting up the times on a separate piece of paper. At the moment, things are looking pretty tight if it's all going to be wrapped up before the car is seen again on the A43 at 12.35am.

'I've no bloody idea. I'm the Facilities Manager here. I didn't need a PhD to get this job. I just deal with cleaners, site workers, security, the toilets. I'm not called upon to help them with their quantum mechanics homework.'

'Let's assume,' says Hayes, 'that these guys knew what they were doing and that they needed four hours and three minutes to do it in.'

'Hang on,' says Ridder. 'I've just had a reply to my email. Someone did use the equipment on Sunday night. It ran for twelve seconds with a ninety-seven minute power-up. The pulse was activated at 11.58pm.'

Carlisle stares at her piece of paper. 'So, by my reckoning, they were in the Beam Hall and the Control Room for a good two and a half hours before they turned the machine on.'

'I suppose they were having to set some of the equipment's parameters. All I know about this stuff is, if you go off half-cocked, you can seriously waste your time and money.'

'Okay,' says Hayes. 'To summarise. They took time to get something in to the building via the back door. They then went directly to the Beam Hall and spent the next four hours in there, apparently setting up and then running some experiment. It's getting near midnight. What do they do next?'

Ridder looks at the chart once again. 'Then they leave via the south-east entrance. That's the last camera to go on the fritz and it's offline for another fifteen minutes.'

Carlisle smiles. 'Fifteen minutes. That should give them enough time to get back to the car.'

'More than enough, I'd say,' says Hayes. 'It surely can't take more than five minutes to get back to the car park. After all, it only took three to five minutes to get down there from the reception area at the outset. And they didn't have the bother of trying to get back through the security gates in reception.' She stares at the screen. 'Did any other cars leave at or around the time of our suspect car?'

Ridder switches across to the two cameras covering the car park, plays with the controls for a while, then shrugs his shoulders and turns back to the detectives. 'As far as I can see, the Mondeo was the only car that came or went during the time we're interested in.'

'Are you sure?' says Carlisle. 'Didn't we see only one occupant of the Mondeo after it left the Research Park?'

'Sure as I can be.'

Hayes shakes her head. 'Can we account for the other cars in the car park at the same time?'

'I'm pretty sure I can. That one belongs to the Security Guard. That one belongs to Max the maintenance guy—'

Hayes interrupts him. 'What is a maintenance guy doing here at that time on a Sunday night?'

'We have maintenance people on call round the clock. What he was actually doing though was probably sleeping. Just because you're on site, doesn't mean you have to be awake. You just need to be available if anything goes wrong.'

'And the Security Guard?' says Carlisle. 'Where was he for five hours?'

'I don't know. That's something I'd quite like to ask him myself when I next see him.'

Amanda smiles conspiratorially. 'I'll leave that to you. Please let us know when you find out, as we'll need to eliminate him from any enquiries.'

'Will do. The other car belongs to the cleaners who were doing the offices. They wouldn't necessarily have known anything was going on in the Beam Hall. Besides, their car pulls out at 11.35pm, so it's unlikely to be them. Anyway, I know them both and I can vouch for them.'

'So,' says Hayes, 'that accounts for all the cars in the car park during the time we're interested in.' She sits there, gazing into the middle distance. After a while, she speaks, thinking out loud. 'For fifteen minutes, they went out to the car. One person got in it and drove away. One person didn't... one person didn't...' Her voice trails off. The silence is shattered as she slams her hand down on Ridder's desk. 'Got it! Of course, one of them came back!'

'What on earth for?' Carlisle is trying to keep up at this point.

'As Mr Ridder said, it's easier to hack into the security cameras from inside the building. So one man drives off, leaving the other man to stay behind and clean up the tapes. He obviously did that in a spot where there aren't any cameras because we don't have any more time-outs after 12.20am. Or do we?'

She turns to face Ridder. He shrugs. 'I'll check the tapes from that point on.'

'How many blind spots have you got in the building?'

'Thousands. There aren't any in the office area for a start.'

'But he could have got from the southeast entrance to the offices without going past another camera?'

'Yes, there's another staircase just beyond that entrance and that doesn't go past a camera.'

'So,' Hayes continues, 'we can conclude that our man is familiar with this building, he knows how to hack his way into the systems and he knows how to operate the equipment. He's not your common or garden burglar. Two men drove into the car park on Sunday evening and only one man drove out. So, for want of any other cars in your car park, we can assume that the remaining man returned to the offices and, for the rest of the night, edited the security tapes. Which leaves me a few last questions to ask you, Mr Ridder.'

'Yes?'

'Do you know anyone called Ludis Pahars?'

'Ludo? Of course. He's one of the technicians here. I've known him for about two or three years. I can provide you with his contact details if you like.'

'That would be useful. We have some addresses for him but it's good to confirm.'

'What else do you want to know?'

'Did anyone find a large package discarded on the premises yesterday?'

'What sort of 'package?'

'I'd rather not say, but if you'd found it you'd know what I was talking about.'

Hayes didn't want to ask if anyone had found a body, as it wasn't certain that Otto had indeed been brought to the facility in the Mondeo. It might all have been a terrible wild goose chase or misidentification and mentioning bodies would result in rather too much egg on her face if Otto turned up safe and sound the next day.

'To my knowledge,' said Ridder, sounding like a parody of some official declaration, 'there have been no reports of "packages", unidentified or otherwise, being received by this department in the last two days.'

'Then that just leaves us to work out who stayed behind after the car left,' says Carlisle. Hayes nods at her. 'And that means trawling through the camera feeds until we find someone leaving who hadn't arrived.'

Hayes smiles. 'I bet I know who that might be.'

Ridder winces. This had already eaten into his morning and it didn't look like it was going to end any time soon.

Carlisle turns to Ridder. 'I'm afraid I am going to have to ask you to continue to assist us. I am going to get some of my CID colleagues to come in and review these tapes, and I'd be grateful if you could show them to a suite where they can operate the system without having to bother you more than is absolutely necessary. And I am going to have to ask you to suspend all operations within this facility until it has been searched by my uniformed colleagues.'

'Won't you need a warrant for that?' Ridder has seen enough police procedurals on the TV to know that this is what one is supposed to say at this juncture.

'Not if you invite us to search it,' says Hayes, smiling sweetly.

CLAUDIO GIACCHERINI

Liechtenstein. October 1941.

Come in, your highness, come in. And may I say what a pleasure it is to welcome you back to Eschen und Schaan Privatbank. I hope that life has treated you well over the last year and that you have not been affected too adversely by the unfortunate situation around here.

No, we haven't had any real problems to speak of. A few minor items that are now hard to come by, but compared with many countries in Europe, we do quite well. Liechtenstein is a small island, really. Just off the leeward shores of Switzerland. Any importunate weather that blows our way will have been tempered long before it makes landfall here. If anything, we are blessed with a fine and temperate climate and, being so small and remote an island, we are seldom bothered by troublesome external forces. And anyway, we are tethered to other shores to maintain an upright posture, so our position here is more than tenable.

But, may I ask, how have you found the journey here from your homeland? Surely the road from the Arabian Peninsula is beset with obstacles? I'm thinking particularly of the situation in neighbouring Bohemia and the Sudetenland. Our little island has had to give up quite a few assets due to the unrest there, and I'm sure that anyone attempting the journey through those lands would have found their way blocked. I'm glad that it does not appear to have affected you too much. If anything, you seem to be doing very well on it. You are just as fresh-faced as ever. I hope you don't mind my saying such a thing. May I offer you some tea or coffee? Coffee. Very well, then. I shall ask my assistant to bring us both some coffee.

As always, I have prepared a statement of the accounts in the investment fund you asked the bank to manage in 1930. As per your instructions to Eschen und Schaan, I have been assigned the sole responsibility of managing this fund and, apart from menial duties concerned with the day to day running of the bank, that is all I have done. Also, in line with your instructions, I have made the proscribed investments and disinvestments and I am delighted to report that, as before, the fund has continued to grow and flourish. At the time you entrusted the account to us, the bulk of the fund was concentrated in precious metals, since equities were performing poorly in most of the markets around the globe except Germany and Japan. However, since 1931, the fund has become ever more diverse with a more even spread between stocks, bonds, equities and commodities. This more balanced portfolio has yielded both considerable growth in value and additional growth through dividends, all of which have been reinvested, as per your very detailed instructions, back into the fund.

Therefore I am delighted to confirm that, as of last year, the fund has grown by 87.6% and, since 1930, has grown a little over tenfold. Given the challenging nature of the investment sector these past twelve years, that performance is unparalleled, as I'm sure you would agree.

I must say that your highness has great foresight and wisdom when it comes to investments, and if only all our clients and indeed our own advisors had your rare gift. Please do not worry. My activities on your account are kept strictly confidential, even within this establishment. No one else has sight of your instructions and nor shall they. You have my word. Except…

Your highness, I am not getting any younger, I'm afraid. I have served with this bank now for twenty-five years out of a total of nearly forty years' experience in private and investment banking. I shall be due for retirement in less than two years' time and therefore I feel it judicious for me to advise you of this and to put into place some plans to appoint my successor. Whilst I do not believe that anyone with any talent for the industry will have any difficulty in managing this extraordinary fund, I do feel it wise to allow the new incumbent some time with which to become accustomed to the, ah, how shall I put it?, *peculiarities* of the role. May I therefore press you on how you would wish to proceed? Do you have someone particular you would wish to assign or are you confident enough to permit me the task of assigning someone myself?

You are happy for me to find the successor? I am flattered by your faith in me, your highness. Naturally, I shall still be here, God willing, for our next two meetings, but I hope that you will have the chance to meet my replacement at our next meeting in twelve months. In fact, I already have a young man in mind. He is very skilled, very detailed in his work and possesses rare discretion for a man of his age. There is, however, something you should know. He is based in our branch on Grand Cayman. We have certain reservations about continuing to hold all the papers relating to your fund here in Liechtenstein given the situation over the borders and we are keen to transfer them to a safer place, one where ill fortune is less likely to visit. There are certain issues within the principality that are attracting unwelcome attention, especially the issue of the Prince's wife, the Countess of Wilczeck. The *Jewish* Countess of Wilczeck. Whilst our little nation has asserted its neutrality, we do regularly entertain visitors for whom this neutrality is a convenience, nothing more. These visitors have certain expectations regarding who they are likely to, er, bump into. Therefore, just to be on the safe side, I would recommend the fund be transferred, at least in part, to our George Town branch. If you are in agreement with this proposal, I shall commence organising the transfers immediately.

No, I myself shall not move from here. This is my home, despite my Italian name, and this is where I was born. This war will not last forever and I am sure that I will be able to live out my remaining years in relative peace. But thank you for asking. I shall insist that my replacement meet with you here in these offices this time next year. I am keen for him to do so and, anyway, transport between here and the United States is relatively uncomplicated. What is this? Why would you think that America would want to join the war between now and next year? You cannot say? How intriguing. In that case, maybe our next meeting should be between the two of us here and, before then I might inform you of the young man's name. Maybe you will visit him over there. This is entirely at your discretion. Just say the word and we will make all the arrangements.

Now. May I turn to the matter of your instructions for the forthcoming year? May I see, please?

ROB TILLING

Grand Cayman. Saturday 10th.

[Headline]

THE THREAT OF AN OCTOBER STORM: WHO IS GORDON McALLISTER?

[Copydate: Monday 12th October]

Grand Cayman is well known as a tax haven: a honey-pot of fund managers, shell companies, brass plates and a major intersection for the world's money launderers. It is also one of the bases of a quiet operation that has been conducted since the beginning of the 20th Century; that operation goes by many names including the October Fund.

Readers of my column over the years will know that I have been peeling back the seemingly endless layers of this mysterious onion since the late 1980s. Information has been extremely hard to come by and few people know much about this secretive fund. Those who do know anything will not be drawn to comment.

Nonetheless, George Town in Grand Cayman is a small and well-connected community of less than thirty thousand souls and, given the even tighter nature of its financial district, gossip is a highly-valued commodity here. Naturally, people who work in the industry will never discuss specifics with outsiders but they are more than happy to talk about each other. And a curious story has emerged.

The manager responsible for the Cayman Islands end of the operation I have been tracking all these years operates out of a small office block just off Albert Panton Street in the heart of the financial district. He works there alone, has no assistant and occupies a single-room office. His furniture consists of a desk, a phone, a computer and some filing cabinets. Decoration is limited to a couple of prints of photographs by Freeman Patterson and Ansel

Adams, a man famous for his chilly, high-altitude panoramas of the Yosemite Valley in the California Rockies. Quite a contrast from the tropical swelter of George Town.

Why is this so astounding? Because, for nearly thirty years, this office has been rented by the same company—a Private Bank in Vaduz, Liechtenstein—and staffed by only one man (it has always been a man). Nobody I have spoken to in this town is sure how many men have worked here in their time, but a few know that the last incumbent left his post four years ago and disappeared without trace.

His name was Jeremy Fulford and he was, like many financiers here in George Town, an 'incomer', having been born in the UK. He'd worked for a major clearing house bank in London in the 1970s and then managed to secure a job with a merchant bank in their offices in Kuwait. He'd married and divorced and, finding himself suddenly unattached and footloose, landed this strange position in the Caymans working at a branch office for a fund run on behalf of some nameless clients by a Vaduz bank. And there he stayed for what appears to have been the rest of his career.

People who say they knew Jeremy report that he was an affable enough man, although he largely kept himself to himself. He had a well-appointed house in the fashionable area of Seven Mile Beach, was a member of one of the more exclusive golf clubs, was a keen scuba diver and owned a succession of sizeable yachts which he would sail, sometimes in the company of a few friends, around the islands of the Caribbean.

He had barely turned sixty when, one morning four years ago, he was no longer there. The house and the latest yacht had been put up for sale, the membership was cancelled and no forwarding address or contact details of any kind had been provided to anyone. Prospective purchasers of his property were not told who the vendor was, even if they asked. The sale was handled by a local agent and, curiously, in the agent's name.

So, what of his replacement? The branch office still operates; as far as the Cayman Islands Companies Registry in concerned. However, since there is no income or corporation tax in the Caymans, it is difficult to determine the revenue of the company, despite the signing of an agreement between the UK and the Caymans in November 2013 to improve international tax compliance.

This is in line with the efforts made by the US Inland Revenue Service to implement the Foreign Account Tax Compliance Act (FATCA) of 2010. A number of other countries have agreed to cooperate with the US on FATCA implementation, including the UK, France, Germany, Switzerland and Japan. The upshot was that FATCA would, directly or indirectly, make it harder for so-called tax havens to operate in total secrecy. In short, if you are earning money as an individual or as a company—whether it be a salary, interest on a deposit account or the revenue from a major money laundering ring—you have to pay tax on it somewhere.

The George Town rumour mill has it that the present incumbent at the October Fund has one main job: to emigrate all activities to any or all locations on the globe beyond the reach of FATCA or its kind. That includes states such as Argentina, the Seychelles (which enjoys one of the highest Financial Secrecy Indexes in the world, bettered only by Samoa and Vanuatu), Venezuela, Russia, most of Africa and North Korea. The question the rumour mill has on its lips: why is it taking so long for this new man to complete the job?

The answer is both simple and obvious: there's a lot of work to do.

As readers of my columns over the years will know, I have long held a suspicion that the October Fund has been single-handedly manipulating markets for nearly ninety years and that its transactions have been growing at a measured but nonetheless exponential rate. Whereas the fund might have generated merely billions of dollars of profits from its investments from the 1920s to the 1940s, these have transmogrified into literally trillions of dollars today.

So, if the information I have received over the years is to be trusted—any good journalist will check and re-check his facts, but the opportunities to do so in this matter are rare—the financial transactions being managed by this tiny branch office will have to *be wound up and transferred to a non-FATCA state rapidly. My guess is that it will be Russia.*

Lastly: who is the present incumbent at the October Fund, Cayman Islands? His name is Gordon McAllister, a native New Zealander who arrived in George Town about a week before his predecessor left (presumably). As one would expect, he has a very low profile on social networks: no Facebook or LinkedIn. That said, he had worked for a major trading house in Hong Kong for fourteen years prior to his move to the Caribbean and, like Jeremy Fulford, is reportedly unmarried and likes to make few waves socially. He too has a property on Seven Mile Beach but has not found the time to indulge any hobbies such as golf or yachting.

If he is managing trillions of dollars of funds on behalf of a private client or clients, then he is single-handedly generating revenues equivalent to the Gross Domestic Products of some significant countries. For example, the GDP of the UK is approximately $2.5 trillion (£1.56 trillion).

Therefore, I call on Mr McAllister in this column to meet with me and consent to an interview. The funds he is managing have global significance and can have seismic influence on the financial markets around the world. This level of influence is far and away beyond the right of a few individuals to possess as they can affect the wellbeing and the way of life of literally billions of other people. They can impinge on our pension provisions, the money we set aside for charitable donations, tax receipts that are employed on behalf of nations to build roads, hospitals and schools and therefore to feed, maintain and advance our populations.

This concealment of power should not be allowed to go unchallenged. It is not known whether the October Fund is a force for good or ill. Either way, it is a potentially monumental force and one we should all fear. Our governments have not overtly done anything to mitigate this threat. Perhaps because they don't know or have not yet assessed its potential impact. That's why I call on Mr McAllister through this column.

Meet with me and reassure us.

[End copy]

MICHEL DUPUY

St Aubin de Lévéjac, Provence. October 1958.

There is a knock on the door. Who can this be on a sunny Tuesday evening? The day has been long but productive for Michel who has been tending his vines and checking for signs of infestation. A few dead branches here and there have had to be pruned to prevent the spread of any disease but all in all, it is going to be a reasonable crop this year. Sadly, he doesn't think it will be anything like the glorious summer of last year; that will have produced a vintage of true note, at least for the *Grands Chateaux.*

He has been washing dishes in the kitchen and is still wiping his wet hands down with a small towel as he opens the door.

'*Monsieur le professeur!* What a surprise. Won't you come in?' Michel waves his hand in the direction of the beckoning hall and the kitchen beyond.

'That is extremely kind of you, Monsieur Dupuy,' says the bearded figure in the doorway. It is almost as though he hasn't changed since their last meeting fifteen months ago. He still wears the faded Panama hat, the slightly elegant but creased beige summer suit and the silver buttonhole, this time sporting a small chrysanthemum. The Professor steps up to the threshold of the cottage and follows his host toward the kitchen where he is invited to sit on a rickety ladder-backed chair by the table. Michel offers him a glass of white wine—he was in the process of pouring one for himself—which is graciously accepted. It is last year's cru and it is delicious. Professor Croce smacks his lips with profound pleasure. 'You, sir, are an artist!'

'I cannot lay claim to it all, unfortunately. It is the combined output of the *commune*. But my grapes are in there somewhere.' He gives a barely concealed smile and sips the golden liquid. The professor notices but chooses to let the matter rest.

'How are your studies?' says Michel, after an appreciative silence.

'They are going very well, monsieur. Thank you for asking.' The professor knows that the time for talking business has not yet arisen. 'We have restored the throughput of students to pre-war levels. It was difficult at first as no one had any money for education. There were more pressing issues to attend to. However, it is a delight to have the faculty back to… well, almost normal. Not everyone is still with us, of course. Some were displaced, some fled to join other family members elsewhere in the country and some…' His voice trails off. The silence finishes the sentence for him, so he takes another sip of the wine.

'We were fortunate, I suppose, here in St Aubin de Lévéjac. The Germans had little use for a small Provençal village. We didn't bother them and they didn't bother us.'

'I heard things were not so pleasant elsewhere.'

'Quite! We thought all we had to do was sit here and let the Vichy government run things but, after *Case Anton*, it got very bad. Marseille…' Michel sighed at the thought of how the Germans had flushed the resistance out from the port area by simply blowing it all up. Why go to all the effort of street to street fighting when you can just remove the streets? 'I had a cousin who lived in Marseille. I haven't heard from him since 1944. I fear that he did not see the conflict out.'

'That must be a worry for you, monsieur.'

The professor drains his glass and, in a break with traditional protocol, holds it aloft and looks expectantly at his host. Michel does not need to take so blatant a hint; he was already keen to follow that first glass with a second. The wine replenished, he gets down to business.

'How can I help you, professor?'

'I'm glad you ask, monsieur. Actually, I am here to impart some information as well as ask you to perform one more service for us.'

'One *more*? I don't do anything *now!*'

'Yes, you do. It is very valuable work. You allow us access to your cave and you do so without any hindrance.'

'I am well paid for it!' Michel wonders if he should have said that; he doesn't want his stipend to be cut from its present generous level.

'Very gracious of you to put it like that,' the professor begins, 'you may recall when we first met that I was keen to impress on you the need to keep unauthorised people from going near the cave. We don't want any of the artwork to be damaged before we have had the chance to study it properly.'

'I remember,' Michel confirms.

'Good. But we need to put in place a system whereby you can tell who is authorised and who is not. We have various students and post-graduates who will need to have access and I can't expect you to know who they are by sight. Can I?'

Michel shakes his head in agreement.

'Okay. So here is what I propose. Do you know the poem 'Matin d'Octobre' by Francois Coppée?'

'No.'

'No matter.' The professor fishes a piece of paper from his jacket pocket. 'I have written it down for you in full. I hope you enjoy it; I think it is truly lovely.' Michel takes the paper and begins to read.

'*C'est l'heure exquise et matinale...*' It is the exquisite and early hour. The professor interjects with the next line.

'*Que rougit un soleil soudain...*' Reddened by a sudden sun.

'It is a call and response,' says the professor. Michel looks confused. 'Permit me to explain. When you see someone you do not recognise, *call* out to them the first line of the poem. If they *respond* with the second line, then they have my personal authority to go up to the cave. Call and response! Is that clear?'

'What if they don't know what to say?'

'Well, then. Not to worry. But I would be grateful if you could note down the exact time and date you see anyone walking up the path and we will sort everything out from there. Just write the details down on a piece of paper and leave it under the flower pot on your front step. I will ask my colleagues and students to check the pot regularly whenever they come here. Is that alright for you?'

Michel regards the professor for a short while. He has an open and kind face, blue eyes and hearty cheeks under that beard. He seems genuinely concerned about the site not being disturbed and there does not appear to be any other reason for his caution.

'To be honest, professor, I don't imagine that my flower pot will ever trouble you. I virtually never see anyone come across my land. But I will do as you ask. It is the very least...' He shrugs his shoulders, his palms upturned. The classic Gallic gesticulation.

'That's marvellous. Thank you very much. That is all I ask.'

The two men continue their conversation in the kitchen and then saunter outside to enjoy the last of the day's light. Michel shows off his vegetables and his vines and the professor revels in the delight of seeing food and drink sprouting from the warm Provençal earth. An hour or so later, they part company and it is the last time Michel sees the professor. But thereafter, he catches sight of men—usually in pairs—striding past his house. As instructed, he challenges them with the first line of the poem and they oblige by responding with the second. After that, they go on their way.

Sometimes these men are carrying wooden packing crates. In fact, most times. Usually they are carrying the crates up to the cave but not down again. Michel reasons that they are erecting some equipment in the cave to protect the paintings and he leaves it at that. He is paid handsomely for what little he does; he isn't required to ask questions to which he might not understand the answers.

To begin with, there is a fair amount of activity; nearly every day two men and a crate go up and two men come down. Then, after about three months, the site visits become more infrequent and by the year's end, cease altogether.

So, six months after his meeting with the professor, it is with some surprise that Michel spots a young couple strolling across his land. The girl and boy cannot be more than eighteen years of age and it is quite plain to Michel that, whatever their academic objectives, they enjoy each other's company beyond the pursuit of palaeontology. They have come from a different direction than is normal; they have approached along a track from the direction of the church up the hill. This obviously requires some further investigation, and Michel wanders out to intercept them.

He waves and calls out the first line of the poem. The two respond with a cheery *bonjour* but nothing else.

'*C'est l'heure exquise et matinale...*' Michel insists. The boy looks at him strangely and glances at his watch. It is four-thirty in the afternoon; there is nothing *matinale* about it.

'I'm sorry, monsieur,' he says. 'I don't understand.'

'I'm sorry,' says Michel. 'My mistake. I thought you were someone else. Have a good afternoon.' He turns around and walks off to his house. As soon as he gets in, he heads for his writing desk and dashes off a brief note about the young couple, being careful to stipulate the time and date as instructed. He folds the note and places it under the flower pot. Geraniums this year; not quite fully in flower yet, though.

He returns to the house and closes the front door behind him.

As the door latch clicks into place, Michel thinks he can hear a distant gunshot and some shouting, but it is the hunting season after all.

DR BARNABY WATTS

Oxford. Monday October 12th, 1830hrs.

It is evening and Barney is marking the work of his second-year students in his rooms at college. It is close, warm and comfortable there; the room is snug with old carpets, a voluptuous Chesterfield sofa and a couple of elegantly moth-eaten armchairs. He sits in his favourite armchair with his back to the glimmering light, a tumbler of scotch—Talisker, his preferred single malt—on the table before him and Chopin murmuring away on the stereo. This is one of Barney's favourite times and activities. It carries an almost monastic grace for him—appropriate for a university lecturer—in which he can gain satisfaction both from his work and his own company. The febrile gropings for meaning of the students' essays somehow enhance the atmosphere; he is there to nurture their talent and lead them to explore new concepts within their study, and they are doing their best. But they are not quite there yet. Give them time…

He is reaching for his glass when his reverie and comfort are shattered. The door to his rooms twitches against the insistent and robust assault. This is no request for attention; this is urgent, an emergency. Barney leaps to his feet and rushes to the door with the full intention of flinging it open and demanding in no uncertain terms to know what the hell is going on. At the last moment, he hesitates; this door has not been hammered upon in this manner for as long as he has stayed here. He shouts through the door. 'Who's there?'

'It's Nick. For God's sake, let me in!'

'Nick?' Barney is astonished. Nick didn't need to resort to histrionics to gain access. Barney unlocks the door and swings it open to see Nick, an arm outstretched gripping the doorframe for balance, his face bruised and bloodied.

'What on Earth has happened to you?'

He helps his friend into the sitting room asking if he's been mugged, had an accident, demanding to know who did it. Whatever it is.

Nick slumps into a sofa and Barney rushes off to the bathroom to fetch some water and a sponge. He dabs his friend's face as Nick tries, between winces of pain, to impart what he knows.

'I don't know what... I was at the office and... I remember walking down Summertown... Some people, I think... After that, it's so confused.'

'Confused?' Barney has finished his attempts at nursing. He sits back to assess the worst of it. Apart from the bruising, there are only a few cuts and he won't be disfigured for life. Nothing too dramatic, anyway.

'It was black. I think they blindfolded me.'

'Nick. Who's "they"?'

Nick screws up his face, trying to concentrate. The pain of doing so causes him to wince, which also hurts. 'I honestly don't know. I don't remember seeing them. I was blind—'

'I know, you were blindfolded. But why would they do such a thing?'

Nick's head reels around the room, looking for inspiration. 'I honestly can't say.' He furrows his brow. 'White noise. The room was filled with white noise.'

'What sort of white noise?' It's an absurd question, but none of this is making any sense.

'What sorts are there?' Barney feels the urge to snigger.

'Anything else you can remember?'

Nicks pauses and strains to recall. 'The programme.'

'What about it?' Barney is trying hard not to sound too intense.

'I'm sure they wanted to know about the programme. How we made it.'

'Dear God! You didn't *tell* them, did you?'

'I don't really know…' Nick trails off. Barney paces around the room, wringing his hands.

'I know this is hard for you, my old fellow.' He tries to sound soothing. Nick has had a bit of a battering, after all. 'But do your best to dig deep and bring back whatever it was you might have said.'

Nick grimaces and grinds his teeth. 'No.' He says at last. 'I really can't.' He looks imploringly at his old friend. 'Please. It's no good trying to ask. They must have done something to me.' He speaks slowly, emphasising every word. 'I really. Can't. Remember. At. All.'

'I'm calling the police,' says Barney. Nick looks at him blankly. 'I'm calling the police. You've been assaulted, for fuck's sake. Look at you!' Barney strides over to the window where the phone sits on a small occasional table he had picked up in a dusty old bric-a-brac shop in Cowley. Mock Regency.

He stabs the number nine button on the phone and waits for the answer which comes promptly. 'Emergency. Which service do you require?'

'Police.'

'Putting you through, caller.' A wait and a new voice on the line. 'Police?'

'I have a colleague who has been assaulted. Someone has beaten him up.'

'Can I have your address please, caller?' Barney stares out of the window down into the quad which is darkening rapidly as the day fades. Barney gives the address to the officer at the end of the line.

Movement.

'Can you give us more details of the assault?'

Barney outlines the bruising, the contusions, the confusion. His voice becomes more mechanical. Something down there has caught his eye; over in the corner to the right, behind the scout's lodge.

'Do you require an ambulance?'

It's a figure: a man. He doesn't look like a student and he isn't behaving like one. They don't stand in the quad by themselves. Not unless they're on the phone, which this one isn't. He's wearing jeans and a jacket of some sort. Quite athletically built. But he doesn't look… well, quite right. Not entirely authentic. More like some kind of worker. How did he get in? Didn't the scout stop him?

The police take the details and offer to send a patrol car and an ambulance over 'straight away'.

'One last thing,' says Barney. 'I think I'm being watched.'

'Excuse me?'

Barney repeats himself, only more tentatively. 'I could be mistaken, but I think I'm being watched.'

'Can you give more details, sir?'

'Only vaguely. It's getting dark and hard to see clearly. Can you get here a bit more quickly than 'straight away'?'

'We are doing our best, sir.'

'Yes, quite possibly. But given that my friend has been assaulted and that it may be connected to a project we were jointly involved in, I wonder if this chap…' He trails off. It sounds outlandish even to himself. 'Anyway, can you come as soon as you can? This looks very odd.'

Nick twists round in the sofa and looks in Barney's direction. 'What? What can you see?'

'I'm not sure. But I think we should turn off the light in this room for a while.' Barney strides across to the switch and flicks the room into darkness. He turns on the light in his bedroom and returns to the window, crouching and gesturing at Nick to keep his head down and to stay quiet. The figure is still down there and isn't moving.

It's not long before the sound of distant sirens drifts across the ancient university buildings; a strange soundtrack for dreaming spires. Barney holds his breath as the figure startles at the advancing noise, abandons his position and walks away. Not hurried, nothing of note. No reason to take an interest here.

And he is gone.

PROFESSOR DAN SIBLEY

Oxford. Monday October 12th, 1615hrs.

He replaces the receiver on its cradle. He does it perhaps rather hard. He has tried all the numbers he knows: his home landline, his mobile (which he practically sleeps with), the office, the labs in Abingdon and the labs in Oxford. No joy.

And now he has called Matt. And Matt has had difficult news to impart. No, he has not seen Otto for some time—at least a couple of months—and he was due to hook up with him on Sunday night. But Otto didn't show and his house looked like it had been broken into. Matt has visited the police station and told them what he knows about Otto and his life and work. He's tried to get hold of Otto on his mobile, but it didn't seem to be ringing; it was as though the number had been disconnected. No. He doesn't know where Otto is.

And now Dan is worried. Otto always turns up: usually late, but he always arrives in his own sweet, academically fuzzy time. The fact that he was a no-show for Matt and that there has been no contact with him for so long is a huge concern. Dan has tried Otto's mobile and, although it hadn't registered with him at the time, it did sound like the disconnected or unobtainable tone: a long, despondent, metallic whine. Dan tries the number one more time to be absolutely sure, but only gets the whine again. This is more than just unusual; it's like a law of physics being broken.

He knows that Otto had (has?) a girlfriend but isn't sure of her name or where she lives; they weren't yet on co-habiting terms. Otto was not a fast mover when it came to women and they tended to leave him faster than he could hook up with them. Feverishly, he scans the top of his desk looking for clues, inspiration, something that might give him a lead, a spark. Something that might put him back in contact.

Nick!

Of course! Nick will know his whereabouts, surely. Nick had been talking about a second series of *Witness: History* and he and Otto were in the early stages of getting ideas together. The first series had apparently been a major TV event and channels from all over the globe had been falling over each other to buy the rights to broadcast it or distribute it in their regions.

The Chinese had been particularly enthusiastic. Dan leafs through his address book and stabs the numbers into the phone. He waits. A female voice on the line.

'Oxford History Unit.'

'Oh, er, hi.' Dan is never fluent at speaking to telephone receptionists. Just when he's decided what he's going to say, someone he hadn't expected answers the phone and he loses his train of thought and rhythm. 'Can I speak to Nick, please?'

'Can I ask who is calling?' The voice is remote but mellifluous.

'Can you tell him it's Dan? He knows me.'

'Will he know what it's concerning?' Dan knows this is a script. He feels a rising anger.

'It's a personal matter. It's alright, really.' Dan is pleading with the girl, although she probably doesn't understand. She certainly doesn't understand the gravity, the peculiarity, of the situation.

'One moment. Just putting you through…'

A pause as buttons are pressed and phones ring. There is a click and Dan draws breath to speak. Before he can utter his first word, the phone cuts to some on-call music: a jaunty, Caribbean-style calypso-synth-rock fusion thing. Dan tries to steady his breathing which is broken rhythmically by his own heartbeat. Another click. Dan draws breath in vain for a second time. The music returns. Dan tries to enjoy it, shakes his head a little from side to side. But he is starting to lose hope.

Finally! The girl's voice returns. 'I'm sorry, but Nick appears to be away from the office right now.'

'Have you got any idea where he might be?' Dan is getting wound up and he knows it is beginning to resonate in his voice

'No, I'm sorry. Would you like to leave a message?'

'Erm… I…' Dan stammers through pursed lips. 'I really need to speak with him. This is the only number I have. Can you give me his mobile number?'

'I'm sorry, sir.' The long, drawn-out 'sir'. 'It's not company policy to give out staff mobile numbers.'

'I appreciate that and, normally, I wouldn't have a problem with it. But this is an emergency.'

'Well, all I can suggest is if you leave a message…' The sentence is left hanging like the victim of some vigilante lynching; no chance of redemption, no closure.

Last chance. 'Is there anyone there who might know when Nick Young is expected back?' Dan looks at his watch. 4.30pm.

The receptionist sighs quietly, almost inaudibly, but Dan catches it and it does little to quench his anxiety or his rage. 'He stepped out about lunchtime and hasn't been back since. I can only assume that he won't be back until tomorrow.' And then, to brighten proceedings… 'Would you like to leave a message?'

Dan agrees to leave a message and dictates his phone number to her twice because she mixes up the numbers the first time, and hurls the phone down at the end of the call. He knows that his message is going to disappear inexplicably, and now he is getting more tense. No Otto and no Nick. Where in God's name is everybody? And what is going on?

He pushes the chair back from his desk, cluttered with piles of unread scientific papers and theses he is peer-reviewing. He launches himself from the chair and paces the room, stroking his ponytail as he goes. He only ever does this when he's lost in thought or stressed. Today he is most definitely stressed.

He parted company with Otto on bad terms; the police had to be called to get them to pipe down. It was an argument about how fucking thick he'd been in going off half-cocked without thinking to involve other people, especially the CEO of the company he chaired. In any other organisation that would have been enough to get him removed from the Board. That might yet happen after all this.

He just hopes to God that Otto hasn't done anything reckless. Images of railway lines flash through his mind. He shakes his head to fend off the thought. Otto isn't that histrionic. Although he was bloody angry on Saturday night, and—this is the bit that Dan is seriously fretting about—he had said he was 'going to do something about it'. Probably not a terribly bright thing to say when one of them is standing in front of you.

Dan glances out of the window across the road from the lab block to the Gothic edifice of Keble College chapel, all red brick and pinnacles; a confection of heavy, over-egged Victorian uber-architecture. Some lucky fellow is just standing there, without a fucking care in the world. Here he is, enduring all this turmoil and there's some feckless shithead coasting blissfully through life.

There's only one thing for it. He lunges back to the desk and punches more numbers into the phone. A ringing tone—long, single—and the faint crackling of a distant call. A click and the ringtone is interrupted. 'Yes?'

'Mikhail? It's Dan.'

'Dan…' The voice sounds like the speaker is wearing a smile that hasn't quite made it as far as his eyes.

'Has Otto spoken to you recently?'

'Otto? When?' the voice is circumspect.

'I don't know. Since Saturday. Yesterday, perhaps?'

'No…' A long 'N' and a drawn-out vowel, as though he is looking around the room for a lost stapler. Then, more assertively… 'No, I don't think so.'

'He hasn't spoken to any other members of the team?'

'I don't know. I'll check.' The speaker draws breath to shout, but then changes his mind and talks back to the phone. 'Dan, is there something wrong?'

Dan stares at the phone on his desk, rifling through all the possible answers in search of the one which would create the fewest ripples. 'No, I don't think so. But I'm trying to get hold of him and he isn't on his usual numbers.' There is a silence at the other end. Dan cannot tolerate the vacuum. 'So I was just wondering if he'd made contact with you at all. He did say he was going to call you.'

'Oh, yes? Do you know what that might have been about?'

Great. One question is now succeeded by another. Mikhail is a past master at diverting the course of conversations and discussion. But this isn't the time for him to start playing games.

'Not precisely.' A towering lie. 'But we had a get-together down the pub on Saturday and the upshot was he was going to call you to get a third opinion.'

'So you *do* know what the call would have been about.'

Fuck! How to get out of this one?

'I think it had something to do with certain funding streams he was keen to explore.' Which is the size of it, basically.

'Well, I'm sorry.' Mikhail is doing his best to sound apologetic. 'But Otto hasn't called. Would you like me to get him to contact you if he does?'

'Mikhail, that would be very good of you. Yes, please.'

This conversation in now concluded. They bid each other goodbye and Dan replaces the receiver. He regards it for a few seconds, then beats it with his fists like a blacksmith. Dan swears until he is out of breath, then he sits stock still, rubbing his chin. Think, dammit! He sighs long and deep and leans back from the desk, hands clasped behind his head. The view from the window has changed little: still the same dull October sky; still the trees along Park Street, their leaves mottled green, gold and brown; the passing cars creeping behind the arrogant bicycles that claim dominion over the city; the lonely man leaning dejectedly against the chapel across the road. How long has he been there? Doesn't he have somewhere else to go? Poor bastard. Dan allows himself a weak smile; maybe someone else is having a shit day after all.

He slaps the top of the desk decisively. This day is a non-starter. May as well go home as bugger-all else is going to happen here today. Not now. Surely, some of these people will show up before too long.

With resignation, he packs the materials he needs for the evening into his black nylon backpack: new papers on quantum mechanics, dissertations to be reviewed, marked and commented upon. He levers his jacket over his sweater, swings on the backpack and makes for the office door. He tramps downstairs to the front entrance and grunts his goodnights to the security officer in the foyer.

Outside, into the refreshing air: he realises how stuffy his office has become, especially today. He walks round the side of the building and gathers his bike from the storage frame.

He swings his leg over the saddle, hoists himself up and pushes off towards the road. He snatches a final glance at the man standing opposite the entrance to the physics labs, leaning against the wall of Keble College. He appears to be talking with some conspiratorial urgency into his phone; an important message being relayed with tense delicacy. A girl in tight jeans and a bomber jacket with earphones strides down the pavement crossing Dan's path; she is walking heavily as though she is trying to march at the pace of her music.

It is a short bicycle ride to Dan's home off Turl Street in the cobbled centre of Oxford; no more than ten minutes. He'll call in to the King's Head on Broad Street; it's one of Otto's haunts. Maybe he'll be there.

Dan shakes his head. Why would Otto be in the pub without any of his phones? It doesn't make sense. Dan swings his bicycle into the Parks Road traffic and begins to pedal. He clicks up through the gears, the rhythmic ticking of the chain on the back wheel sprocket stopping like a breath held, each time the gears disengage with a murmuring whirr.

His head is still whirling with notions on where Otto—or, for that matter, Nick—might have gone. It's out of character for both of them. The autumn air on his face is helping to calm him down, along with the musty smell of the leaves turning above him. A small hatchback creeps nervously past, and, with the confidence of space, revs its engine and speeds off towards the traffic lights. Dan continues to pedal.

To his left is the confection of the Natural History Museum, a large-fronted building with tiers of dormer windows inset into a steeply pitched roof. Dan glances at it, thinking how much it reminds him of a town hall in some rural part of Germany: Hanover, the Black Forest, maybe. Next to that is the ugly Science Library, doubtless designed by the same lumpen hand that built the modern extension to the Bodleian. He muses on how Parks Road is lined by one university building after another: across the road is Keble College with its red brick and sandstone cross-hatching. Oxford University doesn't have a campus *per se*; the city itself is the campus. And this is the centre.

In front of him are the traffic lights and a left turn to South Parks Road with more university buildings: laboratories, libraries, faculties, lecture theatres, more colleges, sports grounds.

A queue of cars is waiting to join Dan's road from the side and, as he nears the turning, the lights turn red. Dan usually likes to try and beat the lights, but today he has too on his mind to care. So he slows and comes to a halt, planting his left foot on the ground. The cars file meekly in from the left. A white van pulls up alongside him and positions itself so that Dan's bicycle won't impede its launch when the lights turn amber. Dan's home is straight on; the road ahead penetrates ever deeper into the old heart of Oxford and is lined by the walls of more ancient colleges and their parks. It's a pleasant view. And there they sit, waiting.

The lights turn. Dan levers himself back to his bike and pushes off; he hasn't bothered to change the gears down so he has to push extra hard to gain any momentum. The white van's gears crunch and it revs its engine to try and pass, but an oncoming car blocks it. Dan cycles past the left-hand turn and looks ahead, toward the jumbled university: the Radcliffe Camera, the spire of St Mary's beyond. He glances down to avoid a grating by the kerb and something catches his eye.

Dan looks up with a start and sees a van, similar to the one trying to overtake, approaching from the other direction. It veers across the white lines, heading directly at him. The overtaking van brakes hard and ducks in behind his bicycle. The oncoming van accelerates towards him. The other van is obviously trying to take evasive action but has ended up a few centimetres from his back wheel. The oncoming van lurches to Dan's left, mounts the kerb and grinds to an abrupt and violent halt. The suspension digs in over the front wheels and the whole vehicle rocks back and forth.

Dan has had no time to apply his brakes and anyway, doing so with that idiot van on his tail would be dangerous. Instead, he clicks up one more gear and tries to pedal out of the situation by circling to the right, round the back of the van blocking his way. The back doors spring open and two men jump out; one of them is holding something that Dan can't recognise. For the first time he realises that this is not an accident and that he may be some sort of target. It is as though a switch has been thrown. Dan suddenly has complete clarity: he needs to escape.

He tips the bicycle over onto its right side, skids the back wheel along the road surface and pushes off as hard as he can, narrowly missing the front wing of the trailing van. Another oncoming car has to squeal to a halt to avoid hitting him and the driver, upset and impotent, blasts his disapproval on the horn. Dan speeds back up the road towards the traffic lights again as more men emerge, this time from the other van. There's four of them, not counting the drivers. Where to go? Where's safe?

He draws up to the traffic lights. Behind him, the sound of trainer-clad feet, moving quickly, fit enough to outrun a bicycle being pedalled by a fifty-seven-year-old professor of physics.

Even one who is in good enough shape for a man of his age (Dan is a regular enough attendee at his gym). The lights are red; cars are filing in from the right and splitting: some crossing in front of him, the rest turning left and crawling towards the two vans which are noisily reversing across the road to give chase.

Dan springs into the oncoming traffic and the cars shriek as their brakes bite and the tyres scuff the asphalt. He weaves past the first car, mounts the kerb and bumps his shoulder against the trunk of a yellowing ash tree before careering along the pavement and turning right into a side turning. Before him is a line of near-stationary traffic waiting for its turn to cross the lights, each car budging forwards. A gap opens and he throws the bicycle off the kerb in front of a creeping car, oblivious to any other vehicles that may be trying to drive down the road. He's not looking, but he can hear the protests of the car he cut up. With a spine-jarring jolt, he mounts the pavement on the opposite side.

The four running men have split; two are over to his left trying to block him from getting back on to Parks Road, while the other two have followed his desperate course through the traffic. There are shouts from outraged drivers as they slide over bonnets. The assailants are attempting to perform another pincer action, similar to the one they attempted with their vans. Dan knows the key thing is to keep moving in a direction that doesn't allow them to get in position. The way forward is blocked by the Science Library and the two men over by Parks Road would have no difficulty scooping him up. The only way is to do a hard right and make a dash for it down South Parks Road.

He is riding pell-mell along the pavement; he can hear the footfall of his pursuers and they gain on him. He may have twenty or twenty-five yards head start, but it can't last forever. A couple of pedestrians jump grudgingly from his path. Dan drops the bicycle from the kerb on to the road. Ahead of him are more university buildings but he doesn't know the passages well enough to be confident of losing himself among them, and half of the buildings have security gates which would leave him at a dead end.

To his right is Mansfield Road, but that just leads back to the centre of the city. He could get to Holywell Street and, if he took the left turn, he could squeeze through the traffic barrier at the end. That would get rid of the vans. No! They'll be sending one the other way and he'll meet it halfway down Mansfield Street.

Straight on, then. The feet are getting closer and he can hear air being sucked over his pursuers' teeth and blown out again, like the rapid chugging of a locomotive. This is going to be a matter of time.

Dan notices that he is tiring; the air is whooping in and out of his burning lungs. His vision is tunnelling to an ever finer point and the sweat is dripping down his arms, back and forehead. He wipes the moisture from his head; if any gets into his eyes…

Past Mansfield Road. An oncoming bus, open-topped. Tourists being regaled with the history of 'this great city'. On the opposite kerb… On the opposite kerb! Of course!

Dan veers in front of the bus; it brakes, knocking the tour guide off her feet. Squeals of alarm issue from the passengers. The bus clips the back of Dan's wheel and he is pitched off the bike and onto the pavement. He rolls twice over the concrete slabs and collides with the spiked railings that surround the building. The men giving chase have little time to change direction and they have to run around the bus. Dan senses them splitting up, moving around both sides of the bus. They think that the trap is now sprung. They have him.

Alongside the bus is the main entrance to one of the newest university buildings, and he darts through the plate glass doors and up to the security barrier beyond. He still has his university pass around his neck and he waves it at the sensor. The first of the two men splays himself against the glass door as a van crunches to a halt beyond. The sensor light blinks from red to green and a click enables Dan to push open a second glass door ringed with stainless steel, and he is through. His pursuer hurls himself against the security door but Dan has had just enough time for the door to acquire its own momentum and it clicks irrevocably shut in the man's face.

Dan is sitting on the floor beyond the door facing back at his pursuers, and, for the first time, he sees them. Young, fit, muscular, thick necks. For all that, they are red and heaving for air, regarding him through the reinforced glass with loathing.

'The one that got away!' Dan shouts, taunts through the glass at them. 'Who are you?' He gasps, fills his lungs and bellows. 'Try getting in here, you fuckers!' A security guard hurries across the stone floor to where Dan is sitting and grips him by the shoulders. Dan, now unable to speak for lack of air, fumbles for his pass and waves it at the guard. 'Police!' he eventually spits out. The guard rushes back to his station and summons help. Dan stumbles to his feet, collapses against the security door and watches his pursuers slink away. The last pursuer turns to give him one final threatening glower before climbing into the back of the van. And they're gone.

The guard stammers. 'Are you... What was all that about?' No 'sir'; no 'professor'.

'Sorry about that.' Dan starts to retch. The guard runs off to find a wastepaper bin to catch the vomit. He is too late, and Dan is riotously ill over the floor and himself. He chuckles. He may be covered in sick, but he's on the right side of a very secure door; the one that leads to the Biological Science Building where they perform the small animal research; the one the Animal Liberation Front tried to burn down. Nobody gets into this building without a pass or a tank, and the place is ringed with high resolution cameras. Drop a cigarette butt outside and security will be able to tell which brand you smoke.

The city air fills with the sound of sirens and, before long, there are two police cars wreathed in flaring lights parked outside. The police officers help Dan to a chair and sit with him whilst someone from the building runs off to find a wet cloth to clean up the floor and the wheezing professor.

Tea is administered. Police officers check the security camera feeds. They note down registration numbers and take detailed descriptions of the pursuers. A female officer asks Dan if he is feeling okay and hopes he hasn't sustained any injury. Dan says he thinks he may have sprained his ankle when he fell off the bike in front of the bus. A member of staff materialises with a mop, bucket and wet cloth, and the female officer dabs at the vomit on his jacket and trousers as best she can. Don't worry, they assure him, they will get a bulletin out and they will track these guys down pretty quickly.

A radio crackles into staccato life. A blaring woman's metallic voice announces something that spurs an officer to approach Dan. He informs him that a Detective Sergeant is on her way and will be here in a short while, and can he hang on until she arrives? Dan confirms that he doesn't plan on going anywhere just now.

Five minutes later, there is a tap on the security door and a small female detective dressed in a flowery, but predominantly brown, dress displays her warrant card to the security guard.

A physiology professor who Dan knows ambles into the lobby to see what the fuss is about. His face drops in alarm. He spots Dan and rushes over to him. Dan, Dan, are you alright? What has gone on? What are you doing here? Why are there all these police here? Why? What? How? Tell me!

Dan is still too breathless to reply and the female police officer gently guides the other professor to one side as DS Hayes is clicked through the door. She makes a beeline for Dan.

'We need to talk' she says.

'I need somewhere safe.'

DI PAULINE CAMPBELL

Bicester and Oxford. Tuesday 13th, 1045hrs.

The driver is hammering the car up the A34 as fast as the traffic will allow. Trees, meadows, rivers, cattle and hedgerows stream past the windows. Despite the sirens and the promenade of flashing lights, some drivers have not yet noticed there is a vehicle bearing down on them at nearly one hundred miles per hour. Those who do realise snap to attention: brake lights flare and cars weave and slow as they try to squeeze into the same lane.

'Our man Ridder has come up trumps.' Hayes' voice crackles over the police radio.

'Fill me in.' Campbell doesn't have time for words. They should be in Bicester in fifteen minutes and there are enough things to occupy her mind as it is.

'It's pretty certain that Pahars did doctor the video files at the Exatron. He can be seen leaving the building just after 10am on Monday morning, but the security records show no sign of him entering the building that day. The last record was for his leaving the building the previous Thursday at…' Sound of paper being rustled. '16.45.'

'So he left the building twice without entering it between times.'

'Check. He had to stay in the Exatron over Sunday night because he couldn't wipe the records from outside it.'

'Any sign of how he left the science park?'

'No, sorry. If he had a car, it was off the camera grids.'

'In which case he could be in any car on any road pretty much anywhere.'

'Sorry,' says Hayes again. She is trying to sugar-coat the news. 'It's also possible that he got a local bus to Didcot and caught a train to somewhere. I've got White checking up on their surveillance. You never know…'

'Indeed.' Campbell sighs. 'You never know. Let me know how you get on. We'll be arriving at Bicester North Station in a couple of minutes and we can knock our heads together after that.'

And the call is over. The car powers round a series of roundabouts, vehicles scattering before them, drivers on the motorway below staring up to see what is happening on the bridges. Campbell smirks to herself in the knowledge that some of those drivers will have had a small heart attack with the anxiety that the police car is going to chase them for speeding.

'When's the first train from Bicester North to London?' she asks Reynolds in the back of the car.

The detective constable thumbs at his smartphone. 'Between quarter past and twenty past six.'

'If he left the Exatron at quarter to one that morning, it won't have taken him more than half an hour to get here. Forty minutes at the outside. That means there's about five hours we can't account for.'

The car pulls abruptly into the station forecourt where two marked cars are already parked, lights circling. Four uniformed officers loiter by their vehicles trying to look busy by cocking their ears to their radios periodically. A third vehicle in the car park—a silver Ford Mondeo—is surrounded by yellow tape, fluttering in the wind.

Campbell strides from her car without shutting her door. She addressed the uniforms. 'Who called this in?'

A constable steps forward and stakes his claim. 'We were doing a patrol this morning and, as part of our rounds, we checked the car park. Usually the cars that are here for the night are, well…' he trails off. Campbell knows; it's either someone who'd over-indulged and took the wise decision not to try driving home, or it was hanky-panky of one sort or another. The constable continues. 'We ran the number through plate check and your name came up. The engine was cold when we got to it.'

'What time was that?'

'About four this morning.'

Well, that just about figures. The car is unlikely to have been anywhere yesterday, which means it was driven here early Monday morning and dumped. 'Have you questioned any of the platform staff about the occupant?'

'I've spoken with the ticket office manager and he didn't notice anything unusual.'

'The first train would have gone about 6.15am and our suspect would most likely have been on it.'

Unless he just drove to the station and got a lift from an accomplice in another car; in which case the whole thing is scuppered.

'Check the CCTV for the first few trains for yesterday morning. I'm looking for someone who doesn't fit in.'

'Any more details, ma'am?'

'I don't have any details at all! But those early trains tend to be full of the usual suspects.' The constable looks at her blankly. 'It's the same people who use it every day. Those red-eyes are almost like private clubs, so a newcomer is going to stick out a bit.'

'I'll get on it right away, ma'am.' The constable swivels on his heels and jogs over to the station platform.

Campbell shouts across to the other uniforms. 'I want that car uplifted and brought back to Oxford for full forensics.' The uniforms all stiffen at her command and all say, 'Right away!' She can hear them redoubling their efforts on the radio to expedite the car's removal.

She strolls over to the silent car. What does it want to tell her? What can it say?

She peers through the windows; there's nothing on any of the seats. Campbell snaps on a pair of rubber gloves and tries the boot lid. The car is locked and immobilised so there's no way of getting in without destroying evidence. The local dealer or the car hire company should be able to provide replica keys with the necessary security codes. She reminds herself to get one of the team back at the office to sort that out.

She paces around the car checking the wheels, the trim, the panels; any unusual wear or dents? Any blood? Any marks in the dirt of the paintwork? It hasn't rained over the last two days, so finger marks would still be fresh. There are a couple of dents in the nearside rear door panel and the rear wing on the same side. Other than that, nothing much. That said, the car looks reasonably clean. In fact, really *very* clean: on the outside, anyway.

A thought dawns: what if he'd…

'Constable!' She calls across to the uniforms again. 'How many all-night car washes are there around here?' The police constable rubs his chin for a moment and says.

'There's one near the Shopping Village.'

His colleague speaks up. 'Otherwise, there's one at the service station on Junction Ten up the motorway.'

Campbell strides back to DC Reynolds. 'Doug, I need you to check with those guys over there and get me a list of all the twenty-four-hour car washes within a reasonable distance of the route from the Exatron to here.' Reynolds scribbles some notes down, nodding. 'How soon can you let me have that?'

'Ten, maybe fifteen minutes at worst.' Campbell calls in with a request for the car key. That's the here and now taken care of. As soon as the tow truck arrives, she'll head back to Oxford.

She is drawing up a list of things to do in her head when she is interrupted by the constable who found the car.

'I think we may have him, ma'am.' He looks pleased. And so he should; that was quick work. Campbell nods a 'well done' to him and he perceptibly fills out a bit. 'As you said, the early passengers for the 0619 to London Marylebone included a first-timer. He doesn't look right. He's wearing a hoodie and carrying a large bag. Luggage. Like he's going away somewhere for a while.'

Absolutely. Everyone else will be suited and booted for a day at work, and the most they'll be carrying will be a laptop and a briefcase. Campbell requests a print-out to be emailed to her, together with a detailed rundown of what the man was wearing when he took his early morning train.

Reynolds walks over. 'There are two of them. One down the road here at Bicester Services and the only other one is the Cherwell Services on the M40, but that would take him out of his way.'

'Well, he did have five hours to kill. Maybe he wanted an all-night burger or a coffee.' She gives a thin smile which Reynolds doesn't catch because he's concentrating too hard on trying to read her expression through her glasses. 'Go with one of those cars and get the service stations to share their tapes with you.' Reynolds disappears without another word.

She knows how this is going to pan out; she has pieced crime scenes together in her head too many times to have many actual surprises when the results come back from forensics. Parsons was abducted from his house in Jericho sometime early Sunday evening; he put up a struggle; he was bludgeoned or shot or stabbed and, either dead or unconscious, he was carried to a waiting car—this car—where he was probably wrapped in some kind of blanket to keep any blood off the trim; in their hurry, they inadvertently bashed Parsons against the side of the car; they took him to the Penrose Science Park. Parsons then disappears.

Then, four hours or so later, one of the two men leaves the science park with the car they brought Parsons in. He drives up toward Bicester with the intention of catching the first available train to London. On the way he puts the car through the car wash, presumably to remove traces of matter that would show up during forensics. The car wash would dispose of any fingerprints, blood, DNA. So whoever they are, they're cute enough to cover their tracks as best they can given the circumstances.

What *are* the circumstances? Are they in a hurry? If so, what for? Campbell sighs and throws her head back; maybe the fresh air will give her some inspiration. Jake!

She should call Jake. She pulls her smartphone from a pocket and taps out a number. After a short while a voice answers. 'DCI Golding.'

'Jake. It's Pauline.'

'Pauline!' As though they hadn't spoken for decades; it was last week. They had both gone through police college together and had parted ways professionally at least. The two of them had done well in the police, but Jake... Well, Jake was male for one thing and, for another, he had something of a spark about him. 'To what do I owe the pleasure?'

'I need your help.'

'Always happy to help, my angel.' Jake is a card. He likes to model himself as some sort of 'cockerney' wag; a throwback to seventies' TV shows which he was probably too young to watch the first time around. 'We never have anything to do here at the Metropolitan Police. Quiet as the bloody grave.'

'You're being ironic aren't you?'

'No. I'm lying. I can't do ironic and you know that. I didn't go to a posh school like what you done.' This banter is great fun in the pub, but right now it's taking up a bit too much time.

'I'll have to get to the point here, Jake. We have a suspect in an abduction case we are working on. It's pretty urgent as we are concerned for the safety of the abductee.'

'Go on.' Jake turns off the badinage.

'We have grabs from CCTV of one of the suspects and he would have been heading in your direction. He probably went through Marylebone Station yesterday morning at around quarter- to half-past seven.'

'Do you want us to apprehend him?'

'Absolutely. He is wanted urgently as we are certain he can "help us with our enquiries".' Pauling trots out the usual press line; few people who fit that classification are keen to offer any 'help'.

'I also need to know where he's been since yesterday morning.' She sighs again. 'There's a high probability he has headed for the airport. He was carrying a bag that looked like luggage. Obviously, anything could have been in it, but that's our best guess at the moment. I'll send the images across to you as soon as I've got them. Should be any moment now.'

'Okay. I'll get on it right away. I've got a couple of guys who can pick this up for us. If he's passed through our manor, we'll have him.'

'Jake, *you're* an angel!'

'And you, too. Talk soon.'

It is five o'clock and, back at the station, Campbell is about to wrap up for the day. She has been scrutinising the early reports from forensics and she is on the verge of brewing a headache. There are tell-tale specks of blood on the back seat of the Mondeo and they match the bloodstains found at Parsons' house. What they don't confirm at this stage is whether or not it is Parsons' blood, but that shouldn't take too long to find out. There's a pretty good chance that it is. At the very least, the perpetrators are looking at charges for abduction and grievous bodily harm, assuming Parsons is still alive.

She has phoned her partner to let her know she is coming home on time for once and is replacing the phone in her pocket when it vibrates in her hand. The timing is so unexpected it makes her jump. It's Hayes.

'Guv, this is starting to get a bit odd.'

'Sorry?' Campbell's brow furrows. 'What's 'odd'?'

'I've just had a call about a disturbance off Parks Road. An attempted abduction in broad daylight.'

'Tell me this isn't a coincidence.'

'I don't think it is. The abductee was known to Parsons. In fact, they work together.'

Campbell's heartbeat accelerates. 'Bring him in and don't let him go. I want to talk with him, whoever he is.'

'Medical's with him at the moment. He was a bit cut up. They're taking him off in the ambulance and are talking about keeping him in overnight for observation.'

Campbell clenches her fist and gesticulates at the phone. 'Don't leave him for a second. I want you to go after him and make sure someone's with him until we can interview him. Is that clear?'

JAKE GOLDING

London. Tuesday 13th, 1030hrs.

Jake squints at the two photos.

'When was this taken?' he points at the photo of the man entering the target's hotel. The subject is wearing a green hoodie with yellow lettering, a red baseball cap and a pair of black sneakers. He's carrying a large bag.

The sergeant peers at the image. 'About 8.15am. Yesterday.'

Jake rubs his chin and looks at the other photo. 'Does that, or does that not, look like the same bloke?' Jake stabs the second photo. then the first.

'How many other blokes are there with that outfit running around London?'

'They're not both taken in London,' says Jake. 'This one was taken in Bicester Station about two hours before he shows up at our target's hotel.'

'Do you mind me asking how you came by that one, Guv?' The sergeant points at the Bicester photo.

'I don't think that's important right now, do you? What is important is that this man is a suspected felon and he turns up in the middle of what we thought was an unrelated operation. All of a sudden I feel I want to know more about him. Have we got any other shots? One with his face in it?'

The sergeant runs off to rifle through the hundreds of digital photos on his laptop. After a while, he returns with two printouts. Golding places them on the desk in front of him. It seems that the man briefly turned the right side of his face toward the camera as he pulled open the hotel door.

'Absolutely no idea who the hell he is!' says Golding. 'Does anyone know what happened to him afterwards? Go and trace his movements.'

The sergeant returns to his desk and is back again twenty minutes later. 'He was in the hotel for about seven minutes. He walks away from the hotel and round the corner towards Grosvenor Square. After that, can't say.'

'Find out if he caught a cab or something. A bag that size means he's either going somewhere or returning. Unless he's homeless. But I don't think so to look at him.'

This poor sergeant is going to need new shoes if he runs up any more mileage today. Still, it keeps him busy and that's always a good thing. Jake picks up the phone and punches a number on the keypad.

'Roger? It's Jake. I've got a strange one for you.'

'Go on,' the voice on the end of the line is non-committal.

'I've got a suspect in a possible abduction turning up in the middle of yesterday's photo shoot. Does this mean anything to you?'

'What ties him in with any abduction?'

'A friend of mine in Oxford sent it to me just now. It's got to be the same bloke.'

'Oxford?' The voice is startled. The backs of Jake's hands start to tingle: a sure indication that there's more to this than meets the eyes and a good reason to feel suspicious.

'Roger. Is there something you're not telling me?'

'Jake, I guarantee there's something I'm not telling you.'

'Yes, but what's the Oxford connection?'

'What connection is that, Jake?'

'With the greatest of respect, don't fuck me about. I do work for you, you know.'

The caller chuckles; he loves it when Jake plays the hard nut with him. 'I tell you what. You send me the photos and I will give them my fullest possible consideration.' Jake suspects that's the last he'll hear on the subject, but he sends an email, attaching the two clearest shots from his team together with the one from Pauline.

The sergeant returns, brimming with good news. 'We've got him getting into a cab and we've got the cab's licence number.'

'And?' The sergeant looks crestfallen.

'And Hannah is contacting the cabbie to find out where he took the fare.' He sounds hurt, like a twelve-year-old wrongly accused of stealing sweets.

'Fiver says it's the airport. As soon as you know which terminal, trace him through it and let me know where he was travelling.' The sergeant is heading off when Jake's voice lassoes him to a halt. 'Any word on the target?'

More than one voice replies. 'No, Guv.'

'Who's on the ground?'

Hannah shouts from her desk; she is already on the phone waiting for her call to pick up. 'Smith and Williams, Guv.' That's good, those two don't miss much. If the target moves, they'll pick him up. Hannah calls again. 'Terminal Five. He was in a hurry, the cabbie says.' Two other officers tap numbers into their phones and within fifteen minutes, there are five of them seated around Jake's desk. Jake holds court.

'Okay. This is where we're at. Our new target, Hoodie Boy, is suspected of an abduction or attempted abduction in or near Oxford. He turns up at 8.15 yesterday morning at the target's hotel and stays for seven minutes. He then walks out and, four minutes later he's sitting in a cab bound for Heathrow.

'Forty-five minutes after that, he is striding into Terminal Five and is checked through on a flight bound ultimately for George Town Grand Cayman. He's cutting it fine; the flight leaves at ten thirty and the gate closes twenty minutes before that. Hoodie Boy is bigging it up on First Class so they'll hold up the airport if he's running late. Which he isn't, because he has fifty-nine minutes to get from the door of the terminal to the door of the plane. He's waving a solid gold boarding pass, so he'll go through Fast Track and sail into his mink-lined rocking chair before you can say "Dom Perignon".

'According to the airline, his plane arrives at Grand Cayman, having bounced in and out of Nassau, at 16.40 local time or twenty to midnight last night in our money. So he's already there. I've spoken to the powers-that-be and they're taking it from here. Maybe. Maybe not.'

ROB TILLING

London. October 1987.

It is the last round before Armageddon and everyone wants to line them up. The air is saturated with fear and the clamour for drink is unconfined. Nervous faces glance from person to person; each face seeking out the truth behind the eyes of the other before passing on to the next. It is all too obvious who works for a financial house with a large US exposure and who does not. Those who do are all too aware that their time is measured in hours not days; those who do not are still standing on the thin ice of chance, listening with mounting horror at the cracking beneath their feet.

Rob Tilling has not slept for thirty-six hours. Yesterday was Black Monday and the news has been unremittingly bad, worsening since the previous Thursday. He had known that a hard landing was on the cards, but this! The Footsie had lost over three hundred and fifty points in one day, about eighteen percent of its value; the Dow Jones had free-fallen by over twenty percent. Today saw a bouncing back of equities, but all the traders knew that this was the fabled 'dead cat bounce'. One or two dealers have emulated that effect in person; this crash has a death toll.

The rumours are rife. Automated trading in the US is running amok, with suggestions that it's been triggered by the unexpected closure of the London Stock Exchange on the previous Friday due to an exceptional gale, or by the attack on a supertanker by the Iranians the previous Thursday, or overvaluation, or mass hysteria. Who knows? But the panic is etched deep in the lines on the faces in this bar, and this bar is crammed; there's barely any room to stand, let alone find a place to sit. Somehow, Jason has managed it, and has kept another seat for Rob; he must have a gun or something to keep this mob at bay. He has also managed to buy a whole bottle of Cabernet and get two glasses to the table without having them jostled from his grasp. Rob is in the mood for a drink. Actually, he's in the mood for some kip, but history is being made today: ugly, brutal, desperate history. Sleep can wait.

Rob squirms through the seething mass of humanity and wrestles his way to the seat Jason has reserved. He nods a greeting, pours himself a large glass of the deep ruby liquid and takes a much-deserved mouthful. Jason is already halfway down his glass and gives a weak smile to his guest; he can appreciate what sort of a day he's had.

'Quiet, isn't it?' Rob is tearing his throat out in order to be heard.

Jason nods, chuckling and raises his glass at Rob. 'Just another ordinary day in our little village.' Jason is a classic exponent of the New City. Once, the Square Mile was the exclusive preserve of the wealthy and titled, where one could get a leg up provided your father knew somebody or you went to the right school or university and you were the Right Sort. Play up and play the game and the game was *Dictum Meum Pactum*: my word is my bond. Today, the City of London is run (some would say overrun) by the new breed of trader: young, thrusting, aggressive. Winning. Except today, for the first time, many are losing, and they find it incomprehensible.

Jason, on the other hand, has a different expression on his face. It's not fear and it's not panic, but it's not vanquishing either. Rob isn't sure but it looks like confusion. Bemusement, at the very least.

'What's on your mind?'

'I'm not sure…' Jason looks around him, pointlessly checking if he can be heard. 'I've had a rather odd day and I wanted to check a few things with you.'

'Check what, exactly?' Rob is thinking he has a fair bit on his plate at the moment. The newspaper wants in-depth analysis of what is happening in the markets and he feels as though he is skiving off just by having this drink.

'I got hauled over the coals today.' Rob looks surprised; what with the chaos that is raining down on the world's financial centres, it seems strange that any senior manager would have the time to hand out a bollocking.

'It must have been serious.'

'It was. Insider trading.' Rob's expression changes from surprise to concern. This is a serious charge and one that reverberates up and down the management structure, ending with formal announcements by the CEO to the Stock Exchange. The law has been in action for seven years now and it has already claimed a number of eminent scalps, especially from the old school who were more used to a City where 'tipping the wink' was established practice.

'Jason, what have you been up to?'

'Nothing. Well, nothing criminal.'

'Tell me what happened.'

'Moncrieff called me into his office this afternoon. His boss Talbot was there, too. They wanted to know why my position had made such a massive profit yesterday and, specifically, why I had been selling short on Thursday afternoon.'

'You made a *profit* yesterday?' This is extraordinary. Unless he had advanced notice that the market was going to fall out of bed quite so dramatically.

'Yeah, a big one. Moncrieff didn't like it and said so before my arse had hit the seat.'

'What did Talbot have to say?' Talbot has a reputation for being one of the most aggressive people in the City and will tear up anyone who displeases him, usually for having a loss-making position. An insider trading charge could displease him more, though.

'He didn't say a thing for the whole time I was in there. Moncrieff looked like he'd been through the wringer, so I suppose Talbot had already said his piece. They wanted to know why I started selling when everyone else was still buying. Moncrieff said it looked as though I knew the Stock Exchange was going to be shut on Friday and that Monday morning was going to be too late. In short, they wanted to know what I knew, if I'd been tipped off.'

'What *did* you know?'

'As you're aware, Rob, it's hard to say who's buying and who's selling at any particular time, but you get whispers and hints and, after a time, you get a nose for certain trades and traders. I know I've only been doing this for three or four years, but there's something about this that sticks out for me.'

A couple of traders swept on the tide of humanity swamping the bar just avoid falling over onto Rob and Jason's table. They regain their balance and carry on talking without turning to look.

'I'd spotted this investment fund. It's based in Liechtenstein, and they have an uncanny knack at calling the market. I've noticed them do it a couple of times before and they are never wrong. Never.'

'Do you know who's running it?'

'It's all a bit vague, really. As far as I can tell, it's some bloke who works for a private bank, moving his client's cash around. But he's really good. He knows when to move in and out of equities, commodities, gilts, futures, everything. Do you know how much they made from oil futures in 1973? Billions. The same goes for the last gold bubble. So when I heard that they were unloading equities on Thursday afternoon I took a punt and sold everything in my position short.'

'How did you get on?' It would be interesting to write a good-news story in the midst of this meltdown.

'Made a fucking mint. It's not due to be reconciled until tomorrow but I'll get a handy bonus at the end of all this, assuming they don't sack me for insider trading.'

'Or the bank goes under,' says Rob darkly. Jason's bank is badly exposed to the US markets and this is going to hurt them. Heads will roll. 'Did you explain this to your boss?'

'Of course. Most of what I've been doing is in the public domain, even if it isn't exactly common knowledge. I suppose I'm the only one who's joined the dots.'

'Well, I hope things work out for you okay, Jason. These are uncertain times.'

'Tell me about it!' Jason laughs and pours himself another glass of wine.

Rob takes out his notebook and makes a few jottings before turning back to Jason, 'Look, I'll have a dig around and see what I can find. If there is a fund manager with a crystal ball, I'd like to interview him. Do you have any other information about the fund? Something I could get my teeth into, journalistically speaking?'

'Like what?'

'Its name, for starters. That would be a help.'

Jason looks up with alarm as the same traders teeter precariously over him. They have had a bit too much to drink and are beginning to become a pain. 'I'm not sure but I heard of it being referred to as the October Fund.'

JULIA KITAGAWA

New York. Monday October 12th, 0945hrs.

David Koscielski endeavours to be the soul of discretion wherever possible, but he has made no effort to hide his hatred of this building.

While the skyscrapers tumble down toward the southern edge of Central Park like a crumbling cliff, this newcomer is totally out of place. In proportion with the surrounding architecture, it resembles an industrial chimney speared into the heart of an ancient village. It clearly states the position of its sponsors: we have arrived and we are the new overlords. To that end it looms over Midtown Manhattan like the visitation of a sinister spirit, casting its long bony shadow across the lawns of Central Park. David gives an involuntary shudder as he crosses the threshold. They proceed into the room.

'Mr Rebrov!' David is in effusive form. 'Delighted you could make the time.' David shakes the man's hand warmly but not too tightly. David is well mannered in every sense of the word: his dress sense; the precision of his hair, teeth and nails; his etiquette; the delivery of every word he utters; and the intensity or subtlety with which he makes physical contact. The client is similarly well appointed, with a little more ease.

The client enjoins David in the protocol of small talk; no one should exhibit or display a sense of impatience for an important event. The gravity of an occasion is most often inversely related to the speed of its conclusion. The two men stand together in the middle of the plush hotel suite, a deep sculpted carpet beneath their feet, hands clasped together as if in a fatal embrace; they are both locked in eye contact and are smiling with the expectation of greatness.

Julia stands against the wall of the suite, next to the door. Beside her is the hotel's Deputy Manager who has personally escorted them to the client's room. The room is pregnant with plump furniture, all in a faux-European style possibly modelled on Louis XIV. It's opulent but not entirely gracious. It's an affected luxury rather than an innate feature. The bloated furnishings are in contrast with the owner's face which, Julia thinks, seems pinched and rather mean-spirited. Rebrov has piercing green eyes that fix on subjects like searchlights. He looks like a rat that has spotted its next meal.

David finally loosens his grip on the client's arm and gestures in Julia's direction. 'Mr Rebrov, may I introduce you to one of our rising stars at Armstrong's? Julia Kitagawa.'

'*Ohayo gozaimas,*' says Rebrov, bowing slightly.

'*Ohayo gozaimas. Anata wa nihongo, hanasemasu ka, Rebrov-san?*' She smiles at him and he relaxes. No, of course he can't speak Japanese; he only knows how to say 'good morning'. David looks uncomfortable.

'Julia will be handling the painting's authentication in the run-up to the sale as she did with the van Gogh. The difference is, this time, with your approval, she will be your personal point of contact.' The client bows once again at Julia who responds to him by bowing slightly lower as is the Japanese protocol once hierarchy has been established.

'What part of Japan are you from?' Rebrov asks Julia, taking care to enunciate his words.

'Buffalo, New York.' The client is taken aback at this and Julia steps in to remove any embarrassment. 'My father had Japanese parents but they had both left the country before the Second World War. They were regarded as being unpatriotic and disrespectful because they disagreed with the Tojo regime. So I'm second generation American. Oh, and my mom was American to start with.'

'But you speak Japanese?'

She giggles. 'I like to keep my hand in. I'm not very fluent, I confess.' But Julia is fluent in the cultural nuances. She would shudder at the thought that some action on her part would cause loss of face in another, especially in a client as important as this one. 'I am so looking forward to working with you on this sale. It is going to be so exciting!' Julia silently chides herself for saying 'so' too many times.

David steps in and leads the client to an armchair, taking an adjacent chair for himself. Julia retreats a few steps, leaving the men to take matters to the next stage. A waiter pours out coffees, working his way around the furniture to Julia who politely declines; it's not quite ten in the morning and she's had four coffees already.

'So tell me about your new artwork, Mr Rebrov.'

The client gestures to the waiter who walks quickly to the other end of the room where a painting covered by a sheet rests on an easel. The waiter pulls back the sheet and the painting is revealed. It is an oil on canvas, about two and a half feet square. The background consists entirely of blocks of solid colour—ochres, blacks, porcelain whites— over which have been painted images of fruit—an orange, a grapefruit, a lemon and a lime—all of which are rendered with exquisite clarity but overlapping and mixing like blended spotlights. Behind the fruit concoction is a tall, graceful plant reminiscent of a bamboo shoot laid diagonally across the ground. This takes up most of the background leaving the solid base colours peeking through the gaps in the leaves. At the foot of the painting is a green glass bottle with the light playing on the indentations and imperfections. There is some lettering on the surface of the glass, though this is hard to read. The glass is rendered as though lit from the side by a desk lamp: slightly yellow.

There are also intimations of water—sea or ocean, maybe— and rocks. The whole presentation is sharp, exact and rendered with the utmost draughtsmanship. Each image appears flat but is fully suggestive of a third dimension. It could be an advertisement from the nineteen thirties—it has the same graphic quality—or it could be a collage. But these images are not cut out; they are meticulously painted with imperceptible detail. It is like revealing a universe of complexity in an ice cube: the form is simple, but the intricacy spectacular.

Julia's first reaction is that it looks very nice, but David's reaction is far more marked. It is rare to see him genuinely surprised (although he has often faked it in front of clients to flatter them) and this time he is almost speechless. 'A Murphy?' He turns to Rebrov in astonishment. 'Where? I mean, how?'

'It's quite a story,' says the client. 'That will have to wait for another occasion, but yes, you are right. It is a painting by Gerald Murphy.'

'Which one is it?' David is still aghast. Julia wonders if he's seen a ghost.

'It's called *The Juice of a Few Flowers*,' says Rebrov, and waits for a reaction. It is slow in coming, from David.

'*The Juice of a Few Flowers*. But there isn't a painting that I know of called that. Is there?'

Rebrov indicates the painting before them all. David blows out through his cheeks; he never does this in front of clients, only with colleagues at the auction house when arrangements are failing to come together. He looks up at Julia who tries to smile reassuringly back at him. She is still none the wiser.

'So, let me get this right,' says David. 'You want Armstrong's to sell a completely unknown and uncatalogued Gerald Murphy?'

'That is correct.'

'May I ask how you came by this extraordinary work?'

'That is not important Mr Koscielowski. The important thing is that I have it and I have the documents, bills of sale and whatnot that prove both its provenance and my ownership.' Rebrov reaches down and retrieves a leather wallet from which he extracts a sheaf of documents in a clear plastic folder. He places the folder on the coffee table in front of them. 'Please feel free to examine these at your leisure.' He looks across at Julia who is trying to be as nonchalant and ambient as possible and sees the appreciation and the ignorance in her expression. 'Are you familiar with Gerald Murphy, Miss Kitagawa?'

'I confess that I am not. But if this painting is anything to go on, I like his work.'

'But you don't understand the significance of this man?' Julia shakes her head. Her expertise has been in oriental art and she has been cramming hard to learn as much about 20th Century and contemporary art and artists, but this one has slipped through the net. 'Don't worry about it,' says Rebrov with a slight air of condescension. 'Let me give you a bit more background.'

Julia sits down with the two men as the client runs through a history of the artist.

'Gerald Murphy was the son of the owner of a company that manufactured fine leather goods based in Boston. He had incurred the displeasure of his stern father in almost every regard. He had failed his entrance to Yale repeatedly, mixed with inappropriate characters (Cole Porter was a friend) and had married an older woman, Sara Wiborg, whose only possible saving grace was that she came from an auspiciously wealthy Ohio family with a close relationship to General Sherman, the Yankee hero of the Civil War. Above all, Gerald's principal shortcoming in his father's eyes was that he made little effort to conceal the discomfort he experienced whenever his father tried to groom him as his successor. Not for Gerald the cut and thrust of the boardroom, which he saw as superficial and unimportant. Nor for him the claustrophobic brotherhoods of the various clubs and societies where he could make the contacts essential to the continuation of the family's success. All these were devoid of the spirit and freedom of thought that he as a young boy had discovered in the arts and in Sara.

'They had met as adolescents in the Hamptons and their friendship grew to companionship and thence to romantic love. Neither of their parents approved. Sara's parents were disapproving of the Murphys and Gerald's father routinely disapproved of Gerald. So, after having brought three children into the world, they moved to Paris where the confines of New York society could be cast off with the ship's mooring lines. And there they discovered art and artists and food and drink and life and love. Gerald took up the brush for the first time and began to paint. He had absorbed the new schools of art in Paris but his own output somehow alchemised all that he had seen into a new style of art. One that has stood on its own both before and since.

'The art critics, in hailing his work in later years would ascribe labels such as "Precisionist" and "Precisionist Cubism". Later still, they would reappraise his work and describe it as "Proto-pop Art". But the labels merely described the critics, not the work.' Rebrov pauses to delicately lower a sugar lump from its porcelain bowl into his coffee which he stirs unhurriedly. Throughout, his eyes lock on to Julia standing at the edge of the room. She does her best to appear impassive while suppressing the urge to scratch the side of her neck.

'Gerald and Sara took the radical decision to move to the Cote d'Azur in the summer of 1923 and hired an entire hotel. At this time of year, it was customary for the British 'hivernauts' to return to the more temperate shores to escape the broiling sun, thus bringing life in the region to a close. The following year, they purchased a villa in Cap d'Antibes and named it Villa America. At both the hotel and subsequently the villa, they entertained and they partied and they lay in the sun and they swam in the turquoise sea and they drank cocktails and ate of the fruits of the region, both land and sea. Their guests would stay and paint and write and play music, some being inspired to explore new means of expression in their medium. Picasso's transposition to the south of France triggered a dalliance with more figurative art. He painted Sara many times in a way that was an infidelity to his cubist mistress in Paris. Jean Cocteau, Ernest Hemingway, F Scott Fitzgerald and Cole Porter were among the many guests at Villa America, and they left the company of the Murphys with renewed zeal.' Rebrov once more offers a coffee to Julia who declines. He continues his lecture.

'The Murphys' influence on 20th Century culture can't be understated. It is widely accepted that it was the Murphys and their summer parties that gave rise to Picasso's new approach to art. They inspired novels such as Fitzgerald's *Tender Is The Night* and Hemingway's *Garden of Eden* and plays such as Archibald McLeish's *JB*. And Gerald painted.' He waves an arm in the direction of the painting, resplendent upon the easel. 'Careful, exact, exquisite works of art. Some of them were overpoweringly grand. See his enormous canvas entitled *Boat Deck* of three ship's funnels rigid with grandeur and effortless momentum. Other works were minutely detailed, such as *Watch*. But they were all graphic representations of the age. Jazz, art deco, and the moment itself.'

'I'm getting the sense that this isn't going to have a happy ending,' says Julia.

Rebrov shrugs. 'Artistically, that is the case. Gerald set aside his brushed and returned to America in 1929, having resigned himself to his father's will, and took up his duties in the firm. "When I became a man, I put away childish things." And there he committed himself to his directorial duties and the company flourished under his care. There were personal tragedies, too. One child died from tuberculosis and another from meningitis.

'Gerald died aged seventy-six, some thirty-five years after his return from the Cote d'Azur where he had completed his final canvas. He left behind fourteen paintings of which a number have been lost or destroyed, leaving just eight.

'And this,' he concludes, 'is the ninth.'

The rejoinder *voilà* remains left unsaid.

'This,' says David, after a pause for reflection, 'is an opportunity of such rarity that it can only rank alongside that of the Van Gogh we sold for you two years ago, in terms of its sheer…' He is working himself up to a frenzy of superlatives and is fast running out of them; unusual for an auctioneer. 'Uniqueness!'

Rebrov leans across to Julia. 'The last time a Murphy came up for sale was fifteen years ago.'

'How much did it reach?'

'It didn't sell,' says David. 'The estimate was only three to five million and it didn't even make two.'

'But that was then,' says Rebrov. 'Gerald Murphy has since gained in status and appreciation. And his rarity has fuelled some of the new mystique. There is no demand for his paintings because, until now, there haven't been any to buy. People now look at his work and see the genesis of a number of different artistic movements. Any single person who can generate such evolution and diversity can command considerable respect within the fine art community. The fact that he has done it with just a dozen pieces...' He leaves the implication hanging in the hotel's scented air.

'We would be delighted to offer the painting for auction in our 20th Century Art sale which is scheduled for next May.' David is keen to close this deal and sign the Murphy up for cataloguing. 'Can we rely on you for its inclusion?'

Rebrov regards Julia for a while, then turns and looks at David and smiles. 'What would be your estimate for auction purposes?' he coolly enquires.

'We would need to do some research among our clientele, but I am confident that we would be able to set a reserve in excess of a hundred million dollars.'

Rebrov gives a hint of a satisfied smile. 'Before I agree, can you confirm that Miss Kitagawa will be handling the sale herself?'

'Yes,' says David, a little too quickly for Julia's comfort. Julia finds herself involuntarily rubbing the corners of her mouth. 'She will. This will be an extraordinary opportunity for her and I am confident that she will be more than equal to the task at hand. Her work on—'

'Quite, quite!' Rebrov cuts him off. Julia is now more convinced that her presence on the lot has less to do with her professional aptitude than either she or David might have liked.

'I have already set up appointments with a number of centres over the next few days.' Julia jumps in, keen to re-establish the correct basis for the conversation. 'We need to start confirming the authentication of the painting and validating the provenance before we can announce the sale.'

Rebrov nods. 'May I ask with whom you have made these appointments?'

'Forgive me, Mr Rebrov,' says David. 'But it is not normal policy for us to disclose this information. We need to conduct these checks discreetly, you understand.'

'I'm afraid I do not understand, Mr Koscielowski.' The temperature in the room drops sharply, the fragrance dulls. 'It is not "normal policy" for anyone to sell a Gerald Murphy, especially one that has not been catalogued before.'

'That is why we need to exercise *extreme* caution in our enquiries.' David is trying to sound as emphatic as he can without rubbing this client up the wrong way. This is an immense prospect; it's not just the commission that would be made on the artwork: twenty percent plus taxes from the purchaser. It is also the prestige that would be garnered by Armstrong's for having sold it at all.

Rebrov sits motionless and silent. For once, his eyes have locked contact with David, releasing Julia from their relentless gaze.

David continues unfazed. 'We will provide you will all the necessary receipts and copies of documentation together with our insurance certificates. I want you to feel assured that your property is in the very best of hands and that it will be given the very best of care. In the infinitesimally remote probability of any loss or damage being incurred, then you will receive the full market value.' Still nothing. David perseveres. 'While I appreciate that the picture means a great deal to you, the fact that you are offering it for sale probably means that the route whereby you realise its value is of secondary importance to you.'

And now David sits quietly to await a response. He knows that, in any negotiation, silence is a powerful weapon. After probably ten or even fifteen seconds, the client sighs and a smile breaks across his face.

'Very well. You are the experts. I will leave it in your care.' Rebrov shakes David's hand. 'I am delighted to have Armstrong's offer my painting for sale at the first available opportunity and I await the fruits of your authentications with enormous excitement.'

All rise to their feet. Rebrov shakes David's hand again and kisses Julia on both cheeks whilst resting a hand on her waist. Julia blushes slightly. Somewhere, a champagne bottle opens with a celebratory report and the deal is settled with clinks of glass.

Rebrov proposes a toast. 'To *The Juice of a Few Flowers!*'

Julia chuckles to herself. *And here's to the juice of a few grapes.*

DR JANET HOOPER

London. Tuesday October 13th, 0845hrs.

Dr Hooper is proceeding through the hotel lobby with the purpose and resolve of a warship; she is flanked by her two colleagues and none of them are to be stopped. Beyond the rotating doors and the floor-to-ceiling windows are the street and the waiting car. The engine is running. Single-mindedness brings with it the dulling of the senses: tunnel vision, the filtering of sound. But it is still difficult not to react when your own name is used and you are not expecting it.

'Dr Hooper!'

Five metres from the door, she breaks her stride.

'I'm sorry, Dr Hooper, but I really advise you not to leave just yet.' The voice is firm but affable. She stops dead, her shoulders drop and she slowly turns around. The two men with her snap round in the direction of the voice.

'Roger!' It's Roger Ingham, her British opposite number and the very last person of all the seven or so billion on the planet she wants to see at this moment. She tries to sound pleased to see him and realises she has done a poor job of it. 'How lovely to see you.' She stretches a smile across her face; it almost causes her pain. 'I'd really love to stop and chat but I'm in a frightful hurry.' You can tell when an American is being disingenuous, Janet thinks to herself: the British idioms come out.

'I'm so sorry,' says the gentleman with the grey hair and moustache and the brilliant, laser-blue eyes. His soft, measured voice has a regional accent that Janet doesn't have the experience to place, but she is told that it is from somewhere in a remote part of England called Yorkshire. They probably all live in caves there. 'I did so want to have a quick catch-up with you.'

'Roger, any other time… I've got an urgent meeting with the Ambassador.' Janet motions to the door and the waiting car. Her two bodyguards move silently between her and Roger.

'Oh, that's alright. I'll get one of my people to give one of His Excellency's people a call and let him know you're going to be late.' Janet's strained smile cuts to a frown.

'How late?'

'Oh, let's say fifteen minutes. Maybe twenty. No more, I'm sure.' Roger directs her to a table circled by easy chairs. One of the chairs is occupied by a younger man dressed in a suit and tie. His clothes don't fit him very well and his shirt collar is too tight. Roger raises his chin. 'I do hope your colleagues would be happy to accept a cup of coffee on my account, over there.' He points to another table some distance away.

'My colleagues are keen to hear anything you might have to say, Roger.'

'I'm sure.' Roger smiles. 'But I'm not! I'd be surprised if you hadn't noticed a couple of my men standing outside by your car. Please be so good as to request your men to do as I ask and that will avoid a lot of unpleasant melodrama that could place a strain on the Special Relationship.' Roger's mouth is smiling; his eyes are not. Janet sighs and nods at her colleagues to do as they are told. 'Thank you. Coffee?'

Janet slumps into a chair like a petulant teenager. 'Oh, why not?' Roger's associate pours the coffee and offers milk and sugar, both of which Janet declines. 'So, Roger…' She crosses her legs and relaxes into the back of the chair with her coffee. 'Why are you so keen to intercept me in the centre of London? What's wrong with the telephone?'

'I like the personal touch. That's why you and I get on so well.' Janet is starting to feel uncomfortable and is doing everything she can not to show it. Her chief concern is that these efforts will betray her anyway.

She flashes Roger an insincere grin. 'I think you should know I am travelling under diplomatic immunity.'

And you do it so often that, back in Section, we call you the Diplomatic Bag.

'And I think you should know, my dear Janet, that I don't give a twopenny damn. And I speak with the authority of Her Britannic Majesty's Government, and I have an army of Civil Service minions who will gladly spend days trying to sort out the avalanche of paper that this encounter will generate.' He noisily slurps at his coffee. 'Jesus! It could be weeks before they find the right form which details where you and your jolly chums over there have been mistakenly confined.' He leans forward to her, smiling all the while. 'Now, are we going to play nicely or is this thing going to get theatrical?' He flops back, by way of a rejoinder.

Janet speaks slowly and quietly. 'It is always a pleasure to see you, Roger, as you well know. Is there something I can help you with?'

Roger claps his hands together and sits upright. 'There! I *knew* you'd want to help out!' He nudges his associate who doesn't move or change his expression. 'I wanted to ask you, in the spirit of mutual cooperation as part of our Special Relationship, what you think you are doing?'

Janet sits, lips pursed.

'Too hard for you? Okay, let's try this, then.' Roger bends down beside his associate and retrieves a cardboard folder which he opens on the table. He removes a sheaf of photographs and places them, one at a time, in front of Janet. Janet keeps her gaze fixed on Roger. 'This is you arriving at Heathrow on Sunday morning. This is you having lunch at the Randolph Hotel in Oxford on Monday. They do a very good buffet lunch there, I'm told. This is some friends of yours in Summertown. Meeting with a well-known TV producer. And this is them manhandling him into your safe house in Harrow. You know which house I mean, don't you, Janet? The one with the high laurel hedging and the long driveway? The one no one can see from the road?'

Janet's has settled on trying to look bored. Which isn't hard.

'Now, what have we here? Oh this is a good one! This is you, yesterday evening, in another car, sightseeing at the Penrose Science Park Exatron. Pity the place is infested with police. That must have pissed on your cornflakes.'

'Roger, is this going to take much longer?' Janet brandishes her watch at him without looking at it. 'You did say that I wasn't going to keep the Ambassador waiting more than twenty minutes.'

'I always find that when one is having such an enjoyable conversation, time can take on a rather elastic property, don't you?' Janet moves to stand up. Roger's associate tenses and the two American agents sitting by the window rise to their haunches. Roger raises his hands and waves them palm downwards in a calming gesture. 'Janet, I really wouldn't go right now. It would cause all sorts of problems. Let me cut to the chase. You come to this country brandishing your immunity and start to kidnap UK citizens. That is an offence here, in case you weren't sure. Then you interrogate them, drug them, assault them and dump them in the streets of Oxford. I will concede that you had the good grace to dump your man close to where he lived and where he could get help from a friend. But, Janet, this all constitutes bad manners in my book, and, in more official circles, it could be deemed "behaviour inconsistent with your diplomatic status".

'Next, you order your goons to stake out the premises of an eminent and prominent academic with a view to possibly removing him from circulation, too. Were you going to give him the third degree as well?' No response. 'Yes, I thought so.

'I've always been a fan of yours, Janet. In fact, my colleagues at Section think I have something of an infatuation where you're concerned. I regard you as more of a hobby, actually. Still, when you set foot on my shores, I make sure that you are well looked after. What is that quote of Sun Tzu's? "Keep your enemies close, but your friends closer." Janet knows full well that Sun Tzu didn't say it quite like that, but this isn't the time to start correcting Roger's misquotations. 'I like to give you my undivided attention. I know you might think it's a bit creepy but, hey, that's me for you.'

Janet rises and, without saying a word, turns and makes for the door.

'Are they wearing body armour?'

She stops again and turns back to face Roger. She tilts her head. Roger repeats the question. 'Are they wearing body armour? Your, "friends"?'

Janet slopes back and retakes her seat. 'Tasers?'

'Yes, something like that. My men have instructions that if you set foot on the pavement without my blessing, the lot of you will wake up with a headache a long way from here.' Roger isn't smiling now; the bonhomie has evaporated.

'You have the professor?' says Janet.

'No. The police do, or they will when he's discharged from hospital.' Roger slumps back and folds his arms. 'Really, Janet! Of all the gilt-edged cock-ups! Broad daylight, a fifty-seven-year-old hippy on a bicycle, and six of you in two Transits couldn't apprehend him. I bet the air was a choice shade of blue when you found out.'

Janet's eyes narrow.

'And another thing. We have all the main contacts of your targets under surveillance, so don't get any inspired ideas that we've kissed and made up. I'm dedicating a sizeable chunk of my counter-intelligence budget to you and your operations. Which means: whatever you're up to is blown.' Janet has been trained for this sort of thing: avoidance of 'leakage', tell-tale glimmers of body language or facial expression that reveal what you are thinking. But she can't resist the urge to look acutely pissed off. Roger motions to his associate to pour some more coffee and glances over at the two Americans; they are glowering at him but seem no longer ready to spring from their positions.

He offers her another coffee which she declines. She is seated, legs crossed, arms crossed, lips pursed, brow furrowed, regarding him with a gaze of smouldering rage. She seems close to losing control but Dr Janet Hooper never actually does so; at least not in public.

'Tell me, Janet. What is your doctorate?'

'I fail to see—'

'Economics, wasn't it? Yale, I think.'

'If you say so, Roger.'

'We are going to have to work together. You know that, don't you?'

'Work on what, Roger!' It is a question enunciated without an interrogatory inflection. It is a challenge.

'The conjecture.' Roger leans forward dropping his voice conspiratorially. 'Work on the conjecture that all the maroons went up last Friday when that programme about the assassination of Kennedy was broadcast, and that lots of senior somebodies were rabid with excitement at finding out how a gnat's-prick TV production company from Oxford cracked the biggest political intrigue in American history. And that you decide it is easier to gatecrash your way in here and start waterboarding—'

'We didn't waterboard anybody, for fuck's sake!'

'At last, we're getting somewhere!' Roger is exultant. 'That you decide it is easier to gatecrash your way in here and start interrogating UK citizens rather than speak to one of us and politely ask for permission, as is customary in our Special Fucking Relationship, Janet, for fear that you might have to share your scoop with the farts in the Old Country.' Janet draws breath to speak, but Roger hasn't finished yet. 'Oh, and the conjecture that you know there is more to this so-called TV programme than meets the eye and that we know it, too.' Janet relaxes and switches her gaze back to Roger.

'Go on.'

'Our professor is obviously tied up in this. We also know another academic has had a major hand in the programmes, at least. That was where your... interviewee went after you so kindly dropped him off.'

'They found out who did it. They found out and they didn't just not tell us first. They went and told the whole American nation that Kennedy was murdered by his own bodyguards, aided and abetted by Southern white supremacists.' She stabs the table top with the nail of her garishly painted forefinger. 'That sort of thing has repercussions, Roger. That sort of thing has National Security implications. Big ones.' She shakes her head disbelieving. 'I cannot begin to tell you what kind of a shitstorm has gone down. They're right now tearing up the Warren Commission. They are going to have to conduct a review of the current security arrangements around the White House, Capital, and Jesus knows what else.' She is panting with pent-up rage now. 'I mean, for Christ's sake! We got reports of at least seventeen suicides. *Seventeen* people have killed themselves, Roger, because it turns out that Roswell was nothing more than a close encounter with a big aluminum balloon; it was not First Contact with creatures from beyond our galaxy. *Seventeen*. It could be more!' Roger is doing his best not to smirk at this news; there's always an upside to every cock-up.

'Well, I hate to be the bearer of ill tidings, Janet, but we have information that there may be way more to this than just some silly shows on the gogglebox.' Janet looks quizzically at Roger. 'I'd like to offer you an olive branch.'

'What for?' She is starting to feel uneasy again.

'I've not been entirely gentlemanly with you today. I know I'm a plain speaking Yorkshireman and we in God's County have a reputation for calling a spade a bloody shovel, but we like to exercise a generosity of spirit.'

'Oh God, Roger. I hate it when you talk in riddles.'

'Alright. I'll put it simply. What we are dealing with is international. We need to pool resources and we need to work together.' He pulls another photograph from the folder and lays it before her. 'This fellow is tied up in all this.' She picks up the photo and pores over it for a moment.

'Him! How is he involved in this?'

'I haven't got the foggiest. All I can tell you is that he emerged from the Exatron about nine hours before you turned up there and, seven hours after that, strode down the platform of Marylebone Station. The local police in Oxford called in a few favours from a detective in the Met who is currently on secondment to Special Branch. And one thing led to another and… here we are.'

'But if he's in London, that means—'

'Yes, that's what that means!' Roger's smile is back. 'Time to reinstate the Special Relationship. But if you go behind my back or if you keep anything from me, Janet, I will clip your wings and you will never fly again. Do I make myself clear?'

'Yes, Roger,' she says, meaning, 'Not necessarily, Roger.'

JULIA KITAGAWA

Long Island. Monday October 12th, 1430 hrs.

It takes about two hours to complete the drive from Brooklyn to East Hampton along the Long Island Expressway and, beyond that, the West Sunrise Highway. The Expressway is a grandiose name for a vast sweep of asphalt where nothing seems to move expressly. It's just a long conveyor belt; you sit on it and it gets you there, but in no particular hurry. Julia doesn't mind driving, though. It's a chance for her to get out of the office, listen to some music on her iPod and get some sun in her eyes; a rarity in the canyons of midtown Manhattan.

It's a lovely day; a fresh, bright October morning with a deep blue sky clashing flamboyantly with the autumn tones. Nowhere other than nature can the juxtaposition of two such jarring colours be so delightful. On top of that, the roads are open and fairly clear; the bulk of the morning traffic has cleared and, anyway, it was headed the other way.

Having a few hours to herself is a good thing right now. Yesterday had been manic. After the meeting with the client—a funny little man, obviously very powerful but somehow insubstantial as a human being—the painting had to be crated up and shipped back to the Armstrong warehouse ready for dispatch to East Hampton. Julia had set that up in advance of the client meeting on the basis that it is good to be prepared for a successful outcome. She had already set up the preliminary appointments with the labs and had met with them that afternoon and fixed all the necessary tests: X-ray, spectrophotometric, carbon dating, any test that would confirm the painting to be genuine.

So, over the course of the next six weeks, Gerald Murphy's forgotten canvas and its attendant paperwork would be criss-crossing New York State as it passes from one eminent academic institution to the next. Each would validate, confirm, cross-reference and authenticate. Every step of the provenance would have to be double-checked. An artwork of such rarity cannot be sold at auction with any assumptions or suspicions hanging over it.

Julia's first port of call is Dr Eliot Langer, the archivist for the Murphy estate. He has the glorious fortune of living surrounded by the low dunes, clouds and ocean airs of Long Island, close to where the Murphys' enormous mansion once stood. A contact at the Whitney had introduced her to Dr Langer with a glowing reference as the foremost authority on Gerald Murphy's paintings. She felt a certain envy for a man who spent his life surrounded by wonderful art in a location so close to the sky as on this magnificent island. On such a day, what a sky!

When Julia finally arrives, Dr Langer is already in waiting on the front drive of a modest but delightfully picturesque cottage hung with silvering wooden shingles and buttressed at each gable end by two generous brick chimneys. The house is ringed by a low post-and-rail fence and beyond it a screen of plane trees rises like a chorus. The Atlantic wind rocks their topmost branches and flurries of golden leaf scatter with every gust.

Julia pulls her car onto the drive and Langer walks up to shake her hand. He is a slight man with receding curly hair and thick-rimmed glasses and he gives off an academic if not bookish air.

'A pleasure to make your acquaintance, Dr Langer.'

'Likewise. Please, though. Do call me Eliot.'

Langer has a ground-floor extension built onto the side of the old house; it is modern and light with large plate-glass windows and contains his office, a light table and bookshelves. The limited wall space is adorned with a few choice works of art; some are early 20th Century works which Julia can't identify and one is a delicate, petite Russian Orthodox icon in gold and blue. A saint looks on from the icon, observing proceedings with a circumspect eye.

By the double doors at the end of the extension is the Murphy on an easel; its back is to the room so that the northern light can softly illuminate it. Julia steps around the easel and takes the opportunity to appreciate it in detail by herself: at least without the attentions of the client.

'This was quite a departure for him, you know,' says Langer. 'Prior to this, his subjects had been more, well, industrial. *Engine Room, Turbines, Boat Deck*. All of those early canvasses are missing.'

'I've seen photos of them taken at the Paris exhibitions. They seem to owe a lot to Fernand Léger's work, wouldn't you say?'

'Possibly. But one can never be certain. The two men were certainly friends, and Léger is known to have stayed with the Murphys in the South of France during the 1920s.'

'So, Eliot.' It is time to get down to business. 'You've had a short time to examine the canvas; what is your first impression?'

'I'm confident it's by Gerald Murphy.' Langer looks straight at Julia as he says this. He isn't smiling.

'I'm thinking you're going to use the word "but"…'

'But… I need to examine the provenance more closely.'

There is a pause. Julia breaks it. 'Go on.'

'Take a seat.' Julia takes the chair by Eliot's desk. He sits facing her, takes a deep breath and leans in. 'There's a problem with this painting.'

'I thought you said—'

'Oh, yes. I'm convinced that this was painted by Gerald Murphy. But I am not convinced that the current possessor of the work is the rightful owner.'

'How do you mean?'

'Julia. As you know, I am employed by the corporations that acquired the Mark Cross Company which Gerald Murphy and his father before him both ran. I am responsible for maintaining the company's archives and I deal with issues arising from the estates of the Murphy family. Therefore, the artworks of the late Gerald Murphy fall within my purview.' He shifts in his seat a little uneasily. 'I freely admit I am not an art historian, but I have had to become something of an expert in the few works of Gerald Murphy that survive to this day. I have had unfettered access to these works and that has been easy because they are all to be found in museums in the United States. Some in New York, some in Dallas and Minneapolis. Apart from those that are missing, or those that are known to have been destroyed, none are thought to be, or have been, in private hands.

'The other thing that is suspicious about this painting is the name and subject matter.'

'*The Juice of a Few Flowers*,' says Julia, the image of the rat-faced Russian springing to mind.

'Do you know the relevance of the title?' Julia shakes her head. 'It was the name Murphy gave to his favourite cocktail. A recipe he concocted himself. I've tried it and, you know, it's not bad. From what you've told me, this was painted in 1925 which matches the time that Murphy stopped painting industrial subjects and began to represent more organic images such as in *Doves*.'

'Yes, but why is any of this "suspicious"?' Eliot is obviously an enthusiast who doesn't often get the opportunity to share his enthusiasm with anyone. Maybe that's why he is at the far end of Long Island.

'Because, according to his diaries for 1925, he did indeed complete a painting with this subject and title, and it was stolen.' He pauses, partly for effect, partly because he is having trouble absorbing the enormity of it all. 'It was apparently removed from his villa by a guest. Gerald was so frustrated by the episode that he painted a new version the following year which he called simply *Cocktail*. In my opinion, he did a better job of it the second time around.'

'That's the one in the Whitney, isn't it?'

'That's right. So, the problem we have here is not whether it's a Murphy. I can pretty much guarantee it is, and a bit more close examination will confirm it. The problem is whether or not your client has the right to sell it in the first place.'

'Isn't there a statute of limitations for stolen works of art?'

'Yes, and no. Yes, a statute exists and, in New York State, it's about three years. No, because the statute only commences from the date at which the artwork is *discovered*. This rule was brought in to help those families trying to recover works of art stolen during the Holocaust.'

'So, in this case the clock would start running from today?'

Eliot shrugs. 'I'm sorry about that.'

'But the client provided a comprehensive dossier of papers which confirm the work's provenance and, I assume, his right to assert ownership.'

'Very probably and I assure you that I will review the papers in fine detail.'

'The client tells us that the artwork was acquired in a card game.'

'Quite so. But I will still need to examine the documentation to be absolutely sure.'

'May I suggest that we get the papers copied so we both have access to them?' Julia can see the dossier sitting on Eliot's desk and, right now, she would like to reach out and get hold of it; advantage comes with possession.

'That's a good idea. If you do the photocopying, I'll get the coffee organised. The machine is just through that door on the right.' He indicates a small alcove just outside the main office area, with shelving for stationery and an up-market photocopier.

Julia copies the sheets entrusted to her by Rebrov. As the machine whirs and clunks hypnotically, she wonders if she should call David. The sooner this matter can be hushed up the better. David has few faults but, sadly, firing from the hip is one of them, and the risk is that he will already be telling the world what a coup Armstrong has scored just when it turns out that the sale cannot proceed. The embarrassment would be inestimable. But, then again, the documents might show that the painting was legitimate after all and, in that case, she would be the one with egg on her face if she pressed the panic button prematurely. But, to be on the safe side...

She pulls out her cellphone and dials. There is a delay as the call connects and then a woman's voice at the end.

'Hi, Pam. Can I speak with David, please? It's kinda urgent... No, I really think he'll want to take this call...' A wait. Why are personal assistants so protective of their stupid bosses? He's her boss, too, and she doesn't smother him in goddamn bubble-wrap.

'What's the problem, Julia?' Even wreathed in the metallic fog of the phone network, David sounds worried. 'Pam said it was urgent.'

'I think we've got a major issue here.' Julia is half whispering, half speaking in the way that we do when we are trying to say something about someone else when that person is in the room. 'I'm with Eliot Langer right now and he reckons the Murphy is genuine—'

'That's great—'

'And stolen!' The line goes quiet.

'Oh, holy shit!' David blows out a long, forlorn sigh. 'Why does he think that?'

'He's got the Murphy diaries from 1925 and that's what they say. Some guest just walked off with it.'

'What about the provenance?'

'He doesn't know yet because he hasn't in any detail. I'm copying the documents right now.'

'For God's sake, make sure you keep the originals.'

'That's a good point. He's going to want to hang on to the painting so it's a trade I'm sure he'll agree to.'

'Thanks for letting me know anyway, Julia.'

'No problem. I just wanted to give you a heads-up before things get outta control.'

The call ends and Julia gathers the original documents and copies them into separate piles before returning to the office where Eliot is waiting at his desk.

'Here you go,' she says, and passes the copies to Eliot who regards them with poorly concealed distaste.

'I'm so sorry. Would you mind if I had the original documents?' he asks, a little too politely.

'If you have no objection, we'd like to hang on these for the time being,' she says, soft but polite. One good thing about her Japanese upbringing is being able to erect a rubber wall which no one can knock down but causes little pain in trying.

Eliot shrugs, admitting defeat on this issue. 'Okay. But I am going to have to hang on to the painting. If it is stolen, then it's legally the property of the Murphy estate, such as it rests.'

'I expected that. Of course, the painting had been entrusted to the care of Armstrong's and we will happily surrender it in exchange for the usual receipts and copies of insurance documents, shifting the liability to you in case anything should go awry.'

Eliot agrees easily enough and the conversation moves away from Gerald Murphy and the goings-on at the Villa America to life on Long Island, the coming winter and the splendid isolation of the place when the summer seekers have returned to hibernate in the city.

Julia sets off in her car. At the T-junction with Ocean Avenue, she waits for a car to pass before lifting her foot from the brake pedal to move out into the road.

That's when the penny drops. She stamps her foot back on the brake pedal and peers more keenly to her right where, in a driveway, a man is bent over the open hood of a silver SUV. She had made no connection until then, but it now dawns on Julia that every time she has looked in the rear view mirror, the silver-coloured SUV was there.

Why is he working on the engine? The vehicle looks brand new for one thing; for another, he doesn't have his hazard lights on. Also, he's not looking at the engine; he's looking at her. He drops his gaze in the way that men do when Julia catches them eyeing her in bars. The peak of his baseball cap covers his face. What to do? She hesitates a second and looks at the map on her satnav.

She accelerates away from the side-road, turning left onto Ocean Drive. The rear view mirror reflects an empty road behind her, at first. Then, a glimmer, some lights and the sun glinting off the roof of the SUV. She takes a right turn; the SUV follows. She takes the next right turn, and the next, heading back to Ocean Avenue, almost at the point where she had first joined it. The silver vehicle matches her with each turn.

Julia makes one more right turn onto Ocean Avenue and takes an immediate left back down the small road to Eliot's house is situated. She is at his door within thirty seconds, knocking urgently, taking out her cellphone. Eliot peers through a side window and opens the door to her.

She steps inside as a vehicle swishes past the property.

'Pam! Get me David! And get him now!'

DAVID KOSCIELOWSKI

New York. Monday October 12th 1830 hrs.

'I'm so sorry to have to call you like this at such short notice.' David strides across the deep carpet of the rooftop bar with his hand outstretched. 'But I needed to check something out with you rather urgently.'

'Of course, of course. Please, let's take a seat.' Rebrov is effusive, suave and immaculate as ever. He pulls back the cuff of his exquisitely tailored Italian jacket and glances at his antique Swiss watch. 'I'm afraid my time is rather limited as I have to fly off to London later this evening. But I'm sure I can make time to offer you a drink. The sun is over the yardarm, as I believe they say.' David requests a glass of Pinot Grigio and Rebrov orders a Manhattan.

'How are things progressing with the sale of my Murphy, Mr Koscielowski?'

'Mr Rebrov, I have a direct question to ask you.'

'Ask away,' is the blithe response.

'Have you or anyone associated with you been following Julia Kitagawa?' Rebrov's expression does not change. He does not tense, he does not shift uncomfortably in his seat. He simply sips his Manhattan, gives a satisfied sigh and locks eye contact.

'Yes.'

'May I ask why?' David is affronted by his candour and is finding it hard to hide it.

'Naturally,' Rebrov purrs. 'I am ensuring the safekeeping of my property.' David allows the pause to hang in the air. As far as he is concerned, the ball is still very much in his client's court. But Rebrov can play this game, too, and wordlessly twitches his head with a wink of a smile as if to say, 'That's all you're getting'.

231

David has to get the conversation going again. 'I would like to express my discomfort to you that you found it necessary to resort to such underhand methods.'

'What's "underhand"?'

'With respect, having her followed constitutes an overt lack of trust in our services. It has also caused not unreasonable alarm for the person concerned.'

'David,' Rebrov calls in his best comradely tone; he might as well have called him *tovarich*. 'The "person concerned" is Julia Kitagawa. Why the anonymity?'

'Alright. Julia Kitagawa was upset. Justifiably, in my view. She felt threatened.'

'Okay, okay. I'm sorry!' It is more a concession than an apology. 'For your information we did exactly the same thing when you were getting the van Gogh authenticated. But on that occasion it all happened within the confines of big cities such as New York and Amsterdam. It was harder for your people to spot my people. Stuck out in East Shitville, Long Island, it's a lot harder to blend in.'

'Do you normally follow people who are working for you?' David is having to use every last ounce of his diplomatic reserves.

'When they are toting over a hundred million dollars' worth of my artwork around, yes.'

'What about when they are not "toting" it around?' David throws Rebrov's words back at him like snowballs with rocks in.

'Excuse me?' Rebrov looks puzzled.

'Julia didn't have the painting with her when your "people"'— another snowball with a hard centre—'were following her.'

'May I therefore ask where it was?' The question is issued with the menace of a low threat.

'It was still with the archivist.'

'Why would she leave the painting with an archivist in a private house on Long Island? A painting which you have valued at more than a hundred million dollars? Why would she do that, eh?' Rebrov's words acquire a rising whine, like a jet engine winding up before take-off.

'Nobody knows it's there.'

'My people know it's there!' His voice is raised now. A few drinkers turn their heads.

'No, Mr Rebrov. Apparently they don't! That's why they were following Julia, isn't it?'

Rebrov's voice drops to a snarl. 'But, that still doesn't answer my last question, Mr Koscielowski. Why did she leave the painting with the archivist?'

'He's still doing some checks.'

'*What* checks?'

'Excuse me, but why do you ask? I thought that you had chosen Armstrong's because of our matchless reputation in auctioning lots with impeccable provenance. The very fact that something is in one of our catalogues is testament to the almost infinitesimal care we take to ensure that the buyer is obtaining the genuine and unsullied article.' Rebrov is weaving his head sarcastically throughout David's homily on professional exactitude.

'Please, David. I fully understand and appreciate your ethical stance. But you have to accept my position as someone whose priceless work of art has been left in a private house on a remote part of Long Island. Why is it there, please?'

David takes a mouthful of wine and swallows it like medicine. 'Because we still need to authenticate it. There have been some issues which have cropped up that must be addressed before we can release it for sale.'

'"Issues"?' Rebrov looks alarmed.

'Yes.'

'Such as?'

'There is reason to suspect that, at some point in the painting's history, it may have been stolen.' Rebrov freezes, his glass halfway to his mouth. For a moment, New York stops moving, the traffic noise thirty storeys below ceases and the soft jazz music soundtrack in the bar halts mid-note.

'What?'

'It's possibly stolen.' David repeats with less venom. 'That's why the painting has to stay there whilst the archivist checks the validity of the provenance.'

'What makes him think the painting was stolen?' Rebrov looks crestfallen.

'Apparently the Murphy diaries recount the theft of the painting after one of the dinner parties at his villa. I don't know more than that at this stage.'

'But it was won over a game of cards.' Rebrov is searching the floor as if some answer may lie beneath the table. His face his lined with incomprehension.

'If that's what the accompanying documents prove, then there is nothing to worry about.'

Rebrov looks up. 'What if the accompanying documents don't prove that?'

David scratches the side of his head and sighs. 'Then the painting will be retained by the Murphy estate until all disputes over legal ownership are decided.'

'But…' Rebrov stammers with mounting rage. 'It is *my* painting. It has been in the family for ninety years!'

'As things stand, Mr Rebrov, it has been missing from the Murphy family for ninety years. You may need to engage legal support with this issue, but Armstrong's cannot intervene in this process until it has run its course.' David regards his desolated client.

'I'm sorry,' he adds, even though, deep down, he isn't. He has rather gone off Mikhail Rebrov.

ELIOT LANGER

Long Island. Monday October 12th, 2130 hrs.

The SUV crunches to a halt, blocking the driveway. It's late but not so late that Eliot has turned in for the night. He is still examining the Murphy and the noise of the unseen car outside shatters his reverie. He turns off the lights in the extension just as the security sensor washes the front of the property in a harsh blue glare. His eyes aren't fully adjusted to the darkness yet, but he can see the silhouette of two men, one obviously holding a silenced pistol to his side.

Eliot grabs his cellphone and thrashes his way through the interior of the house, extinguishing every light as he goes. He doesn't have much time; he must double back to the extension, slip out into the night and lose himself in the dunes and scrub, even if it means submerging himself in the brackish pond. He must get away, and quickly.

He hears the voices of the two men. Bronx, maybe. They have split up and are planning to cover all the exits from the house. It's too late to get to the extension, so he veers into the kitchen at the back of the house and throws the window open as quietly as he can. He dives inelegantly through the opening and lands heavily on the gravel outside, jarring a shoulder. The pain is forgotten in the realisation that the noise of his landing has alerted one of the intruders. A voice summons the other one and two sets of feet pound the ground on either side of the house.

Eliot hurls himself towards the dunes, remembering to vault the low hedge at the back of the property. He misjudges it in the darkness and nearly trips up completely; the sound of the twanging wire and snapping twigs will have given his pursuers another clue to his location.

He doesn't have much time. He holds his cellphone close to his chest and dials 911 as he stumbles and lurches over the uneven ground. He must duck for cover; the light on his phone will be a beacon.

The operator picks up the call and before she can say anything, Eliot is pleading with her in an urgent whisper to send some police over as quickly as possible; there are two armed men and they are closing in on him.

'Hurry! Please. Hurry!'

The operator acknowledges the call and tells him a patrol car is on its way. Eliot disconnects and peers up from behind a small mound of sand and earth. He can see one of the men silhouetted against a maroon aurora, backlit by the distant lights of New York City over the horizon. He moves inexorably towards him, veering from side to side, but always closing in.

Eliot dials Julia's number. She must know they might come for her, as well. It has to be the Murphy. The call goes through to voicemail.

'Julia!' he whispers. 'It's Eliot. As soon as you get this message, go to a police station. I am being pursued by some men. They are in the house. Get out!' He ends the call, places the cellphone face down on the ground and crawls away.

He is aware of a new light nearby: orange and flickering intensely. The light rises into the night sky and Eliot realises what is happening: the men have set the house ablaze to illuminating the scrub ground. He needs to keep as low to the ground as he can. He knows that if he lifts his head to get a look at either the burning building or his pursuer, he will reveal his position. A mistake he will make only once.

A row of sandy tussocks rises before him. They are only a foot or so high, but it's enough cover from which to plan where to go next. He slithers over the sandy soil. As he goes, he can hear the man with the pistol pacing around nearby. He is getting closer and Eliot needs to find a position where he can open up the number of options for escape.

Within a few seconds he is among the tussocks and allows himself a brief period to relax. His heart is pounding and he is worried that the sound of his breathing will give him away. He peers through the long grass, hoping to spot either of the assailants. Although the house fire will have lit up the area, it will also back-light them. It will be all the information he needs to decide which direction to flee.

To the left, nothing. To the right, a gentle breeze rustling the scrub and the crackle of the fire. In the distance, a howling siren.

And directly behind him, the dull click of a safety catch being disengaged.

ROB TILLING

London, November 2002.

[Headline] *WHO BURST THE DOT-COM BUBBLE?*

[Copy] *Hindsight is a wonderful thing in finance. If one looks back at the performance of a share or a market more generally, one can consider a point on the graph and wish that one had bought then. Or sold then. Because today it would be worth...*

If hindsight in finance is a wonderful thing, then foresight is much, much better.

Imagine waking up in late 1990 and, after a scan of the financial press, deciding that you should invest the bulk of your fortune in tech stocks and that the NASDAQ quoted companies all look like good bets. So you start investing. And you put in one hundred million dollars, then two, then three. Pretty soon, you have several billion dollars invested in the new tech stocks and, before you know it, the first of the new companies dedicated to commercialising the newly invented worldwide web come along.

So, what do you do? It's 1995/96 and some of these young, fresh, vibrant companies are starting to make a mark. They have weird names like Google or eDigital or Boo and they look like they are going to utterly disrupt the corporate landscape and change it forever. So, you think, 'I want to be a part of this brave new world. I want a piece of it.' You start shifting your tech portfolio across to these mavericks.

By now, your investments are paying off big time. So big time, in fact, that the sharks that prowl the depths of the financial markets have woken up and smelt the fresh blood of easy profits. So they pile in, and the value of your holdings grows exponentially. And by 1999 you are coasting. Everyone else is doing all the hard work for you, and all you have to do is count how much more money you have today than you did yesterday.

Then, on another morning in, say, March 2000, you decide that enough is enough and you pull the whole lot out and the entire house of cards comes crashing down. In that time, the NASDAQ index has swelled from 292 to over 5,000. All the Boos, eDigitals and InfoSpaces implode. You take your money and put it somewhere safe, like gold, while the major banks hold endless crisis meetings in order to calculate how many staff they have to lay off.

But you're not finished yet. Oh, no. By September of this year, you're back in again. The NASDAQ is down at 1,100 and within two months it's at 1,500. Piling back in again is turning out to be a really good idea. And do you know how you've managed to call the top and the bottom of the market each time? No.

But somebody somewhere is really very good at it. Because one fund has been calling the market time and time again. And it's not just the NASDAQ. They've managed to do it in commodities, gilts, currencies and equities. They have called the market's collapse almost to the day every time since the 1980s, including 9/11. So who are these people?

As you would expect, tracking down the identity of these prescient investors isn't easy. I first heard about them round about the time of the stock market crash of October 1987—Black Monday—when a friend of mine who was also a trader made one of the few major killings from the fall. He did that by following what one of the funds had done the previous Thursday. He dubbed the investors the October Fund.

Since then, the fund has gone under a multitude of names— Avestan 2000, Houston, Eisenstein, Rheostat—but the pattern has always been the same. The day before some dramatic correction in the market, one enormous trade will be executed and this will quite often be the trigger for the chaos to follow. Below is a short and far from exhaustive list of the major trades that have coincided with tumultuous market corrections.

October 1973. An unnamed fund executes a massive oil futures trade, pinning the barrel price at the pre-crisis level. This meant that, when the option matured, the value of the stock had risen four-fold within six months.

September 1976. The Rheostat Fund buys into gold heavily at $109 per ounce and sells again on 30 January 1990 when it hits a high of $691 per ounce. It then buys similar amounts in September 1999 at $253 per ounce which has not been resold, begging the question: what do they know?

October 1987. The October Fund undertakes a massive shorting of stocks two days before Black Monday.

July 1990. Houston Fund shorts stocks on the Japanese Stock Exchange just in time for the crash which halved the value of the Nikkei.

August 1998. Avestan 2000 Fund shorts the rouble two days before the Russian government devalues the currency.

There are many more.

Naturally, lips are tight if not completely sealed when it comes to discussing the identity of the people behind the trades. All that it has been possible to glean so far is that a number of the funds are based in Liechtenstein and some are dotted in other tax havens around the world, including the Cayman Islands, the Seychelles and, closer to home, the Isle of Man.

The other thing that has become abundantly clear is that, despite these trades being made by a number of different funds— or, at any rate, a number of funds with different names—the pattern and the proficiency of these trades coupled with the limited points of origin strongly suggest that a small number of individuals have been behind them.

The key questions now remain.

Who are they and what is their next move?

[End]

MICHEL DUPUY'S ESTATE

Provence. Monday October 12th, 1600 hrs.

Ninety-four years old. A good age. Although a long time to live on your own. Michel was found by the local nurse who came every week to deliver his medicines and check up on him generally. He had been getting rather weak and confused, so it was likely that his time was going to come any time soon. A pulmonary embolism, the doctor reckoned. One of the better ways to go. A few moments of breathlessness, dizziness, then you black out and a couple of minutes later, that's that.

The nurse has made all the necessary telephone calls and the ambulance and Gerard, the *notaire publique,* arrived later the same day. It broke up an otherwise relaxing Saturday morning but he was back home later that morning, tidying up his garden in preparation for the winter.

Gerard sits at Michel's old kitchen table waiting for Docteur Frey from the university to arrive. He looks through the papers; he has the old man's will which seems to make no sense at all, and his bank statements, which are also nonsensical.

The key questions: why would an old widower with no surviving family leave his entire estate to the University of Avignon and why would a private bank in Liechtenstein be paying a regular monthly amount into his bank account? It wasn't small beer, either; it was enough to keep a family of four well fed and well-heeled. Michel had assiduously squirreled the money away, spending next to none of it and living, as far as Gerard can tell, on the output from his smallholding. As a consequence, Michel had died a cash-rich but asset-poor man living in a crumbling old farmhouse with rising damp, the plaster falling off the walls and the staircase riddled with some sort of rot which meant that it was no longer safe to venture upstairs.

There is hardly any wind today, but Gerard can still hear a chill whistling through the cracks in the walls and seething through and around the frames of the doors and windows. The panes are nearly black with dust, soot and cobwebs, so the kitchen is submerged in a grey gloom. It is as though the house died many years before and Michel has just been wandering vaguely around through the final years of his life. Still, Gerard never knew him personally; all Michel's legal affairs were undertaken by his predecessor, and he had been one of his longest clients, if not the most active active.

Gerard rises from the table and saunters down the hallway to the front door, listening to the sounds of the bereaved house: the faint clicks of the plumbing, the delicate knocks of windows and doors as they rock plaintively in the moving air, the delicate tapping of birds' feet on the tiles, the shuffling tendrils of a wisteria that has been allowed to run unchecked. The dust on the linoleum floor crunches under his feet and he can feel the smell of the death clinging to his clothes. Michel must have been dead for at least four of five days and one never forgets that smell; it's like a musk, and it lingers long afterwards.

Gerard notices the vines beyond the front door; they have yet to be harvested and the bunches of grapes are swinging pendulously in the wind. They should be about ready by now, but he's sure the local commune will have it under control; they must have been responsible for picking the last few years' crops. Michel certainly could not have done it by himself. But then again, he was known as being self-reliant to the point of reclusive. According to the nurse, he only ever ventured out on Sundays when he attended church, put flowers on his wife's grave and sat in the village café drinking Pastis. For the rest of the week he kept himself to himself and chased away any potential visitors.

And that was a strange feature of this man's deliberately unremarkable life. It wasn't that he was antisocial. Quite the opposite. He was moderately convivial, though no one would ever go so far as to call him gregarious. But anyone who was so ill-advised as to venture onto his land would find themselves ushered off, usually at the point of a shotgun. A few trespassers had complained to the police, but their view had always been that, if one was ill-mannered enough to traipse over another man's land uninvited, you should expect a frosty welcome. They would exchange the traditional Gallic shrugs and the police would promise the complainant that they would take the matter up with the owner, which they usually did albeit not very convincingly. Michel was in his right to protect his land and as long as he didn't actually shoot anybody, he was technically in his right to wave a gun at them. Other than that, Michel hadn't been a problem to the authorities; he was viewed as 'local colour'.

Gerard can hear the approach of a motor car; it whines and hiccups as it trips up and down the gears in order to negotiate the narrow lanes and tight bends. Before long, a hatchback pulls up to the farmhouse and a bemused looking man dressed in a sweater and jeans steps out. He strolls over towards Gerard, taking in the view of the farmhouse, the rolling hills and the limestone bluff beyond. He holds his hand out and introduces himself as Docteur Frey from the University of Avignon. The two men exchange business cards and, after the usual pleasantries, stroll off up the path toward the bluffs and past the small vineyard. Gerard had wanted to start the proceedings with some joke about how all this will be his someday, but decided against it; this is a serious matter and has to be pursued with the appropriate level of decorum.

'Monsieur le Brocq,' says the docteur, 'do you have the remotest idea why this man should want to bequeath his estate to the university? Not that we're ungrateful, of course.'

'I was rather hoping you could shed some light on that for me,' is his reply. Gerard raises his eyebrows in the hope of enlightenment. The university man shrugs.

'I've dug as far as I can into the university records looking for some reference to a Monsieur Dupuy and we have a few, but none have any connection with this address nor are they anywhere near as old as this gentleman.'

Gerard hums as he tries to find the correct form of words for his next question. 'Forgive me for prying and please tell me to mind my own business.' He holds up his hands in a defensive gesture. 'But was the university paying the former owner some sort of retainer?'

'A retainer?' Frey looks aghast. 'What on Earth for? The university is more geared to accepting donations rather than handing them out. Why do you ask?'

'I'm not sure I am in a position to answer at this stage.' Gerard hates asking leading questions that serve only to raise the suspicions of the other party; all it does is create frustration. But he is clutching at straws here. He veers off the path and steals a grape, chewing appreciatively. 'Hmm. Not bad. Should be ready about now.' He makes a mental note to inform the *commune*.

'You have my curiosity now, monsieur le Brocq.'

'I may have to bear with it for a while longer.' Gerard replies absent-mindedly; he is formulating the follow-up question. 'Again, please forgive the nature of my next question. Does the university use a private bank in Liechtenstein to manage disbursements of any kind?' The path has steepened now and the two men are looking at their feet; neither is wearing the correct shoes for this, but the estate is charming and the view from the top of the incline next to the bluff will most likely be rewarding.

Frey thinks before answering and then he stops, feet bent up against the side of the hill. 'Liechtenstein?' He wrinkles his face as he tries to conceive of any situation where the university would have resorted to such a measure. The frown clears with a shake of his head. 'I honestly wouldn't have thought so, no. After all, why would we do that? The university is a *de facto* charity, so it actually benefits us to ensure that all our transactions are conducted here in France.'

'That's what I thought.'

And that's the end of that line of enquiry.

'Liechtenstein.' Frey is feeling genuinely confused. 'Are you totally sure that the late Monsieur Dupuy had some connection with the place?'

'Absolutely.' Gerard turns to his walking companion. 'Can I tell you something in confidence?'

Docteur Frey nods.

'Good. You'll probably get to know all of this soon enough once the estate has been properly valued for tax. Not that you'll pay any, of course.' Gerard runs a finger around the collar of his shirt; he is going out on an unaccustomed limb. 'The late Monsieur Dupuy was receiving a monthly payment from a private bank in Liechtenstein of around two thousand five hundred euros. As far back as I can see, he has received this payment; it used to be a bit less but the amount has obviously grown with inflation and what have you. I don't yet know how far back the arrangement goes but, since he had no family or anyone else to whom he could have bequeathed his estate, and since he left it all to your establishment, I naturally thought that you might be connected with this in some way.' The docteur looks blank. 'It would certainly help to clear up one... conundrum.'

The docteur's expression has deepened to incomprehension. He shakes his head. 'I'll have a good look in the records as soon as I get back, of course. But, truly, I...' He gropes for the right words and then gives up altogether. The two men continue their walk in silence until they crest the rise. They turn and survey the smallholding. It is a delightful view; the hillside is peppered with small bushes and the occasional black pine, and below in the valley by the farmhouse sit the serried ranks of grapevines, their leaves yellowing and shimmering in the autumn breeze. To the right, a craggy face of limestone looms over them, pitted and grooved by the passage of time and the cruelty of the Provençal climate: white hot for half the year, blistering cold for three months and lashing rain for the rest of the time. A thorny bush of some kind stands before the bluff like a prisoner awaiting the firing squad. Gerard thinks he sees something next to, or behind, the bush and saunters over to have a closer look.

'Have you found something?' Frey asks casually. He is still gazing at the lovely view; the sun is glowing more golden as it sinks in the western sky over the village, the church steeple puncturing the skyline. He waits for a reply and is surprised when none is forthcoming. He turns to follow Gerard's direction and, for a moment, his confusion returns. The *notaire* has vanished.

'Monsieur le Brocq?' Still nothing. Frey ventures after him and sees what it was that first attracted the lawyer's attention. There is a cleft in the rock, big enough for a man to walk into. Frey follows, calling the lawyer's name as he goes. After a while, he hears a response in the darkness.

'It's okay. I'm down here!' Frey can just make out a faint glow ahead of him; le Brocq is obviously using his smartphone as a torch. 'I think I may have found something.' Frey gets his own phone out and illuminates the walls of the cave with a pale blue light. Before long he makes out the lawyer standing next to a large stack of thin wooden crates. One of the crates has been opened and le Brocq is examining its contents.

'What on Earth are those?'

'I think,' says the disembodied voice of the *notaire,* 'that we need to call the police.'

'Whatever for?'

'I'm not an expert, you understand,' murmurs Gerard, couching his words carefully. 'But I think this is a Kandinsky.'

JAKE GOLDING

The concierge of the hotel has been on the payroll of Special Branch for a dozen years now. It's not like he gets a retainer, but he is certainly on the receiving end of Her Majesty's largesse whenever he passes useful information their way. The last four days, he has been stacking up a reasonable amount of bankable goodwill as he has passed snippets and details at regular intervals about the target's schedule, who has been coming and going and who he has met with, where and when.

At three in the afternoon he had let it be known that the target was planning to check out in the next couple of hours.

At six-thirty he gives the tip-off that the entourage are on the move. He says to follow the black Merc, not the decoy Maybach. Jake asks for confirmation and, five minutes later, he gets it. There are no details of where they are heading but it's a good guess they'll be aiming west where the majority of likely airports and airfields are situated round London.

Jake has vehicles posted along two main routes out of town: one on the A4 before it merges into the elevated section of the M4, after which any stationary cars would be both suspicious to anyone wary of who they encounter and conspicuous in their illegality. There's nothing more embarrassing than being arrested by the uniformed mob in the middle of a covert operation. Two other vehicles—a car and a motorcycle—are stationed close to the more northerly A40 and another one in Chiswick. This last location is where the motorcycle is positioned; Jake knows DC Collins' abilities to weave through London traffic at speed, so placing him with easy access to the two main routes out of town enables the team to cover a large arc of West London.

The Maybach bursts out of the hotel's underground car park and Jake sends a car to follow it; not to do so would be suspicious. If they have gone to the trouble of organising a decoy car, they will be expecting an official retinue. It's not long before the tailing car reports that they are heading towards East London; probably City Airport in the Docklands. Jake and his team sit tight and, ten minutes later, a nondescript black Mercedes inches out of the car park and onto the streets of London.

This car does not want to draw attention to itself; it courteously obeys the speed limits and slows before every pedestrian crossing and traffic light. This is a car that, outwardly anyway, is in no particular hurry. There are two possible reasons for that: either they have left plenty of time for their scheduled flight; or the flight is not scheduled and can leave any time of the passenger's choosing.

'Five quid,' says Jake to the three others in the car. 'Five quid that they're heading for Northolt.' No one takes him up.

The sergeant on the back seat calls ahead to Northolt tower. 'Private plane being readied, boss. No flight plan filed yet.'

'Well, get them to press for one sharpish!'

The sergeant relays the message and is told that they will do everything they can to assist. The Mercedes threads its way through the streets and by the time it is heading north up Park Lane, Jake's unmet wager is confirmed. The motorcyclist is called to the A40, covering the route to Northolt; the other car is ordered to stay put just in case their target is playing games.

Jake's driver has done this sort of thing countless times before and he knows to keep a respectful distance. Slipping behind at traffic lights is always an effective ploy; if you appear too keen to jump the amber then you make an unwanted spectacle of yourself and your cover is blown. If you have a reasonably good idea where the target is heading, then you can afford to be a bit more relaxed.

Park Lane is flowing freely but Marble Arch is the usual bunfight and they briefly lose visual contact, but soon pick it up again down Bayswater Road, as expected. Jake's driver decides to follow by taking the road through Hyde Park, a route that follows parallel to the Mercedes. Embarrassingly, the police vehicle ends up crossing the Mercedes' path at the next set of traffic lights but Jake orders the driver to lead the way, which he does before looping around behind the target after a few blocks.

The road wends its tortuous way through streets lined by crumbling crescents of Edwardian terraces and finally up an insignificant side turning which takes them over a brutal iron bridge over railway lines and up a ramp onto the Westway, an elevated section of road. They are no more than twenty minutes from Northolt Aerodrome; it's a straight road from here: strewn with traffic lights and major intersections, but straight enough all the same.

The sergeant and motorcyclist, Collins, are in constant contact; he has picked up the target and is keeping close tabs on it, enabling Jake and his team to drop back a bit. Jake has called the other car in as well and directed it to arrive at Northolt at the same time as everybody else. It's a tall order—the traffic has subsided from the evening rush hour but the roads are far from deserted—and so he activates the blues and twos. So far, so all going according to plan.

Jake briefs his team in all vehicles to converge on the executive jet terminal at the aerodrome and to arrest all occupants of the Mercedes, once the main target has been clearly identified. He has already contacted Security at the terminal to ensure that the target's check-in is slowed down sufficiently for a formal identification to be made. After that: well, firearms have been issued for this operation so all personnel will be expected to resort to the appropriate SOP for an arrest of this nature. The driver of the Mercedes will be pulled over once his vehicle has left the aerodrome and he will be detained pending further investigations into his activities. Usually, the driver will turn out to be little more than a swanky limo hireling in which case they can let him go uncharged and with the minimum of paperwork.

The sergeant's mobile phone rings and he answers briskly. After a perfunctory conversation largely consisting of monosyllabic grunts, he clicks the phone off and announces the destination of the only jet requesting departure in the next three hours: St Gallen-Altenrhein, Switzerland. Jake asks if anybody has the first fucking idea where that might be and, after a bit of smartphone research, the sergeant informs him that it is on the south shores of Lake Constance towards the eastern edge of Switzerland.

'What does he want to go there for?'

The sergeant continues to fiddle with his phone. 'Liechtenstein?'

'Sorry?'

'Liechtenstein. It's the nearest airport to Liechtenstein.'

Within minutes the cars and the motorcycle brake to a shuddering halt in front of the terminal building, the Mercedes having pulled away. The eight men and women stream into the building to see the target and one other man strolling towards the departure gates. Jake directs four officers to give chase whilst he heads toward the check-in desks to get hold of Security. He doesn't at first notice the two men and one woman standing by the desks.

He slams at full pelt into one of the desks brandishing his warrant card. 'Police. I need to speak with the Head of Security.' One of the two men—a gentleman with white hair, a moustache and piercing blue eyes—walks over to him.

'Are you Head of Security here?'

'In a way, I suppose I am.'

'I'm sorry, sir, but if you are not—'

'Inspector Golding,' says the man, cutting him off. 'Can you please call your officers and order them to stand down.' There is a pause. 'Now.'

'Roger, what is this all about?' says the woman, American.

The white-haired man stands resolute and gives Jake a rather pathetic look as if to say, *I'm sorry, son, but this is how it's got to be.*

Jake does as asked; there are some cries of incredulity but all comply. The officers turn and lope back in the direction of their guvnor. The white-haired man puts his hand on Jake's shoulder and leads him to one side.

'Apologies for doing this, but we have different fish to fry here.'

'We have been working with agencies in other countries,' says Jake through clenched teeth. 'We, they, have spent eight years chasing this character down. Do you have any idea what he has been mixed up in?'

'I have a very good idea,' says the white-haired man. 'An even better one than you do, most probably. And we, myself and my colleagues, have been working with other countries' agencies, too.' He nods in the direction of the woman. 'We would like him to arrive at his destination safe and sound, where he will be taken good care of. In good time.'

'Do you know who this is?' Jake indicates the second man, standing with the woman at the desk.

'Yes, thank you. He is an associate of your target. Our target, also. But still someone of interest to our various agencies.'

The team return to Jake and clamour to know what has happened and why the operation has been called off. Jake waves them away and suggests they go and get a coffee; he'll get back to them. Ingham looks stern. 'No you won't, Inspector Golding. You won't tell them a damn thing. Do I make myself quite clear?'

'Unless I get authorisation from a superior to that effect, I will do what I like.'

The white-haired man clicks his fingers and the other man offers Jake a mobile phone. The voice on the end of the line settles the issue with one crisp sentence.

'Inspector, I want you to obey any and all orders you are given by this man. Is that clear?'

'Yes, sir.' Jake hands back the phone.

'I'm sorry to have spoiled your operation, Jake, but as I said, we have other fish to fry and I need this man to arrive where he wants to go. Thank you for your understanding.' He nods. 'Oh, by the way, you might want to let your colleague Inspector Campbell in Oxford know that Pahars, the other man she has been seeking in relation to the disappearance of a scientist, is the one boarding that jet with your target.' Jake's face flushes; how in God's name did he know any of *that*?

The white-haired man nods at his companions and the three of them walk out of the building, leaving Jake the onerous job of explaining to his team why all their work has been for nothing, without offering any explanation. As he walks over to them in the coffee bar, he has a flash of inspiration. He pulls out his phone and dials a number from his list of contacts.

'*Mit Bröcken, ja?*'

'Sven? It's Jake.'

'Jake? Great to hear you. How's things?'

'Look…' Jake turns away from his team, hiding the phone. 'Something's come up and I need your help.'

'I'll see what I can do. What's up?'

'There's a private jet on its way to St Gallen from Northolt, London.'

'I'm not in a position to interfere with it, Jake. My jurisdiction does not extend beyond the Zurich canton.'

'Okay, but do you have any friends who could keep an eye on the occupants of the jet?'

'I certainly have friends in the St Gallen *polizei*. I can give them a call. But why?'

Jake takes a deep breath; he's going to get it in the neck for this but he can't just let the bastard get off scot-free. 'One of the occupants is an Emirati Sheikh. Mohammad Zayed. He is wanted in a number of countries, including this one, for terrorist-related activities. Mostly funding terrorism.'

'Is he wanted in Switzerland, to your knowledge?' The question Jake was dreading.

'No, I don't believe so.' There is the hint of a sigh on the other end of the line. 'But anything you can do to keep him in your sights would be greatly appreciated. Is that okay?' The request sounds lame, apologetic.

'Funding of terrorism. That is something the authorities in Switzerland take very seriously indeed. Especially if money laundering is implicated.' Sven is getting into his stride here, Jake can sense it. 'I will call my colleagues in St Gallen. Leave this to me, my friend. I owe you a favour anyway, don't I?'

GEMMA BAYLIS

Grand Cayman. Wednesday October 14th, 1030am.

She arrived with about an hour to spare. London rang the High Commission and the call percolated its way to her. Get on the next flight to Cayman. There's one in fifty minutes. No, you don't have time to pack. Buy what you need when you get there.

She was met off her plane by a callow youth who introduced himself as Simon Something-or-other-posh and announced he worked for the Head of the Governor's office. She presented her identity card, declaring her to be the Information Officer a title that belies the fact that her role is the acquiring rather than the imparting of information. The first bit of information she notices she is in danger of imparting is that she is wearing a T-shirt, shorts and canvas shoes while he is dressed in suit and tie.

'How quickly can you get changed?'

'What's wrong with this?' he says, a little hurt.

'You need to look like a tourist. *I* need you to look like a tourist.'

'Right-o!' he says and runs off to his car. Gemma is not sure about his being her 'boyfriend' for the next couple of days. She is one of the first in the new generation of embassy workers: young, bright, lively and from Stevenage, with a degree in Sports Psychology from Loughborough. He obviously went to public school and has had a rod up his backside since the age of five. They're not exactly compatible. But all she needs is to create the image that they're an item. (Anything more than that will *not* be happening.)

Simon returns, still wearing his suit trousers but he has changed into a more casual polo shirt. They walk off toward a small jeep-like vehicle in the car park; the roof's down and the sides are open. Perfect transport for a tropical island.

'We spotted him when the flight arrived yesterday afternoon,' he tells her once the car is on the road. 'We've been keeping tabs on him ever since. He's been staying at a B&B in Hell.'

'Where?'

He smiles. 'Hell.' The name of that place always startles people; the idea that anyone would establish a town and call it that is certainly pretty amusing. 'It's a district of George Town on the cape. It's not the best part of town. He went to a local bar as soon as got settled into the B&B, stayed there long enough to have a drink and then went back to his room.'

'He didn't go anywhere else?'

'No, that was it. He left the B&B this morning at 8.45 and got a cab to the centre of town. He got out near Albert Panton Street, sat in a café for a bit and then went in to one of the offices there.

'Can you take me there now?'

'That's exactly what I was planning.'

'Anyone watching the place?'

'Yes, I managed to get one of the secretaries to—'

'Secretaries! Are you mad?'

'This isn't downtown Manhattan, you know. We all have to double up sometimes.' He looks hurt again. A small part of her wants to give him a big hug and make it all better. But only a small part.

The jeep arrives in the financial centre; the two of them leave it in a car park and walk a couple of blocks to where Jocelyn was waiting at an outside table behind a large latte. She is pretending to read a book. Gemma is quietly impressed at her resourcefulness. Simon and Gemma sit at an adjacent table and order two coffees. While they are looking at each other, Jocelyn speaks from behind her book.

'He's been in there for about ninety minutes now.' She half-whispers, covering her mouth with the book. 'That is, unless he's managed to slip out of the building by a back door.'

'Nice one, Joss,' Simon says, apparently to Gemma. She nods in appreciation.

'If you have no objection now you're here, I'll be getting back to the office.'

Simon thanks her for the help and says he'll make it up to her soon. Jocelyn tuts, gathers her things and wanders away.

The coffees arrive and Gemma and Simon sip them whilst scanning the two ends of the street as well as the entrance to the office block. The sun is broiling the upper storeys of the block but down at street level among the shadows, there is a cool and satisfying breeze.

Simon is the one who spots it. A taxi cruises from behind the buildings on the crossroads. A man wearing a black leather jacket sits in the back. Jocelyn was right; the target had used the back exit after all. Gemma directs Simon to follow the cab and report back to her as soon as it arrives at its destination. Under no circumstances is he to intervene in anything. Simon promises he will do no more than follow and observe, and dashes off to retrieve his car.

Gemma crosses the street and enters the office block. She looks up and down the list of companies behind the reception desk and finds the one she is looking for: second floor. The receptionist seems untroubled by the fact that she has not presented herself and carries on writing something in a book. Gemma takes the lift to the second floor and steps out. The door to the branch office of Eschen und Schaan is about halfway down: a nondescript wooden door with a louvre'd glass inset. She knocks and walks in.

She is expecting to be accosted by another receptionist or a secretary or someone but there is no one there and no sound other than the whirr of the air conditioning unit and the faint sounds of the traffic in the streets outside. The first office has a waiting area of sorts: cane and rattan armchairs, a low glass-topped coffee table, walls lined with filing cabinets, a large indoor plant (a Swiss-cheese plant, Gemma thinks). There is a door to one side which is closed. Everything seems orderly apart from the total absence of life.

She calls out to attract the attention of anyone through the door, but there is no response. She tries the door and it opens easily enough so she enters the main office: nice desk with a computer terminal, easy chair and sofa arrangement around yet another coffee table, impressive photo of Yosemite, and a body which has obviously been stabbed some time ago given the amount of blood soaking the carpet. The dead man is sitting in his office chair, head back, eyes and mouth wide open in a morbid expression of disapproval. Gemma sighs. On reflection, they should have picked McAllister up as soon as the newspaper article broke on Saturday, but the attitude on the island is not to intervene if no obvious laws have been broken.

Well, one has now! She gets her phone out and calls Simon.

'Where are you?'

'I'm heading in the direction of the airport.'

'Call the police and get them to close the airport to all traffic until we know he's not going there. McAllister's dead. Stabbed. I reckon he did it almost as soon as he arrived and he's been ferreting around for something ever since. Or just biding his time.'

That probably makes more sense; if he has a flight arranged off the island, he will want to board at the last possible moment to minimise the amount of time he spends hanging around where he can be picked up.

Gemma disconnects and calls the police from the office phone to report an incident at the Eschen und Schaan offices. No, she doesn't want to leave her name. She replaces the receiver and vacates the premises. It's not in her job description to be around to answer lots of police questions and fill in forms. Not right now, at any rate.

Outside, she hails a cab and heads off towards the airport. The driver wants to engage her in some conversation about the weather because she is obviously a tourist and doesn't get weather like this where she comes from. Little does he know, she's from Kingston and the weather is a poor topic of conversation unless there's a hurricane coming. Thankfully, it's only about ten minutes from the centre of town to the airport so she doesn't have to endure this happy-smileyness for too long.

She gets her phone out and dials. 'Simon? Any news?'

'I've spoken to the airport chief. Our man has just got on to a private flight. The jet is taxiing toward the runway as we speak.'

'Is there anything the police can do to stop it?'

'Take-off clearance has been denied by the tower, I've heard. But short of driving a vehicle out on the runway to block it, there's little we can do.'

'Find me a vehicle!' Simon snorts at the other end.

She runs through the terminal building waving her ID at anyone who tries to accost her and emerges at the other side to see the executive jet, engines limbering up at the end of the runway, the air boiling behind. A police officer runs up and demands to know what she is doing. She holds up her ID and he asks how he can help.

'Can you get the tower frequency on your walkie-talkie?' He tweaks the frequency knob and, before long, the tower conversation crackles into life.

'Kilo X-ray, this is George Town Tower. I say again: clearance to take-off is denied at this time. Please break off and return to the terminal building. Over.'

Nothing.

'Kilo X-ray, this is George Town Tower. Radio check. Over.'

Still nothing.

'What's he doing out there?' The police officer looks nonplussed. 'Can we get a car out there?' His expression has not changed. 'Now?' she presses.

The policeman returns his walkie-talkie to the correct frequency and calls up a colleague for a car to take him and one other passenger out to the jet. Gemma is sure that some sort of altercation is taking place on there; it's likely the passenger is keen to leave while the pilot wants to keep his licence and follow the instructions from the tower.

The police car turns up as requested and Gemma jumps in, ordering the driver to take her out to the jet. He looks aghast but her expression confirms that she is not joking. He revs the engine and sets off towards the plane. As soon as the car is on the main taxiway, some decision is reached on board the jet. It lurches forward and starts to accelerate. Gemma has a rush of blood to the head and instructs the driver to drive the car across the runway and into the path of the jet.

'Not on your nelly!' The driver lifts his foot from the accelerator pedal and steers the car over to the side. The jet tears down the airstrip, its front undercarriage lifting from the concrete. Gemma is past screaming with rage; she winds down the window of the car and stares with deep, deep frustration after the diminishing plane. She calls Simon.

'What happened?'

'The pilot claimed the passenger was threatening him with a knife. The tower wanted to let him go but the police tried to insist that clearance was denied. I think the guys on the plane saw you driving out there. I don't know, maybe they thought you were going to block the runway or something daft.'

'So did the tower give clearance or not?'

'Not! The pilot just said, "He's going to kill me, I must go now." And that was it.'

'Any flight plan filed?'

'Havana.'

Roger won't like this.

PROFESSOR DAN SIBLEY

Oxford. Tuesday October 13th, 0230 hrs.

His arm hurts. It's dark. There are machines beeping. They keep him awake. He can't sleep.

Whenever he feels himself slipping away, either his arm begins to throb again—the painkillers they've given him don't seem to be working or they've not given him a big enough dose—or a patient in an adjacent ward starts to howl in pain. He then starts awake again. He lies there staring at the polystyrene ceiling tiles, side-lit by a ghostly fluorescent light through the glass pane over the top of his door. All round the ward there are little points of light: the red machine blips. Thankfully, none of them are connected to him. There's more light: in ceiling fittings (fire alarms?), on electric sockets in the walls, light switches, emergency cord. The place is a galaxy of coloured stars.

He's feeling a bit pissed off. All he did was graze his arm and bash his knee when he fell off that bike. The casualty nurse did a bloody good job patching him up with gauze and bandages, and the police and the hospital were careful to ensure that every inch of him was scanned and X-rayed; no bones were broken. The most significant damage was to his dignity and that will recover in time. So why did they feel the need to keep him in 'for observation'?

The only observation that's going on round here is the observation of the constellations of tiny LED lights. He could easily have gone home and slept it all off there. Unless, of course, the police felt that he was still in danger of being abducted. That's always a possibility. But wouldn't it be cheaper to put him up at home with a police guard rather than in a private ward at the John Radcliffe?

So, he muses, who were they? Is this what happened to Nick? Or Otto? And where were Mikhail and the Sheikh? Why was it so hard to get hold of anybody? It all seems unreal, like the whole thing is unravelling around him and he can't see how this might have happened or even if he was actually involved.

Still, the whole project has been running with minimal contribution from himself. Maybe that was the intention: to squeeze him and Otto out of the way and to let them take over it all. They've had numerous Board meetings which he has chaired and all the members have paid due deference to his chairmanship. The meetings have all followed the proscribed agendas and reported to the investors as set out in the Articles and Memoranda of Association, and it's fair to say that he has acquitted himself of his fiduciary duties as Chair of the Board and that he's been nicely rewarded for it, thank you very much.

But he has been sensing the growing disquiet that the Board meetings are tableaux for his and Otto's indulgence and that the real decisions are being made by Mikhail and Ludis and the rest of the cabal. They know how to operate the apparatus; they don't need him or Otto. It begs the question: what are they doing with it?

More importantly: what's this going to mean when it all comes down to him? The buck notionally stops with the CEO and that's Otto. But Otto has gone AWOL. So the next best person to lay the blame on will be the Chairman. What blame can they attach? Has the cosy little clique done anything reprehensible? And how much of it is going to stick to him?

He sighs.

It's over. It's all over, isn't it? This marvellous adventure. Science is so often about peeking over the fence and glimpsing what might lie beyond; here, for the first time, they had vaulted the fence and roamed around freely in the glorious, forbidden lands. There had been no let or hindrance; they had just done it. More than that, they had discovered more about the nature of the universe than had been thought possible in this lifetime.

Thanks to Otto's genius—and his clumsiness—they had been able to glimpse with greater clarity the mechanisms of the origins of the universe. More work was needed, but it now appeared that the notion of a 'Big Bang' was based on flawed assumptions about the nature of space-time. Dan and Otto were closer than ever before to showing how existence began. It was like, to paraphrase the John Gillespie Magee poem, holding out a hand and touching the face of God. It was beautiful, it was simple, and it was breathtaking.

The question now is whether they'll ever get the chance to publish. Most of the data is there but there are still some pieces of the jigsaw missing. The others had all but completely taken over the equipment. And now, Otto was missing. *Missing*.

Ludo had to be at the bottom of this. Otto had really got under the man's skin, he could tell. And that Russian friend of his doesn't look the type to brook any dissent. He is worried about his former student and he doesn't know what he can do about it.

On reflection, Otto was probably right and they would have been better off if they had done things his way, and he hadn't gone off on his own. It was pride on his part that had got them in this mess: he wanted to be seen to be the breadwinner; he wanted to be seen to be shepherding the next generation of genius into the light. Dan realises that perhaps that is all that's left for him to do. The great discoveries are almost behind and beyond him; it takes the fresh eyes of the young and unencumbered to see past the clutter and declare the future. No old man ever queried the Emperor's clothes.

Is it over? He asks himself the question again. And in how many ways? They were so close to unwrapping the greatest conundrum in physics, in all of science. How did we get here? Did God bring forth the universe from nothing or did he design it so that it would renew and regenerate itself endlessly? Does our notion of the infinite now move from distance or time to sheer repetition? He snorts half-derisively: infinity as a number! There's something to get philosophers' knickers in a twist for all eternity.

The policeman standing guard peers through the window at the side of the door and sees him lying awake. He whispers through to ask if he needs anything. Dan replies that he is fine, thank you.

He wouldn't mind seeing that ward sister again, but for less than professional reasons. But maybe that's over as well.

Here he is: a fifty-seven-year-old hippie-*manqué* having been merely nine years old during the Summer of Love. He has acquired the affectations of hippiedom: the long hair, the suggestion of a beard, the jeans and the homespun waistcoats and jumpers. He enjoys the countercultural statement it projects. Here he is at the very heart of the academic establishment— one of the greatest universities in the world—and he can only serve it by breaking as many conventions as he can, by pushing the boundaries of acceptable knowledge even if the pushing is within the constraints of good scientific practice. He once boasted that to be an original thinker, you have to be able to prepare a good hamburger using the most sacred of cows.

In his early days in Oxford, he had been incandescent with original thought, insight and creativity. But now, he is the sounding board for others' incandescence, the silver screen on whom their brilliance is projected. He challenges and mentors and nurtures as best he can, but he feels his power waning, the edge blunting.

Now he has been the midwife to one of the most radical mistakes in human evolution which was instead supposed to completely change the way we view the universe and our ability to understand our place in it.

But that opportunity, fleeting as it was, is slipping from his grasp, and he knows he will never get it back. He turns over on to his side in a physical attempt to shrug off this terrible thought and inadvertently rests on his damaged limb. The pain shoots up his arm and he arches back, in acute agony. He grimaces and wonders which is worse: the pain of injury or the pain of loss and the knowledge of the nearly-was.

PROF DAN SIBLEY

Oxford. Wednesday October 14th, 1000hrs.

Dan enters the interview room. One of the officers asks if he would like a cup of coffee and politely invites him to sit down. The room is bare, save for a table with four chairs—two either side—and a dual cassette recorder sitting between the interviewers and the interviewees. This morning it will be just him and the two of them.

He snatches the opportunity to quickly inspect them: the older of the two women is dressed austerely, in a beige trouser suit; she has straight shoulder-length hair which gives her a rather forbidding air not helped by the scary glasses. The younger one is more petite: girly, even. She wears a brown and beige floral dress and flat shoes. She clearly doesn't want to appear forbidding or authoritarian; if this was going to be a good cop, bad cop routine, Dan knows which is going to be which.

He sits at the table and manoeuvres his coffee in front of him, so that his good arm has ready access to it. It's going to be counter-intuitive as he's injured his writing arm and his left seems to serve little function other than to provide balance and perform certain sanitary functions.

'Thank you very much for agreeing to come in this morning, Professor Sibley,' says the forbidding one. 'Before we start, let me introduce myself. I am DI Campbell and this is DS Hayes. I would like to state that you are not under arrest and you may leave at any point during this interview. However, we are investigating the alleged abduction of Dr Oliver Parsons from his home on Sunday night and we are interviewing colleagues of his in order to best decide which lines of enquiry to pursue.'

She stops talking for the moment so Dan nods. She begins again. 'For the purposes of obtaining an accurate record of this interview, we are intending to make a recording. Do you have any objection?'

'Do I have a choice?' Dan asks, for no other reason that pure mischief.

'Yes, you do,' she says curtly. 'If you wish to object, we can conduct the interview without the tape.'

Dan smiles and tries to outwardly relax. 'Forgive me. I'm always at my most contrary on a Wednesday. Of course I don't mind you taping this. Although I'm surprised you're still using cassettes, for God's sake! Do you have an eight-track cartridge player in your car as well?' Dan snorts with hilarity at the thought of it; the two policewomen maintain a graceful and benign silence: one didn't find it funny, the other didn't know what an eight-track cartridge player actually was.

'Thank you, Professor,' purrs DI Campbell. 'Getting back to the matter of Dr Parsons' disappearance. When was the last time you saw him?'

'That's easy. Saturday evening at the King's Head. We were having a pint together.'

'Were you alone?'

'We were alone most of the time, but we were joined towards the end by one of the technicians that we work with.'

'May I ask his name?'

'Ludis Pahars. He's Latvian, I believe.' The two women exchange a quick knowing glance.

'Do you have an address for this man?'

'I don't, but I'm pretty sure the management at the Exatron will. That's where he worked, on the Penrose Science Park. Do you know it?'

DS Hayes nods. 'What was said at this meeting in the King's Head?'

'Do you mean before Ludo arrived or after?'

Campbell has drawn breath to clarify her question, but before she can begin, the interview room door bursts open and two men march in unexpectedly and very much unannounced. The older, white-haired man shows the Inspector some ID and declaims that the interview with Professor Sibley is to cease forthwith at the orders of her Chief Constable and that the professor is to be removed from Oxford Police Station immediately.

The younger of the two men, a stocky type with only the merest suggestion of a neck, grabs Dan by his injured arm, causing him to wince and let out an expletive. 'I can fucking walk without your help, thank you!' The man lets go and Dan rubs his sore arm accusingly.

The older man speaks. 'Professor, I would be grateful if you would accompany us. We have some matters we need to straighten out with you. These are serious issues that impact on national security.'

'Do I have a choice?' says Dan, with less mischief this time..

The man laughs. 'No.'

OTTO PARSONS AND DAN SIBLEY

Oxford. Saturday October 10th, 2145hrs.

The beer slopped and pitched in the glasses as Otto pounded the table. Heads flicked round in their direction as he could hold his rage back no more.

'You have not only opened Pandora's box, but you have let the very worst people possible play with the contents, you stupid fucking arrogant cunt!'

'Gentlemen, if you don't mind…' The landlord called out in a mollifying tone.

'Look, Otto, the project was—'

'The project was doing fine.'

'No, it fucking wasn't! We were down to our last firing. After that, there was no more money.'

'I knew that. I *knew* that! That's why Nick and his team—'

'Nick and his team! Give me fucking strength, Otto!' Dan banged the table this time. 'You seriously think that the revenues from a couple of TV programmes were going to—'

'"Going to"? They fucking *were*! The money was just starting to come in. *Pour* in, for God's sake.'

'Look!' The landlord's tone was firmer. 'I've asked you nicely once already.'

'Who gave you the fucking right to go to Dubai and get that *fucking* jihadi involved?' Otto's face was burning red like a coal. 'And who gave him the unilateral fucking right to go and vote his arms-dealing mafia friend on to the board, as well?'

'Hugo at the Exatron.'

'Hugo is a stupid arsehole. He gets all his money from government grants, university bursaries. And his airhead fucking girlfriend who nurtures the only two corporate clients they have. Asking Hugo for advice is like asking the iceberg to skipper the fucking Titanic!' Otto had tried to keep his voice low, but the emotion welled up behind his chest and ejected the words like cannonballs. The landlord made blustery motions toward the phone as some of the other guests tutted audibly. They could tut all they liked as far as Otto was concerned; they were just collateral damage, caught in the verbal crossfire. The pavement was outside and they could always exercise their disapproval and fuck off and join it.

'The Sheikh is not a jihadi.'

'Oh, read the papers, Dan! Why do you think he brought that nasty little Russian shit on board? Do you think it was Hands Across The Oceans? Brotherly fucking love?' Dan started to speak but Otto cut him off without his uttering a single word. 'You just didn't stop to think what the implications might have been, did you?'

'I think you're being unrea—'

'"Unreasonable"?' Otto's mouth had dried and he angrily threw some beer into it. Even wiping the froth from his lips was an act of rage-fuelled defiance. 'Are you too fucking old or too fucking *stupid* to use Google? Haven't you looked these guys up? Dan, they've been in cahoots for nearly twenty years. The mafia supply the guns and the rocket-propelled grenades and the landmines and the ornate swords to behead people with. And the Sheikh gives them to his friends who want us all to return to the twelfth century.'

'We needed to keep the project going!' Dan hissed back like a cobra summoning up sufficient bile to rear upwards.

'That would have been great if we had been the ones running the project. Think, Dan, think! What have we achieved since you came back from Dubai four years ago?'

'Quite a lot, actually. We now know more about the origins of the universe and the rigid linearity of—'

'And I look forward to reading the published papers once they are peer-reviewed!' said Otto sarcastically. 'Oh! But they aren't going to be, are they? Because Sheikh Yerskyscraper and

Count Kalashnikov aren't going to give you enough time on the machine to finish gathering sufficient data.' Dan tried to speak again. 'That, and the fact that we can't publish how we got the fucking data in the first place. I haven't been able to get anywhere near the Exatron since Ludis got his grubby hands on it, and Hugo isn't going to give a shit because he's actually solvent for the first time ever.'

'Are you quite fucking finished?' spat Dan. 'I don't like being lectured about solvency by some petulant post-grad. This would never have got off the ground if it—'

'"Petulant post-grad"? Is that what it comes down to? The Great Professor Shitley presides over all he sees and all he sees is great? You ineffably arrogant, self-righteous cunt! Anyway, if it had just been about the money, I could have got it for you. All you had to do was come to me. I had the solution as it was.'

'That does it!' said the landlord. 'Either you two pipe down or I'm calling the police.'

'You call *that* a solution?' This time it was Dan with the reddening face; there was a fleck of foam at the corner of his mouth and his eyes were wide with inexpressible rage. 'I call it Drawing Unwanted Attention to Myself. How long is it before the press pick up on what you've been doing? Ah, yes. They already have! And, talking of fucking stupid, you had the inestimable stupidity of buying the tickets in the next street. Talk about crapping on your own doorstep! It's been all I could do to keep them from sorting you out. Do you understand what I'm saying?' By this time, Dan was so enraged that he was bellowing at Otto, oblivious of who could hear, what they could hear and what they could make of it. From this point on, there was no outside world; there was only Otto and Dan.

The landlord spoke into the phone. 'Look, I just want them to go away. My staff aren't bouncers and the language is upsetting people. Especially the—' The landlord tried his best to sound both urgent and insistent, mindful that demands on police time would be high on a Saturday evening.

'I don't recall being besieged by the press, Dan. In fact, my life has been fairly peaceful since I've been effectively kicked out of my own company and had access to the Exatron withdrawn.'

'Hugo was worried you were going to—'

'Well, Hugo is an arsehole. I was never going to jeopardise or sabotage anything. But I'm thinking of changing my mind and I might try practising on Hugo's fucking skull!'

'Yes, please,' said the landlord. 'Before it gets violent.'

By now, Otto was weeping. The futility of his position had sunk in and he began to realise that all he could do was lash out impotently. He was no longer part of the project, the process, anything. Just as it seemed that things couldn't get any worse for him, they were joined by a tall man in a leather jacket with a close-cropped head of hair and a stubbled chin. The man glided over to their table and sat in an empty chair without waiting for an invitation. He looked as angry as the other two but spoke more softly.

'So, Otto. You are unhappy…'

'Go fuck yourself, Ludis.'

'I'd advise you to mind your manners when you are addressing me' was the soft, crisp reply.

'As I recall,' said Otto, 'you were one of my employees. So I'd prefer it if you kept your advice to yourself.'

The landlord was now pleading into the receiver. 'Just get here as quick as you can. They're upsetting some of the girls here. It's not right.'

Ludis leaned closer to Otto. '"Were". Past tense. I'm not your fucking employee now, Otto, so I don't have to do what you say anymore. Any more than I did when you were my boss. Or thought you were.' He turned to Dan. 'You know what the purpose of the project is now, don't you, Professor?' Ludis edged towards Dan who was still red-faced and trembling with rage. He grabbed the front of his large woollen sweater, pulling it towards him like udders. 'And you know what's at stake now, don't you?' he said, half-whispering, half-hissing.

Dan did his best to not move. He tried to be stony-faced but the emotion throbbed behind his eyes and in the blood vessels of his cheeks. Instead of looking impassive and unmoved, he seemed even more scared. 'Sooner or later, you are going to get found out. And when you do—'

'Nothing! Nothing, Dan! That's what's going to happen.' Ludis flicked Dan's face with both his forefingers and slumped back in his seat. 'We've changed nothing. Nothing that wouldn't have happened, anyway. So what are they going to find out?' Dan sat still and glowered at Ludis. Behind him, the street pulsed with blue light.

Otto jumped from his seat. 'Listen to me, you Latvian shit!'

'Oh yes, hard boy! I'm all fucking ears!'

'If you don't—' Otto couldn't finish. Two black-clad policemen swept into the bar, wearing Kevlar security vests bulging with pockets and utility belts. They bound over to the three men's table. The sergeant instructed everyone to be quiet and ordered Otto, Dan and Ludis outside. His constable touched Otto on the elbow to encourage him to rise and leave quietly, and all of them moved toward the door. Ludis leered at Otto and began to laugh mockingly. 'You're so fucked' he mouthed.

'No, I'm not—' Otto started to reply and the sergeant cut him off.

'Keep it down, son, or I'll have to arrest you. We can talk about this outside.' And then, if it wasn't clear enough already… 'You're causing a disturbance and you're being asked to leave.'

The five of them disgorged onto the pavement, into the crisp autumn night air and the golden backdrop of Oxford's oldest buildings. In that historic setting, their names were taken, beside the flashing police van. The sergeant pursed his lips and summoned the remains of his patience. 'Now. All of you. Clear off. I don't care where, but if I hear that any of you are involved in anything else this evening you're spending the rest of the weekend in the cells. Is that clear?' The three nodded.

Dan motioned to Otto to follow him. 'Come on. We can talk about this somewhere less public.'

Ludis shrugged. 'You two lovers run off and talk all you fucking want. It'll change nothing now.'

'Really?' Otto sneered. 'I know what will change everything.' Dan tried to shut him up; he knew what Otto was going to say next and it couldn't be unsaid. Not to Ludis. 'You can only operate freely if I don't tell everyone what the apparatus actually does.'

Ludis' eyes widened in momentary terror; he knew Otto meant it. 'What?'

'I'll make you fucking famous!' Otto was still weeping. 'Everyone will know your fucking name, Ludis. And everyone will know what you have been doing.' Dan grabbed Otto's shoulders and manhandled him into the shadows of Holywell Street. Ludis watched them retreat into the darkness and then reached into his leather jacket for his phone.

'Hey. *Privet. U nas yest' problema.*'

PART FOUR
CHILTERN HALL

IN CHILTERN HALL

The Chilterns. Thursday October 15th, 0830hrs.

What a lovely place. And a beautiful morning.

The sun is starting to dip toward the line of trees hugging the ridge on the opposite side of the valley; the autumn colours are shimmering and burning exuberantly as a light breeze catches the dry leaves. Below him Dan can see the small river sparkling as it tumbles gently along its course; it will soon be lost from view in the darkening valley. A red kite patrols the sky above him, keening and mewling. It describes its long, slow arc towards the trees beyond.

Chiltern Hall, the old house, is sited well, atop a small knoll at the meeting of two valleys and, beyond it, the luscious, smooth mounds of the Chilterns rising above. The house itself is glowing in the afternoon sun, its old red bricks glowing proudly and, from this vantage point, he can take in a serene view of the valleys, two country roads and a sweep of landscape peppered with sheep, swans and low hedges.

Dan sits on a bench trying to gather his thoughts and make sense of the last few days. A week ago everything had been whatever it was that passed for normal. Normal, like this view; the cars that tootle along the little country road below, the walkers in the valley. They are having normal days; they don't look up and see him sitting there, they don't feel his isolation. The gentleman standing just behind him is Dan's reminder of the fact that he is cut off from all that he can see below. He has been told he is free to walk around the grounds for as long as he is not needed, but he must be accompanied at all times. It is 'for his safety', of course. Dan knows this is a euphemism for avoiding harm coming to him should he inadvertently wander beyond the perimeter of the estate. The gentleman, Dan is informed, has no name. And he doesn't speak.

He looks up. The sky is so blue; the kind of blue that glorifies autumn when the air is clean again after the sweat and heat of the summer months, when the trees stand with dark, exhausted leaves wishing for the shade they can only give others. The blue is deep, almost indigo; it clashes magnificently with the golden leaf cover. Dan inhales deeply, savouring the musty smell. It takes him back to when he was a small boy running, jumping and playing in the crumbly and dusty fallen leaves under the line of horse chestnuts along the edge of his school playing field.

A throat clears behind him; they are ready for him again and he and his mute attendant return to the house. They enter the imposing oak-clad hallway in the centre of which is a low table with a splendid flower display. He is met by a white-haired gentleman and two of his 'associates'. The white-haired man is dressed in a sober, grey suit—Prince of Wales check, or something like it—although he has forsaken his tie; maybe he feels that it would lend a more casual air to the forthcoming proceedings, or maybe it was just chafing his neck.

His 'associates'—one woman, one man—are also dressed as though for a business meeting; she is wearing a black and cream coloured trouser suit and he is in a dark blue suit, white shirt and dark grey tie with the hint of some diagonal stripes. He is doing his level best to appear unnoticeable and this serves merely to communicate that he is the junior member of this reception committee. Dan is dressed in his large, pilled grey sweater and jeans; while his hosts are well-groomed, he is unshaven, sporting his familiar greying ponytail and feeling as out of place as he probably looks.

The white-haired man directs them all to a corridor off the main hallway and Dan's mute friend leads the way. They troop to a remote corner at the back of the building, away from the rays of the autumn sun, and into a small room furnished with four relatively easy chairs and a low coffee table in the middle. As soon as they have entered, the silent attendant departs without a word. Dan looks around; whoever decorated this room had no gift for it. The walls are painted an insipid, jaundiced institution green, and feeble attempts have been made to make the room feel cosy with the addition of a mirror and some formless country prints; the kind you can stare at for hours and still have no idea what the subject might have been. Hunting? Some bucolic types out walking along a path with a tree and a cloud? It was academic, anyway; Dan is sure he is going to get little opportunity to study them in any sort of detail.

He is invited to sit in one of the four chairs and is offered a coffee— black, no sugar—which he accepts, along with some biscuits. In turn, the others all take their coffees and biscuits and the white-haired man leans forward in his seat and fixes Dan with his piercing eyes, as though he is about to attempt to hypnotise him. He takes a sudden intake of breath and flops back in his chair.

'Professor Sibley,' he announces, without shifting his gaze.

Dan nods; he can't speak as he has a mouthful of chocolate biscuit.

'Allow me to introduce myself and my colleagues here. My name is Ingham and I work for the Government.' He leaves a pause here, as though expecting a familiar question, but it's not forthcoming. 'I am not the police, therefore you are not under caution, nor are you here to be charged with any offence. You have' he stresses 'been placed under a form of arrest whereby you are required to remain under our care until such time as we deem it appropriate for your release. Therefore you are *not* at liberty, nor are you entitled to any of the statutory rights accorded citizens who have been arrested by the police.' Ingham pauses again to make sure that his words have been received and understood. Dan stares back at him; he is sure the opening remarks have not ended. They haven't.

'You are not entitled to legal assistance. You may not contact anyone outside this facility until such time as we deem it appropriate to do so. Everything you say in this room or in this facility as a whole will be recorded. We will decide what action will be taken pursuant to the recordings of any and all evidence you give us in response to our questions. Should we decide that you have indeed breached any laws then these may be passed to the police for further investigation. Is this clear to you?'

Dan nods.

'Good. I would then like to introduce the other people in this room. This is Doctor Janet Hooper.'

'What are you a doctor of?' Dan reaches out to shake her hand; she withholds hers. He withdraws.

'Politics, philosophy and economics.'

'You're American.' She gives him a thin, condescending smile and Dan moves his gaze to the last member of his tribunal.

'And this,' Ingham continues indicating the precisely dressed younger man 'is Robert Coates. He's an American, too.'

'Why so few Brits?'

'There are more outside this room,' says Ingham with a reassuring grin.

'Why so many Yanks?'

Ingham takes a deep breath to maintain his composure. 'We are being assisted by our American colleagues who have expressed a close interest in this case.' He turns to Hooper and gives her an imperceptibly brief scowl, 'We have decided to pool both knowledge and resources. Now, before we start, you may have noticed that I rejoice in a northern accent. This is because I am from Yorkshire. In that regard, I am congeniality personified unless you try and pass off any bullshit as fact. If you do try, then my sense of humour is likely to fail and this encounter will take on an entirely different tone. And please don't think that you are smarter than us, British or American, as we can all spot bullshit ten minutes before any of it even starts to come out of your mouth. Clear?'

Dan nods.

'Good. Let's get cracking, then.' Ingham places four photographs in front of Dan. 'Recognise any of them?' Dan scrutinises the images and looks up at Ingham.

'That one,' he says, pointing at a grainy photo of a man in *dishdasha*, 'is Sheikh Mohammed Zayed.' He points at the photo of a man climbing into a car. 'This is Ludis Pahars and that one is Mikhail Rebrov.' He nods at the photo of a small man in dark glasses drinking some sort of cocktail.

'And that one?' Ingham points at the fourth photo.

'I don't know his name, but I have seen him at the Exatron with Ludis a couple of times. We were never formally introduced.'

'Do you know anything about him at all?'

'Afraid not, no.'

'Very well, then' Ingham returns his attention to the other photos. 'How did you come to know the three people you have identified in these pictures?'

'"Know" would be putting it strongly, but I was first introduced to the Sheikh back in 2011. At least, that's when I first made contact with his associates.'

'And how was that contact established?'

'By phone, initially.' Dan thinks he's being helpful.

'I mean, how did you come to be calling his office at all?' Ingham's teeth are lightly clenched.

'The director at the Exatron, Hugo Patterson, put me in contact with the CEO of a private equity house with bases in both London and the Emirates. They have a network of high net-worth individuals who were looking for somewhere to invest their money.'

'And what was the *name* of this private equity house?' Dan will have no opportunity to misinterpret him this time.

'Manama Equity Group. Their office is in—'

'Thank you. I think we can find it for ourselves. Was he the only taker, or were there others who expressed an interest in investing in your enterprise?'

'One other person reportedly showed an interest.'

'"Reportedly"?'

'MEG only told us about him. We were never given his name.'

'So the Sheikh was the first person you made contact with in Dubai?'

'Yes. He was originally proposed to us as a local sponsor. As our means of gaining access either to the angel networks or the Dubai Stock Exchange in advance of a pre-IPO. At first, contact was made by telephone conference and then, when we outlined the proposition, he quickly arranged a face-to-face meeting.'

Ingham presses his finger to his ear; he is obviously being briefed by someone in another room, possibly behind that mirror over there. It dawns on Dan that the room is probably the centre of a lot of people's attention.

'Tell us about the proposition.'

'Okay' Dan begins. 'We were developing a means of neutralising the effects of Earth's gravity in a confined field.'

'Forgive me...' Ingham wrinkles his nose. 'I'm having a problem trying to work out why that would be an exciting investment opportunity.'

'Do you know how much it costs to get anything into low-Earth orbit?' Ingham shakes his head. 'Anywhere between five and fifty thousand dollars per kilo of payload. This means conducting low-gravity scientific research using equipment that weighs about twenty kilos would cost you up to one million dollars before you even start to perform the experiments. One million dollars!

'So, Otto Parsons had determined that a field we called "the X-ray cage" or just "the cage" placed directly in the path of a very high energy beam would result in the gravitational effects we desired. We set up Oxford Gravity to undercut all the space agencies and grab their business for ourselves. Think how much could be saved in terms of resources and material, let alone the cost, if the experiments could be conducted safely here on terra firma.'

Ingham tries to look impressed but cannot summon up the sincerity. Dan continues.

'The Sheikh listened to our business plan and was impressed enough to offer an investment that we couldn't turn down.'

'Very interesting, Professor.' Ingham turns to Hooper. 'Does that sound right to you?' Janet offers a wry smile and Ingham returns to face Dan with a dark look. 'Remember what I said about bullshit, Professor?'

'It isn't bullshit. It's absolutely true!' Dan looks genuinely hurt.

'It may be factual, Professor, but it's not actually *true*, is it? When did His Highness the Sheikh finally part with his investment?'

Dan moves to speak but is stopped in his tracks by Janet Hooper's intervention. 'According to our information, it wasn't until the middle of 2013. That's about eighteen months after your first meeting. Isn't that correct, Professor?'

Dan is feeling sheepish and is trying his best not to show it.

Ingham picks up. 'By which time you'd found something out about your little anti-gravity machine, hadn't you?'

Dan tries to regain some of his composure by moving the topic to ground on which he can feel relatively secure. 'Well, first of all, it wasn't an anti-gravity machine *per se*. What it did was to neut—'

'This isn't one of your physics tutorials!' barks Hooper. Ingham holds his hands up to try and calm the situation.

'Thank you, Janet.' He's going to get merry hell for using her first name in a debriefing. 'Professor Sibley, we aren't terribly interested in the minutiae of your research. But we are interested in its implications. Tell me about when you found out that it didn't work as a gravity neutraliser.'

'We discovered that the first time we switched it on,' is the reply. 'We placed a target payload within the field and activated the beam. It's a very high energy X-ray beam using exa-electron volts of energy which we can split so that the photons are entangled…' Dan looks up to see six blank eyes staring at him. He takes a breath and starts again. 'The beam is split in a way that it is synchronised. It forms a sort of tube around… Look, it's a big deal if you know anything about quantum mechanics.'

'I'd be grateful if you'd try and keep it simple for us, Professor.' Ingham smiles, reassuringly. 'We do have scientific chaps who I am sure will want to quiz you about the theory of the thing after we have finished with you.' Dan looks disturbed; yet more questions to answer. 'So tell us: what happened?'

'The payload vanished into thin air. Except, it didn't. Not really.' Dan has their attention again. 'We did some analysis of the data we'd collected from the X-ray cage. We discovered that the payload had effectively stopped moving relative to a fixed point in space.'

'What fixed point?' Coates is wishing he hadn't spoken before the words have even left his mouth, but it's too late now and a sharp sideways glance from Hooper tells him he is going to be in trouble for that. His orders were to keep his eyes and ears open and his mouth shut.

'Do you know the speed we are travelling now?' Dan says to the room.

'Right now I like to think I'm stationary,' says Ingham. 'I'm certainly going no further forward at any rate.' He feels slightly pleased with himself for his witty sarcasm, but no one else has acknowledged it.

'You're stationary relative to that coffee table, Mr Ingham.' Dan leans forward in his chair and picks up his cup in preparation for a gulp of what must be, by now, cold coffee. 'But the planet rotates at about a thousand miles per hour. Relative to the Sun, we are moving at about sixty thousand miles per hour, and relative to the centre of our galaxy, we are moving at about five hundred thousand miles per hour. What happened was that the payload ended up in a position that was, relative to us, moving away at about half a million miles an hour.'

Silence. The three look at the physicist with one question in their minds. Ingham, the Yorkshireman, asks it. 'So what?'

Dan runs his tongue over his lips as he attempts to scale the unconquered heights of answering this in layman's terms.

'So…' He begins slowly, as though taking a run up to a high bar. 'It means we stumbled on something central to how our universe functions. Something quite unexpected.' All six eyebrows are raised in anticipation. 'It means that the expansion of the universe is not bound in with time. It means that time is affected by *local* anomalies, not universal ones.'

'Well, thank heavens for that!' Ingham declares. 'Can we get on with the important answers before I develop a headache?'

Dan raises his voice, trying the hammer the obvious into their little skulls. 'It means that we can create a highly localised field and anything within that field can be repositioned along the space-time continuum.' No one is breathing. 'Oh, for fuck's sake!' Dan bellows. We invented a fucking time machine! Okay?'

'Glad you finally brought that up,' dead-panned Hooper.

'We'd wanted to build something where gravity could be compensated, but instead we built something where you could reposition a payload back in time.'

'How easy was it to travel in time?' says Hooper.

'You don't "travel" in time. The act of repositioning yourself in time is not even instantaneous. It's simultaneous. You're here one moment and there without any time, as we would measure it, elapsing.'

'Yes,' says Hooper. 'But if you are currently moving through space at five hundred thousand miles per hour, it must be hard to "reposition" yourself at a place and time of your choosing.'

'It took a bit of careful code writing, but it wasn't too hard. We needed to rediffuse the entangled beam around the cage such that it was positioned where we wanted it to be.'

'And when exactly did you make this astounding discovery?' Ingham is back on the subject and he is keen not to let go of it again.

'The repositioning? About March 2012.'

'So, about fourteen months before Sheikh Zayed committed his investment,' Ingham confirms.

'That's correct.'

'So why the gap?'

'I'm sorry?' Dan cocks his head to one side like a spaniel.

Ingham shuffles in his seat. 'Professor, you have a working time machine—'

'I do wish you wouldn't call it that.'

'What would you prefer?' Ingham is making an effort to keep his temper.

'I don't know. But don't call it that! It's melodramatic!' Dan shrugs dismissively.

'What I am hoping to elicit,' Ingham continues, 'is how you hoped to keep the experiments running when you had no funding.' He opens a file containing a sheaf of papers. 'According to my information, your grace-and-favour usage of the facilities at the Exatron, thanks to the university imprimatur, had long since expired and you were having to fund the use of the Exatron through the monies invested in Oxford Gravity by Illumina Innovations. Is that correct?' Dan nods. 'And how much did each use of the Exatron cost?'

'About four thousand five hundred pounds.'

'Not exactly chicken feed, is it, Professor? How much funding did Illumina Innovations grant you to get Oxford Gravity off the ground?'

'A quarter of a million.'

'So, by my reckoning, Oxford Gravity was going to run out of cash after using the facility about fifty-odd times. Is that correct?' Dan nods again. 'At what rate were you using the facility? How frequently?'

'About once a week.'

'So, you'd have run out of goes on the fairground waltzer within a matter of months of you going cap-in-hand to your Sheikh. And given he didn't put his hand in his pocket for quite some time, what happened next?'

'What happened next' Dan replies 'is Otto's friend, Nick Young.' Janet Hooper manages to keep her face set like granite. 'Otto thought we could finance the research using the revenues generated by the *Witness: History* series. I wasn't convinced, but when I saw the footage, I thought we could really make a go of it.'

'But?'

'But there's a major lag involved in getting the revenues and, by the time the programme was being broadcast, a lot of time had passed and we were down to our last few "goes on the fairground waltzer" as you put it so elegantly, Mr Ingham.' Dan allows himself the brief luxury of acting intellectually superior. 'Fortunately, we still had some last funds left before the project had to be canned and, in the interim, the Sheikh saw what we had done and came up with the full amount.'

'Which was?' asks Hooper.

'Ten million. It's what we needed to expand the project so we could continue with to generate revenues through the TV productions and still carry on with the research.'

'Excuse me...' Coates interjects. He is keen not to incur further displeasure. 'What research were you hoping to conduct?' Hooper, to Coates' relief, nods appreciatively. Good question.

Dan looks astonished at the sheer stupidity of the question and then realises that he alone in this room has known what the research meant to science. 'We've unravelled a lot of the conundrums that exist about space-time. We now know that time is largely uni-vectoral.' Blank looks again. 'You can only reposition yourself back in time because there is no Forward. It is like a red carpet being rolled out on a pavement. Where the carpet has been, it will always be; where the carpet has yet to be, it isn't there and it doesn't exist. We also discovered something else.' Dan drops his gaze to the floor, then looks up. 'Look, can I have some more coffee?'

Ingham decides this is a good time for a break and waves at the unseen souls behind the mirror to fetch more coffee.

During the hiatus, he and Hooper step outside the room with Coates lurking close by.

'What do you think?' he asks her, half-whispering.

'I think he is just about telling us everything we want to know,' she replies softly and carefully. 'Apart from the start, he's not left very much out. If anything, it's hard to get him to shut up if the topic veers too close to his beloved physics!'

'I agree,' says Ingham. 'How does his story agree with what Young told you in between beatings?'

'Roger, can we keep this civil?' Ingham holds his expression neutral despite his feeling pleased with himself at his dig. 'Young's account does bear fairly close correlation. Obviously he isn't a physics don so his account is not quite so... nuanced.'

'Quite, quite.'

'Young told us that he and his friend the history lecturer Barnaby Watts used the cage about twelve times in the course of filming the four programmes. He also told us about the speed at which the cage would get them to where they were going and back. He said it was disorienting.'

'One other thing he told us,' says Coates, 'is that the further back in time you want to go, the more energy is needed from the X-ray beam. So about the furthest back they could get was one hundred and fifty years. The late 1860s. Which is why the Oxford History Unit could do a programme on Jack The Ripper but not one on, say, the American Civil War.'

Ingham is appearing to pay attention but is really considering how such a device might be used in his stock-in-trade and who else in his profession would want to use it for their ends. It is crystal clear to him that the specifications for the apparatus have to remain within the UK. At all costs. He is also considering how Dr Hooper might be thinking the same thing as well. Suddenly, the existence of Professor Sibley's research project is causing him some ill-ease. He looks at his watch, wonders briefly at the futility of doing so in the light of what he has just heard and then decides to accept what the watch is telling him: it is half past eleven.

He and the two Americans return to the room where Sibley is sipping his coffee and nibbling the contents of the replenished biscuit tray. He looks up at him imploringly. 'How long are we going to keep going?'

'This, Professor,' Ingham declares, 'is what we in the trade call a debrief. We try to maintain the momentum of the information being dispensed so that we minimise the risk of anything being missed.' Or anything being concealed. 'So, in answer to your question, as long as it takes. Or as long as I can keep going. Or as long as it amuses me.'

Ingham sits down and the two Americans follow his lead. 'You were saying?'

Dan looks bemused. 'What was I saying?'

Ingham puts his finger to his ear and recites. '"We also discovered something else". What was that "something else", Professor?'

'There is no Grandfather Paradox.'

'I'm delighted,' Ingham coos sarcastically. 'Now would you have the slightest aversion to spelling out what the bloody hell that actually means?'

'You can't change the past. You can observe it. You can *exploit* it. But you can't change it.' Dan takes a moment to compose his next few words. 'As far as we can tell, because you can't prove a negative, any attempt to alter the course of history is doomed to failure, if not impossible. At least using this equipment.'

Hooper cuts in. 'Surely that can't be right.'

'That's what we would have thought,' agrees Dan. 'You go back in time, kill your grandfather and your existence is instantly erased as is every instance of anything he might have influenced, caused to happen, and so on and so forth. But every attempt we have made—'

'You've *tried?*' Hooper is almost open-mouthed in astonishment and exasperation. 'You actually *tried* to change history? Wasn't that reckless? Stupid, even?'

'That guy in the photo…' Dan points in the vague direction of Ingham's file, now returned to his briefcase. 'He was Russian. I'm sure of it. He was pretty thick with Rebrov, anyway. He and Rebrov wanted to eliminate Hitler before he could kill however many Russians he killed in World War Two. He used the cage to go back about a dozen times and each time, something would go wrong. The gun would jam, the round would misfire, the target would move at the last moment, something else would move into shot. Whatever he tried, the Russian couldn't kill him.'

Ingham and Hooper are speechless.

'When did the Russian arrive on the scene?' says Coates.

'About six months after the Sheikh committed to the investment. And that's when things started to get out of control. Mine and Otto's control, anyway.'

'We'd like to hear more about that time, if you please, Professor.' Ingham restores control over the debriefing. The Americans are supposed to be observers only; Hooper and her director had given their assurance that this part of the operation would be led by the British.

'About three months after the Sheikh invested, we had a Board meeting with him in London. Swanky hotel, wall-to-wall vintage champagne and bling. Otto and myself are about to outline our revised Business Plan to him and his Non-Execs when he calmly interrupts the proceedings and says he wants to introduce us to a new VP Commercial Operations. Before I could explain that commercial roles fell within Otto's purview as CEO, the door opens and Rebrov strolls in, flanked by a Swiss guy called Bernhard Croce, Ludis Pahars and the Russian. Have you any idea what he was called, by the way?'

'Yes, thank you,' says Ingham. 'Please continue.'

'We are told that Rebrov is going to be in charge of day-to-day affairs and that we are to take our instructions from him. We were upset by this turn of events and Otto reminded the Sheikh of his commitments to the scientific programme we had set out. The Sheikh calmly told Otto that the scientific programme would remain unaffected because his new apparatchiks were going to ensure a healthy revenue stream that would pay for the research.'

Ingham nods. 'And did he?'

'At first, yes. As time went on, though, time allocated to the scientific research was squeezed more and more by Rebrov's "commercial" exploits and both Otto and myself were concerned that we'd be squeezed out altogether. It became obvious that our days with the project were numbered when it transpired that Pahars was some Latvian technical genius who had been quietly learning how to operate the apparatus all by himself and had been relinking the workstations so that the Exatron could be set up and run by one person instead of the original design's six or seven.

'This meant he could come and go and do what he liked with wild abandon and with no recourse to anyone else. Least of all me and Otto.'

'What about the other clients of the Exatron? Surely they had something to say about their facility being monopolised by you?'

'Patterson is a grasping little shit. I expect they paid him off quietly. So he's got a back pocket stuffed with cash and the facility is running at a healthy profit. He's still making just enough time, but only just enough, for the university-funded research. But, any sign of them running overtime and the plug gets pulled sharpish. Meanwhile, Rebrov and his boys are doing whatever it is they are doing.'

'Did you ever determine what that was?' says Ingham leaning forward in his chair. The key to a thorough debrief is for those questions to which you know the answer to predominate so that the questions to which you don't know the answer can be included without rousing any suspicion or interest in your actual line of interrogation. This is one where the answer has so far eluded him.

'No. Not really.'

'Not really?'

THE OCTOBER MEN

'I did overhear something about six months after Rebrov got his hooks into the project. Something about the October Fund and the account in Liechtenstein.'

'And what did you draw from that?'

'That they were using the apparatus to fix or fiddle financial transactions of some sort.'

"Fix or fiddle", "of some sort". Ingham senses that Sibley is flannelling. 'What sort of financial transactions?'

'I can't be sure.' *Yes, he is being deliberately evasive.*

'Well, indulge me, then.' Ingham gives him a thin smile. 'Speculate.'

'If I can't be sure, any speculation I make is liable to be wide of the mark.' *Now he's being defensive. We're getting somewhere.*

'Try me!' Ingham pushes. Dan hesitates for a moment and then shakes his head. 'Come on, Professor. I know and you know that Rebrov and his cronies were using the Exatron for nefarious purposes. And it wasn't just to shoot Hitler. What do you think they were doing?'

'I already said. Financial transactions!' His voice is raised and cracking slightly; Ingham is sure he has hit on something that Sibley thinks might be a problem for him personally and Ingham knows what that might be. Time to offer some insights of his own.

'Very well. Let me try and offer some more specific responses.' Dan starts to look distinctly uncomfortable. 'You know that Rebrov and his cronies were using the apparatus to exploit a number of financial markets. Yes?' Dan says nothing. 'You are reticent about giving more fulsome answers to questions on this topic because you are worried that you might be accused of some sort of complicity in perpetrating a fraud of literally historic scale.' Ingham pauses to give Dan time to respond. Still nothing. 'Am I close?'

After a time, Dan replies, 'I told you—'

'You told me what you hoped I would be happy to swallow. Unfortunately, we already know about the funds in Liechtenstein and the Caymans and the Seychelles and even

290

North Korea; we even know how much the gang has amassed and my busy colleagues at the Treasury are in the process of sequestrating the lot of it. Now…' He leans forward accusingly. 'You mentioned the word "Liechtenstein" unbidden. I want to know *why*.'

'Did I?'

Ingham presses his finger to his ear. 'Your precise words were "something about the October Fund and the account in Liechtenstein". Ring any bells?'

'Okay, but that's all I knew. Honestly!' *When a man feels the need to say "honestly", then he is surely lying.*

'Professor Sibley. You probably don't know what happened to Nick Young at the hands of my enthusiastic American friends here. They were extremely displeased when some titchy little British film crew barged into their backyard and told them it was the Secret Service working in collusion with the Ku Klux Klan who assassinated JFK and not Lee Harvey Oswald. It was Young, I believe, who told them. Well, Dr Hooper, why don't you tell the Professor here what Mr Young told you?'

Janet Hooper squirms in her seat; she is not accustomed to reporting the outcome of her interrogations to parties other than her Director. Ingham nods at her encouragingly. The Director has already sanctioned this, so she clears her throat.

'Mr Young eventually told us about the time— I mean, the cage at the Exatron and how he and Dr Parsons and Dr Watts had used it to observe actual events in Dealey Plaza. They had made three trips to the United States in order to undertake their clandestine filming and their interviews. Once to Dallas, once to Montgomery, Alabama and once to Washington DC.

'It also transpired that he and his companions had made other unauthorised visits to the USA, to locations including Hawaii and New Mexico. We indicated our concern to Mr Young that he should have gained access to the country so easily and without completing the necessary entry procedures.'

'It might have been a bit difficult for him to get a visa if he hadn't been born,' Dan cuts in sarcastically.

'We take infractions of our immigration regulations very seriously,' purrs Hooper .

'Oh, do fuck off!'

Ingham steps in. 'Could we please conduct this in a civilised manner?'

Hooper nods her head and continues. 'We are concerned, as will all our alliance partners, that this apparatus represents a threat to all our nations' security. The fact that you can reposition someone or something in any location or time of your choosing renders our existing security precautions obsolete.'

'You can't use the Exatron to beam into someone's office today,' says Dan. 'That would mean being in two places at the same time.'

'But isn't that possible in quantum mechanics?' says Coates. Dan does a double-take at the audacity of the question, coming as it does from a spook.

'Only in probabilistic terms. And it's one thing to be an electron or a photon with quantum entanglement, but quite a different prospect for a whole human being.' He shakes his head. 'No, it's just not possible.'

Ingham breaks in again. 'Anyway, the issue remains that we do not know to what extent you aided Rebrov and his cohorts in the pursuit of their trillions.' Dan looks astounded at the mention of the word 'trillions'. 'Now, I know you're not telling me the whole truth because you have been giving yourself away and I am trained to notice these things.' Ingham's expression becomes more threatening. 'Either you just tell me or I turn you over to these people's more energetic methods of enquiry. Do I make myself clear?' Dan nods nervously. 'Now tell me *exactly* what you know or knew about their activities and your part in them.'

Dan clears his throat. 'I worked out what was going on about a month after Rebrov joined the team. He and Bernhard spent a lot of time at the Exatron and Ludis had also been lingering about the place like a bad smell. Bernhard had returned from one of his trips and removed his overcoat. A document fell out of a pocket dated October 1929. It all clicked into place then and I knew that you could use the cage to make a fortune with almost no outlay up-front.'

'Did you know about the artworks?' says Ingham.

'Yes. I did. I saw them loading paintings into vans outside the Exatron one evening a year or so ago. I couldn't see what they were but when I read about that van Gogh selling for God knows how much, I put two and two together.'

Hooper scowls at him. 'And you did nothing about it?'

'Like what? Rebrov's Russian friend wasn't a nice person. There had been a disappearance at the Exatron shortly after he turned up on the scene. One of the technicians. I'm certain he was involved, if not directly responsible. Also, he was the one they kept sending back to try and wipe Hitler out of history. He looked pretty serious and I didn't have any immediate plans for disappearing myself.'

'You could have reported your concerns to the authorities,' says Hooper.

Dan laughs hollowly. 'Can you see that happening? I bumble into Oxford Police Station and tell them there's a bunch of crooks using insider trading to manipulate the financial markets in the nineteen-twenties? I'd be rolling around inside a rubber room by now if I'd done that!'

Hooper nods; it's a fair point.

'So what did you do?' says Ingham.

'Me? Personally? Nothing.' Dan takes a sip of coffee. 'Actually, it was Otto who tried to do something. I suppose it was his actions that unravelled the whole show.'

'Why? What was it he tried to do?' Ingham can feel the sudden change in the direction of this enquiry; there is something that none of them had seen, that none of them had taken into consideration so far.

'He tried to outbid them for the use of the Exatron.' Dan looks at the three people sat around the coffee table and considers the ridiculousness of the situation. It looks like some sort of Christian Society meeting: earnest people in business dress (except for him) all sitting around a table laden with non-alcoholic beverages and biscuits. Everyone is leaning forward in their chairs as though they are about to break into prayer. 'He used the equipment to buy lottery tickets. Winning ones. I believe he did quite well.'

'He did,' says Ingham.

'About a year ago, he managed to persuade one of the other technicians to help him run the cage overnight and finished off the next morning with more money than he had the imagination to spend.'

'Why didn't he spend it?' says Hooper.

'Because Patterson was not only being bribed by Rebrov, he was being threatened as well. I think the disappearance of the technician had spooked him. Justifiably so. What do the French say? "*Pour encourager les autres*"?'

Ingham turns to Hooper. 'I gather from the police in Oxford that parts of a body had been discovered around the city about three months before Mr Parsons won his lottery jackpots.'

'So Rebrov could have shown Patterson the body,' says Hooper.

Ingham nods. 'Or parts of it. So, Otto couldn't regain control of the Exatron and his scientific programme is being squeezed more and more out of the picture. Is that right? What does he try and do then?'

'He tried to threaten Patterson. But that was like banging his head against a rubber wall. Patterson denied everything and challenged Otto to get proof. Otto didn't have proof, did he? Otto was getting more and more morose about the whole thing and I arranged to meet him at the King's Head last Saturday to talk it all over.'

'What were you hoping to achieve at this meeting?' says Hooper.

'To be honest, I wasn't sure. I think I had sort of planned to tell him to get over it, basically. He had more money than he would ever need. He could effectively go off and do whatever he wanted. Scientific research, a life of leisure, whatever. He could live off the income for the rest of his life.' Dan shakes his head as if he is trying somehow to change the outcome. 'But it was like he was mortally offended by the others. He wanted them to *lose*. He wanted to regain the upper hand, both morally and in terms of getting control of the Exatron. That way he would be able to ensure that it was used for more palatably scientific endeavour.'

'What went wrong?' says Ingham.

'Two things, basically. Firstly, we both rather lost our tempers. I don't see myself being welcomed back to the King's Head any time soon. The landlord felt constrained to call the police. Secondly, Patterson had told Pahars about Otto's threats to him and he showed up unexpectedly. Otto was so incensed that he threatened to spill the beans about the Exatron and what they were doing in it. I knew right there and then Otto had crossed a line. Ludis had a face like fucking thunder. It was the one threat that could really upset their plans and he stupidly made it in front of the wrong man. The next day, I gather, Otto disappeared.'

'Do you have any idea what became of Otto?' says Hooper.

'No. No idea at all. All I know is that I haven't been able to get hold of him for the last week and his mobile is coming up as "number unobtainable". It's as though he doesn't exist. Do you have any idea?'

'I'm afraid we do.' Ingham's hands are clenched together, his shoulders hunched. 'We think that Ludis Pahars and the Russian abducted him and used the Exatron to… lose him. Some time in the past.'

'So he could still be alive?' Dan's face brightens.

Ingham looks dolefully at the physicist and shakes his head. 'We are fairly certain he was killed in his house in Jericho. His body was then moved.'

'So was it the same gang who were trying to abduct me outside the laboratories two days ago?' Ingham shakes his head again. *This is getting rather embarrassing.* Hooper wriggles in her chair again. 'We know all about that. It's turned out to be something of a misunderstanding.' Ingham glances across at Hooper who nods vigorously. 'We have been able to clear that matter up satisfactorily.'

'We think that the gang dispersed,' says Hooper. 'Shortly after Mr Parsons' abduction. They may have been concerned that he might have already notified someone about their activities.'

Ingham gives a satisfied smile. 'We have been tracking both Pahars and the Russian for the past few days and it seems as though they have been tying up loose ends and trying to liquidate their various assets. Our various agencies have managed to prevent most of that from happening.' Ingham spares a brief thought for the unfortunate Gordon McAllister.

'What about the other three?' says Dan asks. 'The Sheikh, Rebrov and Croce?'

'That's not your concern,' snaps Ingham.

'And me?'

'That is outside of my control.' Ingham sits back in his chair and regards the Professor coldly. 'As far as we can tell, you have not actively collaborated with these criminals but you have done nothing to impede them, either. You were instrumental in bringing them on board and you were negligent in not having conducted sufficiently thorough due diligence on, particularly, Sheikh Zayed. Had you done so, you would have discovered that he has a number of connections that have troubled global security for some ten years or more. His presence alone in this project has rendered you a suspect.'

'What makes you think his clandestine activities would have come to light in any due diligence I conducted? What makes you think I didn't conduct any due diligence on him?'

'Because, if you Google the Sheikh's name, it's surprising what dirt pops up.' Ingham flashes Dan a scowl and continues. 'The addition of Mikhail Rebrov in the mix has meant that you have a suspected sponsor of terrorism colluding with a known Russian gangster. And suddenly your precious anti-gravity project takes on a different hue. Wouldn't you say, Professor?' Dan notices Ingham only calls him "Professor" when he's being patronising. He nods.

'So, you can understand that what happens to you next will be decided by minds far superior to my own. I will however notify the powers-that-be that you have cooperated fully with our investigations and that you have given your commitment to do so in the future.' Ingham raises his eyebrows at Dan, interrogatively. Dan nods again, this time sullen. 'I am sure that will mitigate your situation.

'In the meantime, myself and my colleagues here would like to thank you for your time and would like to invite you stay here at our lovely estate for a few more days whilst we iron out any last details. In addition, a number of my more scientifically minded colleagues would like a comprehensive tutorial on your recent work. I am sure that you will be happy with that, won't you?' Dan nods, although he fully understands that Ingham's "invitation" is nothing of the sort. Ingham waves at the mirror and, a moment later, Dan's wordless handler enters the room and leads him away.

COLOGNY

Geneva. Friday October 16th, 0830hrs.

This area is select. It has *chemins*, not *rues*, and they curl around and between mansions, not houses. This is an area of the city where those who have worked hard for their rewards can enjoy them in an atmosphere of calm and good order. The streets are regularly swept so that the residents may marvel at the scintillating autumn colours of the manicured trees, but will never find their leaves underfoot.

From the upper floors of one's mansion, one can revel in the splendour of the sunlight playing on the slopes of the Jura mountains across the lake; and one can be delighted as they turn golden to ochre and then magenta in the fade of the dying day. This is a place where ambition, nature and fulfilment converge; where you can just *be*.

The noise and the rush of the city are left far behind and, yes, one might hear the occasional horn blaring on the Route de Thonon, the odd police siren even, but they seem distant and unworldly in this delightful place. Unlike the less salubrious districts of the city, there is next to no trouble here in Cologny. In fact, the only time the police ever venture round these sweeping *chemins* is in response to concerned citizens reporting the sighting of potentially undesirable people seen snooping or loitering.

When they do come, the police never use their sirens and they only come one car at a time. So, if more than one police car should arrive in the district and they should have their sirens wailing, then it would be unprecedented. It would also be unprecedented for them to use two of the cars to block either end of the *chemin*. This, of course, does not happen. Cologny is not that sort of place.

The residents are all pre-eminent in their chosen professions and are, by their very nature, serious people who shun frivolity or prurience. They will always shy away from any act that might seem intrusive or rude. The fact that four police officers have strode up the gravel path of the mansion opposite and have commenced beating on the front door is not something with which one would concern oneself. Nor the officers with guns drawn and trained on the front door giving cover.

The owner and occupier of the property is well known and much liked in the community here in Cologny. He has a cheery disposition and is recognisable thanks to his trademark trilby or Panama hats. Many years past, he has been called upon to play *Père Noël* because, with his beard and his happy smile, he so resembles him. He is smiling now, even with his hands in the air. He is going to be decent about this.

The police officers are making him lie face down on the ground and they are approaching him cautiously, their pistols trained on the back of his head. Now they are taking his hands and putting them behind his back so they can apply the handcuffs. He is putting up no resistance even though his wife and grown-up daughter are remonstrating with them. He is being phlegmatic about the whole thing, while the women are making a rather unseemly fuss about all this.

He is driven away, and the police cars have cleared and the *chemin* reverts to being unobstructed. All that's left behind are the retreating howls of the sirens and the sobs of the two women on the front lawn. Naturally, of course, it is all some terrible mistake and order and calm will return to Cologny once more.

In Cologny, one's privacy is a given; this is not a community for gossip-mongers or the curious. One does not linger on street corners discussing the goings-on in other people's houses. After all, no one wants to be the subject of this tittle-tattle? It would be unpleasant. Monsieur Croce is an upstanding member of the community and it is beholden on all of us to pay him the same respect he would undoubtedly pay us in turn.

What a spectacle. Cologny has not seen the like of it before and, while no one wanted to be seen to be watching, this was something that was happening on one's own doorstep and it is important to be *au fait* with local matters. Naturally, it is all some terrible mistake.

KNIGHTSBRIDGE

London. Friday 16th, 0945hrs.

'Police! We require access to Flat 41, please.'

It is not a request; it is to be complied with immediately. The security guard at the desk of Hyde Park Tower is in no doubt of what he must do.

He is also in a state of confusion; his instructions are to advise residents when visitors present themselves to the lobby of the apartment block. He has a good idea what the answer is going to be, but he has to ask anyway. 'Should I ring and let him know you're coming?'

'No! You will step away from your desk.'

'We would like the security key to the apartment.' Another policeman: this one has a firearm. In fact, half of them have firearms. He hands over the key. The first policeman grabs him by one shoulder and leads him outside into a van. Something about answering some questions. The others head for the fourth floor: some using the staircase, others using the elevators.

They are outside Flat 41 in less than a minute, let themselves in using the security key; brute force would not have worked on these reinforced doors. Four officers stride into the apartment and four more guard the door. Rebrov is sitting on a low, white leather settee watching television and half staring at the view of the park through the floor-to-ceiling windows.

'Mikhail Illych Rebrov?' Rebrov nods at the officer holding up a warrant card and a piece of official-looking paper. 'I am Detective Chief Inspector Jake Golding and you are under arrest for fraud and conspiracy to murder. You do not have to say anything, but it may harm your defence if you do not mention when questioned something which you later rely on in court. Anything you do say may be given in evidence. Do you understand?'

'Conspiracy to murder who exactly?' Rebrov acts cool.

Jake glances at his notes. 'Eliot Langer of Mecox Pond Road, Tuckahoe, Long Island on Monday the 12th by two men. Pavel Shirokov and Valery Melnik.'

Rebrov sighs and crosses his legs. 'I don't know these men.' He tries to blot out the vision of his apartment being dismantled by countless police uniforms.

'Well, they say they know you,' says Jake, triumphantly. 'More than that, New York ballistics matched the bullet that killed Langer to the gun carried by Melnik and the shot was recorded on the voicemail of someone at the auctioneers you had met with a day earlier.'

'That's all circumstantial, surely?' Rebrov's smile hangs on his face like a veil.

'We'll just have to see about that.' Jake beckons two policemen over. 'Also, I imagine you're going to have to explain it to the Americans. You're likely to be extradited from here before the day's out.'

'They can't extradite me. I'm a Russian citizen.' The officers grab him, wrench his arms behind his back and cuff his wrists. Two more officers join them, front and behind, and they march him off to the waiting vehicles.

Jake beckons the other officers inside. 'Right, then. Tear the place apart.'

WHITEHALL

London. Friday October 16th, 1130hrs.

Ingham is irritated. He dislikes being summoned at short notice and he especially dislikes it if it involves having to trek into Central London. The behest of ministers notwithstanding.

As usual, he is a good half-hour early and uses the spare time profitably by sitting in his office reviewing the draft report he has already sent to his superior. It is with some satisfaction that he notes the report contains no spelling or grammatical errors, which seem to be the things that most exercise his section head. The content will pass muster, too, leaving aside its unique qualities. And all this undertaken after midnight. Ingham has had three hours sleep and is feeling his age; he hopes that adrenaline will keep him going through the next couple of hours. After that, he can reward himself with a good nap somewhere: one of the local hotels probably. He doubts he is going to be allowed too far from the office for the next few days.

He glances at his watch: another ten minutes before it is due to start. He methodically gathers up all his papers, checks he has a functioning pen in his inside pocket and quietly begins the slow walk up two floors. He is certain that proceedings would have commenced without him but he doesn't like being late for his allotted slot and endeavours to be five minutes early. The worst they can do is ask him to wait outside; more likely, they will carry on talking as if he is not there and only acknowledge him once their topic has been exhausted.

Sure enough, as he approaches the room, he can hear men's voices from within. He knocks discreetly and enters without waiting further. Section and the minister are deep in conference about something and Ingham is not interested enough to try and work out what it might be. He takes a vacant armchair.

303

Before long, the two men both turn to him and greet him curtly. Section turns to the minister once again.

'Minister, you have read the interim executive summary on the Exatron affair, I believe. Ingham has come from Chiltern Hall to answer any immediate questions you might have.'

'Thank you, Section.' The minister pauses, then addresses Ingham. 'This is the most extraordinary matter. How do you see this affecting our national security?'

Ingham clears his throat. 'I would like to be able to give you a definitive answer, Minister, but I'm afraid I can't.'

'Why not?'

'There are too many directions this thing could go off in.'

'Can you give some examples?'

'Certainly, Minister. Firstly, there is our relationship with our allies. They now know that our scientists have developed this machine, and they will want to know how it works. Probably with a view to building one of their own. The Americans are upset that UK citizens have been able to pop in and out of their country undetected and are rightly concerned that we might have been making more excursions than we have admitted. Naturally, they would like to enjoy the same facility.'

'And they have told you this themselves, Ingham?'

'Not in so many words, Minister. But if the boot were on the other foot, this is how I would feel. With one difference. If the Americans had the equipment, I wouldn't expect them to share it with us. But, because we have it, they will expect us to share it with them. In short, since it is inconceivable that we should allow this technology out of the UK, our Special Relationship with the US is about to deteriorate.'

'What other directions do you foresee?'

'There are two major residual pieces of evidence that will need to be disposed of carefully. These include the art collection the French police uncovered earlier this week. It is undoubtedly connected to the fraud perpetrated by the gang, given its unexpected bequest to Avignon University.

'More sensitive is the outstanding fund from the group's main activities. From what little we have managed to piece together with the help of the police in the Caymans and in Switzerland, the combined value of the funds is in excess of seven point three trillion US dollars. This is roughly equivalent to the public expenditure of this country for the next six years. We can't keep it all. We know that a large proportion of it arises from frauds committed in the United States at various times. We are going to have to share it.

'We could use the funds as a bargaining chip of sorts. The Americans are likely to try and coerce us using economic means. Lines of credit, exchange controls, that sort of thing. Just like they did when the UK refused to commit men to the Vietnam War. But I would advise in the strongest possible terms that the potential spread of this technology is contained with all means at our disposal.

'There then comes the thorny issue of what to do with the money once it has been apportioned to the various interested parties. Firstly, most of it is tied up in equities and commodities and some gilts. If everyone were to liquidate their assets all in one go it would have a material effect on the individual stocks and the markets more generally. Secondly, too many people would have to know about this and would start asking questions. Returning to my point that it is inconceivable that this technology should be allowed to leave these shores, this then risks compromising the secrecy we must maintain in regard to this affair.

'It is as though Pandora's box has been opened, but, before the ills of the world have had time to escape, some of the nastier elements have crawled in there with them.'

Ingham stops and waits for the next prompt from either the Minister or Section. They are taking a few moments to absorb what they have just heard. Section breaks the silence.

'What are the chances we could continue to use the equipment unilaterally?'

Ingham rubs his chin for a moment. 'I'm sure we could get away with it for a while, especially if we ensure that we don't use it on our Special Friends. If they find out there's no telling what they will do. Nuke us, probably.' This doesn't get a laugh. 'We might use it to spy on recent activities of some of our less desirable antagonists. But, sooner or later, we will get caught and, each time we use it, we risk giving away the specifications of the equipment, and then it will be a free-for-all.'

'But will it matter?' says the minister. 'If you can't change history with this machine, if you can only observe it, then who's to say that there aren't hundreds of Exatron cages whizzing around already? All our allies and our enemies might be photographing our most intimate secrets from the last 150 years. And it has changed nothing. We are where we are.'

Both Section and Ingham are stunned, and try not to glance at each other in front of the politician. 'I might say, Minister,' says Section, slowly, 'that is a very interesting philosophical point. And probably factually correct.' He pauses; there is something in his argument that contains peril. 'But, from a Defence point of view, I would consider it reckless if we made this information available to third parties.'

'Why? Tim Berners-Lee made the internet freely available to the planet. In doing so he revolutionised and democratised the flow and ownership of information. We know that the invention of this machine has not altered our situation. We sit here today and whatever we do, whatever decision we reach today, will not affect that. So why don't we make it freely available? At least to our allies.'

It is customary for a respectful pause to follow the pronouncements of a minister of the Crown. Ingham dispenses with custom and jumps down his throat. 'Today, yes. Tomorrow… Well, what can you say about tomorrow?'

The minister frowns. 'I'm afraid I don't follow.'

'Supposing some information pertaining to the security arrangements for the Prime Minister's visit to Brussels next month was to be 'observed' in a secure office three days ago?

By persons we would rather didn't see them? You are correct to state that we are where we are, but that doesn't account for where we will be tomorrow. Do you follow me now?' Ingham finds it hard to keep a tang of desperation from cracking his voice. The minister sits there dumbfounded.

Section seizes his chance. 'If I am correct, Minister, you are to review a new military outpost in the Middle East on the twenty-fifth of this month. The plans for it were finalised about three weeks ago and the copies are kept in four different locations around Whitehall. The plans include your transfer from your ministerial office to RAF Lyneham, the details of which air transport you will be flying in and the transport's flight plan. It includes in-depth information on the motorcade once you arrive and which vehicle you will be allocated to, together with details of your bodyguard, strength, armaments, etcetera, etcetera, etcetera.' The minister starts to look uncomfortable. 'How secure would you feel if those details had already been observed and reported to an unauthorised if not undesirable third party?' Section and Ingham don their stoniest of faces. The silence is eloquent.

'Yes, but…' The minister has one last attempt. 'If we adopt a more transparent policy, then any potential arguments with our allies will be obviated.'

'Absolutely, Minister.' Section has taken control of the exchange. 'But that still leaves us with the Tomorrow Question, doesn't it?' The minister looks blank. 'Your security plans for the Middle East trip?'

Ingham sees an opportunity to turn potential base metal into gold. 'The Tomorrow Question is actually the lever we need to persuade our allies of the wisdom of not sharing this technology. It applies equally to them as it does to us.'

'Can we put the genie back in the box?' says the minister. 'Can we uninvent it?'

'You mean, can we destroy all designs, references, records and physical materiel?' Section confirms.

'Exactly!'

Ingham looks at his superior and shrugs his shoulders. 'I don't know. No one has ever uninvented anything like this before as far as I know. Because of Rebrov and Zayed's control on the distribution of technical information, the amount of mopping up could be relatively straight forward. There are a few individuals who will need to have the frighteners put upon them. Sibley, for one. Also, Young and his cohorts, and Patterson and everyone who works at the Exatron facility. Thankfully, they're all UK citizens and we can tie them up in Official Secrets Act red tape till the cows come home.' Ingham is feeling much more cheerful. 'Yes, we can do it. But we need your sanction to move right away.'

'Right away, you say,' the minister parrots. He thinks for a moment, balancing on the fulcrum of fate. He turns to Section.

'Destroy it. Uninvent it. Now!'

VADUZ

Liechtenstein. Thursday October 15th, 0800hrs.

It is 8am and the car alarm system bleeps cheerily as the owner of the big, luxurious Audi strides up the gravel drive of his house to open the door. He grips the door handle and opens the door; it gives a rich, dark click which coincides with the cold jab of the pistol muzzle against the nape of his neck. He freezes.

'Get in, Herr Grusz.' The words are soft and unmistakeably American. On the opposite side of his car, a young and well-built man in a suit and tie swings open the passenger door and seats himself in the plush leather interior. He too has a small gun and it is pointed at Grusz's solar plexus. He does as he is told, and his assailant climbs in to the back of the car. 'We want you to drive to Munich,' the voice behind him says.

'But I'm expected at the office. I have important clients. I'll be missed.'

'Let us worry about that for you.'

Grusz engages reverse and the car swings gracefully out onto the residential road. Within twenty minutes they are travelling north out of Liechtenstein and across the border into first Austria and then Germany. They're not challenged at the borders; there's nothing suspicious about three men in business dress heading for Germany. It is still only eight in the morning, so the perfect time for a business trip.

Grusz does not know it, but he is not going as far as Munich and he will be away for the next two days.

It is 2pm and the front entrance of the Eschen und Schaan Privatbank has two foreign guests. One is a Middle Eastern gentleman immaculately attired in a silk Savile Row suit. His companion is wearing a shirt and tie and a dark jacket but is feeling distinctly out of place in such august surroundings. They are standing around, trying to look as though they are being patient when they feel anything but.

The Sheikh is put out; he has never been treated this way before and, ordinarily, he would not tolerate this. But today is not ordinary. Today is—or should be—an extraordinary day. Today they should be concluding their business with Eschen und Schaan.

The receptionist is most apologetic; Herr Grusz has not showed up for work today and has not left any messages to explain his absence. She asks if there is anyone else who can help the gentlemen. The Sheikh sighs with irritation and vigorously shakes his head. No, there is absolutely no one else who could help; Herr Grusz would understand that. His companion sits on a sofa and clicks the knuckles of his hand while chewing his lower lip. The Sheikh turns and throws him a caustic glare; he stops the clicking.

The manager of the bank arrives to apologise most profusely and to say that every effort will be made to locate Grusz. Naturally, this is most inconvenient for their esteemed client; but they are rather concerned as this behaviour is completely out of character. Would the gentlemen mind returning to their hotel and, as soon as they have found him, they will be in contact?

The Sheikh states categorically that Herr Grusz will be in tomorrow morning at 9am and he will return then to meet with him. And the manager had better not be in any doubt about that. He mutters some Arabic oath and storms out of the bank lobby, his companion trailing in his wake.

The manager hurriedly instructs the receptionist to contact the head of HR to meet him in his office; Herr Grusz must be found right away.

The departure of the two clients is watched keenly by two men dressed in business suits sitting in a café across the street from the bank. On the table in front of them is the usual array of commercial accessories: tablet computers, notepads, mobile phones, keys. One of them picks up his phone makes a call.

'They're on the move,' he says quietly; he doesn't want his American accent to attract too much attention. The voice at the other end of the line speaks for a while and the man responds. 'Tomorrow morning we expect... Don't worry, we have the pilot covered... Yeah. Tonight.' He clicks the phone off and replaces it on the table.

The other man turns to him. 'You flown one of these things before?' His companion smiles.

It is 6.30pm and Herr Grusz is in his locked bedroom in the farmhouse in the Bavarian Alps. He is starting to get hungry now as he has not eaten anything apart from a small bread roll for breakfast. That was before he left the house and this intolerable day had begun. All they have left him with is a bottle of water and the threat that if he tries to escape, the man outside the door had orders to shoot. The abductors, he is sure, are American.

As soon as he gets back, he will see to it at there is trouble at the highest possible levels. It is unacceptable for foreign nationals to just barge into Liechtenstein and remove people against their will from in front of their houses. Unacceptable!

A key rattles in the lock and the door swings open. There are three men are in the living room of the farmhouse; two are sitting at the dining table, the third is standing by the doorway. They invite him to join them. Grusz jumps to his feet and demands to be released immediately. He is angry and frightened. One of the men tells him in Swiss German that he is not to be released until he has made some commitments regarding the funds held in the name of the client he was due to have seen earlier that day; the fund that Eschen und Schaan has tended since 1930.

Grusz stands in the doorway of the bedroom. 'I will make no commitments and the affairs of my clients are strictly confidential and, under Swiss law, protected from state interference.'

The Swiss man stands from the table, walks over and presents his credentials. Grusz glances nervously at the identity card and looks back at the man.

'Nazi gold,' he says. Grusz swallows. 'Mr Grusz, if the fund had not dealt in Nazi gold, this conversation would not be taking place. Your protection from Swiss law and Liechtenstein articles would be sacrosanct. But a line has been crossed here and it carries certain repercussions that transcend state law, state politics and even state tradition.'

Grusz is silent.

'With the involvement of Nazi gold, all notions of banking secrecy are void, and Eschen und Schaan will be required to hand over all records relating to the accounts forthwith. And that is *all* records. For all their clients.'

Grusz continues his mute sentry duty in the doorway.

The Swiss man sighs. 'Mr Grusz, we are sure that you had nothing to do with the decision to taint the accounts with this unfortunate investment. This is something that will come out at the end of the day. Of course, that's assuming you wish to make a public spectacle of this. There are more discreet alternatives that will keep your name and probably that of your employers out of the news. And that alternative would be good for Liechtenstein as a whole, don't you think?'

Grusz weighs his options. 'Why have I been brought to this place against my will?'

'For your own safety,' says the Swiss man. He gestures towards the table. 'Please…'

Grusz is led over to the table. There is a sheaf of papers laid out on top. The Swiss man hands him a pen. 'This affair can be handled quietly and discreetly. In the Liechtenstein tradition.'

10pm. After he has signed, the two Americans step outside the farmhouse.

'Right,' says one. 'We can move on to the next phase.'

'Okay. I've tracked the pilot down to a hotel near St Gallen. We can pick him up right away.'

'Excellent. Grusz stays here till the dust settles.'

'I'll give the captain a lift back to Police Canton Headquarters on the way.'

ST. GALLEN–ALTENRHEIN AIRPORT

Switzerland. Friday October 16ᵗʰ, 1115 hrs.

The Swiss Police are interviewing the staff in the airport tower; it has been two hours since the executive jet took off into the blue-grey light of morning and banked over Lake Constance in the direction of the high Alps to the south-east. It has been one hour forty minutes since it disappeared from the radar screens. Ten minutes after that, the first reports of an explosion are received from people trekking in the region.

The airfield is closed to all traffic whilst the police try to determine whether there had been any defect or malfunction that could have caused the aircraft to crash. The officers in the tower are polite and cooperative but not helpful. The aircraft appeared to be okay and the pilot must have made the usual pre-flight checks. Otherwise, the safety of the aircraft itself is not their concern; they are there to ensure that it is safe for aircraft to land, take off and taxi around the airfield.

It is another few hours before the first police and air accident investigators arrive at the crash site: the upper slopes of an amphitheatre of peaks in the Allgäuer Hochalpen in Germany. Among the wreckage they discover the bodies of two males, one probably Caucasian and one dressed in the burnt remains of a *dishdasha*. Early examination of the wreckage reveals no obvious malfunction.

Two days later, Janet Hooper, now back in her office in Langley, Virginia, receives word that the pilot has been exfiltrated from Germany and is on his way back to the United States.

IN CHILTERN HALL
The Chilterns. Friday October 16th, 1130 hrs.

'Well, that's that!' Golding is reporting back to Ingham on the phone.

Ingham sighs at the other end. 'God, I wish you were right. There's going to be a shitstorm. Make no mistake about that, Inspector. In the meantime you've got your collar: that's the good news for today.'

'What's the bad news?'

'He's never going to stand trial for it. What did you charge him with, just for my records?'

'Breaches of the Terrorism Act 2006. Namely Section 1 – encouragement of terrorism; Section 5 – preparation of terrorist acts; Section 9 – making and possession of device or materials; Section 11 – threats relating to devices, materials and/or facilities; and Section 12 – trespassing on nuclear sites. I also considered doing him for general trespass, riding his bike without a front lamp, being in possession of an offensive hairstyle, the usual.'

'As I said, he's never going to stand trial for it.'

'Thanks for your support, Mr Ingham.'

'Think nothing of it. I'm grateful to you for having the good grace to help us mop this operation up and cover the due process. It's not something we're very good at in my department.'

'Just out of idle interest, why is he never going to court?'

Ingham laughs heartily. 'Because this enterprise of his needs to be buried and quickly. Can you imagine what would fall on our heads if the full story got out? There would be pandemonium.'

'So what will happen instead?'

'He'll probably get reassigned to a dusty corner of some Governmental scientific research programme where he can while away his autumn years... Oh, I don't know. Getting fusion power to work.' Ingham thinks for a moment and a delicious notion crosses his mind. 'On Orford Ness. Or Caithness! He'll like the sea air, I reckon.'

'My men are rounding up everyone who's had contact with the Professor and having them sign the Official Secrets Act. That should be done and dusted by the end of today.'

'Well done, Inspector. As you said. That's that. At least I bloody well hope so. That was a close one.'

SHANGHAI

China. One Month Later.

You don't ignore a call like that. The best part of thirty years' work, edging ever closer to the truth, could be all over if what the caller has said is true. Tickets to Shanghai aren't cheap, but he knew who he could get to stump up an advance, and two days later, here he is.

Thankfully, the paper has put him up in a decent hotel. It's a world away from this rats' nest of a place. It calls itself a hotel but, by the standards of international travel today, it hasn't moved with the times and offers few, if any, modern amenities other than running water and epilepsy-inducing fluorescent lights in every room. All the floors are tiled—badly—and in need of a thorough clean, and an old, rancid smell of cooking oil permeates the walls. Any hope of sleep is likely to be stillborn thanks to the seedy nightclub just across the tiny street; Rob fancies he can almost touch the building across the road if he leans out of any window far enough. If the incessant, deep throb of the sound system doesn't keep him awake, then the bank of garish, strobing neon should do the trick.

Rob sits in what passes for a lobby—a narrow passageway between the reception desk and the wall—and waits for his host, thinking all the while that this had better be worth his time, otherwise he will have a lot of explaining to do once he gets back to London. On top of that, the trip back to his own hotel is going to take the best part of an hour and a half, if he can find a cab to take him to the nearest subway station.

He was told to arrive at the hotel and sit in the lobby until he was called; he has been here for a good hour now, and he is getting impatient. He is also getting irritated: by the harsh blue-white, fizzing, flickering fluorescent light; by the smell; by the echoing halls of this ghastly place; and by the musical clash of the throbbing bass from across the street and the sickly-sweet oriental ballads sung in glass-crazing soprano.

The door from the street opens and the nightclub's bass throb billows into the lobby like a sandstorm. A local man dressed in jeans and a thick overcoat steps inside; he sees Rob and beckons him to follow. He says something to him in Chinese but Rob looks apologetic and shrugs his shoulders: the international sign for, 'I don't speak your language.' The man beckons again and Rob follows after checking to make sure he still has his recorder, spare battery and notepad with him.

They walk off down the street and the throb recedes into the background. After a couple of turnings to the left and right, Rob is shown into a small apartment block. The Chinese man walks him to the lift, presses one of the buttons and steps outside again, leaving Rob to make the ascent on his own. At last, Rob is somewhere quiet with nothing but the meditative hum of the lift for a soundtrack. It is almost an oasis of calm, except for the ubiquitous blue-white fluorescent light.

After a while, the lift jars to a halt and the doors clank open to reveal a westerner dressed in jeans and a dark V-necked sweater. He has smart, combed hair and the look of a preppie: he's gone to the right schools, he's attended the right sort of college, joined the right fraternity, played football for the college, dated the right sort of girls and has been the apple of his mother and father's eye. Rob wonders what he's doing in this backwater of a place. The man's expression and general demeanour suggests furtiveness; he's trying to be upstanding and resolute but the slight hunch in the shoulders betrays the fact that he's not here in any official capacity, and that he knows he is doing something wrong.

Without saying a word, the man turns and walks down a corridor until he comes to a door that is slightly ajar. Rob follows and they are soon both in a small apartment sparsely furnished with a few chairs, a Formica dining table, a few paintings, and, as ever, a bare tiled floor. The man invites Rob to sit at the table while he returns to the front door, peers down the corridor each way and shuts the door firmly. He takes care to put on the chain once he has locked up.

Finally, he speaks. 'Scotch?' The accent is American.

'Thank you. That would be good.'

The man brings over two large tumblers of whisky and sets them down on the table. He sits and looks hard at Rob. 'Remind me. What was the name of the man who first tipped you off about the October Fund?'

Rob is dumbfounded. He was expecting a bit more of a rapport-building session. He flounders, regains his composure and answers. 'Jason Cresswell at Fillmore-Kermode.'

'When was that, please?'

'1987. October. During the stock market crash. Black Monday.'

The man stares hard into Rob's eyes. Rob tries not to flinch. He turns and disappears into a side room and returns, holding a small external hard drive which he places on the table between them. He takes a swig of his scotch and holds out a hand. 'Robert Coates.'

Rob shakes. 'Rob Tilling. Should I know you?'

'I shouldn't have thought so. You might want to get your voice recorder out. I don't want to keep you longer than necessary.' Rob stands up, removes his coat and fishes the paraphernalia of his trade out of the pockets. Once he's checked the battery levels and arranged everything, he sits back down again.

Coates taps the hard drive. 'This is everything you need to know about the October Fund. There's over one and a half terabytes of data here. Probably more than you will ever need or want to know, but it's there all the same.'

'How big is the fund?'

'You mean "was". It's closed now and in the possession of the Americans and the British for the time being. I expect there's going to be a bit of debate about who has what right to it and yada-yada. But, for your information, the fund closed out just north of seven trillion dollars.' Coates pauses for Tilling to draw breath; it's hard to continue a conversation after the mention of so much money.

'How did… I mean…' Rob stammers.

'Yeah, it's quite a windfall, isn't it? Most of it was made shorting stocks at key points over the last eighty-five years and then investing the very sizeable profits in commodities, currencies and more stock. They've been among the largest players in gold, oil futures, tech stocks and gilts for all that time. But the weirdest part of all this?' Rob leans forward. 'It all started as a flaky science experiment.'

The sun rises on a cold Shanghai wreathed in the vapour of thousands of heating and ventilation ducts. The city rises, and red-and-white rivers of light flow from the edges to the centre and back again. In the sky, an orange glow from the east begins to wash over a gull-grey morning.

The taxi has deposited him outside his gleaming hotel and several concierges, doormen and other staff are busying themselves, trying to usher him into the warmth and luxury within. Rob stands and looks at the chrome and steel exterior, half-hears the retreating drone of the taxi and turns to gaze vacantly at the Huangpu River gliding by. He lights a cigarette and begins to wonder. This story he has been chasing for over thirty years: it has been his crusade, his quest. And it turns out that the truth is… 'Shocking' is an overused word in the media; he has been guilty of reaching for it himself when a drab piece needed spicing up, But, this! For the first time in he cannot remember how long, he is truly, profoundly shocked. Stunned, even.

He takes a long, deep draught of his cigarette. He has all but given up, he tells himself, and, indeed, he is down to only one or two a day. But this occasion warrants a lapse of resolve and he needs something to do while he collects his thoughts. He can feel the hard drive in his coat pocket pressing against his thigh; it weighs heavy, like the future of civilisation. Will they even let him print this story? The paper is known for their rebellious stance on most issues; but this might be too much for them. This subject hovers uncertainly over the line dividing the two arguments of 'The People Have a Right to Know' and 'The Public Interest'.

The public may be interested, but is it in their interest? And who has the right to be so patrician-like as to decide that for them? The public may also have a right to know; after all, the health of their pensions rests on what has been going on. But is it right for them to be told? What will happen when the story breaks? And if he doesn't write the story, who else will? And what stance will *they* take?

The key thing is to try and avoid being sensational about this—oh, bollocks!—*sensational* story. He can drip-feed it into the public domain, but the central issue... It isn't something that can gradually emerge; there comes a point when he will just have to come out with it. After that? Well. Who knows? It will be too late for it to be withdrawn or unsaid. It will be like telling a spouse that you've been cheating on her; once out, it can't be retracted. But what if, instead of a spouse, it's the whole world? 'You have been cheated systematically for the last eighty-five years'.

The river creeps on. The people and cars hurry about their business not noticing the large westerner with the world on his shoulders.

It is nearly half-past eight here; London will be waking up and arriving for work in about seven hours' time. That gives him enough time to draft an outline of his article for the paper and send it to them, once they've agreed to the usual issues of intellectual property. This is his scoop. (What a lovely, old-fashioned newspaperman's term. 'Brenda! Stop the presses! Hold the front page!') This is his scoop and he wants to retain as much control of it as he can.

The only question left hanging is that of Mr Coates. He informed Rob that he had made plans for his own disappearance, and he had not objected to his name being used as the source because his position at the Agency was now terminal. They knew he had gone and what he had taken with him; they would be looking for him, and he'd made arrangements to go where they might be able to follow but wouldn't be able to bring him back.

Rob throws the stub of his cigarette into the river, returns to the hotel entrance and takes the lift back to his room. At the desk by the window, suspended high above the maelstrom of the city below, Rob lifts the lid of his laptop and begins to tap the keyboard; random thoughts as first, but gradually they coalesce and take form and direction. Four hours later, he closes the lid and decides he will reward himself with a decent lunch in the rooftop restaurant. Then, he will read through the draft before calling the paper and agreeing terms.

A week later, the first instalment of the story is published in the Saturday edition. By the following Monday the news has girdled the planet and the markets are waiting. The pundits have had their say; minds have been made up. The bells ring in Japan, Shanghai and Singapore and the screens instantly turn red. Soon, the panic fuels itself and the line plunges down and down. The descent is so precipitous that a new rumour starts: they were there for the last eighty-five years, so who's to say they're not still here? Or is someone else at the root of this?

A dreadful day dawns across the globe and, as the front of sunlight advances across the land, it illuminates another market and more red lights.

PART FIVE
FLIGHTS OF ANGELS

REV. JAMES HECHTER

Kloten, Montana. Six Weeks Later.

A hard, grey light washes the ceiling of the chapel. Inside, the congregation sit quiet in anticipation as the reverend steps up to the dais. Apart from a few perfunctory coughs, the only sound is the delicate trill of spindrift snow against the windows. Winter has come to Kloten: an iron-grey blanket spreading over the land like a slick. The air outside is filling with the first light snow, a portent of the assault to come from the north. This is when the grain elevators will be lost from sight, consumed by the storm, lost to nature.

It has been a long and glorious autumn; the harvest has been yet another reason to give thanks to God. He has blessed the people of this region with good land and good air. The landowners and farmworkers who make up the bulk of the community are right to be grateful; they have the comfort of another year's grace on this land, up here on the roof of the nation, where America meets the trackless expanse of the Canadian Shield. They are all sitting here in this modest chapel with their wives and children, along with members of the local community: teachers, librarians, sheriff with a couple of deputies, and a few soldiers from the Minuteman base a mile or so away.

The spindrift beats its tiny tattoo on the glass, like the footsteps of mice. The Reverend James Hechter clears his throat and pauses, just for a moment. He loves this silence; he revels in this brief moment of glory when all eyes and all ears are upon him and he can channel the very word of God Himself to his flock. And today is a special day. Today is when faith shall be justified for, not only is it written, it is so proved.

He begins, slowly at first. 'I shall take as my text for today's first sermon, Corinthians Chapter Two, Verses Six and Seven.

"Yet we do speak wisdom among those who are mature; a wisdom, however, not of this age nor of the rulers of this age, who are passing away; but we speak God's wisdom in a mystery, the hidden wisdom which God predestined before the ages to our glory".' The Reverend stops again to let this sink in. He knows that he will have to spell it out, but he wants the words of St Paul to resonate in the breathless chapel and in the hearts of the hushed congregation. He repeats. '"The hidden wisdom which God predestined before the ages – *before* the ages"' he stresses '"to Our *Glory*"'.

And what does that mean, I hear you ask? What is this hidden wisdom of which the Bible speaks and which St Paul himself wrote?'

A few amens sprinkled among the gathered.

'These last few weeks have been hard, unimaginably hard for some folks in this great nation of ours and around the world. The towers of Mammon have fallen, and in the wake of this upheaval, countless millions have lost their jobs and are downcast in this season of Advent, instead of praising God and expecting the miracle of the birth of his only begotten son, Jesus Christ.' The congregation stirs with a low, rolling cushion of amens and hallelujahs. 'They are looking forward with fear and doubt to a cold and uncertain future. A future without work, without a wage, without a pension. A future where they look forward and see nothing but destitution. "How will I fend for my family?" they will say. "Where can I go to escape this approaching cloud of poverty?"

'For we have known no poverty here. Not real poverty. We have no beggars on the streets of Kloten. We have no abandoned or destitute here. We are a community. We care for each other in this huge and unyielding land. A congregation of Brothers and Sisters, united under God.' *(Amen to that! Yeah, Reverend! I hear ya!)* 'We have the blessings of a bountiful harvest. We will sustain, we will persist and, with God's help, we will thrive.' More salutations from the pews. The wind hums a mournful threnody through the cracks in the window frames.

'Many a preacher has told his flock that they are the Chosen People. Many times those words have gone unheeded or not understood. We, and I am guilty of this, too, we have heard these words and thought, "Jesus! Lord!"' More hallelujahs, some exultant. '"Jesus, I don't feel Chosen. I don't know what Chosen means. Help me to understand and become closer to your Glory".'

Joyous exhortations erupt around the chapel; some people have raised their arms to the roof.

'I have always tried to preach that, in order to be Chosen, we should choose each other first. That way we will become strong together and we will, in our strength, magnify the name of the Lord and praise God in the Highest.'

The Reverend has raised his arms in a sign of benediction; he lets them fall slowly to his side as his resumes quietly. Now he shouts. 'But, in among all the chaos and fear in the world today. Chaos and fear caused by the naked avarice of a handful of wicked men who shall burn for all time in Hell…' He is quiet again. 'From out of their avarice, a wondrous and irrefutable truth emerges. Out of all bad things, comes good, comes the word of God. "The hidden wisdom which God predestined before the ages".'

He nods at the congregation to make sure that this key verse is starting to lodge in their minds. He sees the appreciative, if expectant, faces looking back at him, wide-eyed.

'So,' he shouts, 'what good has come from such acts of evil? Other than learning that greed is no goal and that greed is its own punishment? First, Man has devised and built a time machine. A time machine! Can you believe it? We can now travel back in *time*. Not forward, mark you. Only back. And we have sent men back nearly one hundred and fifty years, to witness the bombing of Pearl Harbor, the assassination of President Kennedy, the Wall Street Crash of 1929. And much, much more.

'And what did man bring back from the past? Apart from a demonstration of his insatiable greed and perversity? The most important lesson we learned, Brothers and Sisters in Jesus, is that you cannot change the past. Let me say that again. You. Cannot. Change. The Past.'

The Reverend paces back and forth in front of the congregation. At first he is staring at the floor as he speaks, eyes screwed shut and rapt in concentration; then he throws back his head to project his glorious words to the rafters of the chapel; then he crouches, locking his flock with a viper's glare; then his hands are clenched to his bosom, as if in prayer. As he moves, the room sways with him and the congregation become lost to the world and lost in his message, borne on his soaring proclamations. Without knowing or will, they exhort, 'Amen!' and 'Hallelujah!' and 'Praise the Lord!' They begin low and soft but soon, as the Reverence Hechter's sermon builds in strength and majesty and his words turn to psalm, they rejoice and their shouts of praise and wonder build and soar as well.

'You. Cannot. Change. The Past. Let me hear you say that!'

They chant the words back at him.

'Again!'

And again they chant in unison.

'Amen to that, Brothers and Sisters. Amen to that. And what you have just said together, here in this humble House of God, is that the past is written. Let me say that again. *The past is written.* There are no alternatives, no other outcomes, no other options. There is no other past than the one we already know. Let me hear you one more time!'

'You. Cannot. Change. The Past!' they all shout gladly.

'So what does that *mean?*' He holds on to the last word until it becomes a musical note. And he returns to the softly spoken contemplation of his sermon's first few words, and the wind's chorus returns to the congregation's ears. 'What does that mean? Well, people, I struggled long and hard trying to figure that out. I spent hours every day since I heard the news trying to dig out the truth behind it. And do you know what I found myself saying?'

'Tell us, Reverend!'

'Amen!'

He takes a deep and noisy breath and his voice lifts again. 'It was something I heard some scientist say. He said, "Time is like a great big carpet all rolled up. When you unroll it, there's your past with the future, *the* Future, still rolled up waiting to be unrolled. And there, in that simple explanation, is the key to the *importance*, the single greatest importance of this whole affair.

'When you unroll that carpet, you know where it is going. Or in this case, when God unrolls that Carpet of Time, He knows where it is going. God knows what will happen. And He knows this because it is *written*. His almighty hand has written the future already. "But we speak God's wisdom in a mystery, the hidden wisdom which God predestined before the ages to our glory". It's right there in Corinthians. St Paul was right, people!

'We have been guided along the path in all our days. To this very day, here in Kloten. And God will guide us on our paths for all the days to come. He is our guide. "The Lord is my shepherd," it says in Psalm Twenty-Three. "I shall not want. He leadeth *me* in the paths of righteousness".

'Brethren, we are here today because we carry out God's work. And we have always hoped to live in His divine grace, but now we *KNOW*.' The Reverend is yelling as hard as his lungs will let him; the very windows of the chapel are pulsating with the boom of his voice. 'We KNOW that what we do is God's work. And GOD'S WILL. We are his vessels and we are truly blessed.'

The congregation erupts. They are upstanding and they hold their arms to the heavens shouting, 'Amen!' and, 'Hallelujah!' and, 'I believe, it is all true!'. The reverend throws his arms and his head back and chants.

'Thy will be done on Earth as it is in Heaven. Let us pray. Let us pray now. Everybody on your knees before God!'

And the rejoicing and the shouting and the praise subside and the wind's lonely moan returns to fill the hall, now quivering with excitement. And quietly, and with dignity, the reverend leads the congregation in the Lord's Prayer.

Amen.

M/SGT. PHILO JENSEN

Kloten-Canadian Road, Montana. Six Weeks Later.

The four men are standing in the snow waiting for him, their rifles slung over their shoulders; he's received the text message as expected. The Deputy Missile Combat Crew Commander is dead and Jensen is holstering his still smoking sidearm. He presses a button on the console and, on the surface, a large reinforced metal door swings open to the sky. The men above trudge through the snow, bodies bent against the serrating wind, and duck into the shelter of the silo entrance.

They wend their way through the tunnels and elevators, their boots clanking arrhythmically on the concrete floors and metal gratings. Eventually, they file wordlessly into the Command Centre where Jensen is sitting at the Mission Control console, urgently tapping new commands into the computer. He turns to the oldest of the four men behind him.

Jensen recites the names of each of the three targets. As each city is named, the man nods. Jensen returns to the console and continues to program the coordinates into the guidance system.

'You can get three targets with just one missile?' the man says.

'Yes, sir,' says Jensen without looking up. 'This is the LGM-30H Minuteman IV intercontinental ballistic missile. It's an upgrade on the Minuteman III.' He continues to tap away at the keyboard as he talks. He is reciting the specifications impassively as though he is training recruits. 'It can carry an increased payload of three nuclear warheads each with a yield of 500 kilotons. Gentlemen, that's forty times the size of the Hiroshima bomb in 1945.' The men stand there and try to take in the scale of it all.

'How long is this going to take?' says the older man. Jensen finishes his programming with a flourish and swivels round in his chair to face them all.

'Once you and I complete the launch sequence, sir, the missile will take about three minutes to reach apogee at which point it will release the warheads. After that, it's about another ninety seconds to two minutes. I've programmed all three warheads to detonate about one thousand feet above the targets.'

'What do you need me to do?'

'This system is designed so that one man cannot execute a missile launch by himself. It will require two men and for that we have two keys. We place them in the two locks at each end of the console. As you can see, that's about fifteen feet apart. We have to turn them simultaneously on my command to activate the launch sequence. After that, sir, you have to read some alpha-numeric code to me that you will see appear on the screen in front of you over there by your key. I will punch that code into the validation module on my side of the console.'

'After that?'

'After that, I press that big red button over there.' Jensen points to a button protected by a large metal thumb cover. The designer of this system was careful to ensure that clumsiness would not trigger a launch.'

'Okay,' says the older man. 'Let's do this thing.'

'Are you sure you want to go ahead with this?' Jensen asks if only to make absolutely sure. 'You can always pull out if you want.'

'You heard what the reverend said today, Philo. This is all written. This is God's will. And anyway...' He nods in the direction of the dead serviceman. 'I reckon we've all come too far to back out now.'

CAPTAIN HENRY PARFITT

Dammartin-en-Goële, France. Sept 1914.
(Excerpt from Captain Parfitt's memoirs,
published privately in 1932.)

We had erected the Field Ambulance in a barn on the outskirts of Dammartin and remained there for three days. The forced march from Le Cateau by way of St Quentin, Noyon and Compiègne had been gruelling due to the lorry breaking down irretrievably. The poor horses had borne the brunt of this inconvenience and it was a miracle that none were harmed or even lost by their terrible burdens. Those of us who would have ridden to this point were, of course, obliged to unsaddle and walk instead whilst the medical equipment and the barest minimum of canvas was borne by all the horses.

The barn, therefore, was a godsend as it afforded us the luxury of both space and shelter without the exertions usually called for in its erection. It may not have been the cleanest FA in France, but, if only due to sheer relief on our part, it was probably one of the jolliest.

The Great Retreat as it was being called even then had dissolved into a chaotic scramble in which soldiers from both the French Army and the British Expeditionary Force were shuffling past our position in search of someone who could issue them with coherent orders. The casualties we had seen in Saint-Quentin were markedly reduced in number and, for the first time since leaving Dover, we all felt we could relax slightly. There was some talk (wishful thinking most likely) that we might be ordered to retreat to Paris which by now was only about thirty miles away. Tantalisingly close! On some nights we could see the searchlights of the city trying to pick out the enemy planes wheeling in the velvet sky.

I had been billeted in a pleasant farmhouse as part of my *delogement* and the owners were very accommodating and looked after myself and two of my fellow officers with good humour and great hospitality. My schoolboy French was complemented by my more skilled colleague Captain Jarvis who, it transpired, had several French relatives and had summered in the country on many occasions. So, for a few days, my attendance at the FA had become something not unlike a normal job: reveille at 0730, breakfast at 0815, report for duty at 0900 and dismiss at 1800.

On the morning of the third day, I presented myself for duty and was introduced to my new servant for the duration. He had been seconded from the Queen's Own Cameron Highlanders— the 'Camerons'—and he looked rather relieved to have been assigned such duties. Although our first engagement with the Germans had been encouraging (if only because it showed the professionalism and skill of our own boys), their sheer strength of numbers meant that a retreat was inevitable. One wonders if we might have been able to nip matters in the bud had we met the Hun on equal terms and with matching force. That said, McCullough, as he was called, was not as keen as many I had encountered to give them what for, so his new duties evidently suited him admirably.

After a fairly arduous day of near inactivity (I always find it taxing trying to find Things To Do as opposed to having them presented to me), myself and Jarvis were dismissed and we began the return walk to our billet which was approximately half a mile from the barn where we'd established the FA. McCullough, not knowing the way, walked with us and, before long, we were exchanging life stories.

We learned he was originally from a village close to Inverness on the Muir of Ord and was the eldest of six siblings; his father worked in the local distillery and this was the first time he'd ventured any distance from the city of his birth. I, in turn, gave him a potted version of my life and then the course of conversation turned to that of the war and our experiences.

I told him that I had experienced one lucky escape near Le Cateau and thought twice about recounting, lest I become some dreadful War Bore especially as the action hadn't even finished.

McCullough in turn recounted how he and a detachment from his regiment had engaged the enemy near a small bridge over a canal—he told us what a beautiful place it might have been—where they were able to hold their position and repulse the onslaught. They then had to hold the position overnight pending reinforcement, which McCullough was not too proud to admit was a terrifying ordeal. He said that the fighting left very little time for anyone to stop and consider their predicament; the periods in between, on the other hand, were worse as one's demons would come and torment you as you waited for the tumult to begin again.

By the time we had reached our billet, we were all ready for a light supper. This was taken *en plein air* under a late summer's evening sky; McCullough had prepared it with the assistance of Madame who supplied a bottle of *vin ordinaire*. It was most welcome and I confess Jarvis and I consumed the whole bottle. After the meal, as McCullough was clearing up around us, Jarvis asked me why I had been so coy about recounting my story of what happened at Le Cateau. I told him I didn't want to brag, especially as McCullough was the one who had seen the real action and engaged the enemy face to face.

Jarvis then said that my tale about the strangely dressed civilian was a curiosity worthy of retelling and I replied that I really hadn't given it a second thought from that day to this. Jarvis then spoke across to McCullough who was, as I recall, still clearing the plates and glasses, and asked him if he'd seen any curiously dressed civilians wandering about the battlefield. Both of us were expecting him to say that he hadn't. Instead, he stopped in his tracks with some crockery balanced on his arms and paused for a moment, clearly deciding whether to tell us something or not.

Jarvis gave him some encouragement and McCullough turned to us and spoke in his soft Ross accent.

'Begging your pardon, sir, but we did see something. Something out of the ordinary.' Jarvis obviously relished the prospect of a mystery and beckoned McCullough to put down the dirty dishes and come over and join us. This he did, although he politely declined Jarvis' offer of a seat. I can imagine that, this being his first day with either of us, he was reticent to fraternise with officers. I asked him what he had seen and he replied that it was not just him, it was all of them. And, since that evening, there had been others who had reported the same thing.

Jarvis and I were both perplexed by this and asked him to say more. 'I find it difficult to put into words exactly, sir.' His accent was thick: a native Scottish brogue. 'That night I was on watch. The enemy had retreated about a hundred yards behind the cover of a low rise. They had been quiet for a few hours save for a few seemingly random bursts of machine gun fire. As a result, no one had felt secure enough to send stretcher parties out to retrieve any wounded. Our CO had sent a stiffly worded communication back to GHQ to request a ceasefire long enough for our stretcher bearers to do their work but we'd heard no reply. So, all we could do was post watches throughout the night to ensure that the enemy was not planning a dawn attack. It was a fairly boring thing to do as there was no moon and so next to nothing to see, and the land between our two armies was as black as pitch.

'This is when the strangest thing happened, sirs.' He looked at us both imploringly; he was obviously worried that we might take him to be somewhat deranged. 'Out of nowhere this column of light appeared in no-man's-land.' Jarvis pressed him for details and he replied that the light was about the height of a doorway and half the width. 'It just appeared. One moment there was nothing and the next, there it was.' McCullough checked our faces to see that we weren't going to commit him or something. Instead, Jarvis softly bade him continue.

'If you're sure, sirs,' he said, and we nodded. 'What happened next was even stranger. We could see a couple of figures illuminated by the column of light. At first we couldn't be sure what they were doing but when our eyes had become accustomed to the vision—'

'You say "we",' Jarvis interjected. 'Who's "we"?'

'I'm sorry, sir,' said McCullough. 'The others on watch. There were about four of us, but one or two of them woke their comrades to witness what was going on as well. All in all, there must have been eight or ten men seeing what I am telling you now. I since learned that this was also witnessed by men in other positions for about two hundred yards in either direction along the front.

'As I said, when our eyes became accustomed to the light, we could see two figures in no-man's-land. After a while, it became clear that they were carrying a body. They appeared to be drifting among our fallen comrades and…' He broke off at this point and seemed quite distressed. Jarvis and I let him alone for a few moments and then I quietly asked him what he thought these figures were about.

'I don't know, sir. But the lads and me, we all talked about it afterwards. We had no explanation for it. Still don't. But one of the lads, his father is a minister, wondered aloud if they were divine beings sent by God to tend to the sick, the dying and the departed.' McCullough looked embarrassed and stared at the ground.

'How long did this phenomenon persist?' I said.

'I'm not sure, sir. It couldn't have been more than five or ten minutes.'

Jarvis and I both rubbed our chins and agreed that this story was very strange and that we had never heard of anything similar in either of our lives.

McCullough then added a remark that has been echoing all these years since, to the very day I write this memoir. 'The lad wondered if they were angels or something. Who would've thought of angels at Mons?' He gave a disbelieving snort, shrugged his shoulders and resumed his duties clearing away the dinner.

CAPTAIN HENRY PARFITT

October Morning (François Coppée 1842 – 1908)

Matin d'Octobre
C'est l'heure exquise et matinale
Que rougit un soleil soudain.
À travers la brume automnale
Tombent les feuilles du jardin.

Leur chute est lente. On peut les suivre
Du regard en reconnaissant
Le chêne à sa feuille de cuivre,
L'érable à sa feuille de sang.

Les dernières, les plus rouillées,
Tombent des branches dépouillées :
Mais ce n'est pas l'hiver encor.

Une blonde lumière arrose
La nature, et, dans l'air tout rose,
On croirait qu'il neige de l'or.

English Translation:
October Morning
It is the hour exquisite and early,
The sudden sunrise reddens the sky.
Through the autumn mist
The garden leaves fall.

Their fall is slow. We can follow them
With our eyes and recognize
The oak by its leaf of copper,
The maple by its leaf of blood.

The last ones, the most rusty
Fall from the bare branches,
But it's not winter yet.
A fair light sprinkles down on
Nature and in the whole rosy sky
You'd think it was snowing gold.

CPSIA information can be obtained
at www.ICGtesting.com
Printed in the USA
FFOW03n1509040218
44789847-44909FF